YOUTH
A NOVEL

GLORIA
HOLT

Title art by Danny Hirajeta, Iron Clown Studios

Copyright © 2025 Glory Dawn Press
All rights reserved.
ISBN: 979-8-9927344-2-3

To the young, old, and everything in between.
It's never too late.

PLAYLIST

While some of these songs are mentioned in *Youth*, others either were a source of inspiration or just fit the book's vibe ☺ ♪♫

Us – Regina Spektor

Mambo Sun – T. Rex

Fare Thee Well (Dink's Song) – Oscar Isaac, Marcus Mumford

Here Comes the Sun – The Beatles

Helena – My Chemical Romance

From the Edge of the Deep Green Sea – The Cure

Love of My Life – Queen

Fade Into You – Mazzy Star

Never Had – Oscar Isaac

Faithfully – Journey

Bésame Mucho – Andrea Bocelli

Make You Feel My Love – Bob Dylan

Be My Lover – La Bouche

Cruel Summer – Bananarama

Summertime Sadness – Lana Del Rey

Golden Years – David Bowie

Sample the songs at **Gloria-Holt.com**.

PART 1

CHAPTER 1

"You cured aging?"

Veteran TV journalist Wanda Bernette asks the question with unblinking, slack-jawed awe as soon as Matilda Crown walks out from the shadows to reveal her new look.

Her skin is porcelain smooth with a light dusting of foundation and contouring makeup. Her sparkling eyes are framed by liner and mascara-coated lashes. Her auburn hair, styled in a pixie cut, shimmers under the studio lights. And her coral-colored strappy heels clash offensively with her blindingly white pantsuit.

Honestly, she looks like a 25-year-old trying to channel her inner boss.

But Matilda *was* the boss. She was exceptionally wealthy as the founder and CEO of Crown Cosmetics and Youth Services. She was known for her pixie haircut. She was known for her monochromatic pantsuits and impractical heels.

Matilda was also 67 years old and looked every bit her age until that night on live TV.

"Oh, Wanda," Matilda says with a wave of her now elegant, previously veiny hand. "That's ridiculous—and legally inaccurate. We've cured the *effects* of aging."

Goldie mouths Matilda's words with a roll of her eyes. This might be the fourth time the interview has played while she's been in the executive suite waiting room of Crown Cosmetics. As part of the company's twentieth anniversary celebration of its most popular and groundbreaking product, the fully remastered video of the interview is being played on loop on the wall of high-definition TVs.

The Serum, shorthand for the Crown Skin and Hair Ameliorating and Rejuvenating Serum System, is the world's only legitimate panacea for wrinkles and hair loss. Time will march on and illnesses and ailments that come with age can still affect you, but you could have debilitating arthritis and suffer bouts of dementia and not look a day over 25.

It'll cost you though.

The monthly injections are about two thousand dollars each and have to be kept up. If users dare to stop, they'll appear as they naturally would at their age.

"Did you cure your cancer too?" the interviewer asks.

"Nope," Matilda chirps. "Still dying."

"Why do this instead of trying to stay alive?"

"We're all going to die eventually. If the lung cancer doesn't get me, some other cancer will." Matilda pauses. "Or maybe a bus will hit me!" She sounds strangely excited by the prospect.

Wanda seems too stunned to follow up with another question.

"You can't treat all causes of death," Matilda continues. "The signs of aging, though, affect everyone in the same ways. I've been the only one bold enough to confront the issue as the universal affliction it is and to come up with a real solution."

"But even if you were only helping those suffering from your particular cancer, wouldn't that be a more worthy cause than looking young?"

"Oh, Wanda! You're precious." Matilda emits a patronizing laugh and places a hand over her chest. "I'm not heartless for not investing in medical solutions for diseases. I just know it's a futile effort." She leans in closer to the interviewer like she's confiding a secret. "To be frank, I'm a savior. I have come up with a solution to a battle faced by every single person on this planet—aging."

The clip comes to an end with a fade to black and an "In Memoriam" message for Matilda, who died a few weeks after the interview.

Goldie was home from college for the summer during the original broadcast and was forced to watch it by her mother, Sun, who filled their bathroom with Crown products.

"This is ridiculous!" Goldie said. "Spending billions to get rid of some wrinkles? It's a waste!"

"You're 20," her mother said. "Of course you say that now. Wait till you old."

Goldie will never admit this to her, but her mother was right. The older she gets, the better she can understand Matilda's cold logic: If you can't cure death, why not confront something else that everyone faces?

Why not make the world young?

Well, not the world. Again, the stuff's expensive. Only the wealthy have had the option of staying young for a lifetime. Age discrimination and youth bias are normal schools of thought. Self-worth is intrinsically tied to a youthful appearance, and no matter how "good" Goldie might look for her age, she can't pull off 25. Society has no time to waste on her.

Society ... and romantic partners. Goldie hasn't had a significant relationship in her entire life until recently. But she can't think about him right now. She cried enough over the weekend.

Damn you, Teo Estrada.

"Ms. Hays?" the receptionist calls out. "Ms. Crown will see you now."

For a second, Goldie's confused and thinks the person is referring to Matilda, who is still very dead. The clip somehow distracted the *Daily Liberty Press* reporter from her entire reason for being at Crown's headquarters: an exclusive interview with the current CEO—Matilda's daughter, Sarah.

As she gets up, Goldie does a quick comb of her long hair with her fingers, then screws her feet into her heels to make sure she's stable enough to stride across the slick floor toward the wooden doors.

Inside, she finds a vast space with a great view, an expected sight for a CEO's office, but the vibe is more akin to a homey loft apartment. The meeting space is styled like a living room. The large Crown brand logo on the floor is mostly covered by cushy couches with crumpled, slept-on pillows. The coffee tables are littered with papers, used mugs, an open package of Oreos—

Her appraisal is stopped by the squeal of office chair wheels.

Rising from behind a desk in a far corner is a tall, willowy figure wearing a pale pink button-up, straight-legged black pants, and comfortable flats. The casual look contradicts the reporter's more ostentatious expectations: fedoras, feathered boas, fascinators...

Apparently, she's been conflating rich people with early-twentieth-century flappers.

Goldie subtly shakes her head to dismiss the thought. She needs to make a more critical assessment of Sarah Crown, starting with what she knows from her research.

While her mother was known as an innovator, Sarah set herself apart by becoming a logistician with a conscience, ensuring the company was both profitable and charitable. She also differed from Matilda by not using the Serum for several years until one day the news leaked that she showed up at a shareholders' meeting looking decades younger.

As far as appearances go, the mother and daughter have the same auburn hair color ... and that seems to be it. Matilda fought the aging process until her dying breath. Her daughter, on the other hand, despite her complete lack of wrinkles, seems comfortable being an obviously 60-something-year-old.

While Matilda had a short, trendy hairstyle, Sarah's long locks are overdue for a trim. Matilda was known for wearing large, round sunglasses from the usual big-name Italian design houses. Sarah's face currently features the boxy, thick-framed reading glasses you'd find on any drugstore rack. Matilda always stood tall and poised, even in her later years, but Sarah's posture is poor, her neck tilted forward.

"Ms. Hays, welcome." Sarah greets Goldie brightly, interrupting the reporter's observations. The CEO rounds her desk to meet the reporter halfway in the room. "I'm sorry for the wait. I wanted to finish as much as possible before we had our chat."

"Thank you for agreeing to see me, Ms. Crown. I'll try not to take up too much time."

"I insist that you do, Ms. Hays. I've been looking forward to this for a while."

The interview was scheduled a month ago. In the meantime, the reporter's been researching and interviewing Serum users.

Sarah motions for Goldie to follow her to a couch. Once they're both seated and the reporter has her laptop on the nearest coffee table, Goldie fires off her first question. "In regard to your anticipation for our meeting, can I ask why?"

"Yes, you can ask 'why'! You can also ask 'when,' 'what,' and even 'how.' 'Where' might be boring though. Spoilers, but pretty much anything to do with the Serum happened in this building. My mother never took her work home."

"Um, that's great," Goldie says, because having a willing interview subject is, of course, ideal. "But what's happening here?"

"An interview?"

Goldie's unamused by the flippant attitude and isn't afraid to show it since being a newspaper journalist in the twenty-first century requires a thick skin. She's spent years working nights on the crime desk and thousands of hours at boring city council meetings. She's been spit on for an op-ed she didn't even write and had her rear fender dented courtesy of the wife of a dirtbag former judge whom she exposed for taking bribes.

So, yeah, she's got this.

"Why have you asked specifically for me and my newspaper to interview you exclusively? For the twentieth anniversary of the Serum, a TV interview with a big network seems more appropriate."

"I don't want this to be about me," Sarah says, brow furrowing. "Being trans already made me stand out, and after the intense coverage of my transition, I vowed never again to let those media vultures into my life." She snags a water bottle from the table and takes a swig like there's something stronger in it. "This is about the Serum. How it's affected people, whether for better or worse—or a bit of both."

"It's surprising you'd allow the possibility of negative effects from the Serum."

"I'm not oblivious to how the Serum can upend lives. In fact, I was one of the first people to experience it. My mother hid herself from me for three months and let me think it had to do with her cancer treatments and not wanting to show how sick she was. Instead, she stopped treatments, pumped herself full of the Serum, and set the product's launch campaign in motion. I was her only child—her only family member who didn't give a shit about her money—but she didn't have time to waste on me. She couldn't die without making the Serum a reality."

"I'll admit that it sounds shallow of her," Goldie concedes, "but she did leave you her entire company and wealth. That had to be her way of showing her love."

"Money isn't everything."

Goldie can't help scoffing.

"Trust me, I know how ridiculous that sounds coming from someone with my net worth," Sarah admits. "But I didn't want love via money. I wanted my mom."

Goldie's relationship with her mother has suffered too because of money—the lack-of, that is. After her American father left them when Goldie was barely out of diapers, Sun struggled financially as a Korean immigrant with basic English and no higher education.

The reporter shoves the thought aside. Her past and present have no place here.

And yet...

"Why do an interview with me?" Goldie asks again. There's something specific that got her through those wooden doors. She can sense it. "Are you some kind of fan?"

"Not really."

Goldie scrunches her face, her ego surprisingly taking a hit.

"Don't get me wrong. I respect your work, Ms. Hays. And can I call you Marigold? You can call me Sarah. I think we're beyond formalities at this point."

"It's Goldie, actually. I just use my full name for bylines."

"Oh, both names are lovely."

Goldie winces at the memory the comment conjures. Before she can get called out on it, the reporter doubles down on trying to regain some traction with the interview. "If you're not a fan, then why me?"

Sarah sighs and crosses her legs, then leans back into the cushion. "All that stuff I said about not wanting to do a TV interview was true, but there's another factor."

Goldie makes a helpless gesture, imploring her to continue.

"Most TV news personalities, including the ones at small stations, use the Serum. It's part of the channel's budget or their contracts. I know most newspapers don't have to make those same kinds of deals because their reporters don't have to be camera-ready. I decided to go with a local paper because the bigger ones like *The New York Times* pay more, and much of the staff will be Serum users too."

"Why were you determined to get someone who hadn't used the Serum?"

"If a Serum user interviewed me, the person would be right from the get-go biased in favor of it. They'd probably try to bargain for some free doses too. When I background-checked the bylines in your paper, your many years with the newspaper and impressive work made you the obvious choice."

Goldie feels her cheeks heat. "Several of my colleagues would have done great work too."

"Don't diminish your worth like that."

"What?" Goldie reels back. "Acknowledging other people's talents doesn't mean I'm putting down my own."

"I explained why I chose you, and you don't believe me for some reason. Now, is that because you have genuine suspicions that what I said wasn't true, or are you letting some non-journalistic insecurities show?"

"It's both," Goldie says with the slam of her laptop lid. "You're right, Sarah. I'm too insecure to ever claim to be the best at anything, even a job I've dedicated my whole adult life to. But I have enough confidence to trust my instincts, which are telling me that this situation is trouble." She gets up from the couch. "I'm sorry to have wasted your time and mine."

"Goldie, think about what you're risking by walking away. You already know there's something more happening here."

"You admit it!" The reporter wants to jump on the couch while repeating the words, throwing in an "I knew it!" just for the hell of it. Instead, she settles for pointing the typical accusatory finger at her.

"Guilty." Sarah raises her hands in surrender. "There's a big secret."

With her suspicions confirmed, Goldie reassesses the situation. "How big?"

"Re-vo-lutionary," Sarah says with exaggerated flourish.

Goldie can fathom only one thing that could one-up Sarah's mother's innovation. "Holy crap, did you cure death?"

"What? No!"

"Then I'm not interested." Goldie reaches for her purse. (It's a power play and total bluff. There's no way she's leaving now.)

"Come on, Goldie! You'd really be willing to give up on the scoop of a lifetime?"

"Yes! Because you still won't be upfront about everything."

Sarah huffs. "I'll admit that on paper, you seem like the right person to handle this story. But I would like to know more about you before I do my big reveal. It would help me to trust you with it."

Goldie shakes her head. "Whatever you tell me would go into the story and be published for the general public."

"Eh." Sarah half shrugs. "When you hear what it is, you may not want to share it. But I'll leave that for you to decide."

"Let me get this straight," Goldie says, holding up a hand against any possible interruption. "In order to get this interview with you and learn this big secret, which I may or may not want to include, I have to allow you to interview me first?"

"A story for a story."

Goldie takes her time to consider the CEO's proposal. This interview is unquestionably a big opportunity for her professionally. But after what happened Friday night—hell, the past few weeks—maybe she needs to look at what it could do for her personally too.

Because she's got a lot to get off her chest.

Goldie flops back down onto the couch. Sarah grins victoriously.

Scanning their surroundings for inspiration on where to start, Goldie's gaze catches on an old poster advertising the Serum with a butterfly emerging from its chrysalis.

"That ad was used in the intro to advertising course I had to take in journalism school. The topic was how to use symbolism."

Sarah seems to be surprised by the poster's existence. It's

probably one of those things a person has had around for so long that it's gone unnoticed.

"At first, the butterfly doesn't seem to fit the product," Goldie continues. "The Serum makes the person look like they used to or maintains their youthful appearance. It doesn't completely change them."

"Right." Sarah nods. "Instead, the butterfly represents what the Serum can do for the users. It's a new beginning."

"Great marketing," Goldie admits. "New beginnings get rarer as the years go by, and people can get desperate to experience them, doing whatever they can to make them happen no matter the costs. I didn't get that sentiment most of my life. I was afraid of the new, trusted the familiar, always played things safe."

"Did something change?"

"Yeah." Goldie gives Sarah a sad smile. "I turned 40."

CHAPTER 2

ONE MONTH AGO

THE BLINKING CURSOR IS A TAUNTING, OBNOXIOUS THING. IT'S NOT just an indicator of your place in a document but a ticking clock, a reminder of how slow and agonizing the writing process can be.

[BLINK]
Why aren't you typing anything?
[BLINK]
Really? That's what took you so long to write?
[BLINK]
Is your degree even real?
[BLINK]
An 8-year-old could write with more depth.
[BLINK]
You should have stayed in retail.

Hands slam down on Goldie's keyboard. "What are you doing here?!"

"Jesus!" Goldie almost jolts out of her chair.

"Nope, it's just Amber. I'm afraid there's no salvation for us 40-year-olds."

The photographer cackles with her whole body, leaning forward and forcing her voluminous natural hair to curtain her face, then parting the dark curls with both hands as if she were clearing the way for the one last unnecessary "Ha!" she directs at the reporter.

Goldie erases the extra letters that appeared on her document from Amber's shenanigans. "You're so lucky my computer didn't freeze up. This real estate story's almost done."

"There are no stories to finish on your birthday, especially not that boring-ass one. How dare you make me take shots of empty plots of land and rat-infested death traps?"

"Duty to the public, exposing corruption, other important journalistic reasons," Goldie blandly lists as she pecks out the last words of the conclusion. Amber's distraction helps her abandon her previous hypercritical train wreck of thoughts and finish the piece.

"Hays!" Goldie's last name is hoarsely shrieked across the newsroom.

Goldie whips around to see executive editor Lloyd Manning hanging out of his office.

"Quit fucking with the real estate story, and get the fuck in here! There's something fucking big to talk about!"

Newspaper journalists love their F-bombs.

"Prick," Amber mutters before giving Goldie a supportive arm squeeze and going to the photo desk.

Goldie types and moves her mouse at a glacial pace, then finishes her tea while it's warm. Manning and his filthy mouth can wait.

"All right," the reporter says when she finally enters the executive editor's cramped office. "What was the yelling for?"

"What took you so long?"

"I was doing my job," Goldie says, not bothering to hide her frustration from her frustrating boss. "I filed the real estate story."

"Fuck that boring story. You know about the Crown Serum, right?"

"No, I've been living in a cave my whole adult life."

Manning ignores the comeback. "The twentieth anniversary is soon, and I want you to write about it."

"Isn't that more of a lifestyle story? Why aren't you getting Cooper for it?"

"You'd actually pass on this?"

"It's just an anniversary with a nice round number."

"Sarah Crown is willing to do an interview."

Goldie snorts a laugh. "You're joking. She never does interviews."

"I made a few calls," he says, as if he'd been trying to find the best deal on auto insurance.

"Did you threaten her?"

"No, Goldie." Manning rolls his eyes. "I'm not some mafia boss."

"Then this *is* a joke, because there's no way she's talking to us. This is Chris Evans all over again."

"That was a legitimate opportunity."

"You told me, 'Hurry, Chris Evans is downtown!' I broke speed records to get there, thinking I'm going to meet the actor who plays Captain America—my favorite superhero of all time. That he'll fall in love with me, and I'll bear his super babies. But what did I get instead? The owner of Southern Fried Chick-O-Rama scouting a location for a new restaurant."

"They don't open those everywhere," Manning defends.

"There are two in France!"

"Would you let that go already? This is a real interview with the real Sarah Crown."

"Then why aren't you the one interviewing her, Mr. Pulitzer Prize Winner? I agree, it's big, which means *you* would be the one to jump on it."

"Uh, happy birthday?" Manning says pathetically.

Goldie's patented "Bitch, please" expression, learned from her mother, is in full effect.

"All right, I did try to get it," Manning admits. "Even mentioned the Pulitzer."

Goldie nods, because of course he did.

"She only wants to talk to you for some reason."

"When does she want to do this?"

"It's not going to be for another month. That'll give you time for background work and user testimonials. You can get Anderson for photography."

"Of course I'm using Amber. She's the best." Goldie never misses the opportunity to hype her friend's work. "Besides, she's our *only* full-time photographer." She also makes sure to passively give the executive editor grief for the shamefully understaffed photo department.

Manning simply sighs and gets up to signal that the meeting's done. "And for real this time"—he hands her today's paper—"happy birthday, Goldie."

She looks at the opened page and spots what he's showing her: an ad with her security badge photo and the words *Lordy, lordy, look who's 40!*

Goldie stares for several seconds, in absolute awe of her executive editor's prickishness.

"Lloyd, you are the worst," she says as she exits the office. "I'm leaving early. Might not come back either."

Manning waves her off, unconcerned and too busy laughing.

"What happened?!" Amber pounces once Goldie's back at her desk.

"Stop doing that!" Goldie slaps her on the shoulder. "Are you trying to give me a heart attack on my birthday?"

"That'd be tragic, right? Dead on your 40th birthday before you got to celebrate with your hot, young boyfriend."

"It'd be fitting since I made it onto the obits page today." Goldie shows Amber the ad. Silly birthday dedications often end up there thanks to the advertising department's wicked gallows humor.

Amber scans the page, something Goldie avoids. It's not uncommon to use photos of the deceased from their younger years, but thanks to the Serum, they're *recent* photos of baby-faced elderly folks, lending a wrongness to the somber page.

"This is what Lloyd was screaming about?"

"No, it's just his crap sense of humor. But get this: We're doing a story on the twentieth anniversary of the Crown Serum and interviewing Sarah Crown."

Amber's eyes grow wide enough to pop out of her face. "You're shitting me? How did Lloyd pull this off? Do I have to act respectful to him now?"

"Nah." Goldie shakes her head. "Apparently, she was the one to set this up. Asked for me in particular."

"You? No offense, but why you? You don't use the Serum. You don't even use makeup most days."

"I don't know. Lloyd didn't press her. Probably was too grateful she'd talk to anyone at the newspaper." Goldie looks at the birthday ad and frowns at how very 40 she looks. "It's weird. Feels almost like a trap."

Amber throws the paper in the recycling bin. "Fuck this negativity. Think about it later. You've got birthday sex to look forward to."

"Oh God." Goldie hides her burning face in her hands and groans. "Why, Amber?"

"If I didn't have you to embarrass and yank out of your turtle shell, I'd have left this place a long time ago."

"Well, you don't have to drag me out to an obnoxious club this year. Teo and I have plans tonight."

"Good boy." Amber smirks, never missing an opportunity to tease her about her younger boyfriend.

"We're going to see the latest Marvel movie."

"Oh, bad boy," Amber scoffs. "There's nothing better you guys can do?"

"He's a working musician. I don't want him trying to spend money on a fancy dinner or boring theater show. Besides, we've been avoiding spoilers for weeks so we can both get the full experience tonight. It's been killing him not to have seen it already."

Amber waggles a perfectly groomed and penciled eyebrow. "Great ass *and* a gigantic geek. He's perfect for you."

"I wish my mother thought so. I'm dreading tonight. Teo's coming over for dinner before the movie."

"Awkward."

Goldie sighs. "Teo thinks it's an opportunity to win her over."

"I can't believe your mother's not harassing him to marry and impregnate you already. She's been desperate for you to find someone."

"She says she's got a bad feeling about him, and that, of course, I don't see it because I'm a terrible judge of character."

"So, if you like him, there must be something wrong with him."

"Exactly."

"That is the most mom reasoning ever." Amber's phone buzzes. "Speaking of moms, I've got to go be one and answer this. Have fun tonight!" She corkscrews around to return to her desk. "What's up?" she says into the phone. Her daughter says something. "How, Caroline?! How do you keep losing your retainer? Are you spitting it out at people? Dropping it over a flushing toilet?"

Goldie shuts down her computer and heads out the door. It's been an eventful birthday already. Time to see what else 40 has in store.

GOLDIE TURNS OFF THE BLOW DRYER WHEN SHE HEARS A KNOCK.

"What?"

"You use right makeup?" her mother asks from behind the bathroom door. "Use new Crown powder I buy you. No cheap stuff. You have oily face."

"Okay, sure. Let me do one thing at a time."

"You slow. I finish making dinner already," Sun gloats. "Hurry up!"

Goldie growls low but otherwise internalizes her frustrations like a good daughter.

As she returns to drying her hair, Goldie looks down at the variety of bottles and tubes for various skin woes. She gets acne, so she already slathered on medication before applying the under-eye gel patches, which she'll keep on as long as possible to look less goth. Once the medication has soaked in, she can put on the anti-wrinkle moisturizer, then the cover-up foundation for her dark spots and blotchy redness, then—yes, mother—the damn powder for a matte finish.

It's no wonder she takes so long in the bathroom.

When Goldie finally comes out to the kitchen/dining room to check on her mother, she's surprised to see Teo already there.

"Ma actually let you in?"

Her boyfriend looks up from the plate and utensils he's setting. "Yeah, only because it meant she can boss me around without you trying to stop her." He hugs Goldie as soon as she's close. "Happy birthday."

A not-so-subtle cough from her mother breaks them apart.

"Finally, you ready," Sun says, making a point of walking between the couple. "I going to eat cake without you." She places said cake with the numerals four and zero in the center of the table and looks at her daughter with a serious expression. "No more stick candles for you. Don't want house burn down."

Teo covers his mouth to hide his laugh.

Sun waves to order them to sit. "Eat before you get too old and lose your teeth."

Goldie can't help a little smile. There's no denying that her mom's got jokes.

"IF YOU NOT EAT KIMCHI, MY DAUGHTER BREAK UP WITH YOU."

Teo looks at Goldie like he's really concerned. "Is that true?"

Goldie sighs deeply. "Ma, stop it. He doesn't have to eat it."

"I'm not a fan of spicy things," Teo explains.

"I thought you Spanish. All your food have peppers."

"I'm Guatemalan, actually." Goldie's boyfriend is patient with her Korean mother's English limitations and lack of knowledge of Spanish colonialism. "But you're pretty right about the peppers. My stomach is just sensitive."

"You probably disappoint your mommy a lot."

"Ma! You know his parents are dead!"

"I mean before." Sun waves off her daughter's outrage. She's not great with past tense. "Since baby, Goldie always eat what I give her. Not picky."

"We were poor," Goldie grumbles. "I didn't have much choice."

"I'm sorry you had such a hard time," Teo says, brow creasing. "You remind me of my mother. She went through a lot to raise me."

"How she die young?" Sun asks.

"Liver cancer."

Goldie tries to curtail the conversation's somber turn. "Ma, let's just finish dinner and get to the cake."

Sun ignores her words, too focused on scrutinizing Teo, as usual. This time, though, Goldie swears there's some sympathy in her eyes. Her mother picks up her chopsticks and places a piece of kimchi on Teo's plate.

"Ma," Goldie warns.

"One piece," she insists. "It good for you. You too skinny."

Goldie's boyfriend smiles at the peace offering and pops it into his mouth without hesitation (along with a lot of rice).

AFTER A TERRIBLE RENDITION OF THE "HAPPY BIRTHDAY" SONG AND the tiniest piece of cake ever ("You 40 now," her mother said. "You gain weight easy."), Teo and Goldie go to the movie theater. They see Tommy waiting in the lobby as they enter.

Teo whispers to Goldie as they approach her longtime friend. "I feel like I'm taking some kind of boyfriend birthday test. Challenge number one: Survive dinner with the disapproving mother without getting terrible acid reflux. Challenge number two: Endure a movie without getting kicked in the face by the jealous best friend who knows taekwondo like he invented it."

Before Goldie can respond, Tommy sees them and runs over to lift her off the ground in a hug. "Happy birthday, Golden Girl!" When he sets her back down, he looks at her appraisingly. "You know, you're almost old enough to make that nickname fit."

"Haha, everyone's got age jokes tonight." Goldie waits for Tommy to acknowledge Teo's presence and raises a pointed eyebrow when he doesn't even wave at him.

Teo goes ahead and greets him first. "Hey, Tommy. How's it going?"

"Oh, hey, man!" Tommy blinks rapidly, feigning surprise. "Didn't see you there."

Teo rolls his eyes at the smartass jab alluding to their height difference.

Goldie punches Tommy lightly in the arm. "You overgrown child. You're buying popcorn and drinks for that."

"You act like I wasn't going to anyway. But do I really have to get something for Teo? He's a grown man ... I think."

Goldie glares at her best friend. It might be an adjustment to have someone else join their tradition of watching a superhero flick on their birthdays, but she didn't think Tommy would go full *Mean Girls* on Teo.

"Get your ass to the concession stand," she says to Tommy. "Two large popcorns, a large soft pretzel, and drinks for each of us. We'll be in our seats."

"How am I supposed to carry all that?"

"You're tall. Figure out a way to use those long limbs."

Fueled by sheer determination and pure spite, Tommy stretches his ingenuity to bring all the items in one go: covering the popcorn buckets with lids to stack them, balancing the box with the soft pretzel on top, and carrying the drinks in an empty large popcorn box.

Teo applauds the accomplishment (patronizingly, but there seems to be some genuine admiration there). Tommy shoves a drink in between the clapping hands to make him stop.

"Thank you," Goldie says, taking a large popcorn bucket and snatching a few kernels before passing it to Teo.

"Anything for you," Tommy says, looking glumly at the other large popcorn that's meant only for him.

As the movie starts, Goldie gets caught up in the world of fantastic feats and corny one-liners. When Teo eventually wraps his hand around hers, she flinches, honestly forgetting she was seeing this with her boyfriend. He smiles apologetically and gives her hand a comforting squeeze.

Goldie's not a 40-year-old virgin, but her limited dating experiences have left her awkward. No one had ever been right enough to risk her heart for—not even Tommy.

At six-foot-three, the car salesman with tousled chestnut-brown hair and a cocky grin easily caught Goldie's attention the day her old Honda Accord couldn't be revived anymore. Their easy banter about movies and pop culture was the beginning of a friendship that's lasted more than a decade.

With all that they had in common, it should have been an easy progression to dating, marriage, and children during that time. But as much as Goldie loved the guy, their relationship never went further, and there had never been someone to test the strength of their friendship—until Teo.

"That was the lamest ending," Tommy says as they finally leave the theater. The trio stayed through the credits to watch the bonus scenes like good Marvel fans.

"Marvel's going downhill," Teo says. "*Iron Man*'s still the best."

Goldie rolls her eyes. "That was, like, a *hundred* movies ago."

"And nothing compares to it."

"No way," Tommy says. "Marvel movies haven't been good since the original *Spider-Man* trilogy."

Teo scowls. "You're really including the third movie as good?"

Tommy looms over him in an exaggerated show of his entire five inches of superior height. "I respect the overall hard work, vision, and ambition that went into *all* those movies, concepts an Iron Man fanboy apparently can't grasp."

"Is that right?" Teo says, tipping his head back to acknowledge the looming. Then he steps onto a bench, making himself a good head taller than Tommy. "Look, man, I know how you feel."

Tommy scrunches his face. "About the *Spider-Man* movies?"

"No, forget them. I'm talking about your jealousy of my relationship with Goldie."

At the mention of her name, Tommy's eyes flick over to his friend, then back up at Teo. "What the hell are you talking about? And why are you standing on a bench in the middle of a movie theater?"

"Because you love to flaunt your height at every opportunity. Congratulations, you're taller than me. Lots of people are."

Tommy's left speechless.

"Look, I know you're afraid of losing her," Teo says, his voice soft. "And you think jealousy makes your feelings more genuine or honorable. It doesn't though. It's just going to push her away."

Teo jumps down from the impromptu soapbox and returns to Goldie's side.

For a long minute, Tommy's gaze stays stuck on the wall behind the bench. When he finally looks back, there's a defeated dip to his mouth that obscures the deep dimples and perpetual smirk usually associated with him.

"You're my Golden Girl," he says, blowing out a breath. "It's hard not being the one who makes you happy."

The achingly honest declaration has Goldie glancing at Teo, wondering not for the first time why she couldn't have found him sooner. The wait cost Tommy and her too many years of longing and disappointment.

"But Teo's right," Tommy continues. "My biggest fear is losing you. So, as long as you're willing to forgive me for being an ass, then I'm not going anywhere."

Goldie slowly nods and forces her lips to spread into a smile, relieved that he's trying to make amends but sad on his behalf for the unfairness of it all. "Of course, Tommy."

Her best friend offers a hand to Teo. "I'm sorry about everything. Just ... treat her right."

"You got it."

"And if you need anything from me, man, I'm there. Whether it's getting something from a high shelf, cleaning the top of your car, placing the star on a Christmas tree—"

Goldie interrupts with yet another punch to the arm.

"Ow! All right, I'm sorry!" Tommy laughs. "No more short jokes, I swear."

GOLDIE AND TEO HEAD TO HANK'S BAR IN TIME FOR THE NIGHT'S final performances from the Panty Rockers, one of several dubiously named acts that regularly perform on the Helena, the venue's modest stage. Teo's also a regular performer and lives in the building's upper apartment.

Despite the establishment's name, the owner goes by Henry and is an old friend of Teo's family. He's a stout man in his early 60s with closely trimmed hair that's graying. His beard, however, is a cotton ball that stands out against his dark skin. With his quiet nature and inclination toward flannel shirts, Henry's a big ol' teddy bear.

"Hey, old man!" Teo calls out as they claim a couple of bar stools.

Henry waves in greeting before reaching for one of the refrigerators to pull out a bottle of champagne. He smoothly uncorks it and pours the contents into two flutes that seem to appear from nowhere.

"Happy birthday, Goldie," the bar owner says as he places the drinks in front of them.

"Thank you?" Goldie responds with inflection, looking at her boyfriend to silently ask about the fancy order.

"I asked Henry to serve something special for you tonight," Teo says.

Goldie wants to argue that neither of them typically drink and the expensive stuff isn't necessary. She sees how thoughtful Teo's being, though, and takes the glass.

She almost sips straightaway before Teo stops her.

"We have to toast!"

Goldie scrunches her face.

"Stop acting like it's ridiculous to celebrate like this. I still wish you would've let me throw you a party."

"It's just another birthday," Goldie insists, "with a big number that gets overblown."

"It's not about the number. It's about celebrating *you*." Teo lifts his glass and pointedly looks at Goldie's, insisting she do the same. "You're going to have to endure hearing the sappy things I'm about to say set to the romantic sounds of the Panty Rockers."

The birthday girl laughs and lifts her glass without any more fuss.

"To Marigold Hays, the hard-hitting reporter who begrudgingly took a story about the local music scene while the entertainment reporter was on maternity leave and walked into my life because of it."

Goldie smiles at the memory of meeting Teo at Hank's Bar.

"These months with you have made me the happiest I've been in a very long time. You're funny and kind—the best combination. You work too hard. You help anyone in any way you can. You value honest goodness above shallow greatness. And no matter how hard life can get, you never lose hope for that goodness to win out in the end. I'm so grateful to have met you, Goldie. I'm sorry it couldn't have been sooner."

Sniffing hard, Goldie tries to calm down quickly so she can request a slight revision to her boyfriend's toast. "To us?"

Teo's big smile somehow stretches even wider. "To us," he confirms, and clinks their glasses. "Happy birthday, Goldie."

GOLDIE BEGINS STRIPPING HER BOYFRIEND AS SOON AS THE DOOR to his apartment shuts.

"I have wanted you *all night*," she says with a long groan. "We should have just spent my birthday in bed."

Teo laughs, a rumble Goldie can feel with her lips as she

lavishes attention on his neck and chest. "That can be my birthday," he suggests. "How about that?"

Goldie hums in agreement, too busy licking along his collarbone, before looking up. "Wait, when *is* your birthday? Did I miss it?! I am the worst girlfriend. I never asked."

"Relax, you didn't miss it. It's June 7."

"Really?"

"Yeah, what's so shocking?"

"That's not too far away. It's the same month as the Crown Serum anniversary."

Teo seems stunned for some reason but shakes himself out of it. "Why'd you bring that up? Are you going to be too busy for the awesome 'sex all day in bed' idea?"

Goldie rolls her eyes. "No, but I just got assigned a story on the Serum's anniversary. I'm interviewing Sarah Crown."

"That sounds like a big deal. She's the richest human alive."

"It *is* a big deal," Goldie confirms. "But I'm also annoyed I have to do it."

"Why?"

"The Serum's a waste of money that could be better used for literally anything else."

"You can't think of any legitimate reasons for a person to use it?"

"Can you?" Goldie's irked by the non-sexy talk but unable to resist hearing Teo's opinion.

He lifts a shoulder. "Seems similar to cosmetic surgery. It's not always a vanity thing for those who get it. There's confidence that comes from having your face or body look the way you want. With confidence comes motivation to turn your life around or to do what you've always wanted—to realize your dreams."

Goldie's stunned and somewhat ashamed. Here she is at 40 finding ugly cynicism harder than ever to fight and getting the wisdom she needs from her not-even-30-year-old boyfriend.

"How are you real?" Goldie murmurs before kissing him deeply, expressing the excitement and passion and pure joy he inspires within her. She breaks them apart with a softly panted, "I love you."

Teo's panting too, seemingly unable to form words.

"Was that too much?"

"No, it was perfect," he says, a giddy laugh escaping. "Now it feels like my birthday."

"Oh, it's definitely mine." Goldie's face hurts from how big she's smiling. "And I'm making sure it's the best ever."

"Nope, you're not one-upping me." Teo interrupts her indignant scoff by backing her into the bedroom. "I'm going to make sure your birthday is absolutely unforgettable."

Teo removes the rest of their clothes before they lie down on their sides, facing each other, entangling their limbs. He kisses Goldie to the point of dizziness, greedily breathing in the openhearted joy she expressed to him tonight.

When they're fully joined, Goldie holds him in place and hugs him tightly. But despite all the points of contact, the brush of his lips over her ear manages to grab her attention.

"I love you too, Golden Wonder."

Goldie worries that her heart will burst from the intense emotions those whispered words unleash. She's waited so long to hear them. Finally, she's found love.

Best. Birthday. *Ever*.

CHAPTER 3

"You don't deserve God's love."

Hearing those words on a Sunday morning at the local Korean church takes Goldie from half-conscious to fully alert. Everyone else seems just as shocked, too, with one mother unnecessarily covering the AirPod-stuffed ears of her tween son.

The pastor appears pleased with the reaction and remains quiet for a long moment to let his words sink in. Only when the church's head minister clears his throat loudly does he continue.

"I'll explain, but first, I want to discuss 1 Corinthians, Chapter 13, Verses 4–8, in the New International Version. Because on the subject of love, it gets to the *heart* of the matter."

Again, he waits for a reaction to his words. This time, however, he receives blank stares and a sneezing fit from Mrs. Park.

Goldie snorts as quietly as she can at the muted response. There are a few reasons she chooses to go to the English-language service instead of the earlier Korean one. Primarily, her Korean sucks. Secondly, she can sleep in a little later because the Korean mass is earlier, which allows the ajummas—the older women of the church—to make lunch for the congregation for both services. Lately, though, she goes because of the new pastor.

Paul Lee has injected much-needed energy into the little church behind the strip mall with a recently renovated Food Lion. A native of the area, he's a childhood friend of Goldie's and moved back a year ago right after getting ordained.

A shocking development since Paulee had been a tech wiz at Apple.

The pastor opens his heavily bookmarked Bible and begins reading the famous passage. *"Love is patient, love is kind.* I argue that these simple sentiments contain 90 percent of the meaning of love. If you keep these six words in your heart, you're doing love right."

Goldie starts thinking of Teo. Has she been patient and kind enough with him? Maybe she rushed a bit in expressing how she was in love. He's younger and shouldn't be subjected to her middle-aged rush to secure a life partner.

"But relationships, oftentimes, aren't so simple," Pastor Paul continues. "For example, there's this person I know, we'll call him … Saul." He blinks rapidly, clearly surprised he chose that name. "Saul had the life he always pictured for himself. He was known as an innovator in his field, making very good money. Tom Ford suits, Clive Christian cologne, vacations to Bali, courtside Knicks tickets."

He sighs and stares off into the distance. The head minister clears his throat yet again.

"Anyway," the pastor says with a shake of his head, "Saul was smart, but he couldn't have achieved so much without the support of his wife. They encouraged each other relentlessly. Attained the perfect spacious apartment in the super chic neighborhood that, dare I say, even the Almighty couldn't afford. And when they started their family—a girl and a boy—everything was exactly as Saul had pictured for himself."

Pastor Paul takes a breath and barely glances down at his Bible as he recites more of the verses. *"It does not envy, it does not boast, it is not proud.* Saul's lifestyle, his work, his wife, and his family became points of pride, not evidence of love. Thus, he turned to God."

Goldie smiles at Paul's terribly veiled recap of his decision to become a pastor. She was pleasantly surprised when he came back to town after only seeing him for occasional holiday visits. More surprising was his wife, Lily, a financial advisor and Yale graduate, agreeing to the move.

"Saul thought the love he felt while studying the Word— discovering God's patience and kindness—would magically fit around all other facets of his life. Saul was wrong."

The pastor looks down at his left hand and turns the wedding band a few times, like he's fixing its placement on his finger. "After many, many months of trying to live with the new conditions that came with loving him, Saul's wife left."

He sniffs hard and clears his throat. "Back to the love passage: *It is not rude, it is not self-seeking, it is not easily angered, it keeps no record of wrongs.* Turning to anger seems natural after seeing your wife walk out the door. But Saul knew that if he or she had ever truly loved the other, they would never let anger mar it."

Pastor Paul steps down from the dais to the floor. "*Love does not delight in evil but rejoices with the truth.* This is where I'm circling back to that whole 'You don't deserve God's love' pronouncement I led with. Because I want you to ask yourselves how truthful you've been in love."

He clears his throat but can't seem to rein in the roughness of his voice. "They may be separated for now, but Saul and his wife were never more certain of their love than when he made the choice to follow his calling and she made the choice to return to hers. When both parties are completely truthful with each other, that's a show of real love, and only then will we come anywhere close to deserving the perfect love that God shows us every day.

"That love is described in the rest of the passage: *It always protects, always trusts, always hopes, always perseveres.*" He pauses and raises his hand to sweep across the field of congregants. "Now say the next line with me."

"Love never fails!"

Pastor Paul whoops an "Amen!"

THE LINE TO GREET CHURCH LEADERS AT THE END OF SERVICES IS especially long today thanks to the ajummas showing Pastor Paul their sympathies. Currently, two small Korean women are hugging him and sobbing like he told everyone he was dying.

Goldie's so enthralled that she startles when the small arms of a toddler wrap around her leg. "Ty Bear?"

Penny is quick to scoop her son into her bare arms. Goldie likes to have some sleeve on her tops and dresses, but right now, she's envious of her friend's cap-sleeved midi dress. It's perfect for summer at the barely air-conditioned church.

The color's not her taste though. It's a light blue that probably has a proper name like robin's egg or cotton candy and is the color of the day, tinting everything from her supercute wedge sandals and painted toenails to her handmade bracelets and scrunchy-ribbon combo that's holding her hair in a high ponytail.

Heck, even her Bible carrying case is that shade of blue.

"Tyler, baby, you have to stop hugging everyone's legs," Penny says before hip-checking Goldie in greeting and joining her in gawking at their friend.

Paulee's face is between yet another older woman's hands like he's a fussy baby.

"Think we should rescue him?" Penny asks.

"Maybe at lunch. I think he knows he's gotta endure this after what he confessed. Probably wants to get it over with."

They head toward the cafeteria wing and find Goldie's mother arguing amid the hustle and bustle of the kitchen.

"Is everything all right, Ma?"

"How long we do this?" Sun says in English to the ajumma next to her. "Still, no one clean pots right, and we do two-time work every Sunday."

"They're fine!" exclaims Mrs. Kim (one of many with the name at the Korean church). "You just bossy!"

Penny snorts a laugh.

"Ma, can I get a few boxes?" Goldie asks, ignoring the argument. Her mother *is* bossy, and everyone at the church knows it.

"You not eat here?"

"We're going to find a quieter area to eat with Pastor Lee."

Sun opens her mouth to respond, but Mrs. Kim beats her to it. "Oh, I hear what he say in sermon. Too bad." She tsks. "But maybe you marry him now, Goldie."

"What?!" Goldie and her mother both exclaim.

"You single," Mrs. Kim says. "Why not marry good man like him?"

"Because I watch him when he little," Sun says. "He Goldie's oppa, her big brother."

"That's true," Goldie says, agreeing with her mother for once.

"And he not rich no more. Goldie need date him when he have first big job. Now he want her pay everything."

Goldie side-eyes her mother and addresses Mrs. Kim. "Thanks for, uh ..." She pauses to think of any other word besides meddling. "The *support*, but I'm dating someone right now."

"Really?" Mrs. Kim's eyes narrow at Goldie's mother. "Why you not say?"

"They only dating few months now," Sun says dismissively. "Not sure if he good for her yet."

"Ugly? No money?" Mrs. Kim asks. (Wow, ajummas need some form of sensitivity training.)

"Good looking," Goldie's mother says. "No good job."

"He's a musician, Ma."

"I say no *good* job," she clarifies.

Goldie herself wouldn't need a good job if she could monetize every eye roll and sigh she's made over the years after something her mother said.

"Can I get the boxes, please?" she asks again, needing to escape.

Sun hands them over. "Tell Paul I never like Lily. Always stuck up, never help around here. Not like you two," she says, gazing intently at Goldie and Penny.

They look at each other in silent resignation. "We'd be happy to help clean up after lunch," Penny says.

After dropping off Tyler with his dad, they head upstairs to Paul's likely hiding spot: a room with a small balcony overlooking the Dollar General section of the strip mall.

The good pastor is leaning on the railing, wisps of smoke rising above his head.

"Is that weed?!" Goldie shout-asks.

"Jesus Christ!" Paul barely manages to keep hold of his cigarette. After tossing Goldie a glare, he brushes off the ashes on his dress shirt. His suit coat and tie are discarded on one of the many storage boxes that fill the room. "I'd never smoke weed," he insists, then pauses for a beat. "Not at church, at least."

"Hi, Paulee." Goldie smirks.

"Or is it *Saul* now?" Penny asks, also smirking. When it's just the three of them, the old friends tend to revert to their high school selves by communicating with eviscerating honesty and tireless banter.

Paul cringes. "God, that was pathetic. But at least it's out in the open now."

"When did Lily leave?" Goldie asks.

"Last week. She waited for the kids to finish the school year."

"Did she take them back to your old place?" Penny asks.

"Hell no. We can't afford that anymore. She knows someone who knows someone who got us a reasonable brownstone."

"Are you moving back?" Goldie asks. "Are you trying to work things out?"

"I'm not sure." He takes a long, thoughtful drag. "We did couples counseling—the secular kind," he clarifies. "I've been praying about it, of course. Binging on a lot of old episodes of *Dharma & Greg*."

Goldie squints skeptically. "How does that help?"

"Probably doesn't," Paul admits. "I just like the show. If those two total opposites can make it work, maybe there's hope for Lils and me."

"I can see that," Penny says. "When I'm feeling particularly stabby toward Jack, I watch *Sex and the City*. Reminds me that no matter how hard marriage can get, it's so much harder being a wealthy, single white woman with infinite companionship possibilities."

Goldie side-eyes her friend, unsure if she's serious.

"But I can see why you'd like *Dharma & Greg*," Penny continues. "You're the spiritual, lead-with-your-heart one; Lily's the practical, career-minded one. I've never met someone who loves numbers as much as her."

"You mean money," Paul says, stubbing out his cigarette with unnecessary force on an empty Coke can. "Okay, that's not fair. She missed working in her firm's office too. She missed the hustle of big city life. She missed taking the Serum. Seeing how she's supposed to look at 41 was messing with her head."

"She barely has laugh lines," Goldie says. "Maybe one forehead crease if you look hard enough."

"One too many when you've been staying ageless for the last several years. It's sort of like withdrawal."

Now's not the time to gather opinions about the Serum for her story, but hearing how poorly Lily reacted to stopping the treatments has Goldie making mental notes about addressing such concerns.

"How have you been doing without the Serum?"

"I only ever took it because of Lily. I didn't want to look like a middle-aged creep with a trophy wife."

Goldie flinches and looks away, but she still catches the exchange between her friends.

Paul turns to Penny and tilts his head in Goldie's direction in silent question.

Penny mouths, *"Her boyfriend."*

"Oh shit, Goldie!" Paul steps closer to encourage her to look back up. "That's not a judgment on your relationship. It would've been no one's business even if there had been a real age gap between Lily and me. The Serum was how you fit in though. It's just how that world works. I was taking it to meet expectations, and I burned out."

Goldie shakes off the insecurity over her age difference with Teo and focuses on her friend, looking up at his salt-and-pepper hair. "I can't believe you grew up to become a silver-fox pastor."

"I can't believe it either!" Paul smirks and runs a hand through his shaggy locks, indulging in unpastoral smugness, before his gaze drifts to nothing in particular. "You know, there was this one sweet moment after the first sermon when everything felt right. Lily was fully on board with trying to make a life here work; the kids were playing with your kids, Pen; I was surrounded by respected elders and old friends." He looks down at his suit coat and tie, then the wedding ring on his finger. "This is what I'm meant to be doing, I'm still sure of that. It's the where that's gotten muddled. I miss her. I miss *us*."

Goldie wraps her arms around her friend. "Paulee, if anyone can find a way to make it work, it's you two. Just maybe not right now. You might find that this time apart is something you both need— a blessing in disguise."

"Hey, who's the pastor here?" Paul asks as he pulls back, his expression a mix of gratitude and amusement. "I think you missed your calling, Golds."

"Yeah, Goldie, wow." Penny gives an impressed whistle. "Got any advice for my marriage?"

"Like you two need it. I can't believe you and Jack are celebrating ten years already."

"It's your anniversary?" Paul asks.

"On Thursday." Penny flashes excited jazz hands. "We're going to the beach with the kids on Saturday to celebrate as a family, but we really wanted to go out on the actual anniversary, just dinner and some dancing at the piano bar and restaurant downtown." Penny turns to Goldie, eyes wide and pleading.

Goldie already knows what has her friend looking like a freaking anime character. "You know you can just ask me to babysit."

"But I want the reassurance of an offer so I don't feel so bad for inflicting my children on you without monetary compensation."

"Ensuring your special night happens is payment enough," Goldie declares.

Penny knows better. "What do you really want?"

"Let me bring Teo over."

"That's it? Of course he can come. I trust you to make sure the kids are safely tucked in their beds before making out with your hot boyfriend on the good couch. Just keep the clothes on."

"Ah, young love." Paul places a limp hand over his heart and heaves an exaggerated sigh. "You crazy kids are just too precious."

"Ugh," Goldie groans, fighting the blush she can feel creeping over her face. "Let's just eat our cold lunch already."

WHEN WRITING FEATURE STORIES, SETTING THE SCENE OF THE interview is a common practice. Goldie's never been a fan though. After all, why does the reader care that the person you interviewed was sitting in a well-worn leather booth at some overpriced cafe with industrial decor and award-winning bread?

But as she and Amber gaze in awe upon the glittery excess of the Gardner-St. Vincent estate, the reporter is willing to reconsider her stance.

For starters, there's a fountain in the front courtyard with swans. An actual butler opens the monogrammed front doors. Marble columns and a Renaissance-esque statue stand in the foyer. There are wide, red velvet–covered stairs that seem to be transplanted from *Gone with the Wind*. Plus, the birthday party in full swing is mainly being held in the South Wing living room, which is one of five living rooms on the property.

"I just adore quaint country living," says Amelia Gardner-St. Vincent, founder of the Clean Clinic, a brand of luxury soaps, deodorants, and beauty products.

Goldie sweeps her gaze at the veranda they're sitting on for the interview and barely keeps herself from rolling her eyes in response. "Your home is lovely. I have to admit, though, the birthday party was a surprise. If you were busy, we could have done the interview another day."

"It's no problem. This is absolutely the best time you could possibly come with most of my family gathered together—given the subject you want to discuss."

That prompts the reporter to take account of Amelia's appearance. She's dressed in a white and navy-blue striped T-shirt covered with a light shawl, and her pants are wide-legged cargos. It's a casual look that probably costs a not-so-casual thousand dollars and isn't what has Goldie's attention.

The mother of five (grandmother of two) is 58 years old and doesn't have a wrinkle to prove it.

"Tell me about your history with the Serum," Goldie says. "Let's start with how long you've been using it."

"Almost since its creation. That TV interview Matilda gave was powerfully convincing. May she rest in peace."

"You knew Ms. Crown?"

"She was a fantastic role model and incredibly supportive of women entrepreneurs. My business wouldn't be what it is today without her."

"And why did you first choose to use the Serum?"

"I was approaching middle age and wasn't liking the direction my skin was taking. My specialty requires constant scrutiny of appearances. What was there to lose, really? There are no side effects. It only costs a couple thousand dollars a month, which I can easily afford. Plus, I have it to thank for the birth of Angel."

Goldie shakes her head. "I don't think it affects fertility."

"Of course I don't mean it in that way. My husband and I were exhausted running a successful business while raising four boys, so I called off attempts at having a girl. But when you look young, you get this placebo effect of feeling young too. And we sure acted like it in bed."

Goldie's lips quirk. "And that led you to get pregnant like you were young."

"Yes! We were so shocked." Amelia's gaze drifts. "The Serum and the many years since I had last been pregnant made the moment feel new and exciting. Even if we ended up with another boy, we would have been happy to have him."

Amber and Goldie met her two youngest sons, 32-year-old Monty and 30-year-old Mason, in the courtyard "racing" to the end and back. But first they had to chug a full glass of whole milk, then place their heads on the handle end of a baseball bat and spin ten times. If one of them threw up at any time, they forfeited. Amber got an action shot of Mason projectile vomiting just ten feet from the hedges that marked the finish line. After winning, Monty vomited too.

Goldie didn't get much from her interview with them (conducted after they cleaned themselves up). Monty is an actor who works regularly in community theater and commercials and was in one episode of *Law & Order: SVU*. He takes the Serum because it's expected in his line of work.

Then there's Mason's reason for taking the Serum: *"I need to stay hot for my Twitch streams."*

"Right," Goldie said in a flat tone. *"Are appearances that big of a deal for playing video games?"*

He swept his gaze over Goldie's body, then tilted his head back to look down on her. "They matter everywhere."

Goldie refocuses on Mason's mother. "I'm happy you got the girl you hoped for."

"Me too! Thank God for our Angel!" Amelia exclaims, and

motions a hand at the party. Today is her daughter's 18th birthday. "I should go get her. Be right back."

As Amelia gets up, Goldie spots a pensive-looking Amber nearby on a cushy pink lounge chair next to the pool.

"Amber!"

Goldie's friend startles, splashing iced tea on the ground. She curses before gulping down what's left of her drink. "Why is there no liquor at this party?"

"Because it's for an 18-year-old."

"Oh, right." Amber scowls.

"What's the matter?"

"Just questioning my life's work." The photographer heaves a dramatic sigh while gazing at the partygoers. "I couldn't come close to giving Caroline a party like this for her 18th. She'll be lucky if she gets a cake with more than one tier."

"She'll be happy with whatever you can offer her." Amber's usual self-confidence has taken a hit since her divorce two years ago. "Besides, you have a few more years till then. You can pivot and get in on the apparently lucrative soap trade."

Amber snorts a laugh. "And give up the bad pay and shitty hours of working for a newspaper?"

Goldie notices a lovely young woman (although everyone at this party looks young) approach her friend from behind. A colorful dress hugs her hourglass curves. Long braids are bundled neatly over one shoulder, and her full cheeks are dusted, making her dark skin shimmer and glow.

"Here you go, Amber," she says while handing over a Clean Clinic tote bag. "I know you're supposed to be here for work, but Amelia would have no problem with you getting one of these like the other guests."

"Thanks, Connie. That's so sweet of you."

Goldie clears her throat to get their attention.

"Shit, Goldie! Uh." Amber motions next to her. "This is Constance Baker. She's the marketing director for the Clean Clinic. Connie, this is my friend Goldie. She's the reporter for the Serum story we're working on."

"Nice to meet you," Goldie says, smirking at how close together the women are standing.

Connie does a cute, tiny wave in response before her phone goes off. "Sorry, I have to take this." She looks up from her phone at Amber. "I'll be right back."

"I'll be here," Amber assures her.

As Connie walks away to talk about what sound like work concerns, Goldie takes the opportunity to get some dirt from her friend. "She's gorgeous! You seeing her again?"

"Yeah, we're going out to dinner later."

Goldie indulges in a giddy clap. "I'm so happy for you!"

Amber rolls her eyes. "Don't go writing our engagement announcement yet. I need to think of a good place to take her first."

"But you know all the best restaurants."

"Nothing classy though. She's used to things way above my pay scale."

"And if she's interested in you, she'll understand your money concerns."

"Maybe." Amber's eyes flick to the Clean Clinic tote bag, prompting a corner of her mouth to lift. "We really clicked. She said she admires my work."

"Of course she does. You're an amazing photojournalist."

"But if I'd gone into the soap trade, I could have met Connie sooner."

"And if I had gone to law school like my mother wanted, I probably wouldn't have met Teo at all."

Amber looks at Connie, who's in boss mode and making pointed hand gestures. "There's a time for everything, I guess."

Goldie turns back to face the veranda when Amelia returns with her daughter. "Sorry for the wait. This place is too damn big."

Goldie waves off the apology.

"Angel, meet Ms. Hays. She's a reporter with the *Daily Liberty Press* newspaper."

"What's a newspaper?" Angel asks.

The reporter gapes in horror.

"I'm just kidding," the 18-year-old admits. "I couldn't resist playing the clueless Gen-Zer."

Goldie chuckles and inwardly sighs in relief.

"Are you writing about my mom? Or this over-the-top birthday party?"

"I think it's been quite tasteful," Amelia says, raising her chin. "Don't act as if you don't like it."

"Of course I do. My whole graduating class is having a blast, and my favorite band played me 'Happy Birthday.' It's been great. Thanks, Mom."

Amelia wraps her arms around her daughter. "Oh, you're welcome, sweetie."

Angel throws a hand up to pat her mother on the shoulder.

The butler's approach severs the embrace. "Madam, I'm sorry to interrupt, but the swans are flapping about on the guests' cars."

Amelia pinches the bridge of her nose. "Excuse me, Ms. Hays. I need to prevent some domesticated swans from relieving themselves on very expensive vehicles."

After her mother walks away, Angel turns to Goldie. "Are you worried about your car?"

"Not really. I rode with my photographer friend in our company's old VW Bug. It's probably seen worse than swans."

"Why is the newspaper here? You didn't say."

"We're doing a story on the Crown Serum. I'm interviewing your mother and family on their use of it."

"You wanted to talk to me too? I can't use it yet."

"I'd still like to hear about your experience growing up with an entire family of Serum users."

Angel seems to ponder that, ice-blue irises boring into Goldie. "Can I ask how old you are?"

The reporter does her best not to flinch as she answers. "I turned 40 not too long ago."

"Really? I thought maybe you were older."

Goldie thinks puking in the courtyard with the Gardner-St. Vincent brothers would have been less humiliating than this moment. Seriously, she might break down and cry.

Angel tries to do some damage control. "I'm not being mean. You just obviously don't use the Serum, and I'm not used to people who don't look young."

Goldie's face must look more distraught, alerting Angel that she failed miserably at making things better.

"I'm so sorry, Ms. Hays! What I mean to say is that looking at you makes me wonder what the big deal is about using the Serum at 40. I like your face. It looks honest and real."

The reporter tries to shake off her insecurities to understand what Angel is getting at. "Are you ever around non-Serum users?"

"No, not really. Like you said, my whole family uses it. I've never seen my mother look anything but how she does today. Same with my father. My brothers started using it as soon as they turned 25. My 88-year-old grandmother even uses it, and she hardly leaves the house."

"What about at school?"

"All my teachers use it. My friends' parents use it. Movies and TV aren't much better. You might see a genuinely older-looking person, but mostly it's makeup and special effects that make them look that way."

The reporter writes down everything while processing the young woman's situation. "You're saying you can't gauge what natural aging looks like?"

Angel nods. "I feel like such an idiot. I can't wait for college."

"You're just going to be around people your own age though."

"But it's not here, at least." Angel waves at their surroundings. "I know how ungrateful that sounds. There are worse things in the world to be ignorant of, I guess. Poor rich girl, can't tell the difference between a 40-year-old and a 60-year-old. Oh, boohoo."

Goldie agrees initially, which is awful. She'd be a monumental ass if she didn't take the young woman's self-doubts seriously.

"If you're bothered by it, then it's important to address. It's a real consequence to consider as more of the world takes the Serum. Do you think you'll take it eventually?"

"I don't know." Angel sweeps her gaze over the Serum-using guests roaming around. "I should probably know what life is like without it first, you know? I have more growing up to do. I'd like to experience it in every way possible." Angel scrutinizes the reporter once more. "Why don't you use the Serum? And don't say money," she adds.

Goldie huffs at the dismissal of her default excuse. What *is* her reason? Especially at her age. The current state of her life consists of working a high-stress, stagnant position; going to see every superhero movie like it's a monumental event; living with her mother, whose health concerns compound as the years go by; and dating a younger man, who doesn't mind the age difference (for now).

"I'll be honest, if I were your age and had your resources—"

"Money, you mean," Angel interjects.

"Yes, money." Goldie rolls her eyes. "What I'm getting at is that I think you're right. There's no rush for you right now. See where life leads you. But even at 40, you can still feel like you've got more growing up to do. It can take longer than you'd think—and it's exhausting, especially when your body starts mismatching your spirit."

"So, you'd take the Serum now?" Angel asks.

As a reporter, Goldie shouldn't be so personal with her perspective, but the 18-year-old deserves a fair exchange for giving her thoughts so freely.

"I can't believe I'm saying this, but if given the chance to take the Serum today"—she lets out a deep sigh—"I'm not sure I'd say no."

CHAPTER 4

BEING A REPORTER OFFERS GOLDIE THE OPPORTUNITY TO LEAVE the office often. Unfortunately, the trips are less than glamorous: the county jail, abandoned businesses, troubled neighborhoods, natural disasters, etc. This Serum story, however, is giving her a chance to stretch her legs in areas she doesn't often have time for.

Today, she's standing in a floral rainbow at the botanical garden and arboretum outside the city. It's sometime after ten o'clock, so it's not terribly hot yet, and there's a gentle breeze.

"Is that Miss Hays blessing my eyes with her arresting loveliness?" someone says from behind her.

Goldie turns to see Teo leaning against the nearest tree. "How long have you been standing there?"

"I didn't want to disturb the stunning picture you make among the flowers," he says with a smooth Southern drawl.

Goldie groans at the overwrought compliment and clears her throat to join in on Teo's little performance.

"Don't you go pretending that I'm some naive belle who falls for such obviously false airs."

Teo gasps. "Are you questioning my integrity, Miss Hays?"

"I am, Mr. Estrada. The evidence is undeniable."

"What evidence?"

"One." She raises a hand to start counting off. "I have never heard you address me in such a manner."

"But I sing your praises every chance I get."

"Two." Goldie ignores the defense. "A true gentleman would announce his presence immediately upon encountering a lady."

Teo shrugs, admitting to the failure but not looking at all sorry.

"And three, if you want to prove your intentions are virtuous indeed—"

"Most ardently, my lady." Teo's face splits into a grin.

"Then you're to offer an arm for me to take as you indulge me on a walk amongst these beautiful flowers."

Teo holds out the requested arm. "I do declare that you have called me out, Miss Hays. I am an absolute cad, unworthy of your company."

"Shut up," Goldie says with a laugh, unable to keep the act up anymore. "I'm glad you could come out here."

"Of course I came." Teo drops the uppity accent too. "We should have come out here sooner."

"I know." Goldie squeezes her boyfriend's arm. "When Ms. Branigan asked me to meet her out here, I couldn't resist organizing my workday to get a date with you too."

"Who's Ms. Branigan?"

"The director of this place."

"She uses the Serum?"

"Used to," Goldie says a little distractedly as her eyes catch on the bold colors and flared petals of the striking daylilies. "Soledad Branigan was a familiar face in the Scene pages of the newspaper before COVID. She was the lead persona for the garden and organized parties and mixers with local elites to keep this place fully funded and then some. From what I've heard, when the events resumed, she never went back to attending them, although she's involved behind the scenes. She was open to this in-person interview too. She just stipulated that no photos be taken."

"Parties out here must be amazing." Teo stops walking, causing Goldie to stumble a little in her heels. "Sorry, hon, I just need a picture."

When Goldie looks down to see marigolds, she tries to ease away.

"Oh, no, you don't!" Teo's arm shoots out to move her back in front. "How are you going to deny me the perfect shot, *Marigold*?"

Goldie groans at the use of her given name but doesn't try to move again. "Just take the damn picture."

Teo does as commanded and inspects the image. "Such a gorgeous scowl."

Goldie doesn't think she was scowling. She snatches the phone to see for herself, then really scowls at every detail of the image: her closed-mouth smile, her shiny face, her too-wild hair.

"I'm deleting it."

"Don't you dare!" Teo snatches back his phone, clutching it to his chest.

Goldie shakes her head but doesn't complain anymore. Instead, she casts her gaze at their surroundings.

"It's a popular wedding location too," she says, motioning toward the gazebo and the beautiful arching branches of the oak trees.

"Information that is sure to be useful in the future."

"I wasn't implying anything involving us. Although, I'd much rather elope somewhere, to be honest."

Teo scoffs. "Your mother would murder you."

"Not before murdering you first."

"It wasn't my idea to elope!" Teo defends himself like he's already facing the Korean mother's wrath. "I love the idea of having our wedding here. It'll be the classiest affair. Doves'll be released, a string quartet will perform, a horse-drawn carriage will take us away. Henry will serve mint juleps at the reception." He pauses and looks quizzical. "Whatever the heck those are. I've never had one. Do you know what a julep is? Is it just a name or an ingredient?"

Goldie shrugs.

"Never mind, not important. Quick, name something else classy for our wedding."

"Are you planning a wedding or the Kentucky Derby?"

"Says the woman wearing the huge sun hat ringed with fake sunflowers."

Goldie looks upward, going a bit cross-eyed. "Skin cancer is no joke," she says as she pulls out a tube of sunscreen from her tote. "You should wear a hat too, but this'll protect you for now. Come here," she warns before smothering Teo with SPF gajillion.

"Goldie, c'mon," he groans. Despite the weak protest, Teo closes his eyes and mouth as his girlfriend slathers his face.

"I like the string quartet, but we have to have a live band too," she says as she moves on to his neck. "The wedding will just be an excuse to have a concert. I want to hear covers of every power ballad possible."

"So, lots of Journey songs?"

"What wedding isn't playing 'Open Arms' and 'Faithfully'? But we also gotta play Elvis; 'Can't Help Falling in Love' is the best."

"Do I get a say on the set list?"

"You'll be performing a lot of it, so I suppose so."

"You want me to work on my wedding day?"

"Like you'd miss the chance to perform."

"True," Teo sighs, as if it's his great burden in life to share his talent with the world. "But why a bunch of power ballads? Is it just because it's a wedding?"

"Yes and no. You know I love all kinds of music. Classic love songs tend to be on the epic side though. The way they start quiet, then steadily build. More instruments, more intensity, more emotion. Then the crescendo hits you like a tidal wave that you never want to end. It's a kind of high."

"Sounds like an orgasm." Teo smirks. "Honestly, you just described sex."

Goldie opens her mouth for a denial but shuts it to replay her words. "Huh, I guess I did."

"I am learning so much today." Teo takes out his phone again. "Notes to self: 1. Marry Goldie at botanical garden; 2. Put on kickass concert in lieu of reception; 3. Write more orgasmic songs."

Goldie snorts. "You're a little too confident that you'll get a chance to put all that to use."

"You don't think we'll get there?"

"I think we have potential."

"Then what's wrong with a little optimism? I wouldn't change a thing about you, Goldie, but I want to offer you a brighter outlook."

"I said 'potential,' didn't I? You should take that as a win."

Teo looks dubious. "Always so negative."

"Not negative. Just cautious. I've never gotten this far with anyone before."

"It's been great, right?"

"Yes, but you're so much younger than me. You shouldn't have to indulge me in our fantasy wedding."

"I wasn't indulging you! It was fun thinking about that for us. You're not jinxing things by talking about how much better we could get."

Goldie stares up at the beautiful tree they're standing under. The young leaves hanging off an ancient body will be gone by the end of the year.

"You're right," she says. "The better we get, the more scared I get."

Teo turns her back to face him. "I'm scared too."

"So, what's this? False confidence? Fake it till we make it?"

"A little bit, yeah." He shrugs. "You've waited a long time for what we have, and I know you're not going to believe this, but so have I."

Teo's right. Goldie can't understand why he'd feel like he's had such a long wait at his age, but she doesn't want to question it and ruin the atmosphere any more than she already has. "Are you trying to get me to marry you today?" she asks teasingly.

"I would."

Every one of Goldie's muscles tense in response. Teo notices.

"Shit, that was too much." His full lips seal shut and jut out in a thoughtful pout as he regroups. "I would," he says again, "but it's too soon, I know. I want you to be confident about our future together, not trap you into it."

Goldie expels a breath, grateful for his understanding. "I really am a downer, aren't I? Guess every relationship needs one. You're the sunshine and rainbows to balance us. I don't know how you can keep up the positive attitude. It must be exhausting."

"I am a bit tired, now that you mention it." Teo runs a hand through his loose curls, as if doing that could give him an energy boost. "And I don't think you're a downer. It's more of a day and night thing."

"I'm the night, right? Dark, moody, mysterious ..."

"Nope, I'm the night. Mostly because I do my best work at night: helping the bar, performing, writing music. I'm the typical artsy dreamer and probably wouldn't leave the cover of night without you."

"I'm not so sure about this metaphor." Goldie purses her lips, trying to equate her boyfriend to nighttime.

"This is totally a brilliant and very romantic metaphor, because now I'm going to tell you why you're the day." Teo moves his arms out wide, as if to encompass the meaning of day with their current surroundings. "You are the essential one who keeps the world moving and thriving. Your job is about illuminating truths to the public. And to me, your beauty and spirit are brighter than the actual sun." He wraps his arms around Goldie and holds her close. "My Golden Wonder, you light my nights; you are my days."

Their kiss is warm and lush, a physical expression of Teo's ode to Goldie, the sunlight of his day. Goldie's tempted to continue challenging him about that. If anything, Teo deserves credit for bringing the qualities of daylight to her world. She's never felt so vibrant and alive.

Unfortunately, the dreamlike state they've fallen into is interrupted when someone clears their throat.

"I'm sorry to break up the lovely scene, but would you be Ms. Hays?" asks a woman wearing a broad hat that rivals Goldie's. A mask covers her lower face, and her clothing covers the rest of her. She's even wearing gloves.

"Oh, Ms. Branigan!" Goldie separates herself from Teo and straightens her hat, buying time as she composes herself. "Is it eleven already?"

"Close to it, yes. Enjoying the garden?" Her teasing tone can be heard even through the mask.

"I, uh." Goldie flails and sputters.

"It's beautiful, ma'am." Teo speaks up to give her more recovery time. "We're definitely getting married here." His girlfriend shoves him, looking aghast. "Someday," he clarifies.

Ms. Branigan laughs. "Do you work for the newspaper too, Mr.—"

"Estrada," Teo finishes for her. "But call me Teo."

"Estrada," she repeats, but with the pronunciation of a fluent

Spanish speaker, the "tra" sound in the center getting emphasis and flourish. Teo typically pronounces it without inflection. "¿Sabes hablar español?"

"Sí," Teo says.

"Mucho gusto, Teo. Me llamo Soledad."

"El gusto es mío, Soledad," Teo says, a smile playing on his lips. After a glance at Goldie and her non–Spanish speaking mouth, he switches back to English. "And I don't work at the newspaper. I'm just the boyfriend embarrassing her. I'll step away to let you two talk."

"I don't mind if you stay. You'll get to hear firsthand about all this." To elaborate, she waves a hand to her face and body, then toward the garden surrounding them.

Teo looks at Goldie for permission.

"If you want to stay, I don't mind," she says.

"Great, I've always wanted to be a reporter."

"No, you haven't," Goldie says while motioning for him to follow her and Soledad to the gazebo to sit.

"You're right. I could never do what you do. Did you seriously get rear-ended once by a shady judge's wife?"

"Yep."

"That's terrible, Ms. Hays."

"You can call me Goldie. I think it's only fair since Teo's already charmed his way to first-name status with you."

"Honestly, seeing you two together has eased my anxieties about this interview. You're a lovely couple."

"Uh, thanks." Goldie clears her throat and tries to shift into professional mode. "We didn't have to do this in person. I would have understood"—she pauses to ponder her next words—"considering your circumstances."

"So, you know about my condition?"

"It's why I thought your perspective on the Serum would be good to include in the piece."

Teo's gaze ping-pongs between the women.

Soledad sighs before removing the floral-patterned mask. The skin on the right side of her jaw and neck is crosshatched in puffy scars.

"I was burned extensively in Afghanistan when my vehicle was attacked."

"You're a veteran?" Teo asks.

"Army. Joined out of high school." She pauses to study their reactions. "If it makes you uncomfortable, I'll put the mask back on."

"It's what makes you comfortable that matters," Teo says.

"Gracias." She tucks the mask into her pocket, then takes her hat and gloves off as well and rolls up her sleeves to the forearm. "I'm not so much hiding the scars with all this clothing. I just have to worry about sun damage to my skin. Plus, skin cancer is no joke."

Goldie takes a moment to smirk at Teo, who side-glances and rolls his eyes.

"The scarring goes down most of my right side," Soledad continues. "That was the side of the vehicle I was on."

"You were honorably discharged after, correct?" Goldie asks.

"Yes." Soledad's eyes glaze over with the memory. "A war veteran on disability at age 27."

"And when did you start taking the Serum?"

"As soon as my wounds completely healed. Well, healed in the strictest medical sense. I was still puffy and red but no longer scabbed over, and the skin grafts were as healed as possible. So, I had to wait about a year."

"How much of your burns was detectable while you used the Serum?"

"None."

"Really?" Teo beats Goldie to the follow-up question.

"The Serum's not just for smoothing out wrinkles. It can erase second- and third-degree burn scars. It's the greatest creation in humankind's history. It beats the wheel and the iPhone, I swear."

That's hard to argue with, but Goldie's a reporter and has to pry. "If you don't mind me asking, how did you pay for it all those years? Most medical insurers won't cover the Serum, not even the military kind."

"My disability checks."

"Your salary from your work at the garden didn't help?"

"I love this place, but it definitely hasn't made me rich." Soledad looks out at the field of flowers. "One day, there was a job fair here, and instead of applying to any of the companies, I walked to the garden's visitors' center and asked how I could get work here. I needed the complete opposite of the desert in my military past. The garden was the perfect place."

"But not profitable?" Teo asks this time.

"I wish! Besides the council of rich people funding this place, it needs visitor donations and fundraisers. That's why I was always hustling for weddings"—she throws a conspiratorial wink in Teo's direction—"business sponsorships, and anything else I could think of that could be held here to keep this place flourishing."

"Did something change?" Goldie asks.

"Yeah, fucking COVID hit!" Soledad spits out the words. "None of the events were possible. I had to pull from emergency funds and even used my meager salary to help pay for some things."

"That's why you stopped using the Serum?"

Soledad nods. "I couldn't afford it anymore. The disability money had to go to everyday living expenses, and I figured since everyone was wearing masks anyway, I could live with having the scars back and just get a supply of fashionable masks to cover them."

"It's been a few years now," Goldie says. "What's life been like without the Serum?"

"A shit show. My husband left me."

"Your husband left you?!" Teo shouts, causing the women to jump in surprise. "Sorry," he murmurs.

Soledad smiles, apparently pleased with the outrage. "Glen and I met a year after I started using the Serum. Our daughter, Molly, will be planning for college before I know it. Another reason for me to save money."

"Why did you and your husband divorce?" Goldie asks, despite the sinking feeling that she knows the answer.

"He couldn't take how I looked with my scars."

"That son of a bitch," Teo mutters.

"Eh." Soledad tilts her head. "He had never known me with the scars. He knew about my injuries and Afghanistan, but I'd quietly go to my therapy sessions to deal with my PTSD alone. I thought I could take the Serum forever and it would never be an issue. I think even he was surprised by how much seeing me like this affected him."

Teo doesn't say more. Instead, his balled-up fists and clenched jaw do the talking.

"Don't get me wrong, Teo," Soledad continues. "I'm not completely excusing him. Leaving me was one thing, but getting alimony was a dick move."

This time, Goldie can't hold her tongue. "Did he not understand why you stopped taking the Serum in the first place?"

"And that taking money from you would keep you from being able to use the Serum again?" Teo adds.

"Glen was a caretaker here. When he left me, he left the garden too. He does everything to avoid looking at me. On his visitation weekends, he texts Molly from his car so he doesn't have to go to the front door."

"That son of a bitch." Goldie's the one to say it this time.

Soledad ghosts her fingers across her scarred cheek. "When I was burned, I thought my chances of finding love and having a family were gone. But the Serum helped me have all that, even for a short time, after such a horrific experience. I would still be using it if I could. I hate the feeling of being repulsive to the person I love."

Goldie breathes shakily and glances at Teo. His eyes are red-rimmed and glassy with unshed tears.

"I'm sorry," Soledad says with a sniffle. "I've totally spoiled your date here."

"No, don't think about that," Goldie says. "Your experience is important. I'm honored that you'd share it with us."

Teo, still collecting himself, nods in agreement.

Soledad wipes her eyes. "Well, to make it up to you two, I promise to give a discount on your wedding here."

That pulls a surprised laugh from Teo. "Gracias, Soledad."

As they walk to their cars, Goldie swears that Teo is holding her hand tighter than usual.

"Hey, are you okay?" Goldie asks. "I'm sorry that I didn't warn you that Soledad's interview might be upsetting."

"No, I'm glad I stayed to hear it. I just feel so outraged for her. How could her husband treat her that way?"

"It must have been a shock to him, seeing her like that."

"That's no excuse."

"I know," Goldie says. "What I'm saying is that he never knew a Soledad with all her scars exposed."

"Can you blame her for wanting to take the Serum?"

"Of course not. But in a way, hiding her real self from her husband, what she went through, also kept her from seeing the real him."

"Her real self was the director of an awesome garden with a husband who loved her."

Teo drops her hand suddenly, making Goldie think she offended him. He reaches into his pocket for his keys, which is normal, except they haven't gotten to his car.

"I completely sympathize with her," Goldie says, "and I still agree that her husband's a son of a bitch for abandoning her." She needs to establish that with Teo before she fully explains her mindset. "But the reporter in me also has to see it from his perspective, and I know that if someone I loved was basically hiding something that traumatic and life-altering from me, I would be upset—almost betrayed."

"But they were happy," he says, hushed.

Goldie feels guilty for springing moral dilemmas on her boyfriend during what should have been a carefree date in a beautiful place.

"Think of it this way: If she could have kept taking the Serum without fail, and there was no chance of her husband ever seeing her scars, something else could have happened to her—a severe sickness or an accident. Would he have left her then?"

Teo stares down at his feet. "The asshole probably would have."

"I think so too. Soledad's been through more than enough, but when her husband's character was tested, he failed her. I don't blame her for trying to prevent that. I wish the Serum were a real cure, and she never again had to see the evidence of what she went through. That's for her sake, though, her peace of mind. Not for her husband or even for their relationship. Because there's no telling what else can happen to any of us." The next part is hard for Goldie to say after their romantic date. "And no relationship can be kept in an untouched bubble of happiness."

Although he's obviously still troubled, Teo nods.

"You still think I'm your Golden Wonder?" Goldie asks.

Her boyfriend looks into her eyes and again takes her hand. "I do."

CHAPTER 5

NOT TO SOUND MEAN, BUT HANK'S BAR IS USUALLY NOTHING TO wax poetic about. If it weren't for the retro marquee sign Henry invested in several years ago to help hype the acts playing on the Helena stage, the brick building wouldn't stand out at all.

Tonight, the place feels different. For starters, it's a packed house and then some.

"What's going on?" Goldie asks.

Amber scans the crowd. "Is there some big name performing?"

"I don't think so. It was supposed to just be Teo and the other regulars." Goldie turns in the direction of the stage only to find a DJ booth. "What happened to the Helena?!"

The dance floor has changed too. What used to be a modest area surrounded by tables and booths now takes up the expanse of the room, bodies grinding on it like this is the latest club to open.

Amber blows an impressed whistle. "Henry's seriously upgraded the place."

"He would never do all this," Goldie says while looking up to give the new disco ball the stink-eye. "I've got to find Teo."

With Goldie close behind, Amber freely elbows and hip-checks a path through the mass of gyrating bodies. It works until Goldie slams against her friend's back after an abrupt stop.

"Sorry!" Amber steps aside to reveal what halted their progress. There's a redhead in a strapless black satin dress spinning and kicking up her long legs. "But I think that's Melody Honeycutt!"

The woman throws her head back in a perfect recreation of the iconic introduction of the actress's title character in the 1930s noir classic *Gilded Greta.*

"What are you doing here?" Goldie asks.

"You tell me, sugar." One of her amazing legs slides up her faceless dance partner. Her back bows in an impossible arc before rolling slowly upright as she shoves the person away. Arms wave and feet strut in a mix of precision and wild abandon.

Amber's enjoying the display, swaying and seemingly entranced.

As for Goldie, this impossible moment of meeting a long-dead Hollywood legend is completely wasted on her. She has one thing on her mind.

"Have you seen Teo?" Goldie asks the actress. Never mind that she shouldn't know who he is.

"Maybe he's a ghost," Melody says, still dancing. "Isn't that what the kids say these days?"

"You mean ghosting," Amber corrects. "Sorry, Mel, but *you're* the ghost."

Goldie considers the possibility. "Why would you say that?"

Instead of a response, Melody's limbs stop moving to the nonexistent beat. Her head swivels to take in the amorphous atmosphere while her hands run through lush red locks and over her bombshell body parts: full breasts, concave stomach, and curvy hips.

"I'm always this way in dreams," she says with an unnerving focus on Goldie. "But the real me got older."

The actress died in her late 70s. Goldie also knows that gravity exists and that oxygen is a gas. These are facts invisible to her mind's eye.

"You'll get older too." Melody's steely voice reverberates in Goldie's skull. "But if your beau leaves you now, he'll never have to see it."

Amber turns Goldie around to focus on her. "Hey, don't listen to ghost Melody Honeycutt. You can't let your insecurities get the better of you."

"I'm not."

"Then where'd this hill come from?" Amber motions directly in front of them where, yeah, a big grassy hill has appeared in place of the dead actress and crowd of dancers. "It's obviously a metaphor."

Goldie looks upward, a spiteful determination building in her. "I'm going to climb it."

Amber blinks. "You're actually voluntarily climbing over the metaphorical hill?"

"Yeah, I gotta find Teo."

"Don't you realize that if you make it down the other side, you'll fulfill the metaphor and be *over the hill* for a young boyfriend? I can't believe you're not getting this. Jesus, you're the writer!"

"It's a shitty cliché that demonizes aging. I can beat the metaphor."

Before she steps onto the hill, it disappears along with Amber and the dancers. In their place are kids dressed in a rainbow of colors performing martial arts. Tommy maneuvers among them while giving instructions.

"Why didn't you tell me you'd be at Hank's?" Goldie asks, not bothering with a hello. "And since when do you teach classes at a bar?"

"Henry and I made a sweet deal," he says while correcting one of the student's stances. "I can teach here for free, and he'll get customers out of the parents waiting for their kids."

The previously nonexistent bar appears off to the side, filled with raucous adults. Drunk parents driving away with their kids is very wrong, and Goldie should say so.

Again, her mind is on one thing.

"Have you seen Teo?"

"There is no Teo," Tommy says, his focus still on the students.

"I know you guys have had your issues, but if you're going to be working at the same place, you can't act like he doesn't exist."

"He doesn't." The words are blunt and flat, hitting her square in the chest.

"What are you saying?"

"You're looking for someone who doesn't exist." Tommy's voice is sharper now, meant for stabbing. "And you're going to keep looking because you're not as cynical as you act. The serious journalist believes in true love, magic, and rainbows."

"Rainbows are real." Goldie glares at her friend. "Why are you being such an ass?"

"I was the obvious choice, the safe bet. I'm what's *real*." Tommy opens his arms wide. "Look around, Goldie."

The kids, parents, and room disappear. Only the outline of the entrance to Hank's Bar remains. Behind invisible walls and obscured by shadows and fog, she sees what should be people and a band of some sort. Nothing is defined though. Goldie can only see in abstract.

"Even in your dreams," Tommy says, "I'm the most concrete thing. Sweetheart, you need to wake up."

Ouch. It's normal for her best friend to not hold back his opinion when he's worried about Goldie, but the delivery is off.

"Why do you sound like my mom?"

She doesn't mean that Tommy is patronizing like her mother. He *sounds* like her.

"You got work soon." Sun's voice continues to come out of Tommy's mouth.

"No, I don't. Why are you bringing up work?"

An intense beeping noise emerges from her friend.

Goldie's eyes slowly open while her hand gropes for her phone to shut off the alarm.

A knock on her door adds to the rude awakening.

"Get up!" Sun demands. "I already make breakfast. How I get such lazy daughter?"

The tail end of the complaint is quieter, a clue to Goldie that her mother is walking away, confident that her rudeness was enough to wake her.

Goldie takes too long to find her phone and endures the alarm for an excruciating minute before she flips it over to trigger the snooze.

After a few stretches and repeating "This better be a good day" for motivation, she looks at the time: *6:04 a.m.*

She cancels the alarm before the snooze expires.

Despite how unnerved she feels, Goldie tries to recall the dream. All she can grasp is an intense urge to see Teo.

And something about Melody Honeycutt?

6:52 a.m.

"YOUR BREAKFAST COLD," SUN ANNOUNCES (BECAUSE "GOOD morning" is too normal and absent of any underlying criticism). "Omelet no good cold."

"Uh-huh," Goldie intones, expertly biting her tongue. "I tell you all the time that you don't have to make me breakfast."

"So you go hungry? I know you," her mother says, pointing for unnecessary emphasis. "You not worry I work too much. You just want sleep late."

"It can be both reasons," Goldie grumbles. She decides to let the issue drop and maintain some dignity. "Are you working today?" Her mother works part-time at Chang's Asian Market and Korean Restaurant.

"I have to. It shipment day."

"Take it easy today, please. Don't lift anything bigger than yourself." Her mother isn't even five feet tall.

"They just put stuff any place! How hard put cabbage where it always go? You think I want work? They not open one more day if I not there. And I die if I not have good Korean store. You wanna see Mommy die?"

Goldie heaves the long-suffering sigh that comes naturally to daughters of Korean women. "No, Ma. Of course I don't want to see you die."

"They make me work!" Sun grabs Goldie's plate without warning and goes to the sink to immediately wash it. "And *you* make me work! Can't believe 40-year-old daughter not even wash dishes."

Goldie looks at their pristine dishwasher, which has remained untouched for as long as they've lived there. With one last sigh, she gets up to leave for work.

9:30 a.m.

"PLEASE TELL ME SOMEONE HAS A BETTER CENTERPIECE FOR TOMORROW'S front page than today's story about the seventy-fifth anniversary of the shitty dry cleaners in Premier Plaza."

During the morning staff meeting, Manning commonly declares most of the day's edition to be crap as a way to push for better from the reporters and editors. The misguided attempts at being motivational are inspired by a shelf filled with books on realizing your true inner power and saying "F*CK, YES!" (that's how it's written on the cover) to professional success.

"It's a historical landmark," says the story's writer, George Fontaine, "and the family that owns it came from a war-torn village in—"

"You can't defend a story with the boring details that were in the story," Manning says. "Also, did you miss the part about me calling them shitty? They couldn't get the stain out of my favorite shirt."

"You can't dismiss their significance and longevity on your dubious, less-than-satisfactory experience," Fontaine says. "They're not going to get every stain out. They're not wizards."

"Too bad. Imagine dry-cleaning wizards." Manning strokes his chin. "Wait, don't. No one steal that. I can turn it into a YA series. Or maybe something for Netflix."

Amber scoffs. "Think your idea's safe."

Manning spends a whole minute jotting down some notes. "Okay, let's get this meeting over with. I don't want to lose my train of thought. Rider, what are you working on?"

Jenny "The Writer" Rider demonstrates her reputation for being more machine than reporter as she flips open her trusty Steno pad to read from a ridiculously long list.

"The city council election scandal; backlash on commercial zoning near the Sandy Shores neighborhood; the lawsuit against Boats Boats Boats Unlimited for not providing unlimited boats, boats, boats; follow-up on the seemingly indefinite delays for Hotel Princeville renovations—"

"What's the latest on that?" Manning asks.

"Delayed again."

Manning rolls his eyes. He walked right into that one.

"A YouTube doctor doing hilarious surgeries without a medical license; an East Side woman with a thriving nonprofit that trains retired police and military dogs to be golf caddies—"

"Um, Jenny," Goldie interrupts, "do you need help with any of those?"

"Oh no you don't, Hays," Manning says. "You know your priority is the Serum piece."

"I don't need to dedicate every millisecond to it."

"It needs to be perfect. We can't have Sarah Crown suing us."

"Why would she sue us? I'd never write anything libelous."

"What if she just doesn't like the story?"

"You can't sue for not liking something."

"Sarah Crown can! She's the kind of rich that can sue for a misplaced comma."

Goldie has no counter to that.

"So, how's the story going?" Manning asks, nonchalant, like he wasn't being an outrageous asshat less than five seconds ago.

Goldie makes a mental note to check the latest openings for journalism jobs before answering her (for now) boss. "Amber and I are going to the Action News NOW station after this meeting to interview Max Dorian."

"What an inspiration," Manning says while ghosting a hand over his bald spot. "That man's hair makes me want to say, 'Fuck it,' and withdraw my 401(k) early to blow on the Serum. Why are you wasting time here? You should cover the morning shows too."

"I'm not leaving the house before four a.m. to do a day in the life of that shallow jerk." Goldie folds her arms. "I can barely endure a day in the life of *me*."

11:05 a.m.

GOLDIE AND AMBER HAVE BEEN ON THE SET OF ACTION NEWS NOW (tagline: "More NOW than ever!") for less than twenty minutes, and they're already thoroughly done with their interview subject.

"Do you need a shot of me sitting on the edge of the desk looking soberly downward with my arms crossed? You know, to show my gravitas and the weight I carry as the station's star?"

"This isn't *Time* magazine, Max." Amber looks prepared to choke the news anchor with her camera strap. "I have more than enough portraits. I'm just going to take some shots of you preparing for the broadcast, and I'll be done."

"You could be working for *Time* if you wanted. I can make some calls."

Amber opens her mouth to shoot down the proposal, but Max doesn't let her.

"Why are you still with that small-market rag? I told you from the start that you were meant for the big leagues."

In Amber and Goldie's early days at the newspaper, they would often run into Max, who at the time was an AN-NOW reporter with more than fifteen years of experience.

Amber now has the camera strap wrapped around her hands in a truly concerning way. "I do remember you saying that before trying to hook up with me. Then I remember you saying something similar to Goldie before trying to hook up with her. What did he say to you?"

Goldie remembers every stupid word. "'You're too uptight, Goldie. Smile. Flirt more. That's how a shy girl like you gets the real juicy stories.' Then he tried to convince me to practice flirting with him."

"See?! You'd say that kind of shit to all the young journalists."

"Was I wrong?" Max looks more confused than affronted. "Goldie, you were so eager to prove you were a serious journalist back then that your voice wavered with every question. I was gifting both of you with my wealth of knowledge."

Amber scoffs. "Don't pretend you were being altruistic. That was your technique to get young tail!"

"Are you slut shaming me? Oh, Amber, that's frowned upon these days."

"I don't give a shit about you fucking around! You were preying on kids desperate for encouragement!"

Goldie grabs her friend's arm before she can lunge at the news anchor. "No, Amber! Neither one of us has the money to bail you out of jail."

"Come on," Amber pleads, "let me at least mess up his hair!"

Max's face twitches, the threat to the legendary coif cracking his impassive mask for the first time.

"I still need to interview him," Goldie says. "Take a break; go get coffee. See if they have any mugs with the station's dumb tagline to steal."

"Shitty TV people," Amber mutters as she stomps away. "The Serum probably seeped into his brain and removed the few wrinkles he had there too."

The look Goldie gives Max is loaded with disdain. "Have you seriously not matured after all these years?"

"What? She started it." He moves to sit behind the desk. "You better make this quick, Goldie. I have to record a few promos before the live show."

Goldie is glad to oblige. "When did you start taking the Serum?"

"About six years ago."

Goldie does the math. "That's when you became an anchor, right?"

"Yeah, it was a condition of the contract when I took the position."

The reporter shakes her head and pointedly looks at Max's full head of hair.

"What's wrong?" Max asks, bringing a hand up to gently slick back some strays. "If it's a bit off, I'll get a touch-up anyway before we go on air."

"No, it looks great. You've got some great hair."

Max beams with pride.

"I just remember when it wasn't so thick and luxurious."

Max tilts his head upward expectantly, as if Goldie had called upon the hair gods to release his golden strands from their follicle bonds.

Goldie walks closer to the desk. "Why are you lying to me? You're almost 60."

"I'm 57," Max snaps. "Don't you dare round me up in age yet."

Goldie rolls her eyes. "Fine, 57. Besides that, it's well known that on-air talent uses the Serum. Why fudge how long you've been taking it?"

The news anchor's gaze sweeps across the cameras, the lights, the desk he's sitting at. "Growing up, I would always watch the evening news. I'd drive my parents crazy, rotating between the big three networks. The channel hopping only got worse during the Tom Brokaw-Dan Rather-Peter Jennings era. God, the absolute authority they conveyed." The tenor of his voice, trained for clarity from his years in broadcast, resonates with the awe he's expressing. "Those were real journalists, Goldie! Watching the news felt like a privilege."

Max's idolatry is common in the news business. Journalism schools have countless rooms and departments named after prominent figures such as the men Max listed.

"I wanted to be like them so badly." Max looks off into the distance. "I was going to be the public's trusted source for news. The one delivering the sad news of the Pope's death. The one calling the election for the first woman president. The one declaring that humans have finally set foot on Mars."

Goldie bought into a lot of the reverence early in her career too. She held the news in the highest regard as an outside check on those in power and a valuable resource for public information. But the older the reporter gets, the more tedious than vital her profession seems.

Could Max Dorian possibly feel something similar?

"You've made it, Max. You're the lead anchor at the top midmarket CBS affiliate in the country. How does it feel?"

Max takes a minute before answering. He has to put a lot of effort into making his smooth face express the perfect moue of deep thought. He taps his chin, which is raised to signal the poignancy of his ruminations. He exhales as he comes to a conclusion, and with arms wide open, he finally declares, "It's fucking awesome."

Goldie can't help laughing. "I should have expected that answer."

"I'm serious, Goldie!"

"I know you are," she assures him. "Elaborate, though, and get to the Serum's role. That's my whole reason for talking to you."

Max obliges. "I've been working toward this my whole life. Of course I'm glad to be here. My one complaint about getting this gig is how long it took—and how I had to take the Serum in order to ever have a chance at it."

"You didn't want to take the Serum?"

"Tom Brokaw didn't need the fucking Serum to be a great anchor!"

"True," Goldie says, "but it didn't exist for most of his career."

"He still didn't take it when he could have! Not like that fuckwad Nathan Hightower! As soon as the Serum hit the market, that fossil took it."

The former AN-NOW anchor is only a few years older than Max, but Goldie knows better than to point that out.

"And how long have you really been taking it?"

"I held out as long as I could. I thought experience and talent alone could get me behind this desk. But then 50 was creeping up on me, and my hair started thinning. Meanwhile, Hightower's ass was firmly planted in this seat, and his baby face became the new standard for male anchors. I caved ten years ago. May Peter Jennings forgive me." He looks upward. "Rest in peace, king."

Goldie does her best not to scoff. "Now that you are behind that desk, you can change the paradigm," she points out. "You don't have to take the Serum."

"Oh, Goldie." Max gets up from behind the desk to walk up to her. "Still as sweet and naive as you were when you got in this game."

Goldie stands her ground, screwing one of her three-inch heels into the floor to simulate what she'd like to do to Max's foot.

"It's too late to change things now. That mousy-haired hack Hightower and his cohorts already set the standard. Long gone are the days of the wizen and wise elder reading you the news like he would a bedtime story to his grandchildren. No one can look old anymore."

"Funny how that sounds like what women have been facing for decades," Goldie says, "in TV news, entertainment, modeling … practically every industry. Even the ones that don't require a camera."

For a split second, Goldie thinks she can see the barest hint of turmoil flit across Max's flawless face. What he ends up saying is far from empathetic though.

"It's not so bad."

Goldie steps back, recoiling from surprise. "What?"

That seriously can't be the news anchor's conclusion about the Serum after everything he's said.

"I don't know why women complain so much about it," Max says.

"You're not mad that you'll be expected to maintain this facade of youth in order to keep this position that you've studied and trained and sweated for? That none of that matters, and it's going to be your looks that make or break your dreams?"

"Pfft," Max sputters dismissively. "With the Serum, it's easy. Who wants to look old anyway? I would rather lose a toe than lose my hair completely. You don't need all your toes."

Goldie is dumbstruck. *Is it so simple to just accept the new way of things? Is this what progress looks like now?*

"You know, Goldie, you might want to consider taking the Serum too."

"Why do you say that?"

"You've always been too good for that newspaper of yours. It's a dead end, especially these days. It's your Hightower keeping you from where you should be. Think about your future."

Unable to look at Max after hearing that, Goldie's gaze drifts past him as Amber approaches with a mug that actually has the dumb slogan.

"Pluuus," Max continues, dropping his pitch and dragging out the word, "you'd be so hot again if you took the Serum. 22-year-old Marigold Hays was fine as hell."

Before she can respond, Amber dumps whatever she had in her cup over the news anchor's precious hair.

12:40 p.m.

"OH MY GOD, THAT'S FUCKING AWESOME!"

Goldie can hear Teo cackling through the car's speakers.

"I'm gonna high-five Amber the next time I see her. Then what happened?"

Goldie completes a left turn before answering. "Max freaks out about his hair and yells for security. No one tried to throw us out though. The head producer just got him a new shirt and called for hair and makeup to fix the damage." She parks behind the building of the Asian market. "Well, I'm here. I wish you could come have lunch with me."

"Me too. I've been putting off this doctor appointment for too long though."

"Is it something serious?"

"Nah, don't worry. It's just good to get checked regularly. I got stuck with a family history of ailments."

"You still babysitting with me tonight?"

"Of course. I'd never miss the opportunity to perform to a captive audience."

"Not sure performing for my friend's children will be a great stepping stone for your music career."

"But I'll be passing on music appreciation while hanging out with my girl."

"You obviously haven't hung out with many kids before," Goldie says. "The last time I babysat, Serena got really upset after watching *Inside/Out*, Corey was mad at the dog for chewing up his favorite coloring book, and Tyler hated his dinner so much that he flipped the bowl on the table and smeared food around with his hands and face."

"Wait, he used his face too?"

"Yes! Just smashed his cheek down and smothered himself in it."

"Sounds like a great time." Teo laughs. "I can't wait."

"It's hours of nonstop stress and assurance of my continued childlessness."

"Well, you didn't have me before, did you?"

Goldie knows what he means, but her breath still hitches. She shakes her head and dismisses any other possible interpretations. "We'll see how enthusiastic you are after tonight. Anyway, I should go ahead inside and check on my mom."

"Tell her her favorite Guatemalan musician says hi."

"Sure thing. I love—" She stops short.

Should she say the thing? It's been said a few times, but what exactly is the normal number of times to say "I love you" to a boyfriend? Is it commensurate with the months and years together? Is there a chart she can look up?

"Goldie? You there?" Teo interrupts her stream of panicked thoughts.

"Um, yeah."

He clears his throat. "I love you, honey. I can't wait to see you tonight."

A relieved chuckle escapes Goldie. "I love you too. See you later." She tucks her phone in her purse and approaches the storefront.

Goldie's mother and the owner, known as Ms. Chang in the community, have been friends since before Goldie was born. Sun helped her get the business started and has worked off and on there ever since. The store is nestled in a corner of the shopping center that serves as the city's unofficial K-Town.

The windows are covered in old advertisements for various Korean products: the frozen melon bars her mother devoured but always bought with the excuse that they were treats for Goldie; the grape juice in cans with whole grapes on the bottom that Goldie never could completely get out; the spicy ramen she refused to eat in front of anyone because her face would sweat like a glass of iced tea left in the sun.

Goldie walks through the automated doors for the millionth time, expecting to be greeted by her mother in her usual spot behind the counter. Instead, something furry attacks her feet.

"Oh crap! What's that?!" She jumps precariously in her high heels.

"Be careful!" her mother yells. "Don't hurt him!"

Goldie calms down enough to notice the sound of yipping. "*Him?!* I almost twisted my ankle!"

Sun comes from behind the counter to pick up the very small puppy and hug him to her chest. "Oh, did mean lady hurt you? You wanna bite her?"

Goldie squints in confusion over the sight of her typically stern mother cooing and babying the animal. "Where did it come from?"

"Nabi have puppies."

Nabi is Ms. Chang's latest dog, a Chihuahua. She's raised several dogs throughout the years.

Goldie takes a closer look at the animal. His short fur is mostly black with tan and white around the face and underside. The nose and mouth barely protrude. The pointy ears are folded over, and his eyes are big and expressive. All puppies are cute, of course, but Chihuahuas definitely fall in the "So cute I could die" category.

When she offers a finger for him to mouth, he latches onto it as if taking her mother up on the biting offer.

"What's his name?"

"Luck—" Sun starts to say, looking into the puppy's face, "yyy!" she finishes, excitedly stressing the syllable. "Lucky!"

"You named him."

It's a statement, not a question. Luck was always an element in their lives. Her mother worried about what was good luck and what was bad, and not a Friday the thirteenth went by without Sun telling her daughter to be careful.

"It good name. Right, Lucky? Mommy give you good name."

And there it is, the confirmation Goldie was waiting for. The name and Sun's rare show of open delight make the situation obvious—they're dog owners now.

"We've never had animals before," Goldie points out. "Every time I asked for one, you'd complain about having to feed another mouth."

"He small. Not eat much."

A weak but technically valid justification, Goldie grants. Despite her better judgment, she pushes for more. "Why now?"

Sun tears her eyes away from the puppy to look at Goldie, the familiar sternness returning to her face.

"Why you think?" She shoves Lucky into her daughter's hands. "I go get you lunch."

Goldie frowns at the furball, who's struggling to stay awake. She places him in the crook of her elbow, where their new pup pillows his head and falls asleep in an instant.

3:10 p.m.

GOLDIE RIPS THE HEADPHONES FROM HER EARS AND RUBS HER TEMPLES after transcribing the day's interview—the usable parts, at least.

Despite Max's shitty attitude, she finds herself acknowledging some interesting points he had on the Serum's effect on television journalism. There's now an industrywide intolerance for older-looking talking heads of all genders, which begs the question, "If everyone takes the Serum, does it matter?"

An argument could be made that the field has evened out. That taking aging out of the hiring equation means skill and talent have more weight.

Oh, you're young and fresh-faced? So what? So is everyone else. More important: Can you handle the pressures of live television?

Do research constantly and ask informed questions? Work during natural disasters and national crises?

Goldie's gaze sweeps across the newsroom and the faces of her coworkers. As far as she knows, not one of them takes the Serum.

The most recent user had been a graphic designer named Autumn, a skilled professional who added much-needed creativity and energy to the newspaper. But despite the positives, newsroom gossips proclaimed her outgoing personality and confidence to be annoying side-effects of the Serum.

When she brought baked goodies to the newsroom, someone would inevitably joke about her drumming up business for her partner, who was a plastic surgeon. They would, of course, be doing this while stuffing their faces with snickerdoodles so subtly sweet and pillowy that Goldie wanted to cry when Autumn quit bringing them to the office to avoid the comments.

And when a school board meeting conflicted with a soccer game Autumn and education reporter Misty Carson's daughters would be playing, Autumn volunteered to take the teammates. The offer had been firmly rebuffed by Misty, however, with her saying she didn't need Autumn's charity.

In a career field where looks supposedly don't matter, using the Serum also shouldn't have mattered. But Autumn knew better. She quit after only six months.

Goldie starts to put her headphones back on to listen to some music when Jenny's very loud phone conversation reaches her ears.

"We had every right to write that story, Mrs. Lattimore."

"It's nothing but lies meant to disgrace my son's good name!"

Mrs. Lattimore is a frequent caller of the newspaper, either to complain, as she's doing now, or to try to get coverage of whatever random thing is happening with her six children.

And she's super loud. *Wow*, she's not even on speakerphone, and Goldie can hear every word from her desk.

"Even if you think that," Jenny allows, "the fact that he's a county board member accused of misusing public funds makes it a newsworthy story."

"Did it have to be at the top of the front page?"

"It's also a very big story because of your family's history of serving in various offices, and among the accusations he faces is favoritism in getting several contracts for public projects awarded to members of your family."

"You're making more of the situation than it is. He's just new to the position and unsure of how things work. That's all! Not that I'm saying any of the accusations are true," Mrs. Lattimore hastily hedges. "You'll see though! He's practically the next John F. Kennedy!"

Jenny snickers at the mother's boast, covering the mouthpiece to avoid being heard.

"Your paper has always made scandals out of nothing! You never cover the good news in the community."

Jenny puts her glasses back on, a clear signal to Goldie that she's about to shut down this conversation. "If you need to speak more on the matter, I will gladly transfer you to our executive editor, and you can yell as long and loudly as you like at him."

"I'm not talking to that prick!"

The glasses magnify Jenny's eye roll. "Then I suppose we're done here. Now, I have eight other stories to work on. Have a good day, Mrs. Lattimore." She slams the receiver down without waiting for a response.

Still seated, Goldie scoots her chair down to Jenny's desk. "How do you do it?" she asks without preamble.

"What? Put up with idiots on the phone?"

"No, not just that." Goldie looks around the newsroom some more. "*All* of it. How have you done this for so many years?"

Jenny whips off her glasses again and places them on her crown of graying curls. "What is this? A midlife crisis?"

"No! It's, it's just, uhhh." Goldie sputters out instead of finishing the denial and slumps in her chair.

"Goldie, don't be so embarrassed. You'd be stupid not to re-evaluate some life choices at your age."

The 40-year-old cringes, making Jenny laugh.

"Oh God! You're such an age snob!"

"I'm not!" The denial comes out shrill.

Jenny throws an "Are too" back at Goldie.

"Really, I'm not! I don't care about being 40. It's not being where I want to be at the age that's bothering me."

"And where is that?" Jenny asks. "You're our top reporter. You're so good that Sarah fucking Crown requested you specifically to be the only person to interview her. Your hard work has paid off."

"Has it though?" Goldie asks with a groan. "I've done so much in the name of building a career. I kept building and building. I'd work weekends and holidays. No partying, no dating. And before I know it, almost twenty years have gone by. All for a company that could toss me on my ass after the next buyout."

Jenny's lips flatten, her eyes scrutinizing. "Look, I get your concerns. I was like you early on, but once I had the confidence I needed, I said fuck this place and traveled. When was the last time you had a vacation and actually *did* something?"

"Seven years ago," Goldie murmurs. "But there wasn't a chance in hell I was going to miss seeing Queen and Adam Lambert in Vegas."

"There are no buts, no shame in going off to do something that's not work. You had a good time, right?"

"Sure," Goldie says, then shuts her mouth tight.

"What else?"

"Heh," she huffs, "I have another 'but.'"

Jenny sighs. "I have stories to write, Goldie. Out with it."

"*But*," Goldie emphasizes, "I went alone."

Jenny mouths an "ah" of understanding.

"My best friend isn't a fan. My other best friend was busy with her first baby. No one at the paper could spare the money or time away." Jenny's family photos catch Goldie's gaze, especially the one of her hugging her husband in front of a grand locale. "They had plans with family to think of."

"What about now?" Jenny asks.

"Huh?"

"Don't you have a shiny new boyfriend now? Wouldn't he go somewhere with you?"

Goldie shakes her head like she's clearing it. Honestly, she forgets Teo when she's busy. In the familiar autopilot of work, he never enters her mind. She's just so used to having no one to think about.

"Look, Goldie, before you stupidly go taking the advice of the biggest manchild on midmarket TV news—"

Goldie groans. "You heard about that?"

"The whole newsroom did. Amber wouldn't stop bragging about it." Jenny puts her glasses back on. "Anyway, try taking a break from this place first. See how you feel about your life now that you have someone to spend it with."

6:42 p.m.

THE KIDS MET TEO BRIEFLY A FEW WEEKS AGO DURING A SCHOOL fundraising picnic. Penny needed help with getting items that were forgotten or ran out. As rewards for their labor, Teo and Goldie got free Gatorade and the chicken salad that the students wouldn't eat.

This time, they're getting a slightly better meal. Penny and Jack ordered pizza as a treat for their kids in honor of their anniversary before going out to their fancy dinner.

"How old is everyone?" Teo asks, trying to break the ice. The kids were too wrapped up in the pizza to bother with acknowledging the newcomer in their home.

"I'm 8," Serena says after swallowing.

"I'm 5," Corey says with a mouthful.

Tyler is busy squishing his little pieces of pizza.

"How old are you, Ty Bear?" Goldie repeats the question and holds up her fingers. The toddler does as he's shown, proudly displaying two greasy digits without really understanding why.

Teo smiles at the boy and hands him another piece of pizza, guiding his hand to his mouth to make sure he eats.

"Hmm, 2, 5, and 8. Interesting pattern there."

Goldie tries to guess what he means. "They're Fibonacci numbers?"

Teo shakes his head, then furrows his brow. "I actually don't know. Are they? What are Fibonacci numbers about?"

"I don't know either," Goldie admits. "I just remember hearing about them in *The Da Vinci Code*."

Serena pipes up. "It's when each number is the sum of the two numbers that come before it."

The adults look at the girl in shock. "How do you know that?" Goldie asks.

"Wikipedia." The girl holds up her tablet.

"Excellent," Goldie says, side-eyeing Teo to get his support. "You took advantage of a fantastic learning opportunity."

"Which we totally planned for you," Teo says, his serious face selling the lie. "How does the sequence go?"

"0, 1, 1, 2, 3, 5, 8, 13—"

"And without looking at your tablet," Goldie interrupts, "how much is 13 plus 8?"

Serena frowns and starts using her fingers.

"21," Corey garbles out around another mouthful.

Teo and Goldie look at each other and share the awe of being in the presence of a pizza-inhaling math wiz.

"That's right, Corey," Teo says. "This next question should be easy, then. What is the difference between your and your sister's ages? What is 8 minus 5?"

"3," he answers.

"And is that the same number for you and your brother? 5 minus 2?"

"*Duh.* Serena is oldest. When she was 3, I came, and when I was 3, Tyler came."

"Exactly! Good job," Teo praises. "Take another slice."

"Sweet!" Corey grabs a big one.

"What are you getting at?" Goldie asks, although she thinks she can guess now.

"I'm just pointing out a pattern."

"Uh-huh." Goldie tries to be vague about the possibility of another sibling in front of the Song brood. "I don't think it's strong enough evidence for what you're presuming."

Teo shrugs. "It's just a feeling. Ever just know something was right?"

When it comes to feelings? Never. Goldie's always had more faith in facts.

"I have the advantage of knowing Penny very well. I can tell you that she's got her hands quite full and isn't looking to change things."

"We'll see in a few months," Teo says with a smirk.

"It's not happening."

"You wanna bet?"

"On *this*?" Goldie checks to see if the kids are paying attention to the conversation. Luckily, they seem to have gotten bored and started watching something on Serena's tablet (Tyler has returned to squishing bits of pizza). "It's a weird thing to bet on."

"We're not betting on anything bad happening. It's a simple matter of proving that I'm right to go with my gut feeling and proving wrong your cynical, hypercautious paranoia."

"Oh, that's how it's gonna be, Estrada?"

"You gotta trust your instincts, Hays. If not, you'll end up talking yourself out of great things."

Goldie wonders what Teo's really getting at. There's an earnestness behind the playful tone that the reporter wants to investigate. She shoves the urge aside for now. "It's a bet. What are we wagering?"

Teo looks at the disaster of crusts in greasy boxes on the table. "*When* I win, you owe me a Hawaiian-style pizza."

"Eww!" The kids were apparently paying some attention to Goldie and Teo's conversation.

"Oh, just you guys wait," Teo says. "I caved on the toppings this time because I'm a guest, but when your imo loses, you'll see how good pineapple on pizza is."

"Don't worry, kids," Goldie says, low and conspiratorial. "He's not winning. Next time, we'll get the veggie lovers on gluten-free crust."

The kids say "Eww!" again. Corey declares with a pout, "I don't think anyone's winning."

7:20 p.m.

TEO SINGS AND HOWLS (YES, *HOWLS*) LIKE HE'S PERFORMING BACK AT Hank's Bar instead of in the small living room of the Song residence. It's a commanding performance that Goldie won't soon forget despite the noise coming from the members of his band for the evening, who are unpracticed—and under the age of 10.

Serena is banging away on her tambourine, Corey is blasting his kazoo, and little Tyler is trying to sit on his bongos.

Every time the word *you* is sung, Teo's hand lifts off his guitar and points at Goldie, the only audience member for this rendition of the classic T. Rex song "Mambo Sun." He sings a mishmash of the original lyrics, sticking to the animal and celestial references and less to the ones that might have sexier interpretations. And when an alligator is mentioned, Teo makes a pained sound like he's been bitten to make the kids laugh.

Goldie goes to the floor to show Tyler how to hit the bongos. Unsurprisingly, the toddler takes advantage of being allowed to smack something without worry of being told no. Then Teo starts howling again, which triggers Tyler and the dog to howl too. Meanwhile, Corey and Serena try to drown out the distraction with their instruments like they're serious musicians.

Goldie gives her boyfriend her most exasperated glare. Of course, there isn't a hint of guilt on his face. Just a glowing satisfaction at the chaos he's unleashed.

8:20 p.m.
WITH A PASSED-OUT TYLER IN HIS ARMS, TEO FOLLOWS GOLDIE TO PUT him in bed.

"Think we have a future percussionist here," Teo whispers. "Next time, I'm bringing a drum set."

"Penny will kill you." Goldie covers the toddler with the dinosaur blanket she bought for him recently.

They leave the door cracked in case he calls out for them and go to the bathroom to check on the older kids' bedtime prep.

"Imo! We're done!" Corey holds up his toothbrush for inspection.

Goldie acts like she's scrutinizing it. "I see that it's wet, yes," she allows. "Now, show me your tiger face."

The 5-year-old grits his teeth and brings up his hands with fingers curled like claws. "Grrr!"

"Ohhh!" She jumps back. "Very fierce. Excellent job."

Teo giggles from behind Goldie, getting Corey's attention.

"Hey, Teo?"

"What's up, bud?"

"Can we call you imoboo?"

Without warning, Serena whines a "Nooo!" that stuns everyone in the bathroom. "I don't want you to be my imoboo!"

Teo furrows his brow. "What's that mean?"

"Korean for uncle, basically," Goldie answers. "Like how imo means aunt because I'm like a sister to their mom." She leaves out the nuance that it specifically means an uncle by marriage. Korean is very precise with family titles. "Why are you upset, Serena?"

"I was gonna ask him to be my boyfriend."

Teo and Goldie gape at the 8-year-old.

"Uhhh." Teo hesitates. "But I'm your imo's boyfriend."

"She can share," Serena says with a shrug, like that's the most obvious answer.

Despite being an adult, Goldie has to fight the urge to shout "Mine!" and claim the cute new boy.

"Please, Teo! You're just like Tuxedo Mask."

Corey groans. "*Sailor Moon* sucks!"

"Shut up! It does not!"

Teo turns to Goldie, looking for help.

She tries to explain. "*Sailor Moon* is a cartoon."

"Anime!" Serena corrects.

"Sorry, *anime*." It takes all her willpower not to roll her eyes at the girl's outrage. "It's also what the main character's called. Her sort-of boyfriend is Tuxedo Mask."

Before Teo can ask what it's about, Serena goes into full fangirl mode and takes advantage of the chance to talk about her current obsession. "It's about a team of girls who save the world when they're not in school, and Sailor Moon is the main one, and her real name is Serena too!"

"I'm going to bed," Corey declares, stomping out of the bathroom to avoid hearing about the show from his sister for the millionth time.

In direct contrast to the 5-year-old, Teo sits on the toilet seat lid to get to the girl's eye level. "Really? Her name's Serena too?"

"Yeah! I was basically named after her."

"You basically *weren't*," Goldie says. "You were named after

Serena Williams." To answer the likely follow-up question from Teo, she adds, "Her father loves tennis."

"And Appa says that if one of my brothers had been a girl, she'd be named Venus—*and* there's a Sailor Venus. So, I'm basically Sailor Moon."

"I don't think you know what 'basically' means, sweetie."

"*Golds*," Teo says, his tone disapproving of even mildly squashing the little girl's assumptions. "Tell me more, Serena. Why am I like Tuxedo Mask?"

"Oh, he's pretty and mysterious and brave, and Serena doesn't know who he is at first, but he protects Sailor Moon and helps her fight evil with rose darts because he was a prince in another life, and Serena was a princess, and they were in love." The girl concludes her gushing with a dreamy sigh.

Teo nods. "That does sound like me."

Goldie snorts. "You regularly dress like a magician to save the world with floral weaponry? Wow, I really don't know you, Teo."

Teo smirks at his girlfriend before looking at Serena. "That all sounds amazing. I see why you like the show so much, and your moon-themed sailor pajamas make so much more sense now."

"They're cool, right?" Serena turns her hips to make the navy-blue skirt that's attached to her pajama leggings flare outward.

"Very cool," Teo confirms before leaning forward to hold Serena's gaze. "Are Sailor Moon and Tuxedo Mask true loves?"

"Yeah, of course!"

"Then I can't be your Tuxedo Mask."

"But *why*?" she pouts.

"Don't get me wrong, I'll always be there for you when you need me, Serena. I'm your imoboo, definitely." He looks back up at Goldie. "But I'm already your imo's Tuxedo Mask, and she's my Sailor Moon. I wear the mask for her."

9:20 p.m.

"I'M SO SORRY I COMPARED YOU TO SAILOR MOON," TEO SAYS TO Goldie, shaking his head in disbelief as they watch animated Serena's antics. "What is wrong with her? If a magical talking cat tells you that you're the chosen one with mystical moon powers, you don't run away from that kind of opportunity."

9:42 p.m.

"ANOTHER EPISODE?" GOLDIE ASKS.

Despite his complaints about the show, Teo looks tempted. "No," he says slowly, "I've put this off long enough."

Before Goldie can ask what he means, Teo reaches a hand to the back of her head and kisses her flush against her lips.

Goldie catches on and brings her hands up to his neck. Her mouth opens to accept the tease of his tongue, releasing a gasp in the process.

Their mouths have become well acquainted these past several months, but the familiarity hasn't dulled the thrill that runs through Goldie every time they kiss. With each movement and caress, Teo lingers, barely breathing. He seems to savor the moment like it's their last.

Teo likes to call her Golden Wonder, and he treats her as such—a wondrous treasure to cherish and behold.

Goldie's so caught up that when Teo pulls back, a whine escapes her throat, making him chuckle.

"Why the hell were you putting *that* off?" she complains. "You know I have Penny's permission for us to make out on this couch, right?"

Instead of another laugh like she expected, Teo gives a sad smile. "I wasn't talking about that. I'm just trying to soften what I have to tell you."

Goldie sits up fully alert. "What's wrong?"

"It's good news, actually. You know Johnny Fresh?"

"The lead singer of the Panty Rockers?"

"Yeah, great dude. He's been working on something big for the band for a few months now that's finally coming through."

"Is it a new album?"

"Better," Teo says. "It's a tour."

"But they play everywhere all year long," Goldie says. "Their appearances at Hank's are regularly scheduled stops."

"This one's in Europe."

"They have a following in Europe?"

"Yeah, Johnny's English and German. You didn't know?"

Goldie's only had a few chats with the musician on topics ranging from today's awful pop music to the wonders of succulents. "I thought his accent was an act, the way it goes all over the place."

Teo pulls out his phone. "Check this out," he says, and hits play on the band's most-viewed YouTube video, "Resurrect the Living (Chaos Is Free Will)." It has an impressive 5 million views and quite a lot of comments in European languages.

"What does this have to do with you?"

"They invited me to go as an opening act."

Goldie narrows her eyes.

"Okay, more like a secondary opening act for a lot of the stops," Teo admits. "The band is hitching along with a few bigger names, going to some festivals, and mostly playing at old music halls and clubs. I can perform a song or two if I'm willing to be a glorified roadie and help them with gear. Johnny's keeping the budget tight, so it's me and his cousin from Jacksonville helping out."

"That sounds cool," Goldie says. "Why were you so worried about my reaction?"

"It's for three months."

"You're, uh, going the entire time?" Goldie asks stiltedly. Her tongue feels numb all of a sudden.

"Yeah, it's just too big of an opportunity—hell, an *experience*— to travel Europe and perform."

"When are you guys doing this?"

Teo looks away. "In two weeks."

"What?! Two weeks?"

"Johnny dropped the idea in my lap today, and it sounded so good that I said yes without hesitation. I'm sorry."

In the grand scheme of things, this shouldn't be upsetting. They don't live together, so there aren't any expenses to pay or upkeep expected on her part. He doesn't even have houseplants she'd need to water when he's gone. Teo had every right to jump at the opportunity.

"If you're mad about how soon I leave, I could maybe join them a little later."

"Don't you dare! You're not missing a minute of this tour," she insists, mouth quirking slightly to force a faint smile. "I'm just really going to miss you."

"I'll miss you too," Teo says, his voice going a little rough. "It's just three months though. You probably won't even notice I'm gone."

"I'll make sure I do," she says, recalling her earlier conversation with Jenny. "I don't like when I forget that I'm not alone anymore."

"Oh, Goldie ..."

She shakes her head to dismiss his concern. It's not like he's going off to war. "I'll be fine. Just don't run off with any groupies."

Teo snorts, the tension breaking like she hoped. "I'll try to resist the Panty Rockets."

It takes a second for Goldie to process the words. "Are you serious?"

"Yup," he says, popping the *p* to punctuate the ridiculousness. "That's what Johnny likes to call them."

Stomps outside the front door end the conversation, with Jack and Penny entering their home soon after.

"Hey, guys," Penny says, hushed to avoid disturbing the kids. "How did the monsters behave?"

"Perfect angels," Teo says. "Thanks for letting me babysit with Goldie."

"No tantrums?" Jack asks. "No throwing up? No requests for nonexistent Ben & Jerry's ice cream flavors?"

"They were good, Jack," Goldie assures him. "How was your date?"

"The place was amazing!" Penny gushes as she takes off her long cardigan. "It was Italian food, so I ate way too much bread and not enough of the actual meal. And the piano music was just beautiful. She's very accompli—" Penny stops talking when she notices Goldie looking amused and Teo averting his gaze. "What?"

"The back of your dress is bunched in your underwear," Goldie explains, laughing at her friend's horrified expression as she looks down.

Meanwhile, a smug Jack helps his wife pull the material out.

"I'm so winning this bet," Teo whispers into Goldie's ear.

She almost chokes from laughing so hard.

10:50 p.m.

"HEY, MA."

Sun groans as she wakes up and reorients herself, noticing that she fell asleep on the couch with the puppy on her stomach. "What time is it?"

"Almost eleven."

"Shh, not so loud. You wake up Lucky."

The puppy stirs as her mother shifts him to her lap.

"How was the rest of work?" Goldie asks.

"Shoulder sore."

"I warned you this morning."

"I have you after eighteen-hour labor pain. This nothing."

Goldie groans at the well-used maternal guilt trip.

"How's Penny's babies?"

"They're good. Teo and I had fun."

"How Teo today?"

Goldie smiles at hearing her mother ask about her boyfriend. A few weeks ago, she would have ignored the mention of him. "He's great. He's got a big oppor—" She stops herself suddenly, thinking better of revealing more about his Europe plans. It's a little too late to go into it right now, and she's not too sure how her mother will react. "You know what? I'll tell you later. I need to get to bed."

Sun frowns and seems ready to insist on hearing everything when the puppy whines. "Goldie, get towel. Your puppy brother need pee."

Goldie shakes her head, fond and amused, and does as she's told.

11:30 p.m.

GOLDIE CHECKS HER PHONE TO ENSURE THE ALARM'S SET BEFORE climbing into bed. As she stares into the darkness, she rewinds through the day's events.

Before meeting Teo, she often had to block out the awkwardness and disappointments of her wakeful hours in order to fall asleep. Now Goldie feels like she's building a life and wants to absorb every minute. Today in particular felt special.

As she shuts her eyes, Goldie wonders what she'll dream about and what tomorrow will bring.

And she can't wait to find out.

CHAPTER 6

WHEN THE DOORBELL RINGS, GOLDIE ALMOST RIPS THE SHOWER curtain off the rod to avoid falling on her ass as she rushes out of the tub.

"Don't answer it!" she yells as soon as she cracks open the bathroom door.

Too late.

Her mother is moving faster than her 64-year-old feet have allowed her to do for a while. She swings the door open wide without warning, making Teo jump back in surprise, and fills the doorway by standing with her legs spread and her hands high on each side of the doorframe.

"Hi, Mrs. Hays!" Teo says louder than usual. The doorbell set off the puppy, who loyally followed his owner to the door.

Goldie fiercely grips the towel wrapped around her as she leans out of the bathroom door. "Ma, move out of the way, and let him in already! And calm Lucky down!" The little fella's got some lung power.

Her mother doesn't respond—and doesn't move.

Teo's mouth opens and closes a couple times before he makes a straightforward assessment of the cold welcome. "You're upset with me."

Her mother's face must up a notch in scary because Teo steps back some.

"Why you abandon my daughter?"

"Ma!" This is exactly why Goldie didn't want her mother answering the door. (She has got to stop taking so much time in the bathroom.)

"It's only three months," Teo says gently. "I'm coming back."

"Why, God? Why my daughter pick musician?" Sun laments, gaze upward, before pointing at Teo. "This tour gonna make you rich?"

Teo looks down at his feet. "Uh, no."

"Then why you go?! If you not get rich, why leave my daughter? You can just stay here and not get rich!" Her tone makes Lucky yip again like he's agreeing with her.

"I understand why you're mad. I don't want to leave. But Goldie understands that this is a big opportunity for me. If things were reversed, I wouldn't stand in her way."

Goldie's so caught up in the disappointing backward slide her mother's feelings about Teo have taken that she can't disrupt their standoff. She was warming up to him, accepting him as part of their lives. Now all that progress has evaporated.

"My daughter most important person in my life. She most important person to you?"

"Of course," Teo says. "I love her so much."

"If that true"—Sun bends down to pick up the puppy—"be with her. Nothing more important."

She turns around and leaves a stunned Teo in the open door.

"I'M SORRY," GOLDIE SAYS FOR THE HUNDREDTH TIME AS THEY TAKE their seats at the restaurant.

"You don't have to keep apologizing," Teo insists. "*I'm* sorry for upsetting your mother."

"She's just being her usual overprotective self. She'll get over it."

Teo looks down at his menu for a long moment. "I really messed things up with her." His eyes return to Goldie. "Have I messed things up with you?"

"What? No!"

"It's just that I haven't seen much of you since telling you my plans. Did I say the right thing to your mother about what you think? I was reaching for any kind of positive spin in the face of her death stare."

"You were right," Goldie says. "I do understand why you want to go. I'm not upset, just busy with work."

"The Serum story?"

"Ugh, yes. It's ironically probably responsible for a few extra wrinkles and gray hairs with all the interviews I've had to do."

Teo squints and pretends to scrutinize her, making Goldie laugh and cover her face just in case he could see something.

"No hiding that beautiful face, especially since I haven't seen it much these last few days." He bats away her hands to reinforce how serious he is. "Now, catch me up. Who have you been talking to?"

"Is this still a good time?"

Goldie straightens her laptop screen to get the camera to show less of the underside of her chin while her interview subject shoos away the person knocking on her door.

"This is as good a time as any, Ms. Hays. The production schedule is pretty tight on this one."

Thandie Fox is one of the stars of the Netflix series *Tidal Waves*, which is about, you guessed it, tidal waves that decimate the West Coast of North America. It's currently filming a third season.

"Thank you for agreeing to speak with me, especially about such a sensitive topic."

"Oh, please." The actress waves a hand. "You sound like I'm keeping a big secret."

"I know that the use of the Serum among actors is common practice. But the fact that you don't take it and continue to get very prominent roles, it's, well, made you a target for criticism from several of your colleagues."

"Which is why I am more than willing to do this interview, because fuck those assholes."

Goldie's mouth hangs open. "Uh, can I quote you on that?"

"Fuck, yeah. Hollywood is so tiring, Ms. Hays. I've never quite fit in here."

"Okay, let's start there." Goldie tries to establish the interview rhythm. "This isn't a full story on you, but I'd like to get a bit of detail about your industry experience before the Serum and after."

"Hollywood wasn't easy before the Serum, of course. I'm a

dark-skinned Black woman who didn't have connections early on to hook me up with work. I auditioned for everything and took what I could get. That ended up being a blessing for me. I did some of my best acting back then."

"You won an Oscar for your portrayal of a struggling single mother in the indie film *Darkest Before the Dawn*."

"Exactly! After that, I was able to name my terms and get more creative sway. At the time, though, I was disappointed with the timing."

"What do you mean?"

"I was always working to reach that point, and I didn't have the money to live the stereotypical glamorous Hollywood lifestyle while I was still so young. Then it hit all at once in my 40s."

Goldie can't help relating. "As someone who's recently turned 40, I don't want to look at the next decade of my life as being too late for anything."

Thandie's face softens. "You are absolutely correct, Ms. Hays. I felt that way too after dealing with the initial anxieties and worries that come with major life changes. I was going to live my life to the absolute fullest and make up for lost time." The actress pauses and the softness on her face evaporates, replaced with a scowl. "Then the fucking Serum came out."

"Did Hollywood really change that much?" For some reason, Goldie is skeptical of the possibility of any instant change. After all, society as a whole seemed more dented than upended by the existence of the Serum. Just a few more youthful faces everywhere you go.

"I know what you're thinking. Hollywood was already surgically enhanced and filler-injected. What's one more anti-aging product going to do? But the fact that this was a guaranteed fix for wrinkles and grays made it a requirement for anyone looking to maintain a career or status in the industry. And here I was just getting my career well and truly off the ground and coming to terms with my age. I was mapping out the roles I was comfortable taking, the ones that would match my maturity and talent. Being in my 40s meant not being able to take the role of the fresh-faced heroine leading the rebellion. I'd missed my chance, and I learned to accept that."

Goldie tries to grasp the actress's issue. "But the Serum would have allowed you to play such a role again. Why was that so upsetting?"

"Because all that work I did on self-acceptance felt like an absolute waste! And when I was seriously considering taking the Serum, imagining seeing a 20-something Thandie Fox staring back at me in the mirror … it made me nauseous. I've earned these wrinkles. I'm comforted by my gray hair. I don't want to go back to those days of uncertainty and obsession over my looks. That's not me anymore."

Goldie gives a small smile. She appreciates the positive outlook on aging naturally, especially since she's likely never going to take the Serum.

"What was it like being one of the few high-profile actors to not take the Serum?"

"Oh, it was a fucking nightmare. I didn't think Hollywood could be even more youth obsessed, but it happened. Every project centered on teenagers and 20-somethings because those were the only kinds of faces you could get. Early on, the stories hadn't adapted to the new status quo of society either. So, since a grandma with a 25-year-old's face had until recently been unthinkable, you just did away with the grandma roles. It's only in the last ten years that actors who use the Serum have been playing characters that expressly match their real age. Did you ever watch *The Golden Girls* reboot with Serum-using 60-somethings?"

"Yeah, it was pretty awful."

"It sure was!" Thandie exclaims with a chuckle. "And why was that?"

"What made the original so endearing was seeing obviously older women going out on dates and seeking new experiences. It was a nontraditional view of life at that age. It just wasn't the same with the reboot."

"But they're the same ages as the original cast members."

Goldie tries to consider exactly why she didn't like it. "I

guess I was too disconnected from that level of Serum use. Most grandmothers I've met continue to look like old women."

"They look like me?" the 66-year-old asks.

"Um ..." There's no hiding the embarrassment Goldie feels from being put on the spot like that. "You, uh, look your age."

"That's my secret," Thandie says, smiling big, her eyes crinkling beautifully. "You see, the lack of age diversity in Hollywood couldn't be sustained. Audiences got tired of seeing the same flawless faces on their screens. Like you, they couldn't quite relate to a grandmother who looked 25, and unlike most of my peers, I was happy to show my age."

"But makeup and computer graphics have been used to compensate for the lack of diverse ages."

"That's a lot of money and time—and ultimately, it's not the same. Plus, most actors won't stop taking the Serum no matter their role."

"Do you think they're wrong to take the Serum?"

"I know a lot of people who seem genuinely happier after using it. For them, it's like a weight has been lifted. Getting old is no longer a nightmarish scenario despite the multitude of possible ailments it can bring, because at least they don't look old." Thandie gazes down, thoughtful. "Were you able to talk to any actors who use the Serum?"

"No one as well-known as you responded to my requests."

"That's not surprising. It's a known fact that most of Hollywood uses the Serum, but they'll hardly admit to it. I'm all for respecting people's privacy. It just seems to go beyond that for Serum users in the industry. Like they're basically taking their work home with them—because it's all an act, Ms. Hays. *Looking* young will never be the same as *being* young."

―――――――

"THIS SHIT RUINED MY LIFE."

Goldie tries to maintain a neutral expression. "If this is too difficult, we don't have—"

Terrance Bolan holds up a hand, blocking the web camera for a moment, to interrupt her. "I want my story told. People have to know what can happen to them if they use the Serum."

"Well, you've already written a book—"

"Memoir," the 52-year-old wellness guru interrupts again to correct her. "It is a heart-wrenching account of my journey to understanding that true beauty can never be realized on the outside but is within one's soul."

The reporter is trying to be patient and sympathetic, but Terrance's Triple-B Spirituality™ (bountiful, beatific, and blessed) is testing her Single-T Condition—tired. She drives on like a professional though. "You wrote that using the Serum was like a drug addiction. Please explain how."

"I couldn't stand missing a dose. Seeing one wrinkle made me nauseous."

"But it wasn't just the Serum you spent your money on. You've had multiple cosmetic surgeries and liposuction treatments."

"Since flawless skin and hair were possible, I had to make a flawless body to match." He motions to his jaw, which was enhanced to be squarer. "The flipside of all the surgery was not being able to take the Serum for months while healing from whatever work I had done. I would endure the ironic twist of having to see my real age when I was doing all I could *not* to."

"Because the Serum preoccupies the body with its constant regeneration of skin and hair cells," Goldie recalls from her research and the boldly displayed warnings on the Crown website, "which prolongs the healing process for severe illnesses or injuries."

"Yeah, so when you've had some emergency surgery or have plans for anything serious, you're not allowed to take the Serum again until you're healed completely."

"That ended up being sobering for you," Goldie notes, "according to your memoir." She politely uses his preferred word.

"My husband left me after the fifth major surgery. He stood in the living room holding our girls' hands, looked me in the eyes, and said he hoped that this latest surgery would be the one that made me feel beautiful. He added, 'I know it won't though,' and kicked me out." Terrance sniffles. "He was right, of course. I had one more surgery after that; I was down to my last penny, recovering by myself in a hotel room. With only my face in a mirror for company, I looked at it unflinchingly for the first time. The surgeries made me unrecognizable, but there were the wrinkles, at least. The grays of my temples. Pieces of the real me."

"You haven't had a surgery since?"

Terrance smiles wide. "Five years sober."

———————————

"DID HE WORK THINGS OUT WITH HIS HUSBAND?" TEO ASKS.

"No, they're still divorced," Goldie answers before taking a bite of sushi. "He has visitation rights for the kids. Never fought for custody so he could focus on his spiritual healing—and building an impressive wellness brand."

"Really? His husband couldn't forgive him?"

"Some relationships can't recover from that kind of damage." Teo seems strangely distraught over the story, making Goldie feel guilty. "I'm sorry I've been going on and on about work stuff at dinner. This Serum story has just overtaken anything else I've ever done professionally. I never considered the many ways it's affected people."

Teo stays pensive. "Yeah, me neither."

"People can be so desperate to stay young looking that they commit crimes to afford the treatments. Not only selling drugs, but rewriting the wills of ailing family members, using the Serum to pretend to be young so they can convince lonely rich people to be their sugar daddy or mommy and get the money to secretly keep taking the Serum."

Teo mouths a "What the fuck?"

"Credit card fraud is probably at its worst right now; fake Serum administrators are pretending saline solution is the Serum and charging bargain prices—"

"Jesus," Teo murmurs, which stops Goldie's list.

"Oh, Teo, um." Goldie bites her lip. "Sorry," she says yet again. "What am I doing? You're trying to treat me tonight, and I'm dragging down the mood."

"You're not." Teo shakes his head. "I love how your voice gets husky from talking so much, and how your eyes twinkle when you go off about something. I want to soak it in while I can."

Goldie frowns at the reminder of the precious few days they have left until he leaves for Europe. "What are you looking forward to seeing the most?"

"I don't think it's so much the historic places or landmarks that I want to see. I can't wait to experience the culture, the food." He waves a hand, reaching for the right words. "The vibe."

"And what about the music? Got any original stuff you're saving for over there?"

"Well, Marigold Hays of the *Daily Liberty Press*, it's nice of you to ask. I know my fans are dying to know." He places a hand over his heart and heaves an exaggerated sigh. "I have a new song that I'm working on."

Goldie leans forward. "What's it about? Is it up-tempo? Ballad?"

Teo points slightly and clicks his tongue. "That's it. I've been picking at it here and there. You see"—he reaches to take Goldie's hand—"there's this beautiful girl I met a few months ago who's been inspiring me since day one."

"A song about me?" Goldie tries to sound incredulous and not stupidly excited. "Can I hear some of it?"

"You want me to serenade you in the middle of the Sushi Palace? I don't think the staff would appreciate me interrupting the J-Pop they're playing over the speakers."

Goldie rolls her eyes. "Can I hear it when we're not in public? Or are you saving it for the tour?"

"I'd never perform it before playing it for you first. Anyway, it's not finished yet. Probably keep working on it some more while I'm away."

"Then maybe you will get to perform it for me soon."

Teo tilts his head.

"What do you think about me going over there to visit you on tour?"

"You want to go to Europe?"

"Yeah!" Goldie giggles a bit. She's been giddy since she first got the nerve to consider the prospect. "I've wanted to visit England since my *Doctor Who* phase. And the chance to spend time with you there is too big of an opportunity to waste."

Teo's eyes go wide and unblinking. "You barely leave the county lines. And when you do, it's for work."

"True, yeah." Goldie's thrown by how shocked her boyfriend seems. "I'm a workaholic, sure, and I keep a tight rein on my finances."

"And that's *fine*," Teo says with a sympathetic inflection. He must realize how standoffish he's being. "I know how you worry. I don't want you to disrupt your life and spend money you don't want to spend."

"Don't worry," Goldie says a little meekly, almost to herself, trying to fight the doubts creeping into her mind. "It's irrational to hold on to money the way I do. I'm not going to go broke this one time on a dream trip to Europe to watch my boyfriend perform."

"What about work?"

"If I had my way, I'd fly off with you Saturday, but Manning reminded me that my livelihood depends on me finishing this damn Serum story and that the interview with Sarah Crown is on Monday."

"When do you think you'd go?" Teo's voice sounds tense.

"Manning wants me to stay a week after the story goes out to address any queries from other media outlets. I can't imagine what he thinks will come from the interview. What could be more shocking than what they've already done?"

"If he thinks it's necessary, maybe you should stay."

Goldie studies her boyfriend then. His jaw is clenched; his eyes constantly shift away from her. "You don't want me to go," she says as realization dawns. "You never even asked me about the possibility."

"I, uh." He sucks in a sharp breath. "I want you to see me at my best. The tour might be a great opportunity, but it's not glamorous. We're going to be staying in the cheapest of the cheap and playing at some dubious places. I don't want you wasting your first trip to Europe being miserable."

"Despite my name, I'm not a delicate flower," Goldie scoffs. "I can handle a rough road trip, skipping showers, hauling your equipment—"

"I don't want you to," Teo insists. "You deserve to travel in luxury. You deserve to see the sights without worrying about money or safety. I want it to be perfect. Not something you're enduring for me."

"I wasn't going *for* you," she says, her face downcast. "I'd be doing this *with* you. It's time I experienced life outside of this bubble I've been in for the last forty years."

Her boyfriend looks pained. "I am going to miss you so much," he says, hushed, almost haunted in his serious delivery. "Honestly, I want it to just be us over there. I don't really want to do the touristy stuff because I'd want you there with me."

"Then why all this angst about me going?"

Teo pulls his lips inward for a long moment. Suddenly, he scoots his chair to the side of their small table to sit beside her and grabs her hand again.

"I swear I want to experience the world with you and have an adventure of our own making, but this isn't the right time. Just wait a little longer." He brushes his lips against the back of her hand. "Our time will come, Goldie. Trust me."

Goldie crashes her lips against Teo's, keeping him from seeing the look on her face. She's disappointed, sure, but she can't quite hide something else.

Because Teo said to trust him, and at that moment—she really doesn't.

CHAPTER 7

GOLDIE OPENS THE NEWSPAPER'S ARCHIVE AND HOVERS HER FINGERS over the keyboard to give herself a chance to rethink her actions.

For the last few days, she's done her best to work so much that she wouldn't have time to think of her suspicions about Teo, and the battle between sincere doubts about her relationship and guilt about having such doubts is stressing her out.

What happened to the euphoria of love? Are her insecurities behind this gnawing sensation she's experiencing? What real evidence does she have that Teo's lying to her about something?

There's the suddenness of this tour, for one. Second, there's his insistence that she not visit him.

And third? That's the piece she doesn't like analyzing the most and that has her in front of her computer at work about to dig up dirt on her boyfriend. Because these doubts point to a truth Goldie has been ignoring since she started getting serious with Teo.

She really doesn't know him.

Goldie probably wouldn't run out of fingers if she counted exactly how many things she knows about Teo's past. He's originally from Miami. His father died of a heart attack when he was 7, and his mother died of liver cancer when he was 19. He said he managed to finish college despite these tragic losses and afterward moved around Florida, then up the East Coast.

That's it. He's never mentioned any other friends except for Henry. When she's asked about past relationships, he's always managed to skirt the topic and focus on Goldie, and she let him because she was so flattered by his charms.

Before she can talk herself out of it, Goldie types "Mateo Estrada" into the keyword space. The results are disappointing. She assumed that some extra filtering would be necessary to get the right kinds of results. Instead, she only gets an obituary for a woman who died more than two decades ago and a birth announcement that's even older.

Then Goldie slaps her forehead because she's an idiot. Of course, there's not going to be anything about *her* Teo in her newspaper's archive. He relocated because of Henry. She switches to a search of the *Miami Herald* and other Florida newspapers ... and gets way too many results.

The reporter sighs. She really wanted to investigate her way to the truth before she saw Teo tonight for his last performance at Hank's. He's leaving tomorrow to meet up with Johnny Fresh and the rest of the band, who are set to depart today. Teo claimed there weren't any seats left on the same flight, since the band members had booked several weeks in advance. In fact, the Panty Rockers haven't played at the bar since Goldie heard about the tour. Too busy with preparations, apparently.

Goldie figures that her next course of action is to talk to Johnny. She's just not sure what information she expects to get from him. Part of her hopes he puts her doubts to rest, and she gets Johnny's usual mishmash of conversation topics as penance for letting her paranoia get the better of her. As she gets his phone number from the band's Facebook page, she doesn't think she'll be so lucky. Besides, she needs answers.

"You've reached the Panty Rockers. How may we panty rock you?"

Goldie scrunches her face at the terrible overuse of the band's name. "Hey, Johnny? It's Goldie."

There's a long pause and a faint "Oh, bollocks" before he responds. "I'm sorry. Who?"

"Goldie Hays," she says, entertaining the obvious attempt to play dumb. "Teo's girlfriend."

"Oh, *right*." Johnny laughs nervously. "Of course, 'ello, love. I don't believe I've had the pleasure of a call from you before. I hate to be so rude, but your timing is terrible. I'm on my way to the airport now."

"That's no problem!" Goldie forces as much fake cheer in her voice as she can. "I just had a few concerns that I hoped you could address."

"... Concerns?"

"I'm worried about the conditions Teo and you boys will be facing over there."

"Ohh-kaaay," Johnny says, dragging the word out as much as possible. "What is so concerning?"

"Well, Teo mentioned something about some less-than-grand venues and cheap accommodations."

"He said that?" Johnny squawks. "We might not be touring at the level of Harry fucking Styles, but I'll have you know that even the shadiest places in Europe have some historical or cultural quality to make up for the discomfort."

"That's what I thought!" She pitches her voice a little too high. "But that's what he said when I told him that I wanted to go over there to see him perform."

"You're going?!"

"Not anymore since he seemed so worried about my comfort and safety." Goldie swears she hears a sigh of relief.

"Oh no! You're not going after all?" The English-German accent somehow makes the condescension almost entertaining instead of irritating. "That's a shame, love."

Johnny's a true showman, but Goldie's determined to keep her own in this. "That was until you agreed with me about the upsides to going," she chirps. "How could I miss such an incredible experience?"

"Uh, what?" There's silence for a few beats. "I mean, shouldn't you talk to Teo some more about it?"

"I'll surprise him!"

"Goldie, that's maybe not—" The call abruptly ends.

Goldie blinks at her phone, pondering whether it was a legitimate call drop. The musician was unquestionably awkward, a sign that she had reason for her suspicions. It's enough justification for her to grab her purse and run to her car.

GOLDIE SCANS THE WAITING AREAS FOR INTERNATIONAL TRAVELERS and sees the Panty Rockers' lead singer sitting near the windows.

"Johnny!"

His bandana-wrapped head shoots up from the chair he's sprawled on. The neon-pink travel pillow around his neck especially helps him stand out.

"I'm so glad you didn't take off yet!"

Johnny swivels his head like he expects multiple versions of her to come from all sides and ambush him. "How did you get through without a ticket?"

"I know a couple TSA workers. They got airport jobs after being laid off from the newspaper."

"Oh," Johnny says, apparently speechless.

"Are you really going to Europe for a tour?" Goldie's done beating around the bush and doesn't want to waste the chance to get some answers.

"Yes, I'm going on tour!" The deep wrinkles on Johnny's face become more pronounced as he expresses his indignation. "I'll have you know that I had a top-ten hit in Germany."

"When?"

The musician's eyes drift in a way that reminds Goldie of flashbacks on old TV shows.

"The year was 1983," he starts. "'Good Day to Scream (*mein Freund*)' was going to be my breakthrough. It was my magna cum laude of Anglo-Saxon righteousness."

"That's not quite the right wording—"

"But true fame eluded me," he says, ignoring Goldie. "Bananarama's 'Cruel Summer' was too powerful."

Goldie can't resist countering, "Just Bananarama?"

"Can you think of any other good music to come out of the early '80s?"

The music snob opens her mouth to start listing quite a few acts (in alphabetical order), when she shakes her head. She's letting herself get distracted. "Is Teo really going with you?"

"Goldie, they'll be boarding any minute—"

"Attention Flight 39 passengers bound for London," the counter attendant says over the intercom. "The plane has been delayed an estimated forty minutes. We apologize for the inconvenience."

"Bloody hell," Johnny grits out.

"Looks like we have some time to chat after all." Goldie smirks.

The musician hangs his head and motions for her to take a seat.

"As I was saying, success was cruelly ripped from my hands thanks to the majesty of bubblegum pop—"

"Johnny, please just answer my question," Goldie says, using her reporter's voice.

"I am, trust me." He takes a deep breath before continuing. "I toiled for decades without another song getting anywhere close to the top one hundred in any country. I did, however, learn how to make a living with my music through consistency. I traveled all the time, performed everywhere. There was no place beneath me because, like I said before, there's always a bit of history or culture to be gathered. Great folks who want to forget their troubles with some teeth-rattling music. I met my first and second exes while touring, had a small army of children. Eventually, getting a hit and becoming a star were insignificant goals. I realized my own form of success without them."

Goldie smiles, her interest in the musician's tale overpowering her anxiety about Teo for the moment.

"There was one ambition, however, that was always nattering about in my head. And when the children were fully grown, I decided to finally make a go at it. I moved to the States."

"Why was moving here so important?"

"I have to admit, the urge was probably a holdover from my early days in music. Success here would mean legendary status. Don't get me wrong, I had no delusions of making it big. I just wanted to try my brand of success here, start a new adventure. My age be damned."

"It seems like you're doing well. You're constantly performing somewhere."

"Yeah, thanks to Teo."

She flinches. "How did he help?"

"My cousin retired to Florida, so I decided to start there.

Unfortunately, Hamish used to be an accountant and was no help with getting gigs. But since there was no shortage of retirees looking for a break from golf, I managed to form the Panty Rockers as you know them today."

He motions his head as much as the pink neck pillow will allow. Johnny's three bandmates are sprawled on the row of chairs behind them, sleeping or pretending to sleep.

"The only regular gig we could get was at the worst pub in Jacksonville. That's where I met Teo. He approached us about joining him here. Said it was a guaranteed gig in a prime spot for easy access to bigger cities. What did I have to lose? And we've been doing great ever since. But after a few years, I've gotten a bit homesick. Thus, I planned the Panty Rockers' European Comeback Tour and asked Teo if he'd like to join us. It only seemed fair, and I could use the help. Hamish's back isn't great."

"So, Teo *is* really going?"

Johnny stares at her for several beats before sighing. "No, love. He turned down the offer. Said he didn't want to leave you."

If Johnny said anything more, Goldie didn't hear it. White noise fizzes in her ears from the rush of blood. "He lied," she whispers. "But why?"

"I don't know. I asked him to go with us a few months ago; then a couple weeks ago, he rang and asked for a huge favor. He said he needed to pretend that he was going on the tour after all and wanted me to back him up."

"But *why?*" Goldie asks again.

"I don't know. Honest, I don't." Johnny reaches a hand up to scratch the back of his neck but gets blocked by the travel pillow. He rips the damn thing off and hangs it on his carry-on. "I can tell you that he sounded desperate, almost afraid. I hadn't ever heard him like that before, you know? Whatever his reason for lying, it must be big enough for him to leave you for months, which is the last thing he wanted to do. That's a fact."

No, Goldie thinks, *that's not a fact.* She's a journalist; her whole profession relies on facts. The simplest definition of a fact is that it is a true statement. In Johnny Fresh's entire account relating to her boyfriend, there is only one evident, irrefutable fact.

Teo lied to her.

———————————

GOLDIE DOESN'T RETURN TO WORK AFTER SPEAKING TO JOHNNY. She had plans to leave early anyway. Penny, Tommy, and a few others are going out to dinner with Teo and her before going to Hank's Bar.

As she walks through her front door, Goldie is met with the sight of her mother trying to train their new puppy.

"Sit!" Sun practically screams.

Lucky looks up at her without doing as commanded.

"Sit!" she tries again.

This time, Lucky licks her foot. Goldie's mother melts and squats to his level to give him a treat. "Oh, my puppy son! Good boy!"

Goldie scoffs at how much of a pushover her mother is for the dog. "You're not supposed to give him the treat if he doesn't do what you say."

"How I not give him treat? Look at his face." Sun holds up Lucky to Goldie, who gets an enthusiastic tongue bath.

"Eww, Lucky." She laughs. "You're too tiny to have so much saliva!"

Despite her complaint, Goldie doesn't move away. She could use some cheering up.

"Why you home so soon?" her mother asks.

"Gotta get ready for tonight."

Her mother stares for a few moments. "What wrong?"

Goldie winces. She hadn't realized how obvious her feelings were. "I'm just sad to see Teo go." *Not a total lie.*

"For days, you act like you in Korean drama. Why so sad?"

"I've just been busy," Goldie says as she turns away. "I have to shower, so—"

Her mother blocks her. "Really, why you act weird?"

"I'm not acting weird. You're the one who yelled at him for going."

"I check his feelings because you too soft."

Goldie doesn't bother getting defensive about the jab. "And what do you think Teo's feeling?"

"He not want to go, but he hide something."

Goldie's eyes widen at her mother's intuition.

"I not say before because you just think I'm mean. Love make you blind."

Goldie never admits when her mother's right, mostly because she becomes annoyingly arrogant. And she's not about to start now. Instead, she asks a related question. "Do you want to be right?"

Her mother quirks an eyebrow.

Goldie elaborates. "Do you want me to break up with Teo?"

"I want good person for you. Teo seem nice, and maybe he love you. But if he lying, he not deserve you."

Goldie ducks her head and goes to the bathroom. "I gotta get ready," she croaks out before kicking the door closed.

"WHAT'S WRONG?" TOMMY ASKS AS SOON AS GOLDIE REACHES THE table.

"Why do you think something's wrong?"

"Your eyes are red." He frowns. "Like you've been crying."

Goldie's melodramatic sob session in the shower apparently was too powerful for her eye drops. "I'm fine," she says without an explanation. "Are you the first here?"

"Yeah," he says, continuing to eye her warily. "But this is my third bowl of pita chips and fourth serving of hummus." He picks up a chip and scoops up a big glob in demonstration of the damage he's done.

"Are you going to eat an actual meal?"

"Pfft," he says dismissively around a mouthful. "You know I can demolish Mediterranean food. I'm downing three gyros easy tonight."

As if on cue, a server comes around with a plate. Instead of gyros, though, a warm pile of pita and falafel is set down.

"I went ahead and ordered your favorite," Tommy says, grabbing a pita for himself.

"Dude, can you wait till the others get here?"

"Why should I suffer because they're late?"

"They're not late. You're just ridiculously early."

"Yeah, well, I'm starving. I worked through lunch so I could make it to this."

Goldie's being an ass, she realizes. She knows Tommy tends to overwork himself, often rivaling even her.

"Good sales day?" she asks, pushing her plate closer to him as a peace offering.

"Not at all. I have to train up a couple of newbies. One almost promised a new car for way too much off and no money down. The customer said he was a retired six-star general and was owed the deal for his service."

Goldie pauses her chewing. "There's no such thing as a six-star general."

"People will say the most outrageous stuff to get a deal. One time, a guy said he was the Rock's stunt double. I told him that was cool and all, but he should ask for a pay raise if he can't afford the seat warmers he was trying to get included for free."

"Did he look like he could be the Rock's stunt double?"

"Of course not. Dude looked like he'd never seen a gym in his life. I don't know how people can lie so easily."

Goldie drops the pita she was picking up and sinks into her chair.

Tommy's hazel eyes narrow. "Seriously, what's wrong?"

Amber and Connie arrive to save her from more scrutiny—with Paul Lee in tow.

"In a pinch," Connie says as she hands Paul a small Clean Clinic box, "you can put some on dry cuticles or fly-away strands of hair."

"I never knew there were so many uses for face oil."

"Hey, Goldie," Amber says, "look who we found."

The photographer had met the pastor during a photoshoot about the church's famous spring roll fundraiser.

Once introductions and greetings are made, Goldie addresses Paul. "I can't believe you're here. I thought you might be with the kids."

"Lily's parents are up there."

"They're still mad?"

"I gave up six figures a year for 600 dollars a month. To them, that's basically a crime."

"Sorry, Paulee."

He shrugs and takes a seat. "Where's your music man?"

Goldie turns to hide her face and sits back down. "Teo said he'd be a bit late. He's been busy prepping for the trip."

"Amber said he's going to Europe to perform," Connie says. "That's going to be an incredible experience."

"Goldie's going too," Amber says. "She's planning to see him there."

"I'm not."

Amber blinks. "But you went on and on about seeing all the castles and cathedrals and coliseums ..." She trails off before asking, "What's another touristy C word for Europe?"

"Columns?" Tommy throws out. "I think they have decaying columns scattered everywhere."

"I just don't think it's a good time for me to go," Goldie says.

"Did Manning say you couldn't take time off?" Amber jumps straight to outrage and assumes the worst of their executive editor.

"No, he's fine with it—as long as I turn in the Serum story and stick around for any follow-up inquiries."

"Then why?" Amber asks. "This chance is too big for even you to miss."

"Teo and I talked, and we decided it wasn't the right time for us." *Not a total lie,* Goldie thinks. That *was* Teo's weak excuse.

"Is that why you're upset?" Tommy asks.

Before Goldie can give another unconvincing denial, the waiter comes back to take the new arrivals' orders, and conveniently, Penny and Teo show as well.

"I told Jack that I didn't care how great of a deal it was," Penny says to Teo. "We don't need a paint bucketful of Sriracha-flavored cashews. Oh, are we ordering?"

"I can come back if you'd like?" the server offers.

"No, I'm already late." Penny looks at Goldie. "Sorry, the babysitter bailed last minute, so Jack stayed behind."

"Nothing but water for me, please," Teo says as he takes his seat next to Goldie.

As upset as she is at her boyfriend, Goldie can't help checking on him. "That's all? You love the food here."

"Just not hungry." Teo leans over for a kiss but stops suddenly. "What's wrong?"

"Thank you!" Tommy exclaims. "It's obvious, but she won't tell me."

That gets the whole table's attention.

Goldie wishes she could spontaneously combust. "There. Is. Nothing. Wrong," she grits out, then shoves a whole pita into her face.

Everyone stays quiet, probably to see if Goldie will admit to whatever is bothering her.

"It's no use," Penny says. "Goldie's stubborn. One time, she lost an essay contest and played it off. Three months later, I go to get something from her locker and see a stack of notebooks filled with essay after essay in the style category she lost on. Not small notebooks either; those big, fat Five-Star ones."

"What's wrong with that? I needed to get better."

"You never entered the contest again. How were you going to get better when you were locking them away and never planning to show anybody what you wrote?"

The women stand off in a wicked glaring match.

"Sorry, baby," Amber says to Connie. "This night is turning out to be a lot less fun than I promised."

"I have just the thing to lighten the mood." Connie pulls out a bag and presents it to Teo. "I'm Connie, by the way. Amber's girlfriend."

"Teo," he says, slowly taking the gift. "What's this?"

"Some travel-sized Clean Clinic products for your trip. And for you and Goldie, a few things from our new line of personal lubricants."

"Thank you," Teo says as he pulls out the box of cherry-flavored lube. Of course, that's when the servers come with their orders, and he hastily shoves it back into the bag.

Paul snorts loudly, getting Amber's attention. "Glad the gifts aren't making you uncomfortable, Pastor."

"It's just Paul tonight. I'm not on duty." He raises his bottle of beer to illustrate. "And you're looking at a man with two kids who lost his virginity at Vacation Bible School. Some bottles of lube aren't going to make me blush."

Penny whips her gaze at him. "When was that?"

"Before my junior year."

Penny does the necessary calculations in her head. "You were seeing Rebecca ... my bunkmate that summer! Eww!"

Paul rolls his eyes. "It's not like we did it in front of you."

Goldie smiles, grateful for the distraction. "Thank you for the gifts, Connie."

"You're welcome." Her mouth tilts in a devious way before she says, "It's quality stuff, and I'm not just saying that because I work for the company." Connie glances at her girlfriend and seems to wait for her to bring her drink to her mouth. "Amber and I have tried the whole line."

Amber chokes and coughs.

"Oh, baby, you all right?" Connie asks mockingly. "Here's a napkin."

"You're evil," Amber wheezes.

Goldie laughs at her friend's pain. "This must be karma for all the times you've tried to embarrass me in public with random sex talk."

Amber scowls and coughs some more.

"Don't be such a prude." Connie gets in one last giggle. "My God, you act like *you're* the older one."

"Wait, you're older?" Teo asks, eyes wide.

"Oh, yes, I should have said something from the start. I use the Serum. I'm 51."

Goldie notices a cascade of "whoa" faces around the table.

"You didn't have to say anything for my sake," Amber says. "It's no one's business."

"I'm not ashamed of it," Connie explains. "And it's only good manners to be upfront. I'm not about to deceive your friends and pretend to be something I'm not. I take the Serum because I like looking young, not because I want to act like I'm young. I've worked too hard and done too much to not acknowledge my many years on Earth."

"Even when my daughter calls you grandma?" Amber asks.

Connie winces. "I gotta admit, that did sting."

"Sorry." Amber takes her girlfriend's hand. "Caroline's had a lot to work through since my divorce. She'll come around."

Connie smiles and accepts a kiss on the cheek before she looks back at the table. "Oh my goodness, how did the attention get put on me? Baby, help me put the focus where it should be."

"That's right!" Amber looks pointedly at Teo. "We've got a big-time music artist about to make his international debut." She pauses. "I think? *Is* this your first time in Europe?"

"Uh, yeah." Teo sounds like he's straining to say even that much.

"How long have you been performing?" Paul asks. "Have you always been a professional musician?"

Teo draws a long breath. "Actually, I went to school in Miami for business, but music has always been a part of my life. My best memories of my papá were of him teaching me guitar. After he died, I never stopped playing and learning music on my own. A few years ago, I started traveling from city to city to perform wherever I could."

Goldie knows all this already, and in typical reporter fashion, she jumps at the opportunity to find out something new. "But you never used your degree?" she asks.

"What?" Teo furrows his brow and takes another long breath. "I always wanted to play music."

Now that Goldie's really paying attention, his hesitation is obvious.

Paul continues his questioning. "How'd you end up sticking around here?"

"I got a call one day from the owner of Hank's Bar. He's a family friend who needed some help with the place." Teo looks at his watch. "Speaking of which, I better get going and help Henry open for the night." He looks at Goldie with an overripe expression of apology and murmurs "Sorry" before getting up. "I'll see you all at the bar," he tells the group with barely a backward glance as he flees.

The table is stunned into silence after the abrupt departure ... until someone crunches into a pita chip.

With Goldie's eyes glued to the door Teo left through, she sighs and calls out the likely chewer, not needing visual confirmation.

"Really, Tommy?"

She gets yet another crunch in response.

CHAPTER 8

"YOU CAN DO THIS," GOLDIE WHISPERS TO HERSELF WHILE STANDING outside the entrance of Hank's Bar.

But what exactly is *this*?

Is she going to keep her mouth shut and pretend she doesn't know that Teo isn't going to Europe tomorrow? She was going to stay the night with him and have as much sex as humanly possible before driving him to the airport in the morning. That's definitely not happening now.

She also can't barge right in to confront Teo and keep him from performing. Her friends have made time to hang out with them and see Teo onstage for what is supposed to be the last time for a while. By supporting him, they're supporting her, and she doesn't want to ruin their night.

More selfishly, Goldie doesn't want to ruin her own night. She wants to hold on to what she thought was true for a little longer—that she's happy and in love.

"Hey, Goldie!" Amber calls out as she and Connie walk up to her.

With her co-worker's arrival, the reporter is hit with nostalgia. She can't help thinking back all those months ago when they first came to Hank's Bar together.

When Goldie met Teo...

"I CAN'T DO THIS," GOLDIE WHINES, ADDING A LONG GROAN FOR extra emphasis.

"Why are you acting so miserable?" Amber asks.

"We're out at a bar on a weekday after nine o'clock. I'm tired and overworked. First, Manning made me cover freaking sports after Stanley's shoulder surgery. Now I gotta do this music-scene story for Cooper's maternity leave."

"But you love music."

"I love music on my own terms. Subscriptions to multiple music services and carefully curated playlists corresponding to my many moods, the day of the week, whatever I'm working on, and various celestial alignments."

Amber rolls her eyes.

"I want to blast angsty alternative in my car, inspirational film scores in my noise-canceling headphones at work, and classic rock on my record player at home. I do not want to be surrounded by drunk strangers talking over the music and endure secondhand embarrassment watching a college band poorly perform a Pink Floyd song."

"Why do introverts always have to justify their antisocial tendencies with self-righteousness?"

"I'm not being self-righteous. It's cold, hard reality."

Amber scoffs. "Oh right."

"It's true! Look, I loved going to see Queen in concert, but my enjoyment was already a given. They're legends and my favorite band of all time. If I'm listening to some up-and-comer, they're going to be inexperienced. I'm just saving myself from the agony of being among other human beings *and* guaranteed disappointment."

"Or keeping yourself from discovering something new to love." Amber heaves a long, weary sigh, clearly exasperated with the predictably pessimistic outlook of her friend.

To be honest, Goldie's tired of it too. Playing things safe and sticking to proven paths makes for a painfully boring and lonely life.

"We don't have to stay the night," Amber says. "I'll get some shots of the place and the next couple of performances. You go find the owner and interview him as quickly as possible so you don't inadvertently cause yourself aural trauma."

The photographer doesn't bother getting the reporter's

approval and wanders off with her eye pressed to her camera.

Goldie goes to the bar to get the nearest bartender's attention. "Excuse me!"

The man comes over. "What can I get you?"

"I'm not drinking. I was hoping you could tell me where Hank is."

"There is no Hank."

Goldie gapes. "I, uh, mean the owner—Hank Townshend? I'm interviewing him for the *Daily Liberty Press*."

"I know who you're talking about." The guy leans forward, his face almost spotlighted by one of the bar's random lights, and Goldie gets a clear view of a dazzling smile. "It's my terrible way of warning people who use that name that he doesn't go by it."

"But this place is named Hank's?"

"Henry's a junior. Officially, the bar's named after his father. Unofficially, he has unusually strong feelings about the nickname and thinks it sounds better as a bar name."

Goldie takes a second to consider that. "I guess Henry's Bar doesn't roll off the tongue quite as well as Hank's Bar."

"You gave it serious thought?"

"Why not? I'm pretty particular about my name too. I prefer my nickname though."

His smile somehow gets brighter. "Oh, he's gonna love you."

"Okay," Goldie says guardedly. "I'm not looking to make friends. I just want to interview the guy."

"What was that sneer?" He's trying for a playful tone but seems truly curious. "Why is the idea of making friends so offensive?"

"I'm *working*."

"Yeah, *so am I*." As the bartender says the words, he does a no-look pour of something on tap and slides it several inches to the side just as someone approaches. They look at the magical offering, toss some cash onto the bar, and take the drink without question. His big brown eyes never leave Goldie.

The crowd breaks into applause and whoops as the band on the small stage finishes its song.

"Thank you! We're Rat Trapp. Find us on social media everywhere @RatTrapp420 with two *p*'s and the numerals four, two, and zero—because you know what time it is!" More obligatory whoops for weed references. "We're on Spotify and SoundCloud, but don't forget those two *p*'s. T-shirts are out in the alley. We love you! Goodnight!"

As the bandmates tear down their setup, the sound is a little more manageable for conversation.

"Anyway," the bartender prompts, "my point is that you shouldn't shut down a perfect opportunity for making a friend." He stands up straight and puffs out his chest a bit.

Not a bad chest, Goldie notes. "Are we still talking about Henry?"

"Henry is a great friend," he says before swallowing and averting his gaze, looking somewhat shy for the first time since they met. "And I think he'd say the same for me."

Goldie takes the man's words as an invitation to seriously consider him. He's unquestionably handsome with a face that could be found in any cologne ad: shapely nose, chiseled cheeks, strong jawline, subtly dimpled chin. His dark hair is styled short on the sides and longer on top, wavy strands falling around expressive eyes. The crinkle at the edges when he smiles and the arching brows accentuating them belie his otherwise smooth, youthful skin.

The staring must be making him anxious, because he bites his bottom lip and—oh, his mouth is so full and lush…

"Can I get a bottle of water?" Goldie asks, clearing her throat. "I'm suddenly really thirsty."

Hot Bartender complies and turns around long enough for Goldie to let out a frustrated groan. When he hands her the bottle, she barely squeaks out a thank-you before chugging half of the contents and wiping her mouth with the back of her hand.

"Look, you seem nice—"

"Are you shutting me down already?"

Goldie sighs. "You seem nice and probably can 'make friends'"—she air-quotes—"with anyone here. I'm flattered."

"Where's the 'but'?" he asks.

Goldie purposefully doesn't use the *B*-word, instead saying matter-of-factly, "I'm almost 40."

He shakes his head. "Okay, so what?"

She waves a hand at him. "*You* are obviously nowhere near that age. What are you even doing here? Probably working nights while finishing grad school."

He opens his mouth, but she doesn't give him a chance to speak.

"You've got so much to look forward to. Why not waste some time flirting with the obviously lonely middle-aged woman?"

Those stupidly pretty eyebrows shoot up in surprise. Maybe a hint of concern too.

The look unlocks Goldie's need to release her frustrations. Because she might not hang out at clubs or bars regularly, but a kickass pity party? Oh yeah, she's the master of those. All she's missing here is Lana Del Rey's *Born to Die* album on repeat and a stale box of Krispy Kreme doughnuts.

"I, on the other hand," Goldie says, continuing her tirade, "have my work. I mean, look at me: I'm at a popular bar, talking to a hot guy, everyone around me is having a good time, and the band that just performed wasn't as bad as I assumed." The reporter whips out her notepad from her bag. "But I'm working right now, and I will be working first thing in the morning. I work two weekends every month. Then there's the possibility of a late-breaking story that will force me to work even more."

Hot Bartender's expression goes impossibly soft, and his hand lifts before tucking out of sight—like he wanted to reach out to her. Instead, he says, "You need a vacation."

Goldie huffs. "I really do."

"But you probably won't take one?"

She frowns. "Not anytime soon."

"I almost regret convincing Henry to do this interview now. I added to your workload."

"You had to convince him?"

"Henry devotes everything to this place, but he's not the best businessman. He tends to let great opportunities like this interview pass by. I told him that it was free advertising, and not just for Hank's Bar, but for the people who play here. Rat Trapp could use the exposure."

Goldie hitches a thumb at the stage. "It sounded like they were doing pretty good in that area, and being in a newspaper isn't that big of a deal these days."

"Still, it doesn't hurt. Henry was grumbling about how he's not much of a talker."

"I wasn't going to make him give me a speech."

"Right!" Hot Bartender scoffs. "Old man's set in his ways." He looks over at a stout, dark-skinned, bearded man in plaid who's listening with an amused expression to one of the members of Rat Trapp. "He's the reason I'm here."

"Do you mean that he hired you?"

"No," he says slowly. His flirtatious attention turns serious, but before Goldie can ask what's up, he says more. "You're wrong about me."

Her eyebrows knit at the non sequitur.

"I finished school a while back," he explains. "I'm from Miami. A few years ago, I decided I needed a change—a fresh start—but I wasn't sure where to go. I just wandered around, went on I-95 and kept going up. I took jobs where I could and met some cool folks along the way. It was a lot of fun. It was *freeing*."

Goldie feels a pang of jealousy. She's imagined doing something similar: leaving all the work, all the drama, all the responsibilities and expectations. This stranger is describing her greatest fantasy, and unsurprisingly, he says it was an awesome experience.

"Then one day Henry calls me." He pauses, and the barest frown flashes before he continues. "He's an old family friend. He asked me to help him out at the bar. I'll admit, I wasn't jumping at the chance at first. The area's not the most glamorous."

"Thank you for not calling it a hellhole." Goldie might regularly fantasize about leaving the area forever and burning all evidence of her past here, but she's low-key defensive of her hometown. Only natives get to trash-talk it.

"It's not that bad," he says diplomatically. "And Henry always saw potential. He's not originally from here either, but he made this place home, and I started to miss having a place to call that."

"How long have you been here?"

"About three years."

"And I'm only meeting you *now*?" Goldie asks, and instantly regrets the dumb statement. This city might not be as big as New York, but it's not small-town Mayberry either.

Before she explains what she means, the guy beats her to it. "I wish we'd met sooner too."

They hold each other's gaze for a breathless minute, longer than she usually allows when someone shows more than a passing interest in her. This is different though; it's not one-sided. She likes being seen by him—and she definitely likes looking right back.

"Can I ask you a serious question?" he asks, breaking their reverie. Goldie nods the go-ahead. "What's your name?"

Goldie laughs. "Oh my God! We still don't know each other's name!"

He chuckles too. "I've been calling you Pretty Reporter in my head."

"You're Hot Bartender."

He looks strangely surprised by the label. She motions to the bar in explanation.

"Oh, right, you don't know."

"Know what?"

"Never mind," he says with a shake of his head. "Tell me your name first."

"Well, my given name is Marigold." Before she can say her nickname, his eyes grow wide. "What is it?"

"Um ..." He clears his throat. "That's a gorgeous name."

"The flower is pretty."

"No, not just that." His hand twitches again. "The word for marigold in Spanish is *maravilla.* It means wonder or marvel."

The way he'd been looking at her before is nothing compared to the awe he's showing her now. Goldie's heart sputters in response before building a quick rhythm she didn't think was possible.

It's dizzying to feel that weak and unused muscle—that Frankenstein monstrosity—finally brought back to life.

Goldie's revived heart opens her hand, granting the handsome young man his unspoken desire. He softly clasps the precious offering, lifting it slightly, like he's making sure it's real. It's a handshake of sorts, and she uses the gesture to introduce herself properly. "My friends call me Goldie."

It's really a perfect smile he has, especially when it's because of her. "Goldie," he says, trying out the name. "A golden wonder like the sun."

"Okay there, Romeo," Goldie teases. Her cheeks heat from the lyrical words. Hell, her whole body feels on fire, and she prays that her palm doesn't get sweaty in his hand. "You know what? That's what I'm going to call you now."

"Romeo?"

"Yeah, because I *still* don't know your name."

As he opens his mouth, a tap on the microphone interrupts them.

"All right, folks," Henry calls out to the crowd. "Are you ready for our next act?" Whoops and hollers of "Yeah!" follow. "Thanks, everyone, for your patience while he was busy helping me out at the bar tonight."

The bar owner and several members of the audience look in Goldie's direction. Her mouth hangs open in obvious confusion until she feels a gentle squeeze of her hand. She slowly turns back to face the real focus of everyone's attention.

"What did he just say?" Goldie asks.

He flashes a mischievous smile.

"There he is, folks! Welcome him to the Helena stage—Teo Estrada!"

With the cheer of the crowd making it too loud to talk like they were, Teo (*finally*, she has a name!) leans across the bar and beckons Goldie to do the same.

"Don't go!" he shouts into her ear.

Goldie blinks a few times before nodding. "I won't!"

Teo kisses the back of her hand before departing for the stage. He hugs Henry once he's there and says something in his ear, which Goldie figures is about her since the bar owner approaches her once he's stepped away.

"I'm so sorry you had to wait, Ms. Hays."

"It was, uh, no problem." Goldie tries to give him a courteous smile but can't help trying to keep her eyes on the stage.

"One of my bartenders called out sick, and Teo's the only reliable backup I have."

"So, he's not a bartender?"

"No," Henry says, motioning to the stage. "*That's* his real job."

Teo's chatting up the crowd while he double-checks his guitar and amp. There's another stool off to the side with a separate microphone stand, plus a basic drum kit behind him, which leads Goldie to assume that he'll have some company for his performance.

When he's satisfied with his setup, Teo sits on the stool, relaxed under the spotlight. "I typically take a few requests at the start, but I hope you all don't mind that I've decided to kick things off tonight with a Beatles cover." He looks in Goldie's direction. "You see, I'm trying to impress a girl I just met, and I need to play something sickly sweet for her."

The guitar riff he plays is the unmistakable beginning of "Here Comes the Sun." Goldie remembers what Teo said when he learned her name, comparing it to the sun, and she smiles.

"Ms. Hays?" Henry gets her attention.

"Yes?" Goldie responds but doesn't pull her gaze from the stage.

"Do you want to go to the back? It'll be easier to talk."

No way is Goldie missing this performance dedicated to her. "Can we stay till the song finishes?" She feels the need to give an excuse for putting off the interview. "I, uh, I *really* love live music."

The bar owner looks at Teo and back to her, seeming to connect the dots. "Sure, Ms. Hays."

"Thanks, Henry." She catches his surprised look as she fully directs her attention to the stage. "Call me Goldie."

Teo's talent seems effortless as he indulges in a few more refrains than the original Beatles version had and adds flourish on the guitar as he wraps up. He looks at Goldie again with his last strum.

As everyone applauds, Amber comes back around. "I'm almost done. How about you?"

Before Goldie can stop clapping and answer, Amber notices Henry.

"Are you the owner?"

"Uh, yeah."

"Great! I'm Amber Anderson, *Liberty* photographer. Stand over by that neon Miller Lite sign shaped like a guitar and lean forward with your elbows on the bar."

Despite his obvious reservations, Henry does as he's told and grimaces as Amber takes a couple shots.

"Now I'm really done," she announces.

"But I still haven't done the interview yet."

"What's taking so long?"

Goldie looks back at the stage and instantly feels a swooping sensation in her stomach. Her heart's beating impossibly fast, and her face feels on the verge of breaking from how big she's smiling. "I discovered something new to love."

As Goldie sits at the bar waiting on Henry to fill her friends' orders, she tries to will back the feeling from that night. She looks at Teo onstage, performing with his usual passion and flair. At one point, his eyes close at an intense part of the Cure song he's singing with Ruby, who duets and sings backup most nights.

"From the Edge of the Deep Green Sea," a song about the unraveling of a relationship, is somber even by the legendary rock band's goth standards. Goldie asks herself why over and over like one of the lovers does. She was so sure Teo would never hurt her. He was supposed to be the one.

What could he be hiding that's worth risking what they have?

"Here you go, Golds," Henry says to get her attention.

"Thanks, Henry." She grasps the drinks but doesn't move from the bar.

"What's up? You need something else?"

Goldie doesn't answer right away. Instead, she stares like she does when interviewing a particularly tight-lipped subject. "What's it going to be like for you with Teo gone?"

Henry seems surprised by the question but tries to play it off. "Won't be too bad. He won't be gone for long."

"Who's filling in the gaps with the Panty Rockers gone too?"

"Teo lined up a few other regulars to play here. He basically booked every weekend he's gone. Made sure I upgraded the karaoke playlists too so the customers can entertain themselves if anyone backs out at the last minute."

"He thought of everything," Goldie says, trying her best to not sound angry.

"Yeah, I'm glad he did. I hate planning all that. Running this place would be the best job in the world if it didn't have to come with the business stuff."

Goldie remembers her interview with Henry that, yes, eventually did happen the night she met Teo. Hank's Bar was a key part of her article because of the revival it went through. It was barely surviving before it became one of the area's favorites for live music. It found its footing with the new marquee and stage as word spread that working musicians and would-be stars could get a steady place to perform. Henry credited Teo for the turnaround.

"He's that popular?" she asked, not sounding as skeptical as she would have liked. After meeting the young musician, the intense case of heart-eyes she found herself with obscured her objectivity.

"It's not just that," Henry said.

Goldie waited for him to explain, but nothing more came. (He really isn't much of a talker, she mused, remembering what Teo told her.) "Then what else has he done?"

Henry wrang his hands and glanced out the door, where the stage was visible. "Everything."

"How did you become friends with Teo and his family?" Goldie asks Henry, as if continuing the interview that occurred more than seven months ago. "Were you friends with his parents?"

Henry can't hide how thrown he is by the question. "Uh, um." He licks his lips to buy himself time. "No, it was through my sister."

Now Goldie's the one who's thrown. "Sister? You've never mentioned a sister."

"She died a while back."

And there are no more questions when faced with an answer like that. "I'm sorry," Goldie offers.

Henry nods. "I have to get back to it. Let me know if you need anything else." He walks off, easily allowing a few customers to take advantage of being in his line of sight to flag him down.

Goldie bends over to butt her head against the bar in frustration before taking a deep breath and returning to her friends.

"Thanks, girl," Amber says as she accepts a drink from Goldie. "Your man is singing his heart out tonight."

"Yeah, he's so soulful," Connie adds.

"Think we can get him to perform praise some Sunday?" Paul asks.

"I wish," Penny says, scoffing. "But there's no way Sunbaenim would let anyone take her precious baby boy's spot as praise leader."

"What's Sunbaenim?" Tommy asks Goldie, trying his best to pronounce the unfamiliar word.

"It's a term used for anyone senior to you. In our church, it's what young people call the minister's wife."

"I'm not saying I want to replace him," Paul says.

"Well, you couldn't even if you wanted to. Jae has been playing the piano since he was 2!" Penny holds up two fingers like a child. "He can play ten instruments *masterfully*. Juilliard awarded him a triple scholarship." She pauses and goes cross-eyed, looking upward in thought. "Whatever that means."

Even tipsy, Paul manages to console Penny like a good pastor. "Don't let Sunbaenim's bragging get to you."

"It's so awful though! I refuse to be that kind of Korean parent. I will not pressure my kids like that—like our parents did. My kids don't have to be the very best at *everything*. They just have to be really, really good at *one* thing."

Goldie smiles at Penny's special brand of parenting. "Well, you guys can tell Sunbaenim that Jae's church job is safe. Teo's not much of a churchgoer—or so he says."

She curses the need to caveat anything she says about Teo. What does she know? Maybe he is religious. For all she knows, he's a cult leader who claims to be the reincarnation of a sacred duck.

Tommy takes a long pull from the bottle of beer Goldie brought him, then uses it to point at the stage. "He's singing some heavy stuff tonight. What's that about?" He looks at her with the concern he showed at the restaurant.

"*I can see your shadow*," Ruby sings, closely followed by Teo's "*Your memory is all I can see*." They take turns like that for the rest of the chorus.

> *I can feel your shadow*
> *(The cold's all life can be)*
> *I can reach your shadow*
> *(You're far too high on that lea)*
> *I am your shadow*
> *(No sunlight can e'er touch me)*

It's an original song by Teo, the chorus describing a person's misery. It's a stark contrast to the song's fable-like start, in which someone proclaims the person they love to be too great to be with the likes of them.

> *O' little mountain*
> *You're meant for the sky*
> *Ignore my valley below*
> *There's love far greater than I*

Soon enough, you realize that their great love has passed away.

> *You grew too tall too fast*
> *From the heavens you now smile*

There's a sense of futility and desperation.

> *You're my final destination*
> *To all the rest, I'll say goodbye*

But until the time they meet again, the person must find a way to keep on living.

> *I'm still stuck here below*
> *To give life one last good try*

Goldie asked Teo about the song the last time she heard him perform it. She wanted to know the obvious—whether it was based on someone real. He said, "Yes," and kissed her goodnight without telling her more. Tonight's the first time she's heard it performed since then.

She answers Tommy's question about the reason for Teo's somber song choices honestly. "I really don't know."

"THANKS FOR COMING OUT, EVERYONE," TEO SAYS TO THE CROWD after his last song.

Goldie's table joins the clapping, with Paul letting out a surprisingly loud "Woo!"

The bar is technically open another half hour, but with the night's music over, people take the hint and start exiting.

"Is it time to go already?" Paul laments. He tries to take another sip from his bottle and pouts some more when he realizes that it's empty.

"How much did you have, Paul?" Penny asks.

"I just needed this," he says, not directly answering the question. His sad, drunk eyes somehow notice Teo first as he approaches. "Teo! Holy shit, you were amazing, man!"

Teo looks perplexed yet pleased by the praise. "Thanks, Paul. I'm glad you liked it."

"Do you have an album I can buy a hundred copies of?"

"If I did, buying it once would be more than enough," Teo says. "But no, I don't have an album or any music out there."

A few customers pass by, giving him compliments and promising to see Teo the next time.

"You're like a local celebrity," Connie says. "You'd probably get some sales and exposure if you did make your songs available."

"I'm just happy to perform for now."

"Yo, Teo!" Henry yells from the bar. "Grab the mop when you get back over here! We've got a puker!"

The group cringes, giving Teo a sympathetic look, except for Tommy and his smartass mouth.

"Glad I never kept up with those guitar lessons. Your life is way too glamorous for me."

The musician sighs. "I better go help with that. Thanks again for coming, all of you." He shakes hands and gets a few hugs from the women (and his new biggest fan, Paul), as everyone wishes him luck on the tour. He looks at his girlfriend before leaving them. "You're staying, right?"

Goldie only nods, which seems to be enough for him to go off without further delaying his puke-cleaning duties.

"Come on, Paul," Penny says when they've reached the parking lot. "I'll give you a ride home."

"Thanks, Pen." He takes a deep breath of the cool night air. "Thanks for inviting me, Goldie. This was fun. I just wish—"

"Lily were here too," Goldie finishes for him.

Paul nods. "It reminded me of our last real date night before I started studying for seminary school. We saw Coldplay."

"That's cool," Tommy says.

"At the Super Bowl halftime show," Paul adds. Everyone gapes in awed silence, but he doesn't pay any attention while lost in the memory. He eventually shakes out of it. "Guess we better be off," he says, and hugs a still shocked Goldie, who almost misses his whispered, "I'm happy for you, Golds."

She looks at him, eyebrows raised.

"You found love," he explains. "Hold on to it as hard as you can."

Penny says goodbye and leads Paul to her car before Goldie can think much about what he said.

Amber and Connie are next (accompanied by a last-minute recommendation to Tommy about the Clean Clinic's moisture-rich soaps for his dry skin).

Goldie looks up at her last-standing friend. "Are you good to drive home?"

"Yeah, I just had that one bottle. I wanted to be sober to keep an eye on you."

"Tommy—"

"Is whatever's wrong related to Teo?"

Goldie can't lie to him. She can't stand the idea of lies in general for obvious reasons. "Yes."

Tommy's jaw clenches. "Are you going to be okay if I leave you here?"

Goldie knows what he's worried about, and as confused as she is about Teo, she's certain there's no physical danger. "It's not that sort of serious. He'd never hurt me that way."

"But he did hurt you in another way?"

She gives a curt nod. "I need to talk to him."

"And you need to confront him before he leaves?" he assumes.

"He's not leaving."

Tommy shakes his head, brow furrowing.

"Teo's lying about going to Europe." Goldie sighs. "But that's all I know, and I'm not leaving this place until I get the whole story."

She expects an "I told you so," since Tommy wasn't the biggest fan of Teo to begin with. Instead, he pulls her into a hug.

"I'll leave you to it, then. Just call me later to let me know you're okay. And if things do get out of hand, remember what I taught you."

"Thanks, Tommy." Goldie squeezes his waist tightly, soaking in his comfort and strength. "But I hope it won't come down to me kicking him in the balls."

WHEN SHE RETURNS INSIDE, GOLDIE SEES A FEW EMPLOYEES CLEANING up, but neither Henry nor Teo is among them. She goes to check the back area and hears some murmurs.

"Tell her," Goldie hears Henry say. She has her back pressed against the wall next to the open entrance to where a desk and crappy couch serve as an informal office space.

"How am I supposed to tell her now?" Teo asks.

"You should have told her when you found out."

Found out what? Goldie wonders.

"Even before that! You should have told her *everything* the minute you met her."

"I know."

"'I know' isn't anywhere near good enough now. You're kidding yourself if you think she doesn't suspect something's up. Goldie's been asking me questions, and I can't keep lying to her. She deserves better."

"I'll lose her, Henry. I—I can't lose her too."

Who did he lose?

"Look, Teo, I owe you a lot. I'm grateful, and I would do anything for you, which is why I didn't blurt out the truth to Goldie months ago. It was your business, and I thought you'd do the right thing eventually. I *still* think you'll do the right thing."

"I can't," Teo says, leaving the back area with Henry on his heels.

"Come on, man!"

They rush out without noticing Goldie. She stays quiet, waiting for the inevitable realization of her presence.

When Teo turns back to address Henry again, he spots her. "Goldie?"

"What can't you tell me?" she asks point-blank.

"Oh shit," Henry says in a breath and looks around them like he's wondering if he needs to protect his glassware. The employees scattered about take notice of the scene and openly stare. "Just leave it all," he commands. "Go home."

Teo turns to Henry with desperation in his eyes.

"Tell her," Henry insists one more time. "You can do it." He looks at Goldie sadly. "I'm sorry," he says, then shoos the employees out as fast as possible.

As soon as the doors close, Teo tries to approach her. "Goldie …"

"Don't touch me!" She walks toward the stage to get some distance from him.

"Okay," he says quietly. "Whatever you want."

Goldie waits for him to say more, but he looks lost and ready to bolt for the door.

"You're not going to Europe," Goldie says, not asking.

"How'd you find out?"

"I talked to Johnny."

"Ah," Teo says with a huff.

"How the hell did you think you could get away with a lie like that? I was going to drive you to the airport. I was going to see you off at the gates! Were you really flying somewhere?"

"Yeah."

"Where? Why do you need to go away for three fucking months? Why did you lie to me about it?"

Teo opens and closes his mouth like he's forgotten how words work.

"Whatever it is, you can't keep it from me anymore. We're done if you do."

Teo leans back against the bar and exhales a harsh breath. "I lied and broke your trust. We're done either way, aren't we?"

Goldie feels as if the wind were knocked out of her. Despite the turmoil, she hadn't considered breaking up until now. She was holding out hope for some noble reason he lied to her.

"Maybe we are done," she says. "I deserve the truth so I can make that decision."

Teo nods slowly and takes a seat on a stool. "Remember I went to get a checkup that day I told you about the tour?"

Goldie thinks back. "Yeah, you mentioned it on the phone."

"I'd been feeling a little more tired than usual and my appetite wasn't great. I told my doctor, and because of my family's medical history, more tests were done—and they found something."

Of all the scenarios for why Teo would lie to her, Goldie hadn't considered a medical issue and immediately jumps to the worst conclusion. "Are you *dying*?!"

"No! No, it's luckily not that."

"Cancer?"

"Since my mother had liver cancer, the doctor was concerned that might be it. Instead, it turns out that I have benign cysts."

"Benign? So, not cancerous?"

"Right." Despite the seemingly good news, Teo scowls. "But they're still causing me issues, and I need surgery to have them removed."

Goldie tries to comprehend what he's saying. "Why would you hide that from me? Did you think I wouldn't take care of you?"

"No, I know you would have," he says, barely looking at her.

"You lied about going on a three-month-long trip so you could go off and have surgery on your own? That doesn't make sense."

"The doctor says I would need four weeks of recovery, sometimes less."

"Then why?!" Goldie's reached her breaking point. "Goddamn it, Teo! I hate this! I hate not trusting you. What else aren't you telling me?"

Teo seems to have reached his breaking point too. He squeezes his eyes shut and tilts his head back before murmuring, "I can't believe this is how I'm telling you." Then he straightens back up to look directly at Goldie. "When you need a surgery of any kind, if at all possible, it should be done at least a month after your last dose of the Serum."

"Why are you mentioning the Serum?"

Teo holds her gaze, regret written all over his flawless face. "Why do you think, Goldie?"

No, that's not true. That can't be right.

After all these months together, Goldie would have suspected it. There would have been clues. Then she remembers that she doesn't really know Teo that well. The gaps in his history, his vague answers to her questions, his talent for distracting her...

The lie about the European tour wasn't the first, she realizes. He's been lying to her from the start.

She's a fucking fool.

"How old are you?" Goldie asks, voice like steel.

"Goldie, please—"

"How old are you, really?"

Teo dares to get up and move closer to her. "I was so afraid of what you'd think—"

"Don't make me ask you a third time."

Goldie's a volcano long overdue for an eruption. A dam in a flood zone left in disrepair. A forgotten pot on an overburdened stove. A condensed cloud ready to weep. A stick of dynamite with a short fuse.

A pathetic woman tricked into love.

"In June," Teo says, looking down in defeat, "I'll be 62."

O' little mountain
You're meant for the sky
Ignore my valley below
There's love far greater than I

Chorus:
I can see your shadow
(Your memory is all I can see)
I can feel your shadow
(The cold's all life can be)
I can reach your shadow
(You're far too high on that lea)
I am your shadow
(No sunlight can e'er touch me)

You were my mighty peak
I was your down-to-earth guy
The universe has you now
And forever I will cry

You grew too tall too fast
From the heavens you now smile
My trial has yet to be won
But the sands of time quickly pile

Make a path to the top
And lead me when I die
You're my final destination
To all the rest, I'll say goodbye

O' little mountain
You're meant for the sky
I'm still stuck here below
To give life one last good try

PART 2

CHAPTER 9

PRESENT DAY

"THEN WHAT HAPPENED? DID YOU KICK HIM IN THE BALLS?"

Despite the sullen mood from her recollections, Goldie snorts a laugh at Sarah's eagerness over the prospect. "I did not."

"Aww," Sarah pouts. "I would have started tossing chairs at him. Oh, did you do that at least?"

"No."

"Boo." Sarah shoves her second soft-shelled shrimp taco in her mouth and takes a big bite.

Goldie also takes the opportunity to dig into the most epic taco salad she's ever had. The CEO's personal chef made them a buffet of Tex-Mex options for lunch.

"Really, what happened next?" Sarah asks.

"That's it. End of story."

"Come on! You can't leave me hanging."

"I've given you plenty already. I've been talking all morning."

"The time has flown by, hasn't it? You tell a great story. Not too fancy and a respect for realistic dialogue. Your narration isn't overwrought with metaphor or too-detailed descriptions either. Although alliteration might be a bit overused, and you use *but* way too much. Try to come up with more ways to present conditional information."

"There is nothing wrong with how much I use the word *but*," Goldie says, eyes narrowing. "It is the most common sentence construction for the many, many conditions that come with life. And who are you to criticize my storytelling style? Are you a writer? How would you feel if I criticized your beauty products?"

"Well, your whole story has been one big deconstruction of the effect of the Serum, so you already have thoroughly criticized it."

"Fair point," Goldie concedes. "What did you think of the user testimonials?"

"Nothing too surprising," Sarah says airily. "You got a good variety of perspectives, Pretty Reporter."

Goldie glares at the use of Teo's temporary nickname for her from the night they met.

Sarah uses the opening to pry more dirt out of her. "Did you break up with him?"

"Not quite," Goldie admits. "I heard his reasons for lying and left."

"They must have been pretty compelling for you to not outright dump his ass."

Goldie shoves the rest of the taco salad aside. "I thought I was prepared to hate him for hurting me once I got the whole truth."

Sarah guesses the rest. "But you still love him."

Goldie nods, the motion bobbing her body like she's vibrating. "So!" She jolts herself out of her funk. "I've kept my end of the bargain. You got my story. Now, what's this big secret you dangled like a guaranteed Pulitzer?"

Sarah smiles deviously around a mouthful of taco. "How about, first, we take a little tour?"

"Really?" Goldie is unimpressed. "You're gonna drag this out?"

"It's called suspense, my dear. Something you're doing quite well with. Holding off on telling me the entire fallout of Teo's revelation and reorienting with the initial teased secret. Clever."

"Uh, thanks?" Goldie might as well flap her arms like a chicken to illustrate how unhinged this interview has become.

"Allow me to regale you with the storied history of the Crown family and show you the state-of-the-art facilities so I can have a fair shot at outdoing that 'I'll be 62' revelation. Although, to be honest, I could see that twist coming a mile away."

"It wasn't meant to be a big twist," Goldie groans.

Sarah waves off the excuse. "Let's go!"

Goldie tries to pack up her stuff.

"Oh, leave it. Just take whatever you need for notes. We're going to use my private elevator."

"Of course you have one of those," Goldie says with another groan. She grabs a Steno pad and her phone, then motions for the CEO to lead the way.

The small lift takes them to the gallery floor of the building. As the elevator doors part, Goldie's gaze is captured by an expansive wall mural of flowers and other plant life in full bloom and an extremely large monarch butterfly atop a golden, crownlike flower.

Her gaze then shifts to glass displays with etchings commemorating momentous occasions in the company's history, including exhibits focusing on the Serum and the story of Matilda Crown.

One of the largest photos in the room depicts a reflection of the late businesswoman and a little Sarah in a mirror. Matilda smiles wide with a mascara brush raised while looking down at the makeup-covered face of her child.

"I was about 4 here, I think," Sarah says, mouth quirking. "Every morning, without fail, I would sit with my mother at that gorgeous vanity and watch her methodically wash, pat, massage, brush, and swipe every part of her face and neck. It was almost magical. I wanted to do that too and got it into my head to sneak into the room."

"And you got caught," Goldie presumes, since she remembers doing similar things as a kid with her mother's clothes and makeup.

Sarah confirms with a nod. "But I wasn't worried about that. I only wanted my mother's approval and asked her if I did my makeup right. She said, 'Darling, there is no right way to look.'"

"That's really touching," the reporter admits, "and I feel like a total tool for pointing this out, but your mother built an empire on convincing people that they should always look young."

"My mother was complicated," Sarah says with a heavy sigh, gazing back at the photo. "As the years went by, her relationship with that mirror became less magical and more miserable. The wrinkles and sagging skin didn't match how she felt inside. It's a sentiment I could relate to when it came to my gender. She devised a solution for those who felt the same as her. I can't fault her for that, but I'm not giving her a free pass either. With her money and influence, my mother made her insecurity about aging everyone else's insecurity as well. I think about that every day."

Goldie finds herself at a loss for any follow-up and silently follows Sarah along the exhibit's timeline. There are images of landmarks in the company's history: the first factory opening, the first Crown store, and the very headquarters building in which they are standing. There's also a photo of a serious-looking balding man in a tweed coat holding a document in one hand and a Crown box in the other while talking to Sarah's mother, who is wearing another one of her monochrome pantsuits.

"That's Daddy," Sarah says with fondness in her voice. "He was a lawyer for the company. He was mostly retired when Mom started finding success though."

"He was a lot older than your mother?" the reporter prompts, knowing the answer but wanting Sarah to keep talking to get the insider's view of the marriage.

"He was twenty-five years older. They met when my mother was 20 and working at a department store's cosmetics counter. He was divorced and already had three children. My mother had been fully ready for marriage and building her company at that young age but put off having me until age 25, although that still might have been too soon for her. But my father was 50 and already slowing down physically. He passed when I was 15."

"He died at 65?!" Goldie can't help thinking about how close in age that is to Teo. "That's too soon," she whispers.

"He smoked and drank like most men did back then," Sarah says. Goldie's expression must make what she's thinking obvious, because the CEO scrambles for more to say. "But lifespans are different these days! You see stories about centenarians all the time."

Goldie isn't comforted one bit. Now she can't stop picturing Teo shuffling around with a walker, complaining nonstop about the government, and needing an outrageous amount of salt on everything.

"It's true that I didn't get a whole lot of time with him," Sarah says, "but he still loved me and doted on me every hour of every day of every year for the rest of his life. That's all you can do, Goldie. Make the time count with the ones who count." She stares out at the image of her mother and father again. "Trust me, there's no getting those years back."

The advice tumbles and falls gracelessly in the chasm of Goldie's aching chest. Sharing the rest of her life with Teo had been too beautiful of a possibility before. She thought she'd have love and family to see her off when her time came. But the odds are too great that Teo will leave her to endure existence by herself for a staggeringly long time.

The circle of her life always comes back to her natural state—alone.

Sarah turns around and walks away from the photo of her parents, moving to the Serum exhibit.

"Oh. My. God!" someone exclaims from the other side of one of the glass displays. "Are you Sarah Crown?"

Sarah smirks and nods.

The young (maybe?) woman and her companion circumnavigate the display to approach Sarah. "It's really you?! Holy shit! You're a fucking icon! Can we get a selfie?"

"Sure," Sarah agrees.

The woman stretches her arm out before giving it a second thought. "Wait, could you take the photo for us?" she asks Goldie.

She obliges and starts the countdown for the first shot but gets stopped.

"Wait." Her companion speaks up this time. "How do we look?" They're not looking at Goldie for her assessment.

Sarah doesn't take long to respond. "You two look beautiful."

Giddy, they laugh and share looks of awe from being called beautiful by the CEO of Crown Cosmetics.

"Is everyone ready?" Goldie asks.

They huddle close to Sarah, and Goldie takes a few shots to let the two have their picks.

"Thank you!" They shout their gratitude.

"You're welcome," Sarah says. "Have you two been to the

building's store yet?" They shake their heads. "Charles," she calls to a nearby employee, "make sure they get the employee discount for their purchases."

"*Thank you!*" the duo shout louder than before, shuffling off to take advantage of the opportunity.

When Sarah turns back to the Serum exhibit she was about to discuss, she notices Goldie's bemusement. "What?"

"What's it like? The fame?"

"It's something I've learned to live with."

"You don't enjoy it?"

"What's to enjoy? I run an empire that employs more people than the US government. And since I deal in cosmetics, my looks have to come into play, but I was never the glamorous type." Sarah motions to an old ad featuring an immaculate Matilda with smooth skin and a ruby-red smile. "My mother, on the other hand, suited the role of fabulous cosmetics tycoon perfectly. Of course she did; she built this place. I'm the square peg that got shoved into the round, peach-colored hole that is Crown Cosmetics."

Goldie considers Sarah's words before letting out her inner juvenile. "That sounded dirty." Sarah laughs in surprise. "But, seriously, you said it yourself—Crown is an empire. That happened under your leadership. You're not only rich; you run foundations for charitable work and disease research around the world. That person who asked for the selfie didn't call you the child of an icon. She said *you* are an icon. Crown is more than the Serum and cosmetics because of you, and *you* are more than just Matilda Crown's daughter."

Sarah doesn't say anything immediately, sweeping her gaze across the employees and visitors in the gallery, then to the Serum exhibit in front of them. With the exception of its creation featuring her mother, every other notable event involved Sarah.

She clears her throat before finally responding. "That was too kind of you, Goldie. I suppose I owe you that big secret now."

The reporter follows the CEO back to the private elevator, which whisks them to a vast space with a day-spa atmosphere. The palette has opened up from the characteristic Crown peach color to include calming earth tones. Some people are relaxing on comfy recliners and doing yoga and meditation, while others dressed in casual clothes work at monitors.

"Welcome ... to Crown Laboratories," Sarah says with a bit of a dramatic pause after "welcome." It reminds Goldie of the wealthy old man introducing the scientists to Jurassic Park.

"Uhhh." Goldie stalls while looking for anyone in a lab coat or carrying a beaker. "Are you messing with me?"

"Not what you'd expect?"

"You know full well it's not."

Sarah smiles, apparently pleased with the reaction. "We keep things 'chill,' as the kids these days like to say."

"But work on the Serum goes on here?"

"Oh, yes, all the time. We continuously monitor how the Serum is affecting users and ensure that it remains free of side effects or dangers." She gestures around at the different activity areas. "These people have taken their latest dose or received their first round. We keep them in this setting so they have a relaxing environment while we monitor them. We do this all the time since people are so diverse. We have to cover different age ranges, health factors, and ethnic and environmental backgrounds. I don't ever want this company to become complacent about the Serum's performance and safety record. We're also studying the possibilities for improving it."

"In what ways?" the reporter asks as she continues to write her notes.

"Early on, the timetable for taking the Serum was more frequent—every two weeks. The last big breakthrough took four years, when we managed to make the effects last longer and got the timetable to the current monthly requirement. Since then, getting the doses to last longer and keeping it safe and effective have been a persistent issue. Even with the current formula, the effects begin wearing off almost immediately. It's subtle though, and it depends on the true age of the person. Only the user or anyone close to them could tell a difference between the first of the month, when they take the Serum, and the end of the month, when they are due for their next dose."

Goldie thinks back over the months she's spent around Teo.

There would be days she thought he looked so ridiculously young with his skin somehow glowing and his wavy dark locks looking like they belonged in a shampoo commercial. But there had been clues to the truth. One day, with her boyfriend's head in her lap, she had traced every light crease bracketing his warm brown eyes. The next day, the lines had disappeared. Goldie was perplexed and inexplicably disappointed.

"It's been quite a few years since that last breakthrough," the reporter notes. "Is that the big secret? You've extended the effectiveness of a dose?"

Sarah crosses her arms. "I didn't rush you with your big revelation, did I? No, I let you go on and on about how wonderful and perfect Teo seemed, how Serum users were secretly trying to cure their self-loathing, how you overwork yourself but really just have a martyr complex—"

"All right! Sorry!" Goldie scowls. "By all means, continue to spin the Serum as a shining jewel of innovation and human ingenuity."

The CEO scowls back, indulging in their childish standoff and remaining quiet for a few beats before heaving a sigh. "I'm sorry for the bitchiness," Sarah offers. "Now that I've gotten to know you, I'm worried about what you'll think when I tell you everything. I admire you, Goldie. I hate to burden you anymore than you already are."

Goldie gazes over the secret lab parading as a day spa. "You've taken me this far. If you offered me a chance to leave and never know the secret, I wouldn't take it. I've had enough of living an oblivious, inconsequential life. I want to take the red pill."

"A *Matrix* reference? Really?" Sarah laughs. "You just had to make it geeky."

"You have to admit that it fits this situation."

"I'm afraid you're going to be disappointed if you're expecting to find out that your life is part of some grand computer-generated world."

"No, my life was meant to be read on a rainy Sunday afternoon and leave a sweet ache in the reader's chest."

Sarah's eyebrow arches. "Is that another movie reference?"

"Never mind," Goldie says dismissively. "Tell me your huge

secret already. At this point, I'm starting to think you were lying to me before, and you really did cure dying."

"Thankfully, it's nothing so godlike, and you already spoiled part of my big reveal. You were right about us extending the effectiveness of a single dose."

"How long does a dose last now?"

"For, um." Sarah looks upward like she's embarrassed by what she's about to say. "Forever."

Goldie's jaw drops. "I couldn't have heard that right. Did you say 'forever'? As in the rest of a person's life?"

"Yup," Sarah says, like she's confirming a Starbucks order.

"Oh" is the reporter's blank response. Meanwhile, the nearby meditation session is producing a round of *oms*. Goldie tries to channel any residual calm from the sound.

"I told you it was big."

At first, Goldie thinks that Sarah might be bragging, but her smooth face contorts in concern.

"How did you go from barely getting it to last a month to fucking forever?"

"Well, we had originally just been working on lengthening the effectiveness. Having it last two months would have been a major breakthrough. It ended up being harder to achieve than we thought. The Serum, in a way, mimics how we age. Our bodies start out elastic and supple. That period only lasts a small fraction of our lifespans though. It's a fast and extended decline from there. We realized it was going to be an all or nothing effort then. Instead of buying scratch-off tickets for a better chance at the smaller prizes, we went and blew all our money on the jackpot."

"And you won?" Goldie asks.

Sarah nods. "We call it the Forever Serum."

"Wow, real creative." Goldie falls back on sarcasm while her mind whirls with questions and scenarios. "When did you create this? How are you sure it lasts a lifetime?"

"We started testing a formula we were confident with about twelve years ago. We built a cohort of one hundred users who signed NDAs and agreed to be closely monitored for the first two years, followed by exams by my employees four times a year for the rest of their lives."

"People agreed to that?"

"For a chance at being part of the next step in Crown's legendary serum and never having to worry about looking old again? Of course they agreed."

"And it continued to work for every single person?"

"Yes. In fact, I just received this quarter's reports, and none of the users had a negative word to say about the Forever Serum. All glowing reviews about how great it continues to work."

"For more than twelve years? Is that long enough for you to confidently say it won't ever wear off?"

"All my researchers believe it to be more than enough time. Honestly, even one year of successful use was long enough for them. That was the milestone to gauge full effectiveness. The chances of the Forever Serum truly failing at some point with the current average lifespan is .01 percent. Now, if we all start living to 200, then it might start failing."

"What about that whole conflict when someone has a serious injury or medical condition?"

"It's not an issue with this. The Forever Serum convinces your skin and hair that you are 25 no matter how old you are. Although, if you were to seriously damage your skin, you're not going to heal up automatically like Wolverine."

"Nice comic book reference," Goldie acknowledges. "But what if someone like Soledad Branigan takes the Forever Serum?"

"Her scars will go away and stay away because that is the Forever Serum—and the current Serum—doing the rejuvenation that's possible with a dosage, but she can never damage her skin again so severely. The current Serum's monthly doses are like topping off your car's gas tank. With the Forever Serum, it's one and done. Are you going to get wrinkles from suntanning? No. Can you still get skin cancer? Yes. Soledad and everyone who takes it will be subject to the natural healing abilities and limitations of a 20-something."

The reporter ponders the pros and cons. "That doesn't seem like too bad of a downside. If you're not worried about its effectiveness, why haven't you released it?"

Sarah studies the faces of everyone nearby—all Serum users. "I wasn't sure I should."

"What are you worried will happen?"

"You've gotten a taste of my world, Goldie. Absolutely everyone uses the Serum. Not a wrinkle on anyone in this entire building. Picture that *everywhere*."

For the first time since she stepped into the lab, Goldie has become hyperaware of how obviously older in appearance she is to everyone here. "Do you think that many more people will take the Forever Serum than already take the current version?"

"What's the percentage of the global population that uses the Serum? Twenty?"

"Yeah."

"With a one-time dose that is guaranteed to last for the rest of a person's life, even if the price is ridiculously high, like 50,000 dollars, a majority of people will save and sell whatever it takes to pay for it. In ten years, 80 percent of humanity will have taken the Forever Serum. What kind of world will that be?"

"I think you're inflating how many people would take it."

"Would you want to take it?" Before Goldie can get defensive, Sarah raises her hand. "It's why I'm trusting you with this secret. I want to know—now that you have all the information and have researched—would you take the Forever Serum? Would you want to look young for the rest of your life?"

After everything she's been through recently and the Serum users she's talked to, Goldie should probably have a better understanding of her feelings on aging. In some ways, it's true. She can no longer easily dismiss the Serum's use as shallow. Soledad's reasons were understandable, and the others had relatable elements to their stories.

Goldie thinks about how self-conscious she was of her and Teo's age gap. The constant doubt that she'd eventually look too old for his comfort gnawed at her. It still gnaws at her even though he's actually older. And how will she feel about Teo when he looks his true age?

Honestly, her gut instinct is revulsion.

"I would take it, maybe," Goldie says, "if Teo would."

Sarah frowns. "I thought he was someone you wanted to grow old with in the traditional sense. That means accepting each other's wrinkles and white hairs."

"I did want all that—eventually. But it looks like I'm getting that sooner than I thought." Goldie sighs. "I need to either come to terms with what a life with a much-older Teo is going to look like or face that maybe I'm not comfortable at all with it"—she pauses, her voice straining—"and let him go."

Hearing Goldie's dilemma seems to spur Sarah to divulge her last secret. "You wanna know the reason I took the Forever Serum?"

Goldie's eyes grow wide. Shit, she's surprised they haven't fallen to the floor to join her jaw. "Is that why you took so long to take it? You were waiting for the Forever Serum to be developed?"

"Whoa there, Pretty Reporter," Sarah says like she's calming a horse. "It's not so simple. I could have gone ahead with using the current Serum at any time, and I wasn't even going to take the Forever Serum initially. I was fine running the company that produced the Serum, but I didn't want it for myself—unlike my mother. I was determined to run Crown my way."

"What changed your mind?"

"My daughters." Sarah points to a family portrait on what must serve as her desk in the lab. Her wife, Kelly Stone, sits next to Sarah with their daughters, Chloe and Lisa, flanking them. "Mother-daughter relationships are the worst."

Goldie laughs at the random declaration.

"They are! I love my girls to death, but my God, do I wish I could literally smack sense into them."

"And they probably think the same of you," Goldie says. "Trust me, I know."

"Exactly! Why does it seem to always be that way? It was that way with my mother. Then my wife and I had our girls, and the dynamics are exactly the same. We can't agree on anything, including using the Serum."

Goldie looks at the family portrait. The daughters should be about her age, yet there's no way to tell that from the photo.

"Did they take the Forever Serum too?"

"Yes," Sarah says softly. "I understand making such an assured choice with my body better than most, so I wasn't going to stop them. I had my reservations though."

"Why?"

"They're my babies. I wanted to keep watching them grow and evolve, even as adults. But when I discussed the possibility of a Forever Serum with them, they became absolutely fixated on the prospect of staying ageless. In their minds, there wasn't a reason in the world not to take it. Not one shred of apprehension."

Sarah's brow pinches as she looks at the photo. "I don't know what they really should look like now in their late 30s—and I will never know. I will only ever see this static version of my daughters' faces."

"And because they took it, you took it?" Goldie asks.

"My wife and I couldn't imagine continuing to look frail while our children will never know that kind of vulnerability on the outside. I wasn't going to do what my mother did; I wasn't going to abandon my children in uncharted waters." Sarah's grimace while gazing at the portrait subtly morphs into a faint smile. "We'll face the fallout together as a family."

At that moment, the reporter realizes that she is getting a glimpse of what might become the new normal for families.

"Should I reveal the Forever Serum to the public?" Goldie asks.

Sarah turns the faint smile toward her. "I don't know," she says while surprising the reporter with a hug. "And I'm glad you don't know either."

"Why's that?"

"Because then I'll be completely spoiled before your article comes out. I told you, it's called suspense. Every good story needs it."

Goldie laughs at the callback to the CEO's opinions on storytelling. It helps relax her body into the embrace, the exhaustion from the day's discussion catching up to her. "Thank you for listening to me today."

"Oh no, Pretty Reporter, thank *you*." Sarah squeezes Goldie tighter. "I can't wait to read the rest of your story."

CHAPTER 10

TEO KNEW THIS DAY WOULD COME. OF COURSE IT WOULD. Goldie was always going to find out on her own—because Teo was a coward who was never going to tell her the truth. He was going to keep fooling himself by pretending he wasn't too old, too wounded and unworthy of someone as wonderful as Goldie.

"How?!" Goldie practically screams the question. "How are you 62?! The Serum didn't give you that body! Those arms!"

"I've always been into keeping fit."

Goldie continues, as if not hearing him. "You're almost as old as my mother! You're old enough to be my fucking father!"

Teo flinches. "A young father, sure." Goldie's incendiary stare shuts him up.

"You're 62 and use the Serum. You're 62 and use the Serum ..."

Guilt pulses in every part of Teo as he sees how lost she seems, muttering the revelations over and over to try to comprehend the breadth of their meaning.

Goldie takes a few deep breaths to calm herself before going into reporter mode. "How long have you been taking it?"

"Almost five years now."

"Before you moved here?"

"Yeah, when I decided to retire and give music a try."

Goldie's face twitches at the word *retire*. "What did you used to do? How can you afford the Serum?"

"I got a lot of use out of my business degree. I did really well in stocks and securities. I dabbled in real estate too."

Goldie scoffs. "You're secretly rich too?"

"I worked," Teo says, not agreeing with the simple assessment. "I saved, then I worked some more. I know what it's like not to have money. All I wanted was security for my family."

"Y-your family?" Her voice breaks, her already distraught face looking more so.

Teo swallows. "I have a son."

"A son," she echoes to herself.

"And a granddaughter," he follows up in a mutter, knowing this is a lot to take in.

Goldie stares at him for a long moment. "And?" she grits out.

"And what?"

Goldie turns around to climb the few steps of the small stage. Teo thinks he hears her mutter something about prying the truth out of him. She looks down at the stool he was sitting on not even an hour before. "Do you have a partner?"

Whenever Teo let himself imagine this conversation, answering that question was always the hardest part. "I had a wife."

Goldie swivels around to look back at him. "Divorced?"

"Died," Teo answers faintly. He places a chair from one of the tables back onto the floor to sit on. "She died more than twenty years ago in a car accident."

"Oh God," Goldie gasps. Suddenly unsteady, she sits down on the stool.

"Helena was about to turn 37."

Teo's words have Goldie leaping off the stage like it's a hellmouth about to swallow her down. Then she circles it until she finds the brass plate on the top step's side. She reads the embossed letters aloud. *The Helena, est. 2018.* You named the stage?"

"Henry and I both did."

Goldie shakes her head to show her confusion. "Did Henry know your wi—" she starts to ask, then some sort of realization dawns on her. "He told me he knew your family because of his sister."

"Henry's my brother-in-law," Teo confirms. "We stayed close friends after her death despite the distance between us. Their family originally came from Florida, but his father moved them here when Henry and Helena were in their early teens. After Henry graduated high school, he decided to stay here while his parents moved back to Florida when Helena got into the University of Miami. That's where I met her."

Goldie doesn't step back on the stage. She doesn't look at Teo either—just stares at the brass plate.

"Building the stage was my idea," Teo continues. "The marquee outside too. Henry called me panicked one night. He was out of money, and the property's owner wanted to sell the place. Henry was losing the bar. So, I bought it."

Goldie whips her gaze back at him. "*You* own the bar?"

"No, Henry owns the bar. This is his business. I just own the property."

"Oh, that's all!" she sneers. "No wonder you live here. It was a great cover. The friendly bar owner lets the poor musician stay in the building's small apartment. And all this time I thought you were indebted to Henry."

"I *am* indebted to Henry."

Goldie looks unimpressed.

"All right, not moneywise," he says. "In the ways that count though."

"Says someone with money."

Teo knows how sensitive Goldie is about the subject. She overworks herself, partly because of her commitment to her profession, but he thinks most of her drive comes from the struggles her mother had.

"I was like you"—he groans at what he's about to say—"when-I-was-young." He runs the words together to get them out fast. "I worked constantly. I excelled at it, and I thought I would lose everything if I stopped for even a minute." He pulls his lips inward and shakes his head. "I never lost everything, but I lost the most important thing. And when Helena died, I wished it had just been money I lost."

He seems to have struck a nerve. Goldie hangs her head and sits down on the stage steps. She leans forward on her knees, beckoning him to continue.

"Our son was in the car with her. Eli survived with a broken arm. He was 13—and completely traumatized. He underwent therapy for years. Helena's parents tried to offer solace, and Henry would come down to Florida to give him another mentor, but he spiraled eventually. Got addicted to prescription drugs somehow. Alcohol abuse was a natural extension. He would yo-yo. There were stretches when he'd be clean, and I naively thought he was finally healing. Then something else would set him off again. This went on into his 20s."

Teo pauses to gauge Goldie's demeanor. It's an expression he hasn't seen since they first met. Not unfeeling but reserved and wary. It's the wall she erects around total strangers.

"Then his girlfriend at the time got pregnant, and that was the wakeup call he needed. He started committing to recovery. I was there every step of the way. Did whatever I could: went to recovery meetings, helped with tuition for IT training, babysat Jordan. After so many hard years, Eli felt fully stable. He made it happen."

"Where is he now?" Goldie asks.

"Back in Miami. I was going to fly down there tomorrow to visit him and Jordan."

"Are you going to get the surgery down there?"

"No, I was going to come back up here. Well, near here. I'm going up to the university hospital to get it done. They were going to fly back with me to help during recovery."

"You were going to stay out of town to avoid getting caught? What a plan," Goldie scoffs, her red-rimmed eyes moving back to the brass plate.

Teo is a first-rate asshole.

"I think I wanted to get caught. It was a shitty plan."

"It really was," she says, her mouth twisting with the bitterness of her words. "And why a whole three months?"

"Two weeks ago, when I found out I needed surgery, I was having a *superproductive* day and stupidly took the latest dose of the Serum earlier that morning before my checkup, so I have to wait four weeks for the surgery. Like I said, I'll need four weeks of recovery before I can take the Serum again. I'm told the effects wear off really quickly when you don't take the Serum as scheduled. It's a snowball effect. I'll probably look more or less how I naturally would by the time I'm allowed to take it again. Then I'd need several weeks to go back to looking like I do now because I'm fucking old, and the Serum has a lot of work to do to make me look young."

"Good to know you built in some wiggle room," Goldie says, lips curled in a sneer. "Why didn't you tell me from the beginning? How could you let me think you were younger?!" Her voice gets louder with every question. *"How could you hide the whole life you've lived?!"*

Teo's prepared with answers because he's asked the same questions of himself during the past several months. "It's no excuse, but most of my adult life has been wrapped up in my grief and my son's recovery. When I was confident he was in a good place, I started to evaluate the state of my own life. And you know what I realized? I was old, lonely, and *tired*, Goldie."

A hint of empathy flits over her face. Teo knows she can relate. It's what drew him to her the night they met.

"Music was always something I explored," he continues, "but trying to make a living from it wasn't practical. I was too good at the numbers game to ever give it up when I was younger and building a career, and when Helena died, I needed the job stability to keep me from sinking into grief and to help Eli. But with my son settled and happy, I didn't need the distraction of the daily grind or the money it provided anymore, so I hit the road. I was free to pursue anything else, be anywhere else—"

"And be *anyone* else," Goldie interjects. "Thanks to the Serum."

Teo flinches at the implication. "It seemed like the ultimate way to make a fresh start."

A heavy silence fills the space between them. After revealing everything, Teo feels no relief or great weight lifted.

Only shame.

"Why didn't you tell me the night we met?" Goldie asks.

"If I had said I was in my 60s, would you have kept talking to me?"

Goldie opens her mouth to speak, but he doesn't let her.

"Would you have flirted with me and given me your hand to hold? Would you have stayed until closing to watch me perform? Would you have let me walk you to your car and kissed my cheek goodnight? Would you have stayed up on the phone with me until you had to go to work in the morning? Would you have come back the next night? And the next? Would you have made the first move and lunged at me for our first kiss after a week of my hand-holding? Would you have driven out in the middle of the night to the beach to see the first sunrise of the new year with me? Would you have made love to me after I sang 'Fade Into You' at the bar on our two-month anniversary? Would you have gone with me to every blockbuster movie and new restaurant? Would you have been willing to take a long-deserved vacation to experience a different part of the world with me?" Teo pauses to take a deep breath and infuse his last point with raw sincerity. "Would you have fallen in love with me, Goldie?"

Tears pool in Goldie's hard, unblinking gaze until they overflow, cascading down her flushed cheeks onto quivering lips. She licks the evidence of her pain away before speaking. "I guess we'll never know."

Teo gets up and dares to move closer to her. "Lying to you was eating me up inside. I would tell myself that I was just waiting for the right moment to tell you. But every day I spent with you, I grew more in love and more scared of losing you."

Goldie swipes at her tears. "I can't believe I fell for it. I was that desperate for a normal life."

Teo shakes his head. "What's normal?"

"What you had," Goldie says, as if the answer were obvious. "What Penny has. What Paul's trying to hold on to."

"We can still have that."

"Can we? You did it already. You have a son and granddaughter."

"And I lost my wife!" Teo doesn't mean to raise his voice, but her words are making him even more anxious. "Look, Goldie, there is no normal. We just do the best we can with the cards we're dealt. You and I were headed in that direction. We can still—"

"You're 62."

"So?"

"Stop pretending it doesn't matter."

Teo feels the words like a punch to the gut.

"There's nothing wrong with never marrying and having kids, but I *wanted* all that—and it just kept not happening. I was at the point where I thought I'd be better off giving up hope. Accept that this is all I can expect in my life: my job, a few good friends, and my mother. That's more than enough, right? I needed to learn to be happy with it. Then you came along, and I stupidly started to hope again. But you're right. There's no such thing as normal. You found someone you loved early on, got married, had a child, and then lost your wife way too soon. That must have been a terrible pain. So, why would you want that for me?"

"What are you saying? Of course I don't—"

Goldie cuts him off. "I already have my mother to worry about, and you're almost as old as her. Something is bound to happen to both of you. What if the next time you get sick, it's worse than benign cysts? Should I commit to someone who will surely die well before I do?"

Her questions wrench off the blinders Teo wears thanks to the Serum. He's been so reckless with Goldie's heart, pretending that his old age doesn't matter to the point of obliviousness.

This isn't like his relationship with Helena. They married young and planned on celebrating no less than sixty anniversaries in their lifetimes. Losing Helena before Teo even turned 40 was never supposed to happen. But with Goldie...

There's no question he'd make her a widow way too soon.

Goldie gets up from the stage. "I can't take anymore. I'm going."

Teo reaches out again but stops short of touching her. "Goldie, I'm sorry. I never considered how I could hurt you. I—I just ..." He falters when he's hit with the unbearable realization that their relationship might be over. He's been lying to her from the beginning, and if this really is the end, then Teo needs to leave her with the ultimate truth. "I just wanted the chance to love you."

Goldie's control shatters. Her face crumples. Her body quakes. Her hands fly up to cover her mouth in a futile attempt to curb raw, jagged sobs.

The sound lingers in Teo's ears as she runs as fast as possible out of the bar.

"Wow, Abuelo, you f-ed up."

"Jordan!"

"What? I didn't use the whole word!"

Eli glares at his daughter.

"Am I wrong?"

"That's not the point," Eli says. "You don't need to swear to let your grandfather know how badly he messed up."

"Thanks for the support, you two," Teo says, words dripping with sarcasm. "*Really* helpful to be ridiculed by my family. You should have saved yourselves the trouble of coming here though. I'm fine," he says while lying face-down on his couch, hiding his face like a drama queen.

"You don't seem fine, Pops." Eli's phone goes off, and he excuses himself. "Thank you for calling Tiger Computer Repair. How may we be of service?"

"My laptop won't turn on!" Teo can hear the caller shout even though they're not on speakerphone. "It's brand new, and I've barely gotten any use out of it! Now it sits there like an expensive rock!"

Teo's son sighs before asking a follow-up question. "Have you plugged it in since you got it?"

"No! Why? It's got a battery."

"Batteries need to be recharged, sir."

"Why the hell would you make batteries that don't last longer than a day?"

"That's the best we can do for laptops. They need a lot of power, which is why the batteries are rechargeable."

"That's bullshit!"

The call must drop because Eli pulls the phone away to check the screen before putting it back into his pocket and returning his attention to Teo. "Why didn't you go ahead and fly down to

Florida like you planned?"

"I didn't want to leave in case Goldie reached out."

"You dropped a bombshell. She's going to need time." Eli's eyes widen slightly. "Please don't tell me you've been calling or texting her."

"Just one text," Teo admits, "asking her to let me know she got home okay."

"Did she answer?"

Teo flops back over and sits up to pull out his phone and show his son the text. His granddaughter, of course, pokes her head under her father's arm to look too.

"I'm home," Eli reads. *"Don't contact me again. Give me time."*

Jordan makes grabby hands, and Eli lets her have it to look closer for herself. She starts tapping, and Teo worries that she's about to do something awful like reply to the text, but then an "Ohhh" comes out of her mouth.

"You haven't shown me this one yet." She reveals the home screen with the photo Teo took of Goldie in the big hat standing among marigolds.

"We went to a local garden not too long ago," Teo explains as he takes the phone back to gaze at the photo.

"She's so pretty," Jordan says.

"And smart and hardworking and fun. She loves music like me, and superhero movies like we do."

"Yeah? Who's her favorite superhero?"

"Captain America, but Wonder Woman is a close second."

"Do you think she'll forgive you if you invite her to come over to watch the latest Wonder Woman movie with us?"

"I wish that's all it would take, cielo." Teo can't help looking at the photo yet again and sighing like the lovesick dope he is. "Why don't we watch it tonight? Go ahead and turn on the TV and find the movie for us. I'll order some pizza."

"Okay, just don't order the one with pineapples. Yuck!"

Teo frowns at the lack of taste today's kids have and gets off the couch to leave his granddaughter to her task. His son follows him into the kitchen.

"I'm sorry, Pops," Eli says, unprompted, as he leans against the counter. "If I had gotten my act together sooner, you could have fallen in love and remarried a long time ago."

"But then I probably wouldn't have met Goldie."

Eli looks dubious, so Teo rests a hand on his shoulder.

"You can't blame yourself. I needed time to come to terms with your mother's death. There's no bouncing back quickly after losing someone like her. Sometimes, you just gotta have patience."

Eli's gaze drops to the floor as he nods. "And now you have Goldie."

"Had Goldie," Teo corrects. "Fuck, I really hurt her. It's probably going to take the rest of my life for her to forgive me." He sinks into a chair and brings his elbows onto the table to hide his face in his hands.

His son laughs. "My God, you are madly in love. I'm jealous."

"What happened to the actor you were dating? Isaac?"

"He moved to NYC. Finally gonna try to make it big. He was fun, but it wasn't an epic romance for the ages like you and Goldie seem to have."

Teo snorts. "We're not Jack and Rose in *Titanic*."

"You'd give her the door to float on like Jack did for Rose."

"Then Goldie would tell me to stop being stupid and drag me onto it with her." Teo's bemused smile quickly turns into a frown. "She'd probably let me freeze to death now."

"You made a mistake. You're human. I think you should take some of your own advice and have patience; give her the time she asked for. She needs to heal."

"Even if she does forgive me, I'm not so sure she'll be able to accept me."

"What do you mean?"

"I'm more than twenty years older than her. She's not going to want an old man."

"Give her time to accept your age too," Eli suggests. "I love you, Pops, no matter how old—or young—you look. If Goldie loves you like you think, she'll come to terms with it."

"I really hope she finds my old ass hot."

"Oh my God!" Eli croaks out a laugh. "I wasn't talking about that!"

"It's a legit concern! We've had an *active* relationship."

"Shut up, Pops! I can't hear this."

"All right, I'll stop." Teo chuckles at his son's discomfort. "I am being half serious though. I had a beautiful girlfriend who found this version of me really attractive. If she doesn't like what she sees when I stop taking the Serum, I'm not sure how I'll handle that."

"Are you staying off the Serum after your recovery?"

"I don't know." Teo catches a glimpse of his reflection on the microwave door. "I think I have to see myself old again to know how I feel about it. It's been great acting like a 20-something again, but maybe I need to accept my age. I can't stand that I hurt Goldie because I couldn't admit to it."

"And if you felt good about looking your actual age, but she didn't like it, would you take the Serum again?"

Teo keeps staring at his reflection. "I'd do anything for Goldie."

CHAPTER 11

ELI AND JORDAN MEET HENRY FOR BRUNCH AT THE IHOP IN FRONT of what Eli remembers was once a K-Mart. His uncle used to take him here every time they would visit, and though a few years have passed since the last time they visited, the tradition remains. Plus, Eli has an 11-year-old with an insatiable appetite who needs appeasing.

"How's the Miami sun these days?" Henry asks. "Still a scorcher?"

"Same ball of fire there as it is here." Eli's familiar with his uncle's opinions of Florida weather. "You should visit more."

"And endure perpetually sweat-stained shirts? No thank you."

"Just go shirtless like most of the population there."

Henry glances downward at his gut, currently dented by the table. "Think I'll maintain my modesty."

Eli gives an amused huff. "But Auntie Riri loves South Beach and all the high-end shops."

"That husband of mine hasn't worn half the clothes he bought from our last trip. It's a good thing the bar's making money since your dad moved up here."

"Pops is a miracle worker." Eli's work ringtone chirps, and he excuses himself to answer it. "Tiger Computer Repair, how may we help you?"

"Yeah, hi," the caller starts. "My laptop keeps doing a thing."

Eli rolls his eyes at the vague description. "Can you describe the 'thing'?"

"Like, there are all these lines on the screen. I can't read anything."

"Did you drop it?"

After a long pause, the caller says, "No?"

Eli can hear the question mark in the caller's voice and knows what that kind of reluctance means. "Did you damage it in any way?"

"I swear I didn't! It totally did this on its own."

Callers never want to admit any wrongdoing when it comes to problems with their computers. Ultimately, Eli knows that it's because they never paid extra for the service plan, and they want the issue to be declared a manufacturing error to get a new computer. Even so, there's usually a weird vibe of shame and some dumb excuse. "Nothing struck the screen at all?"

"Well ..." *Here it comes*, Eli thinks. "Okay, maybe, uh, my Great Dane sat on it, but—"

"Sorry, sir," Eli cuts the caller off. "You're going to have to bring it in and pay for the repairs."

"Goddamn it," the caller mutters before hanging up.

Eli slips his phone away and glances at his daughter next to him in the booth. "How are the pancakes?"

"Sooo good!" Jordan moans around a mouthful, her lips a sticky mess. "Why are they so good here?"

Henry pats his stomach. "The places around here have no qualms about using obscene amounts of gluten-rich flour and butter." He squints at his nephew. "Have you been depriving my grandniece of good food? What have you been feeding her? Kale and ice?"

"She eats fine," Eli says dismissively, although with the way Jordan is eating like she's never seen food before, he makes a mental note to reassess her meals. "We get pastelitos sometimes," he mentions, as if his uncle was seriously questioning his parenting skills based on the *lack* of starches in his daughter's diet.

"Do they have pastelitos here?" Jordan asks Henry. "I could kill for one."

"How are you still hungry?" Eli murmurs.

Henry laughs. "Unfortunately, no pastelitos. You know, no one made them quite like mi mamá. Rest her soul," he says, wistfully looking skyward. "I do miss good Cuban food though. Miami at least has that going for it."

"I still think Miami has a few other good things, Tío."

"Pfft, there's plenty of good food and entertainment around here without feeling like you're in a slow cooker year round. People complain about this area without really giving it a chance."

"I guess Jordie and I are gonna have to give it one since we got here earlier than planned."

They were only going to stay for a couple weeks after his father's surgery to help him with the initial recovery period. But when Pops called over the weekend to say he wasn't going down to Florida because of what happened with Goldie, Eli decided he needed to be here with him for more reasons than the surgery. Jordan had just gotten out of school for the summer anyway, so he convinced her mother to let her come along early. They're going to be here for more than a month.

"How's your pops?" Henry asks. "He hasn't talked to me since that night with Goldie."

"He's moping like a lovesick teenager. He has a medical appointment today, so that at least got him out of the apartment."

"Teo's pretty wrapped up in Goldie. I haven't seen him like this since, well, your mother."

Eli nods absently and takes a half-hearted bite of his cold omelet. "I wish there were more I could do to help him."

"Can we meet Goldie?" Jordan asks.

Eli looks down to confirm that she only spoke again after polishing her plate. Ever since hitting her tweens, his daughter has become a human Hoover vacuum.

"Uh," Henry stalls, "it's only been a few days since their fight. She's probably still mad."

Eli nods in agreement. "Your abuelo needs to give her some time to think. We don't have a right to bother her."

"But she might decide to stay broken-up," Jordan argues. "We have to tell her how great he is."

"I don't think that's the issue." Eli doesn't want to unload on his daughter exactly how many issues there are. That would keep them at IHOP all day, and they're not that desperate for something to do.

"We have to get them back together. He's too sad."

She's right about that. His father has been putting on a brave face, but the advice about giving Goldie time isn't sitting well with him. It's not sitting well with Eli either. He just didn't want to admit that to Jordan, who apparently also feels the same. Giving Goldie time to think everything out is the sensible thing to do though—isn't it?

"Come on, Daddy! We have to do something."

Eli turns to his uncle for guidance. "What do you think about it?"

Henry opens and closes his mouth like a fish before finally speaking. "Your dad definitely made a mistake that would be hard to forgive. I can't blame Goldie if she decides to break up with him for good."

The possibility makes Eli's stomach drop.

"But Teo also deserves a fighting chance to make it right."

"So, you'll help us?" Jordan asks with doe eyes.

"Help us do what?" Eli asks. "We can't just go to Goldie, introduce ourselves as the son and grandchild of her boyfriend, and beg her to take back your grandpa. We might make her feel worse."

Jordan pouts at the possibility and grabs a biscuit to stuff in her face.

They sit in silence to stew in their own thoughts. Then Henry, surprisingly, is the first to speak. "She works at the newspaper."

Eli quirks his head. "Yeah, I know. Goldie's a reporter."

Henry purses his lips and looks at Eli with a deadpan expression. "I mean, she works there. In a building. Near downtown. It's a weekday, so she's probably there right now."

Jordan's face lights up brighter than Ocean Drive at night. "Let's go! Let's go!"

"Whoa, Jordie," Eli says. "Are you prepared for the very awkward situation you are walking into? She'll probably have the building's security kick us out."

"Then we find some other way to talk to her. We can't give up. Abuelo nos necesita, Papá. He needs our help."

After tackling his personal demons and relying on his father's support, Eli had thought he was prepared to be the one doing the supporting. The responsibilities should have involved keeping Pops mentally and physically active and reminding him to take medications.

Not trying to fix his father's fuckup with a younger girlfriend.

Jordan waits for an answer, doe eyes fully loaded again.

"Fine," Eli caves. "But I'm not above throwing my child under the bus if this goes wrong."

Helena Lucinda Townshend of Miami, Florida, passed away Sunday, November 16, 2001—a couple weeks before her 37th birthday—from injuries sustained in a vehicle accident.

Helena was born November 30, 1964, the beloved daughter of Mercedes and Henry "Hank" Townshend Sr. and best friend and sister of Henry Townshend Jr., a local resident. She was the cherished mother of a son, Elian Hector Estrada Townshend, and wife and champion of her husband, Mateo Antonio Estrada Torres.

According to her mother, Helena could read right out of the womb. Her voracious appetite for books began with secondhand, beat-up copies of Nancy Drew mysteries and the works of Avi; matured to countless fantasy epics by Tolkien and Le Guin; and forged her character with the powerful prose of Maya Angelou, Isabel Allende and Amy Tan.

There wasn't a genre Helena didn't like or couldn't list honest recommendations for. No surface was safe from the weight of Stephen King novels. No bag was big enough for a trip to the bookstore. No ear was safe from her glowing reviews of the latest gothic romance or dystopian saga. Her husband often joked that she loved books more than him. She never denied it.

This great love blossomed into an academic pursuit of literature and library science, which led Helena to a career within the Miami-Dade Public Library System. Her work brought opportunities to serve her community through literacy and education programs such as English as a second language classes and book drives for low-income families.

When her nose wasn't in a book, Helena enjoyed taking her son to NBA games, feeding stray cats, playing (and winning) games of chess and Canasta, and planning her family's adventures.

Memorial services will be held in Miami at a later date, but condolences to local family members may be made at Hope Family Funeral Home Chapel at 11 a.m. Saturday.

What she lacked in height at 5 feet, 2 inches tall, she made up for with her big personality and spirit. The Estrada and Townshend homes mourn the loss of their little mountain and will forever live in the shadow of the one and only Helena.

IF GOLDIE WASN'T AT WORK, SHE'D PROBABLY BE CRYING HER FACE off after reading the obituary for Teo's wife. She remembered finding it among the few results in the newspaper's archive when she was searching for dirt on Teo, but she hadn't bothered reading it before because she couldn't fathom it being applicable to her boyfriend.

Now the journalist in her had to get an outside source to corroborate what Teo told her. Hell, if he lied about his age, then maybe he was lying about his tragic backstory too.

But here's the proof in digitized black and white.

There's love in every line of the obituary. In every word. The small mugshot of Helena's big, bright smile leaps off the page despite the image's graininess. She's beautiful, and Goldie expects to be jealous—like Helena's not dead, just Teo's ex trying to stake a claim on him.

Goldie wishes the situation were so cliché and trivial.

Strangely, she feels happy for Teo. Not for the death of his wife and his grief, of course. She's happy he experienced such a profound love even if it had been with another person.

That's what Goldie's sizing up: the love she and Teo share versus the love he had with Helena. He hadn't moved on for essentially two decades after her death. And when he finally found someone, he thought he had to hide his past to be with her.

I just wanted the chance to love you, Teo had told Goldie at the bar.

With everything out in the open, how does he feel about their love now? How does it compare?

Amber's approach saves Goldie from going any farther down the lovesick rabbit hole.

"Why didn't you warn me about Sarah Crown?"

"What do you mean?"

"She's fucking cool as hell!" Amber says surprisingly. "I was expecting a super-rich Karen with how she didn't let me go with you to the interview."

"It's easy to make assumptions when she's rich enough to buy a continent. But she does a lot of charity work and donates to everything. Her company welcomes unions and offers fair wages and benefits."

"And deep discounts on the new line of eyeshadow!" Amber whips out a large peach-colored palette with the Crown logo. "Connie's gonna love these colors. Sarah tried to give it to me for free, but I told her I wasn't allowed gifts. We had a great chat about the state of photojournalism too." She takes out her phone and waves it in front of Goldie's face. "I even got a selfie with her."

Goldie notices the shot's perfect composition and lighting. Of course the professional photographer had to be extra even with selfies. "Are you a Crownie now? Are you gonna sign the petition to make the Serum anniversary a national holiday?"

"I already did."

Goldie's eyebrows shoot up.

"I wanna be Sarah Crown when I grow up," the 40-year-old mother of a teenager declares with a sigh.

Goldie shakes her head at the fangirling.

"Anyway, where've you been?" Amber asks. "I haven't had the chance to check on you since Teo left for Europe."

The reporter has been making a lot of excuses to escape the office and keep everything bottled up like she usually does. But being confronted with her elusiveness feels like a sign she should let it all out.

"Teo didn't leave."

Amber blinks. "What?"

"He was lying about going on tour with the Panty Rockers. He was going to go to Florida. I'm not sure he even did that though."

"Wuh, what?" Amber sputters. "Why would he say he's going on tour? What happened?"

"I'd suspected Teo was lying to me about something for about a week, I guess. I confirmed it Friday and confronted him about it after the bar closed." Goldie takes a deep breath before diving into the big parts. "Teo lied about going on tour because he was trying to keep the fact that he uses the Serum from me. He needs surgery to remove benign cysts from his liver, and he's going to have to stop using it."

Amber's jaw drops to the floor. "Holy shit!"

Heads around the newsroom turn toward her, but when the exclamation isn't followed by "The [insert name of celebrity, president, royal, or pope] is dead," they turn back to their monitors.

Amber sinks into the spare chair next to Goldie's desk and gets in her face. "He uses the Serum?! Since when? Why'd he lie? How old is he really? Are you okay?"

Goldie's grateful for the concern and answers the last question honestly, her voice cracking a little. "I—I'm not okay."

Amber pulls her into a hug, and Goldie stays in her embrace as she recounts her confrontation with Teo. When she's finished, she raises her head to check on her friend's reaction. "Are *you* okay?"

"No, I'm in complete fucking shock," Amber says, her eyelids blinking like hummingbird wings. "How could none of us have suspected him?"

"I know my excuse. I hate to admit it, but my mom was right. I was blinded by love."

"Have you talked to him since?"

"No, I'm afraid to. I don't know how I'll feel. I don't know what to do."

"That's okay. You don't have to make any decisions now."

"I want to though. I want to be sure one way or another."

Amber indulges Goldie's need to pick apart her dilemma. "Well, he lied to you. There's no getting around how wrong that was."

"But he was right about how I would have reacted if he had told me his age the night we met. I would have shut him down completely. I would have never given him a chance."

Amber looks down at the Crown makeup palette she bought for her girlfriend. "You know how Connie told me her age?"

Goldie shakes her head.

"I was clicking away with my camera at the rich girl's birthday party, completely in the zone, and Connie steps right into frame. I'm stunned by how hot she is, so I don't pull the camera away. Then she says, 'What's a 51-year-old Serum user gotta do to get a photographer's attention?'"

Goldie scowls. "She just blurted that out?"

Amber nods. "No buildup or anything. She said it like a challenge. Like she was daring me to reject her advances over her age."

"How did you react to the age difference?"

"It's just a number, Goldie. We're adults with kids and divorces under our belts. You and Teo were doing great with an age gap. Now the dynamics are just … flipped."

"But Teo's more than twenty years older than me." Goldie hesitates before saying *screw it* to herself and letting it all out. "Before I learned the truth, it had felt good being able to call this young, handsome man *mine*. He could have his pick of any beautiful, carefree person—and he chose me. It made me feel like anything and everything was still possible."

The ring of Goldie's desk phone breaks into their conversation. The caller ID shows the number for the front lobby. "Hey, Miss Dottie. What's up?"

"Hiya, Goldie," the receptionist's Southern twang greets her. "You have, uh, guests up here."

The reporter frowns. "I wasn't expecting anyone."

"It's a Mr. Eli and a Miss Jordan."

"Did you hear that, Daddy?" A girl's voice can be heard in the background. "She called me 'Miss'!"

"Oh my God!" Goldie exclaims before she remembers to hit the mute button.

"What?" Amber asks.

Goldie shakes her head in disbelief. "Uh, I think Teo's son and granddaughter are here."

"Oh fuck!"

"Pretty much, yeah." Goldie's head is buzzing. *Why are they here? What do I say? Is Teo okay? Did he send them?*

"What do you want to do?" Amber asks.

Her first instinct is to run away, of course. If it wasn't for the animal cruelty, Goldie would wish traveling circuses were still a thing to leave town with. She could be a fire breather or barrel roller (that was a thing, right?).

"Goldie? Ms. Hays?" Dottie's voice calls out through the receiver.

Before she can talk herself out of it, Goldie presses the unmute button. "I'll be right up." She sets down the receiver and turns to her friend. "You wanna see my would-be stepfamily?"

"Fuck yes!" Amber grabs her hand to pull her in record time down the hall to the glass doors of the lobby. Luckily for Goldie, she doesn't make her go through them right away. Instead, they stay to the side to spy on Eli and Jordan, who are looking at the newspaper's historical display.

The girl is wearing Ugg boots, purple tights, and a long graphic tee. Her sandy-colored, textured hair is tied almost on top of her head, strands fanning outward like a paintbrush.

Jordan excitedly stretches a hand toward an old typewriter,

obviously about to take a few stabs at the keys. In a sly maneuver, her father takes her hand into his and redirects her to another display case to keep her from damaging it.

Eli looks to be about the same height as Teo. His skin tone is darker though, and his hair is neatly cut shorter. He's wearing a colorfully patterned button-up shirt and fitted blue jeans, a fun, casual style that's completed by a pair of slick-looking black-and-white Nikes.

"God, he looks like an older Teo." Goldie laughs breathlessly. "Or is it younger now?"

Amber snorts but keeps her face serious. "You sure about this?"

"Yes," she says, flicking her gaze to the lobby. "Especially now."

Amber gives Goldie's shoulder a gentle squeeze and wishes her luck before returning to the newsroom.

Goldie takes one more voyeuristic look before opening the doors.

The father and daughter duo turns around at the swish sound and locks onto her. Jordan's smiling with unguarded glee. Her father, however, seems to be checking for all the available exits.

"Hello?" Goldie squeaks out. The raw emotions she's been dealing with are stretching her already paltry people skills.

"Uh, hi, Gold—Uh, Ms. Hays," Eli croaks.

"You can call me Goldie, Eli."

Teo's son flutters his eyelids in surprise and gives a jerky nod. It seems that Goldie's not the only one suffering through excruciating awkwardness.

"No offense," she starts, "but why are you two here?"

"This is all her fault!" Eli blurts out, pointing at his daughter.

Jordan whips her head up, her jaw dropping at being called out. Goldie can't help chuckling at the exaggerated expression of outrage only young girls can make.

Eli arches a brow in challenge at his daughter before returning his focus to Goldie. "We're sorry to intrude. It's just that ..." He pauses, seeming to mull something before continuing. "Jordan and I hoped you would hear our side of the story."

The reporter appreciates the enticing entreaty and smiles a little.

"Hey, uh, Jordan?" The girl perks up at hearing her name. "Do you like boba tea?"

"THIS PLACE IS AMAZING!" JORDAN RAVES AROUND A MOUTHFUL of tapioca pearls. "Daddy, for the next one, can I please get a strawberry-kiwi slush cooler with aloe jelly and lychee popping boba?"

Eli tries not to gag. "This stuff is supposed to be *tea*. I didn't hear that word come out of your mouth once in the last two orders."

"Look at that menu! Why am I getting boring tea when I can get every fruity combination in slushy form?"

"Because the tea's not that bad. It's the little brown balls that I'm still not so sure about."

"Sorry for not warning you to chew them," Goldie says.

"No worries." Eli shrugs off the slight choking incident with a chuckle. "Thanks for bringing us. I've been looking for places to take Jordan. We've been a bit bored."

"When did you get here?"

"Early Monday. Mostly been hanging out with …" Eli hesitates for a second. *Do I call him Teo?* He bats away the thought and decides to speak of his father like he normally does. "We've been catching up with my pops."

"Oh?" Goldie's eyes flicker with interest.

Eli wonders how much he should reveal of his father's current angst. He doesn't want to risk making Goldie uncomfortable, but he doesn't want to be dishonest either. "He hasn't left his place since the weekend."

Goldie looks off to the side, probably trying to control her expression.

"I know it must be really weird to talk to us after just learning we exist, but I thought since we're here ..." Eli trails off when he realizes he has no conclusion. Embarrassed, he sticks the fat straw of his drink into his mouth and risks sucking up another gross brown bubble to keep it shut.

"We want you to forgive Abuelo," Jordan declares, not missing her chance to speak up.

"Jordan!"

"What? It's true!"

Goldie snorts, looking charmed by their dynamic.

"And I really wanted to meet you," Jordan says. "I like your long hair, by the way."

"Thank you, Jordan." Goldie gives a small smile. "I think your hair's great too. I admired it when I first saw you."

"Yeah?" Jordan fluffs the strands out even more. "Abuelo tied it for me."

"He did?" Goldie asks, hushed.

"He braids it for me sometimes too."

Eli notices how Goldie casts her eyes downward.

"He told me about how he helped you do Princess Leia hair buns for a comic book convention."

"I wondered where he learned to do hair so well." Goldie's mouth quirks as she looks back up to Jordan. "Now I know."

Despite the attempt at a smile, Goldie's tired eyes give away her dark mood.

Jordan must see it too, because she frowns before speaking again. "He's really sorry, Goldie. I haven't seen him so sad in a long time. He always tries to be happy and fun with me, but even when I was little, he would get this look that made me hug him tighter. He was missing my abuela, and to feel better, he would tell me funny stories about all the things she made him do. Like the one time he built a chicken coop."

Goldie arches an eyebrow. "Teo can build things like that?"

"No, not at all," Eli scoffs. "He bought whatever the hardware store recommended and laid it all out in the backyard. It took him a month to construct something that didn't collapse at the slightest breeze."

"Then they got the chickens." Jordan picks the story back up. "And they were noisy and smelly and kept escaping. But Abuela still wanted to keep them until Daddy got chased and let them into the house!"

"Wow," Goldie says, an amused curve playing at her lips. "What happened?"

Eli shudders dramatically. "My mother, thinking I was a precocious 4-year-old, sent me to the coop to collect some eggs by myself even though I was barely twice their height and they outnumbered me. I didn't stand a chance. The rooster snags my shoelace, and I keel over and smash the few eggs I had while trying to soften the landing with my hands. I don't have time to cry though because now I'm easy prey for the vultures. I crawl out of the coop and run faster than any preschooler ever has. When I reach the house, the back door is open, so I go right in screaming, 'Mami!' When I don't find her on the first floor, I go upstairs, and the stupid chickens follow me the whole way!"

Goldie is laughing. "Did you find her?"

Jordan's giggling too and answers for him. "In the big bedroom. This is my favorite part."

"Yeah, Pops was still getting ready for work and too stunned by the sight, but Mamá doesn't hesitate. She tosses me on the bed to save my poor legs and feet from any more pecking, then grabs her favorite duvet to lead them out of the house like she was a matador and these were majestic bulls in Spain instead of a bunch of psychotic fowl in South Miami. She sold the chickens a few hours later. We didn't eat eggs for a year."

With the story's conclusion, Goldie's bright smile dims quickly, a solemn, downward turn in its place. "Your mother sounds amazing."

Eli looks off wistfully. "She was."

"I wish I got to meet her," Jordan says. "Abuelo would tell me a lot of those stories when I was little so I could love her like I knew her. And now he does the same with you."

"What?" Goldie asks, sounding alarmed.

"Lately, when he calls, he tells me stories about you and what you do together. Like how he told me this morning about the comic book convention. He talks about you all the time."

"He does?"

Jordan nods. "That's why I'm so happy to meet you. You don't have to be a bunch of stories to me—not anymore."

"Oh." Goldie seems to be fighting back tears. "I'm so happy to meet you too."

"Yeah?"

"Of course, sweetheart. I'm just—" Goldie's voice gets rough, and she abruptly stops talking. She visibly swallows and takes a moment before continuing. "I'm still mad at your grandfather for keeping you from me. You, your father, your grandmother ..." She trails off and blows out a harsh breath. "He hid so much."

"He's so sorry, Goldie," Jordan says again. "Abuelo loves you."

"I love him too," she admits. "But I'm not ready to forgive him."

"But you do want to?" Eli asks, his anxiety no longer allowing him to remain a mere witness to the exchange. "I'm sorry. I'm not trying to pressure you into getting back together with him."

"I am!" Jordan proclaims. "You should totally get back together."

"Jordan," Eli admonishes with a shake of his head, shutting down any follow-up pleas. "What I'm trying to say—and I think I speak for my daughter here—is that Pops is ... just the best," he says with a nervous laugh. "I wouldn't be the father I am today without his example. But *best* doesn't mean *perfect*. He screwed up big time. It's tearing him up that he hurt you, and after seeing him endure so much with my issues and with losing my mother, seeing him suffer again is tearing me up too."

Before finishing his thought, he eyes his daughter, who's looking up at him proudly. "If you don't get back with him, he'll be disappointed for sure. But if you don't forgive him, he won't find peace."

Goldie stays quiet for a long time while staring down at her lap, appearing lost in thought. Eli and Jordan share anxious glances and wait her out. When she clears her throat, their gazes snap back to surprisingly find a faint smile on the tear-stained face.

"Before today," Goldie starts, "I was in so much pain that I didn't think forgiveness was possible. But thanks to you two"—her smile grows wider—"I think it is."

FOR THE NEXT SEVERAL WEEKS, HOME FOR ELI AND JORDAN IS AN Airbnb not too far from Hank's Bar. It's cozy (aka small), which was just fine for the father and daughter duo. They only required two major features: a giant television to watch Jordan's superhero shows and movies, and a kitchen stocked with every pan, utensil, and appliance in existence for Eli's culinary adventures.

Tonight, stir-fried pork and vegetables are on the menu. Eli lifts a wok off the heat to flip the contents in a maneuver honed from watching hundreds of hours of *Iron Chef* reruns. After a couple more flips, his father enters the kitchen.

"Hey, Pops!" Eli waves with the wooden utensil he's using.

"You went to see Goldie?!"

All cooking stops as Eli processes his father's shouted question. "I'm guessing Jordan told you."

"What the *hell*?!" Pops vacillates from the table to the stove. "You told me it was best to leave her alone!"

The pan's getting heavy, so Eli places it back on the burner and reduces the heat to low. "Yes, I did."

"So, how did you end up talking to her today? Please tell me you just randomly bumped into her."

"Jordan didn't tell you?"

"She opened the door and said, 'We met your girlfriend, Abuelo! She's super awesome!' The look of horror on my face must have stopped her from saying more."

Eli sighs. "I really need to teach that girl some chill."

"How?!" All his questions and concerns seem to be encompassed in that single word.

"We went to the newspaper," Eli admits with a shrug, trying to make it sound like it's no big deal.

Apparently, it totally is a big deal, and Pops squeaks out a panged noise in response. "What happened?"

"Relax, it went really well. We had a nice talk."

"How is she?"

"Still upset," Eli says. "But she listened to what we had to say. She was gracious. I can see why she's special to you."

His father finally calms down and plops into a chair after hearing that the meeting wasn't filled with shouting and angry tears like he probably feared. He takes in the meal Eli's preparing, although his eyes look unfocused.

"I had this fantasy about how you all would meet," Pops starts. "You'd cook for us, and Goldie would insist on bringing bread of some kind, since she'd worry that you were doing too much for her. I'd tell her that she was worth the fuss. *They'll love you,*" he says in a whisper, like his father is talking directly into Goldie's ear. The peek into their intimacy makes Eli's chest tighten.

"We'd make easy conversation," he continues, "especially with Jordan at the table asking a million questions. Goldie would be amused, but she'd take every one of them seriously."

Eli smirks, knowing he's right about his daughter. "Even when Jordie asks, 'Which would you save if you could only save one: a school bus full of children or all the world's knowledge?'"

Pops snorts a laugh. "Yeah, even then." His smile fades as he turns pensive again. "Goldie would lay her head on my shoulder while listening to you talk about the weird work calls you get. I'd embarrass you with stories of you as a kid."

Eli tries to scowl in mock annoyance but keeps his expression soft when his father finishes the fantasy.

"There'd be so much laughter and joy," he says, his voice cracking some.

Eli goes to the table to sit next to him. "I'm sorry, Pops. We should have waited until it was possible to meet her with you there too."

He waves off the apology. "I'll get over it. Just tell me what you talked about. I'm dying to know."

"Jordan raved about her abuelo and defended your honor." That earns Eli another snort. "And we told her a story about Mamá and us."

"Which story?"

"The chicken coop."

His father makes a pleased sound. "That's a good one."

"And we both asked if she can forgive you."

"You didn't!"

"Well," Eli clears his throat. "Jordan asked first." He was serious about having no problem throwing his daughter under the bus.

"What did Goldie say?" Pops looks like he can hardly breathe.

"You've got a lot of work ahead," Eli says before giving his father what he hopes is a confident smile. "But there's hope."

CHAPTER 12

On Saturday morning, Eli and Jordan walk through the heavy double doors of a nearby recreation center fifteen minutes early for a taekwondo program recommended by Goldie. She arranged for her friend to allow Jordan to join even though they were in the middle of the second week of classes.

His daughter has never taken martial arts of any kind, and when Eli raised concerns about her newbie status on the phone, the teacher assured him there were several beginners in the class. There wasn't a hint of judgment in his tone, simply an unguarded enthusiasm for the opportunity to instruct someone new.

Jordan not standing out is a relief but not Eli's only worry, thanks to his father's reaction to their plans.

He choked on his water.

"Oh God," Pops croaked out after a coughing fit. "Did you just call him 'Master Rhodes'?"

Eli handed him a napkin. "That's what he's called. He's a taekwondo master."

"Right, so." His father swallowed hard. "I'm going to guess Goldie didn't tell Tommy everything if he was nice on the phone."

"Maybe he's really professional."

Pops snorted. "That's, um, not the issue. There's no way he's okay with you and Jordan going to his class if he knows the whole story. He's, well." He paused like he was holding back something. "He's really protective of Goldie."

Eli looks around for anyone who might be the instructor but only sees parents and students.

"Where's Master Rhodes?" Jordan asks. "I still need a uniform."

"I'm not sure." Eli takes one more sweeping look around before an echoing *ka-chunk* attracts everyone's attention. A tall man wearing a white martial arts uniform like the students enters the room slinging a large gym bag over one shoulder and a mesh pet carrier over the other.

"Master Rhodes!" A few of the kids shout in greeting.

"Hey, everyone!" The man responds as he puts his stuff down. "Sorry I'm not as early as I usually am. I hope y'all have been doing your warm-ups."

Of course, the students hadn't and immediately busy themselves with the tacit command of their instructor.

Eli takes the opportunity to approach him. "Master Rhodes?"

The man is squatting to open the pet carrier for what looks like the smallest dog ever.

"Ohhh my God, a puppy!" Jordan squeals.

Some of the students stop their warm-ups to look in their direction. Master Rhodes shoots a gaze back in silent warning against stopping, then scoops the Chihuahua with one large hand and stands back up.

"Yes, we have a special guest for today's class," he says to Jordan. "This is Lucky."

"Hi, Lucky! OMG, you're so cute. I just want to eat you up." With her appetite, Eli almost worries that she'll try. "Daddy, can we have a puppy?"

"You know the issue. You live with your mom, and she doesn't want one."

"But it could live with you!"

"And then I'd have to take care of it most of the time."

"It'd keep you company when I'm not around."

"I don't need anyone else keeping me company," Eli says.

"We could all use company sometimes," Master Rhodes interjects.

When Eli looks up to meet honey-colored eyes, his breath catches.

Holy hell, he's gorgeous. A brunet with so many shades of brown in his thick, shaggy hair that Crayola will need to come up with new weird names for them. A strong jawline so perfectly angled that Michelangelo could have sculpted it. And don't get Eli started on his height. Not only tall but muscular with broad shoulders that surely could take Eli's weight as he climbed the man like a damn sequoia tree.

In this moment, he can completely relate to his daughter's declaration regarding the puppy—because Eli wants to *feast* on this man.

"S-sorry about that. We're, um, no, wait." *Quit eye-fucking him, Estrada! There are kids present.* He shakes off the horny nerves and starts again. "I'm Eli Estrada, and this is my daughter, Jordan. We talked yesterday."

"Tommy Rhodes," the teacher says with a broad smile (that, besides the height, reveals Eli's other kryptonite—killer dimples). He holds out his puppy-free hand for a shake. "Pleased to meet you. So, you're related to Teo?"

The question completely douses Eli's dirty thoughts. *Damn, Pops was right.*

"Uh, yep, we're … family," he answers stiltedly. Eli keeps going to cut off any follow-up questions. "Jordan needs a uniform."

"Right!" Master Rhodes starts to bend over but looks at the puppy and then at Jordan, handing her Lucky. "Hold him for a sec, could you?"

Of course, Eli's young daughter jumps at the chance and makes grabby hands.

The teacher rummages in his gym bag for a bit. "This should fit you." He holds out a uniform to Jordan in exchange for the puppy (to her dismay). "You can just put it on over your clothes."

She does so on the spot, everything self-explanatory except for the long white belt.

The teacher sets down the puppy and unties his black belt to demonstrate, revealing the tightest abs Eli's ever seen (and coming from Miami, he's seen his fair share). "Pull one end taut across your waist, then wrap the other over and under twice, maybe three times for you, then double knot the ends together to secure them."

When she's finished with the belt, Jordan stands with her fists on her hips and her chest puffed out. "How do I look, Daddy?"

"My little Wonder Woman," Eli says, then flicks his eyes to Master Rhodes to see if he approves of his daughter's work. He's gazing at them with a soft smile.

"Good job." The teacher clears his throat and looks away. "We should join the others, Jordan. I'll show you where to stand and introduce you to the older students who help me out. And Mr. Estrada—"

"Eli!" he blurts out too loudly, and winces at the knee-jerk reaction. "It's, uh, just Eli."

"Okay, Eli." The teacher smirks as the name rolls off his tongue. His voice isn't deep, yet there's a raspy edge that somehow catches every letter of his too-short name and makes Eli's stomach flutter. "You can call me Tommy outside of class. Same to you, Jordan."

Eli arches an eyebrow. "*Outside* of class?"

"Lunch?" Tommy proposes.

Now it's Eli's turn to smirk. "We might need to go to a place with a buffet. This one," he says, pointing to Jordan, "is going to need third helpings after doing anything remotely physical."

"It's true." Jordan nods. "I get hungry breathing."

Tommy chuckles. "A lunch buffet, it is." Then, without warning, he gives Eli a handful of puppy. "I need someone to watch this little guy while we're busy."

"Wait, what?"

"There are pee pads and cleaning supplies in the bag for when he needs to do his business," Tommy says without bothering to confirm that Eli is all right with puppysitting. He places a guiding hand on Jordan's shoulder and leads her to the mats to join the class.

Eli looks at Lucky in disbelief. "What just happened?"

The puppy looks up at him with a "Bitch, I don't know" expression. Chihuahuas are a super sassy breed.

Eli grabs a chair to sit next to the puppy's carrier and lets him wander in and out of it as he pleases. The spot isn't too out of the way from the students, so he's still able to watch his daughter taking in every bit of instruction from Tommy. She seems genuinely interested, which is good news because the martial arts boot camp will keep her busy during their time here.

As far as Eli can tell, Tommy's "master" title is well deserved. In fact, his physical prowess, upbeat personality, and godlike body have Eli drooling so much that he becomes derelict of his puppysitting duties. Lucky wanders among the rows of students performing drills, and Tommy swoops down to save the puppy from getting stomped.

As the furball is deposited in Eli's lap, Tommy whispers in his ear, "You had one job."

Eli catches the curve of a smirk as the instructor pulls away.

The rest of the class goes by without further incidents. Afterward, Jordan is talking with a couple of students and demonstrating what she learned. Her front kick is accompanied by a *thwack!* sound effect, a byproduct of Jordan's superhero adoration. Tommy also is caught up in post-class chats, but Eli swears he keeps looking over at him.

Eventually, Jordan comes back around just as Eli is getting a little frustrated with having only a puppy to talk to. "Daddy! How did I do?"

"You did great. Did you have fun?"

"It was so cool. I'm totally going to be breaking bricks with my face at the end of the month."

"It's good to have goals," Tommy says as he approaches them. "I'm glad you enjoyed your first lesson, Jordan."

"Thank you so much, Master Rhodes."

"It's Tommy now," he says, a reminder of their lunch plans. "Give me a minute to change, and I'll meet you two outside." He looks at Eli. "Do you mind puppysitting a bit longer and taking him out with you?"

It's not a big deal, but Eli can't resist antagonizing him about the request. "Where we're going better have the best food ever. You owe me."

They end up at Fun & Feast, a Dave and Buster's–style place

with video games and twists on games you'd find at carnivals. And, as Tommy promised, it has a buffet.

Eli is first to make his selections and patiently waits at their table for the others to return. Lucky is in the pet carrier keeping busy with a chew toy.

"Daddy, look what I got!"

Eli blinks owlishly at the pile of food on his daughter's plate. "The whole buffet, it seems."

"There's paella and doubles and curry and sushi and—"

"Jordie," he interrupts, "you didn't have to pile everything on one plate. You can get up for seconds."

"Oh, I will," she says, like she's making a sacred vow.

Tommy comes back to the table with a plate just as crammed with food as Jordan's. Eli looks at it, then up at the man. "You too?"

"What? I didn't eat breakfast."

"So this is more than you would usually get?"

"Pfft, no," Tommy scoffs, and takes his seat. "I'm easily crushing another full plate, plus dessert, of course."

"Oh yeah, dessert!" Jordan's eyes search out the bar filled with cakes and pastries.

"The flan's great," Tommy says. "So's the baklava. There are desserts from everywhere. I was so happy when this place opened. I couldn't take another steakhouse or barbecue rib joint. Seriously, I would've cried."

Eli chuckles. "How long have you lived here? Or were you born and raised here?"

"I was an Army brat. Moved a lot until my father retired out. This was his last station. He didn't see a reason to go anywhere else." Tommy looks downward. "'As good a place as any,' he said."

It's not exactly a positive thing to say, nor is it the most insulting, but Tommy seems to be very uneasy nonetheless. Eli tries to shift topics. "How long have you been studying martial arts?"

"Since I could walk. Every new place we'd go, my mom would make sure to find a teacher for me. The diversity in styles helped me gain a broader skill set and figure out my methods for instruction."

"I don't think Jordan could have found a better teacher. You're impressive."

"Uh-huh!" Jordan agrees around a mouthful.

"Um, thanks." Tommy grins.

From that point, Tommy and Jordan dedicate themselves to inhaling their food and giving detailed opinions on each item. And, true to their word, both get up for seconds, making a deal to get a variety and share bites with each other so they can further review the food. Eli can't help feeling enamored by how well the two are getting along.

"Tommy was so right about the flan. Daddy, you gotta try it." Jordan holds up the fork with a bite for Eli.

Once he's tasted it (and, yes, it was creamy with just the right amount of caramel), Eli sees another fork in his face. "Now you have to try the German chocolate torte," Tommy insists. "Freaking. Phenomenal."

His daughter feeding him like that is one thing, but for Tommy to do it—as if he were his date—has Eli flustered and pulling his lips inward.

Tommy, on the other hand, doesn't seem to have such hang-ups and keeps holding the fork. "Do you not like chocolate?" he asks, misinterpreting Eli's hesitation.

Eli sighs over the apparent innocence of the man's gesture. "I love chocolate, actually." He slowly opens and closes his mouth over the morsel and slides his lips off the fork with just as much care. He then checks Tommy's face for any signs of interest in his playful show. Tommy's eyes are locked on Eli's lips.

So, not so innocent after all.

The rich, sweet flavor hits Eli and breaks his seductive concentration. "Oh, that is so good!"

Tommy smiles and huffs out a pleased laugh before taking the fork (that was just in *Eli's mouth*!) and having a slow and savory bite for himself.

Jordan, bless her, is completely oblivious to the shameless flirting. "Gimme a piece too!"

Tommy smirks and looks at Eli for a lingering second before

sliding the whole plate over to her (minus the defiled fork). "It's all yours, kiddo."

After Tommy and Jordan are finally done eating, they roam around the game floor, looking for some activities that will help burn off the calories.

"They're over there," Jordan says, unprompted.

Tommy looks confused. "What's over where?"

"The basketball hoops. Daddy's looking for them."

Tommy turns to Eli for confirmation.

Eli shrugs. "I like basketball."

"He's obsessed," his daughter corrects.

"I enjoy playing basketball and watching basketball. That's not being obsessed."

"He almost named me 'Shaquille.'"

Tommy's jaw drops. "You're joking?!"

"I was going to name her '*Shaquilla*,'" Eli says, "with an *A*. It's a legit name!"

"He was going to nickname me 'Shaqui,'" Jordan says, her face looking like she ate a lemon.

"It would've been cute." Eli pouts.

"You love Shaq that much?" Tommy asks.

"My parents used to take me to as many NBA games as they could. We had the Heat in Miami, but they sucked a lot of the time, so we'd go up to Orlando too. Shaq was with the Magic when I was a kid. I got to see him in his early glory days."

"That's really cool," Tommy admits. "Not 'name my kid after Shaquille O'Neal' cool, but I can respect being a fan of the sport." He looks at Eli's daughter. "I'm guessing you were a Michael Jordan fan too."

"I got to go to a Bulls-Magic game the last time Jordan came back to the NBA. Greatest night of my life, seeing those two on the court at the same time."

His daughter clears her throat; Eli rolls his eyes.

"Of course, that was until my child was born. Hence, Jordan's name."

"Plus, Mami wouldn't let him name me 'Lebron' either."

"Are you serious?!" Tommy laughs. "What were you gonna nickname her?"

Eli looks away sheepishly and mutters, "Lebby."

"Wow," Tommy says with a shake of his head. "Jordan's right. That's an obsession. Do you have any NBA players tattooed on you?"

Eli scurries toward the basketball hoops.

"Oh my God, you do!" Tommy shouts with glee. He catches up to Eli and gets between him and the game booths. "You have got to show me! Or is it on a part of your body that can't be revealed in public? If that's the case, I want to see it even more."

Eli pretends to be more annoyed than he really is. If anything, he's a little too charmed by Tommy's excitable nature. Still, he side-eyes the tall man, tilting his head back to do it right. "Beat me in a shooting match, and I'll show you right here on the spot."

Tommy doesn't require any convincing and moves to the booth next to Eli. "You're on, Estrada."

"We hit start at the same time to release the balls, okay?" Eli instructs.

"Got it." Tommy hovers his hand over the start button.

"Jordie, count us down."

His daughter gets into a position to see both their baskets. "Five, four, three, two, one … GO!"

Despite the balls sliding down to Eli slower than he'd like, as soon as his hands are on one, he's ready and sinks his first shot without issue. And the next, and the one after that. Eli is like a machine. Hardly a ball hits the rim; most slip through the basket with a satisfying swoosh. He's tempted to look over to check Tommy's progress, but that would stop his, and there's no way he's losing.

Eli is so in the zone that when the buzzer goes off, he jumps in surprise. He looks at the scoreboard to see thirty-four glowing above the net. He looks at Tommy's side and sees a significantly lower twenty-two. Eli knows he looks smug, an expression that only intensifies when he sees the shock on his opponent's face.

"How?!" Tommy cries.

"I'm not exactly going to get good at dunking." Eli motions over his head to point out his very respectable but nowhere near towering five-feet, ten-inches of height (and that's without the Nikes, thank you very much). "So I worked on my free throws."

Tommy shakes his head and sighs. "I really can't see the tattoo?"

"Not today, *but*—" Eli's work ringtone interrupts the flirty retort on his tongue, and he turns to the side to answer. "Tiger Computer Repair, how may we help you?"

"Well," the caller starts, "I've run out of space on my computer."

"Okay?" Eli wonders where this is going. "Are you having issues installing a new drive?"

"No, I would just like more."

"You would have to purchase some form of expanded storage, then. If you don't want to install hardware, you can purchase external hard drives or memory cards."

"No, I don't want to buy anything else. I just want more storage space on this computer."

"That would require deleting apps and files from it." Eli does his best not to add a "duh" at the end.

"But I want to keep everything I have on it and add more. There has to be a way of making more space."

"Uh, no."

"But the internet has unlimited space! If it's possible there, how is it not possible to make more storage on my computer?"

"The internet is a more complex system, sir. It's not just one machine running it."

"You obviously have no idea what you're talking about!"

Eli rubs his forehead. "Would you like to speak to a manager?"

"Of course I would! I can't believe you'd try to trick me into buying free storage! I'm not an idiot!"

"Please hold." Eli taps the extension numbers and pockets his phone. When he turns back around, he sees Jordan wandering off with Lucky to a simulator and Tommy standing near, looking at him quizzically. "Oh, sorry, that was work. I'm an on-call IT specialist."

"You just take calls anytime, anywhere?"

"Yeah, my company's pretty flexible. Also, I wasn't supposed to be taking my vacation for another couple weeks, so if I was going to come up here ahead of schedule, I needed to still technically work. I asked for as few calls as possible though."

"Did you really transfer that person to a manager?"

"Heck, no. I banished him back into the queue for anyone on call who's bored enough to pick a fight with a customer."

"Quality service," Tommy says, looking amused. "I wish I could banish the annoying customers I get so easily, but I had to go be a car salesman."

"Really? Full time?" Eli gapes as Tommy nods. "*And* you teach taekwondo? How do you manage all that?"

Tommy shrugs. "I like to keep busy." He looks back up at the scores. "It looks like I'm going to have to work on my free throws on top of everything else."

Eli scoffs. "Why? It's not like I'm determined to learn taekwondo after seeing you kick a speed bag so hard it exploded."

"It's important to show the students the importance of accuracy."

"Is that what that was? You sure you weren't showing off your incredible legs?"

"You like them?" Tommy says with a wink. "Seriously though, I could show you."

"What? Your legs?"

"Those too," Tommy says without missing a beat, "but I'm talking about taekwondo. I could teach you some things."

Eli automatically dismisses the possibility. "I appreciate the offer, but I don't want to be the only 30-something beginner in a class full of kids and teenagers."

"I wouldn't do that to you. It can be one-on-one."

"You're busy, Tommy. And I'm only here for a month or so."

"I wouldn't mind." Tommy steps closer. "I'd like to spend as much time with you as possible."

Eli studies the man, trying to be sure his filthy mind isn't misreading the situation. "Why?"

Tommy hesitates with a response and looks at their surroundings. People are mulling about, and children are randomly shouting and running around. "Let's find a quieter place to talk."

"What about Jordan?"

They walk to where she's sitting in a driving simulator with her eyes covered by a VR mask. Lucky is splayed precariously on her lap as the chair shimmies and shakes.

"Hey, Jordan!" Tommy calls out.

"Yeah?"

"We're going to the patio outside. Can you stay on this side of the room where we can see you?"

"Yeah, I'll be right here winning this race." As she says the words, her car spins out. Jordan takes off the VR set to look at the screen. "Damn it!"

"Language, Jordan," Eli admonishes.

"Mierda," she mutters.

"Not what I meant!"

"You distracted me!"

Eli grunts at his daughter's excuse for using bilingual swears. "Do not leave this side of the room," he commands.

"I'll be fine. If anyone bothers me, I'll take their eyes out like Tommy taught me."

"Jam your thumbs in there as hard as you can," Tommy says, demonstrating with his hands.

Eli shakes his head and motions for Tommy to follow him to the patio.

They take a seat next to the window, away from any other people sitting out there.

"So, why?" Eli asks, wasting no time to pick their conversation back up.

Tommy leans back in his chair and points at the window. "Because of that."

Eli knits his brow.

"The kind of father you are. Before class, seeing your easy relationship with Jordan and the love in your eyes caught my attention. Lunch intensified it."

"Didn't know fatherhood could be such a turn-on," Eli tries to joke, poorly covering up how flustered he is.

"I mean"—Tommy seems to panic—"not in a daddy kink way."

"I wasn't thinking that!" Eli replays what he said, and damn, it did sound like an accusation. "I'm flattered, really. I love being a father. It's nice to hear that I seem to be doing a good job at it."

Tommy relaxes again. "You deserve a 'World's Greatest Dad' trophy. Or a mug, at least."

"A whole mug, huh?" Eli chuckles. "You know if it is a daddy kink, you can just say so. There's nothing wrong with that."

"Shut up! It's not a daddy kink." Tommy playfully kicks him, then looks off to the side, suddenly somber. "My dad doesn't even deserve a stupid mug."

Eli waits for more.

"My parents separated once my sisters and I left the house. My mother stayed with him for so long, thinking that a divorce would hurt us. She never realized that seeing her hurting was worse."

"What was going on with them?"

"After he was forced to retire from the military, Dad bounced from job to job. He never found any footing. And he never could stop 'hanging with the boys' and drinking till he was numb."

Eli was afraid alcohol had some part in it.

"At least he's not a fucking truck driver anymore. That was scary. He stopped working altogether a few years ago. Lives off his military retirement and Social Security."

"What does he do with his time now?"

"Drink, argue with his latest fling, then drink some more but while fishing—because the two seem to go together."

"Have you tried getting him help?"

"How do you help someone who thinks they don't have a problem?"

Even though they only met a few hours ago, Tommy's been honest and upfront about himself. It inspires Eli to be the same way. Maybe it'll do some good. "I'm a recovering addict."

Tommy's eyes widen.

"Always recovering," Eli continues, "but I've been clean and sober for more than eleven years."

"Eleven," Tommy echoes, considering something. "And how old is Jordan?"

"She turned 11 in March," Eli says with a knowing smile.

"Before she was born, I would still take meds and drink off and on. I couldn't commit to getting clean despite my pops' best efforts. Nothing mattered, especially not my life. I mean, why did I get to live when my mother didn't?"

Tommy's mouth opens in a soundless gasp.

"*Mamá* and I were going home from Orlando after a Magic game. My father didn't go with us because he got busy with work. He's also not a big sports fan. But my mother genuinely liked basketball as much as I did." Eli's jaw tightens. Recalling everything never gets easier. "It was dark, but she'd done the drive so many times before. That's a thought I've always had to struggle with. I kept wishing there had been some sign that the accident was going to happen. But honestly, there was nothing unusual—until someone trying to pass us clipped our car from behind. We ran off the road and smashed into a tree. My mom died on impact."

"I am so sorry, Eli."

Eli nods and continues. "I escaped with a broken arm, but I wasn't grateful that it wasn't worse. How could I be? I just couldn't reconcile surviving the same accident that killed my mom. Why should I be alive? What good was my life compared to hers?" He swipes at his eyes. "So, I popped pills, drank. I was in therapy throughout my teens, but it never felt like I could completely deal with my survivor's guilt."

"I'm so glad you survived," Tommy says. "You barely know me, but I'm grateful that we met today. That we can have this talk right now."

"I'm glad too," Eli says with a small smile. Needing a moment, he checks on Jordan through the window. She's moved on to a dancing game and is stomping on the lights as they appear on the floor. Lucky is just as into the game. The puppy is leaping as fast as possible from light to light.

"Having a kid really changed things for you, didn't it?" Tommy asks.

"Yeah, it did," Eli says, slowly pulling his gaze from his daughter. "There's this notion in some recovery programs where a person is encouraged to submit themselves to God or a higher power of some sort. I hated the idea though. In my mind, God had allowed my mother to die. But it's not so much God. It's more about looking outside oneself, because pain is a trap. You live in it, you breathe it, you identify with it. I needed a great purpose to break free from the pain. I needed a reason for my continued existence on this earth."

"Jordan," Tommy says, drawing the right conclusion.

"Jordan," Eli echoes. "Learning that I was going to be a father wasn't some magical cure, of course. I still didn't think I was worthy of surviving that crash, but I finally had the incentive I needed to invest in making myself worthy. I had purpose and drive to recover, to accept my faults, and to make amends."

He looks back through the window at his daughter, who's now given up her part of the game in favor of helping Lucky win by bouncing him around the floor.

"You know, I'm 37 now," Eli says with surprising lightness in his voice. He *feels* lighter after revealing so much of himself to Tommy. "Older than my mom got to be, and I'm genuinely grateful to have come so far."

Tommy looks like he's incapable of speech, his eyes glassy with unshed tears.

"That was a lot. Sorry." Eli half shrugs, contrite. "I guess the whole point was to give you a sense of hope. Addiction is different for everyone, but I think recovery is always possible. It takes finding the right spark of motivation."

"I wish my family had been enough motivation for my dad."

"I'm sorry." Eli frowns, worried his words haven't been of any comfort. "I can relate though. As much support and encouragement as I got from my father, it wasn't enough. I put him through hell, when he was facing the loss of my mother too."

Tommy seems to ponder that. "How are things now with him?"

"I want to keep making amends with him, but he'd tell me that I don't need to. That seeing me in a good place is all that matters."

"He sounds like a good man."

Eli gives him a tight smile to avoid saying anything more.

"Thank you for sharing your story, Eli." Tommy slides his chair close. "You're extraordinary."

Eli sucks in a breath, capturing the man's earthy scent in the process. "You're great too."

Tommy leans forward, eyes hooded. "Can I kiss you?"

"I'd like that," Eli rasps, then closes the distance.

The press of lips is sweet and soft, a caress matching the sensitive conversation and the newness of their connection. No hands reach out, a tacit agreement by both men to keep the kiss from getting deeper. Eli is content with the gentle brush of Tommy's mouth against his. It's a tenderness that feels perfect for a first kiss.

That is until Tommy's mouth practically unhinges while yawning. He scrubs his face with a hand and grunts in frustration. "Way to ruin the moment, Rhodes," he mutters to himself. "Sorry, I didn't get any sleep last night."

"Why? Were you partying?" Eli asks, his joking tone letting Tommy know that he's not offended. "Are Friday nights epic ragers around here?"

"Hey, there's stuff to do. Don't hate, Mr. Miami. But no, I wasn't partying."

"What was keeping you up? The puppy?"

"Sort of," Tommy says, his brow cinched. "Goldie needed me to take him last minute. Lucky's hers—or, well, her mom's."

"Why did she need you to take him? Is she okay?"

Tommy doesn't say anything right away. Instead, he's looking Eli over. "How are you related to Teo?" he asks out of nowhere. "You never said."

"Why are you so concerned?" Eli's protective instincts rear up, making him sound defensive.

"Because he hurt Goldie."

"I know. He's been beating himself up over it."

"You know everything he did?"

Eli nods.

"Do you mind telling me? Because I feel like I'm missing something big here."

"It's not my place," Eli answers honestly.

They're at a stalemate, an implicit wall forming between them and disrupting what had been a fun and enlightening lunch date.

Eli feels a spark that easily could catch fire. He has to commit to stoking and fanning though. To possibly getting burned. "Were you just looking for dirt on Teo when you suggested lunch? I don't appreciate being used."

"No!" Tommy's hand flies out to touch Eli's. "I wasn't using you."

Eli relaxes after hearing the firm denial.

"Huh," Tommy utters in a breath, looking puzzled at their joined hands. "You know, I've known Goldie for a long time, and we've never held hands."

Eli blinks, confused. "Okay?"

"We just met this morning, but I automatically went for your hand."

"Well, we were also kissing a minute ago, so this is actually not so bold."

"Hmm." Tommy concedes with a slight head tilt. "Anyway, I definitely didn't invite you to lunch to get gossip on my friend's boyfriend. I'm sure it's trivial anyway if she's talking to you and suggesting things to do with Jordan. I mean, you shouldn't hate on someone for what their family did."

"Absolutely." Eli nods too energetically. "You should hold on to that belief no matter what you might find out later."

Tommy frowns. "Shit, is it that bad?"

"It's, well." Eli heaves a sigh. "It's complicated."

"IN SUMMARY, YOU HAVE THE HOTS FOR MY SON."

"Seriously?" Eli murmurs at his father, shaking his head.

His father. His fucking *father*.

Teo Estrada, boyfriend of Tommy's best friend, is the father of the fully grown man Tommy flirted and connected with today.

A handsome man he kissed and shared a fork with.

Tommy doesn't know what to think. He always thought of himself as open-minded, which only meant not passing judgments of any kind. We all have our own battles to fight, after all. We're trying to do the best we can with what we've got in this shitty world. Live and let live, c'est la ... whatever the fuck the French say. But what he's just learned about the men sitting across from him has compromised the very core of his blasé philosophy.

There's a technicolor of emotions swirling in Tommy. A blue of sympathy for the loss Teo and Eli have suffered. The golden joy of knowing that they've come out of the inky-black well of grief. There's the purple of pride for the strong family they've remained through it all. And then there's the vibrant orange that's excited for what he's feeling for Eli.

Unfortunately, there's another color that seems to be distorting all the others—the red of anger. Tommy knows he has to deal with it, or he'll lose this beautiful new way of seeing and thinking and feeling.

"Can I talk to you alone?" Tommy requests, his unblinking gaze directed at Teo.

"Are you going to exploding-heart punch my abuelo?" Jordan asks.

Tommy trades his intimidating stare for a look of disbelief at the girl's father. "You let her watch *Kill Bill*?"

"She's outgrown the Netflix Kids profile," Eli says. "At least it wasn't *Pulp Fiction*. Seeing that Tarantino film around her age gave me nightmares."

Tommy turns back to Teo. "You let him watch *Pulp Fiction* as a kid?"

"*I* didn't! That was his mother." Teo folds his arms. "She really wanted to watch it and thought she could make whatever he saw in the movie a teachable moment."

Tommy hesitates with a response and glances at Jordan, trying to think of the vaguest description. "Even the basement scene?"

"She did draw the line there," Eli admits. "But not before telling me about bondage."

"What's bondage?" Jordan, of course, asks.

Eli shakes his head. "Not ever going to tell you."

Tommy cackles at Eli's agonized expression but quickly tries to help him escape the embarrassing topic (which is kind of Tommy's fault anyway).

"Hey, Jordan?"

"Yes?"

"I promise not to use the exploding-heart technique on your grandfather."

"But you know how to do it?"

Tommy gives the girl a wink.

Eli groans at the exchange and gets up. "Come on, Jordie. Put the puppy on the pillow, and let's go."

His daughter grumbles but does as she's told.

"And give us a call later." Eli waves a hand between Tommy and Teo. "*Both* of you. I want to go to sleep tonight knowing I won't have to bail anybody out of jail in the morning."

"Are we already at the 'bailing out of jail' dating stage?" Tommy asks, voice hopeful.

"You wish," Eli says over his shoulder as he ushers Jordan out. "Goodbye, you two."

"Bye, Abuelo! Bye, Tommy!"

All lightheartedness and humor are extinguished once the door shuts. Tommy goes back to staring daggers into Teo, who wisely looks away.

Tommy takes a deep, centering breath. "I'm sorry about your wife."

Teo looks surprised, his nod of acknowledgment delayed. "Thank you."

"I admire how you pulled yourself out of tragedy and helped your son do the same."

The surprised expression intensifies, Teo's eyebrows shooting up. "I appreciate it."

Tommy pulls his lips inward, preparing for his next words. "With that said, I have to ask"—he draws one last breath—"how the *fuck* could you do that to Goldie?"

Instead of bristling or getting defensive like Tommy expects, Teo looks almost relieved by his anger. "I hate myself for it. I can't sleep. I can't … stop seeing the devastated look on Goldie's face. How she cried and ran away from me."

Tommy grits his teeth. "I cannot believe you walked away that night with your balls intact."

Teo nods, probably understanding that getting kicked in the balls is the least he deserves.

"What are you gonna do about it?" Tommy asks.

"What do you mean?"

"Do you want to try to make things right? To get her forgiveness?"

"Of course, I do!" Teo exclaims. "But I was supposed to be giving her time. That was until my son and granddaughter went to see her without letting me know beforehand."

Which led to Tommy's poignant meeting with Eli and Jordan today. What fucking blows is that his good fortune is coming at the expense of his friend's heartbreak.

"Are you serious about it though?" Tommy asks. "Even if she doesn't take you back?"

Teo winces and rubs his jaw, reacting to the words like the fist to the face that Tommy intended them to be.

"Even then," Teo says eventually. "I want her to forgive me not just for the possibility of a second chance. Hopefully, it can help her heal from what I've done."

Tommy takes a long moment to consider Teo's words. He tilts his head back for a quick consult with whatever deities are watching from up there before making peace with what he's about to tell the man.

"Goldie's mom fell last night."

Blood drains from Teo's face. "What?!"

"She hit her head really hard on the floor and passed out," Tommy explains more fully. "Lucky, *luckily*, started barking and alerted Goldie out of bed. She called 911, then called me. I got to their house as the EMTs were getting her mom into the ambulance. Goldie was going with them and asked me to take care of Lucky, which is why—" He stops talking and gestures to the little black-and-tan furball on the pillow to finish his sentence.

"Is she okay now? Goldie's mom?"

"She has a slight concussion and some swelling, but she's been awake and has full cognition, thankfully. The doctor wants to keep her in the hospital for twenty-four hours to rest and for observation though."

Teo breathes out a sigh of relief. "And how's Goldie doing?"

"She was pretty shaky on the phone this morning but sounded

a lot better this afternoon. She asked me to bring Lucky tonight to sneak him into the hospital. She even put her mom on the phone to talk to me."

"What did she say?"

"She said she might not have died, but if I let anything happen to Lucky, she'd find a way to haunt me anyway."

Teo's jaw and neck muscles spasm as he takes in all the information. "I should have been there for Goldie. I should be there *now*."

"Yeah, you should," Tommy says, surprising them both.

Teo eyes him warily. "She's been through a lot today. I don't want to upset her more."

Tommy growls low over what he's about to admit. He's convinced the words will kill him and wishes lightning could just strike him dead now and spare his lips the work. Too bad the only storm cloud nearby is the one hanging above filled with his anger over this whole shitty situation.

Cowboy up, Rhodes. Just say it.

"Goldie … needs you," Tommy grinds out.

Teo is appropriately shocked. His eyes widen and his previously tense jaw unhinges like a nutcracker.

"Last night, Goldie was so preoccupied with making sure her mother was being treated properly that she barely looked away from her. The times she did though, she'd see me and somehow look more distraught than she already was." A lump forms in Tommy's throat, but he swallows hard and powers through the rest. "She kept wanting to see you."

"Tommy, she was just upset about her mother."

"Nah, man," he says with a humorless chuckle. "Trust me, I'm thoroughly aware of the difference between how Goldie looks at me versus how she looks at you."

Teo's expression softens with sympathy, which is all kinds of fucked up since he's the one on the outs with Tommy's best friend for keeping secret his geezer status. Before the asshole can bother trying to make another excuse for Goldie's feelings, Tommy reveals his plan.

"You're going to need my help to see her."

Teo's brow knits. "I could just call her."

"She'd tell you to stay away. Goldie will lie about being fine and not needing anyone's help. She probably wouldn't have even called me last night if she hadn't needed someone to watch the puppy."

Teo huffs. "She's stubborn as hell, that's for sure."

They share amused, knowing looks, surprising Tommy yet again. Their fondness for Goldie might cause friction between them, but it also somehow bonds them.

"Then what's the plan?" Teo asks.

Tommy grins, lips crooked and mischievous.

GOLDIE TAKES A DEEP BREATH AS SOON AS SHE STEPS OUTSIDE THE front doors of the hospital. She hasn't left her mother's side all day and desperately needs the break.

She scans the hospital's modest garden and park for Tommy. There are people enjoying the ever-so-slight drop in temperature as the summer sun begins its descent. As she enters the grassy area, her eyes land on the back of a familiar head of dark hair—but it's not her best friend's.

"What are you doing here?"

Teo stumbles a little as he turns to look at her. Before he tries to step forward, he notices the distance she left between them and stands in place.

It's only been a handful of days since Goldie last saw him, but she gives him a quick once-over, already looking for signs of change. There are no white streaks in the tousled curls, no new creases along his handsome brow. His eyes, however, are hollowed. She recalls her conversation with Eli and Jordan. Teo's granddaughter said she hasn't seen him so sad in a long time.

Goldie thinks she should be feeling some form of vindication. She wants to righteously shout, "Serves you right for lying to me, you son of a bitch!" and escape the whole mess. Instead, the evidence of his sorrow only compounds her own.

"I got lucky," Teo says, his tone upbeat.

And just like that, empathy flies out the window.

What. The. Hell?! Goldie thinks as she looks at him like he grew a second head. *We've barely been apart a week, and he's bragging about getting—*

Teo reaches into the tote on his shoulder and pulls out her mom's Chihuahua, who whines his annoyance.

"*Ohhh*," Goldie breathes out, her cheeks burning. "Uh, right, Lucky."

"Are you okay?" Teo asks. "You look flushed."

"I'm fine!" Goldie squeaks. She is not about to admit where her mind went. "Why do you have Lucky? Where's Tommy? He texted that he was out here."

Teo clears his throat. "He let me bring Lucky so I could get a chance to check on you."

"But he knows you lied to me. I didn't tell him everything yet because I was afraid he'd roundhouse kick your head off."

"I'm surprised to still have my head too," Teo admits. "But I told him the whole truth, and he was really sympathetic and understanding."

Goldie's eyes narrow into coin slots.

Teo's lips sputter as he blows out a breath. "Plus, he wants to get into my son's pants, so he's being nicer than he probably would have been."

"Uh, *what*?!" Goldie has never been more at a loss for words. "Huh?"

"Eli and Tommy hit it off today when Jordan went to taekwondo class."

Goldie takes a moment to consider Teo's son with her best friend. Tommy wields easy smiles and "I gotcha" charms to great effect as a car salesman, but it's hard for him to find people he thinks are worth going beyond a few beers with and carving space for in his busy life. He has so much energy and drive that always need to be channeled.

Eli, on the other hand, seems more reserved, thoughtful, and honestly, slightly befuddled (although that's probably due to being understandably anxious over meeting Goldie). His devotion to his daughter and father and the unflinching self-awareness of his struggles are all signs of great integrity. There's a stiffness to him though. Too hesitant, too careful. He might need some of Tommy's intensity and big-hearted nature. And Goldie knows that Tommy could definitely learn to take it easy sometimes and act more graciously.

Once the initial shock dies down, Goldie finds herself pleased by the news. She can't quite admit it to Teo though, and Tommy still colluded with him behind her back. "I'm going to have a long, uncomfortable, brutal talk with Tommy the next time I see him."

Teo rubs his neck like he fully expects that roundhouse kick to happen after all. Then the puppy starts to whine some more, and he looks to Goldie for instructions.

"You should probably put him in the bag so he can go back to sleep. I still need to sneak him into the hospital."

Teo nods and does as he's told. After depositing the puppy, he steps toward her, slow and easy, his eyes locked on hers.

At that moment, Goldie feels like an actual marigold rooted to the soil. She's missed Teo's presence, his light and warmth. He often compared her to the sun, and she thought the same of him. Without Teo, she's been wilting, withering away.

"Here you go," Teo says softly as he hands Goldie the tote.

She could avoid touching his hand to take it. Instead, Goldie threads her arm through the loops of the handles and brings his hand to her shoulder.

Teo takes the hint and brings his other hand around to her back to hug her tightly. "Oh honey, I'm so sorry about your mom."

Goldie presses herself as hard as she can into him. The wilting flower is now plucked, never to grow as she once did in the sun's embrace—yet still appreciating the warmth.

"How's she doing?"

"Already complaining about the stale hospital air and scratchy bed sheets."

Teo huffs. "That's a relief."

Neither says anything else for a while. Teo seems to need this embrace as much as Goldie, and both indulge in it for as long as the other will allow.

After several minutes, Goldie breaks the hold and steps back.

She scrutinizes Teo from top to bottom. "How old are you today?"

"You know the truth, Goldie."

She gestures to his face and body. "What did you see in the mirror this morning?"

"Do you mean am I starting to look old again?"

Goldie only shrugs.

"I'm not going to start looking older until a month has passed from my last dose. Although, honestly, I tend to look closer to 30 by the end of the month, before I take the Serum again."

"30, huh?" Goldie says thoughtfully. "Do you think you would have seriously asked me to marry you before then?"

Slowly, Teo seems to realize what Goldie's getting at. "I was serious about marrying you in the garden a few weeks ago."

"When would you have tried again? On our one-year anniversary?"

"That's a totally sensible benchmark for two people to be together before deciding to take the next step."

"Recent revelations have taught me that you're not quite sensible when it comes to us."

"No, I'm not," Teo says with a chuckle. "I was going to wait maybe a few more months. Do something romantic like sing that song I was writing for you."

"You were going to propose in front of everyone at the bar?"

"No, don't worry. I know the song would have been your limit for public displays of affection. I'd have asked when we were alone, down on one knee with a ring." Teo pins his gaze on her. "Would you have said yes?"

"Yeah, I would have."

His mouth falls open.

Goldie looks up at the dimming sky, trying to hide how vulnerable she feels. "It turns out that I'm not so sensible when it comes to us either."

CHAPTER 13

GOLDIE'S LATE TO WORK MONDAY MORNING BUT DOESN'T CARE one bit and dares anyone to even jokingly call her out on it.

Upon reaching her desk, she goes about the usual routine: stuffing away her oversized purse, cranking up her dinosaur of a desktop PC, contemplating whether she's exhausted enough to ding the environment by making a better-tasting coffee with a K-Cup instead of her usual instant, skimming the to-do list she left herself Friday, wondering if she can put off opening her email for another hour—

"What the fuck are you doing here?"

Goldie side-eyes Amber for startling her out of her reverie. "I know I'm late, but it's still too early for jump scares."

"I mean it." Her friend puts her hands on her hips. "What the *fuck* are you doing here?"

"I, uh, work here?" Goldie says, pitching her voice into a question. "Or did I get laid off? Goddamn it, was there a buyout I missed?"

"No, Goldie! How come you're here instead of at home with your mother?"

"She's managing. She's sensitive to light on screens but made me turn the TV on to old Lifetime movies so she can at least listen. She likes to come up with conspiracy theories about our neighbor because he owns an old white van the creepy loner-killer-kidnapper-cult leader always uses in those movies. Anyway, Penny should be coming by to check on her in a bit."

"But you've been through hell! You can take a few days off to recover."

"I appreciate your concern, but I don't need time off. I just need to get back to work."

When Goldie reaches for her mouse, Amber grabs it and holds it out of reach.

"No," Amber says.

Goldie scrunches her nose. "What do you mean, '*No*'?"

"I mean you're not burying yourself in work."

"I'm *fine*." Her voice comes out thready, strained, and very much not fine.

Amber puts down the mouse and grabs Goldie's hand to drag her onto her feet.

"Wh-what are you doing? Where are we going?"

Her coworker doesn't answer as she pulls the reporter across the newsroom into their executive editor's office without knocking.

Manning slowly folds over the morning's edition he's reading to see who barged in. "Uh, good morning? What's going on?"

Goldie shrugs and opens her mouth to speak, but Amber stands in front to interrupt her. "Goldie's mom almost died this weekend."

"*What?!*" Goldie and Manning both shout.

"She fell super hard and cracked her skull," Amber brutally summarizes.

"Jesus, Goldie!" Manning puts the paper down and stands up. "Why didn't you tell me? How's she doing? What the fuck are you doing here?" He echoes Amber's question from before.

As if she was the one who hit her head, Goldie blinks dazedly while trying to grasp the situation she's been thrown into. "Well, uh—"

"Have you ever met Goldie's mother?" Amber asks. She keeps talking before Manning can get out a simple no. "Such a fragile, delicate flower of a woman. It's a miracle that her head didn't splatter like a dropped melon."

Goldie cringes at the image. *What the hell is she up to?*

"She's resting at home now. Thank God!" Amber looks upward and clasps her hands together. "Thank you, sweet baby Jesus Savior Lord."

"Uh, yeah." Manning does a half-hearted sign of the cross. "Amen?"

"Amen!" Amber shouts, covering her heart with her hand, her

face overwrought with emotion. "It's going to be a long, hard road to recovery for Mrs. Hays, who left her homeland to sacrifice and toil in the land of opportunity to ensure a bright future for Goldie, her precious little girl and only child, who would surely not be the award-winning journalist we all know and love without the angel on Earth that is her mother."

"Wow," Goldie whispers under her breath. Amber obsessively watching every single thing with Viola Davis has apparently inspired some latent acting ability. Her friend deserves an Oscar.

"How can I help?" Manning asks. "What can I do?"

"It is so heartwarming to hear you ask. And to think that there are some people around here who call you a prick!"

Manning looks surprised. "People call me a prick?"

"Can you believe it?" Amber says with wide eyes and false innocence (and yet again, Goldie fixates on Amber's Viola Davis crush; seriously, she *cried* when *How to Get Away with Murder* was canceled). "But I was never one of them. You know why? Because I knew that when a day like this came and someone like our dear Goldie needed to ask for at least a month off to be with her beloved mother, you wouldn't hesitate to grant such a simple yet necessary request."

"A month?" Goldie mouths. "Wait, no!" she says louder. "What about the Crown Serum story? I still need to turn that in."

"You're almost finished with it, right?" Manning asks. "You did the interview with Sarah Crown?"

Goldie nods.

"Were you planning on doing any other interviews?"

"No, that's it," she admits. "She was the last."

"Then work on it out of the office. The anniversary is still weeks away. That should be plenty of time for you to finish it and have the freedom to do whatever else you need to do. Plus, not being here will keep you from taking any other assignments, which I know you've been doing behind my back."

"But Lloyd—"

"No buts, Goldie." Manning sits back down. "God, you love that word."

"She really does," Amber adds.

Goldie literally bites her tongue.

"Goldie, take all the time you need," Manning says. "When I see you back here, your mother's head better be strong enough to headbutt a goat, and you should be so refreshed that you won't be fazed by covering the upcoming soul-crushing election season."

The reporter is completely lost for words. She stares blankly at the executive editor, who takes the book *How to Win Friends and Influence People* from the shelf behind him. Amber bumps her and motions her head in his direction, willing her to understand her meaning.

"Um, thanks, Lloyd," Goldie mutters.

Manning waves her away without looking up from his book. "Why is there a section about kicking beehives in here? What the fuck does that have to do with making people like me?"

Amber guides a dumbstruck Goldie out of the office, much like how she brought her there. This time, though, she's gentler, holding her hand like she's supporting her weight. When they reach the reporter's desk, Goldie collapses into her chair and dazedly looks around the newsroom.

There's the Writer reliably at her desk with too many document windows to count open on her screens.

There's Sam Fairbanks, senior op-ed columnist and veteran journalist, on the phone, probably sweet-talking somebody to get the scoop on the latest infighting in the state capital.

There's Martin Crane, the sports editor, regaling one of the summer interns about his time covering NASCAR greats Richard Petty and Dale Earnhardt.

There's Dove Cooper, the features editor, trying to brainstorm a story on the local dating scene that works in a *Love Island* angle because she loves every tawdry second of that show.

There's the clacking of news reporter George Fontaine's keyboard behind the precariously piled newspapers and documents on his desk.

And there's Amber, the lone full-time photographer, staring at Goldie with concern. "I'm sorry I had to do that."

Goldie shakes her head in disbelief. "What am I supposed to

do with a whole month off?"

"Holy hell." Amber rubs her forehead. "Only you would treat time off like a death sentence. You need this. A lot has happened to you in a short time. Go figure shit out!"

Goldie frowns. "Okay, you're right."

"Thank you!" Amber sputters. "Now, I've got some photos to edit. I'm giving you five minutes before I look back over here. I better not see you." Despite the stern attitude, she gives Goldie's hand a squeeze. "Call me later."

Goldie nods and offers her friend a lopsided smile. When Amber turns to walk away, she begins to use her five minutes to think about where to start the "Go figure shit out" process.

She definitely doesn't want to talk to Teo right now. There's no conquering that hill just yet. Maybe Eli and Jordan? They were lovely, and Goldie's honestly looking forward to meeting them again, but her ego won't allow her to reach out to them so soon after their initial meeting.

Then there's her mother. That prompts Goldie to check her phone, which, sure enough, shows a few texts:

PENNY
Your mom was trying to make kimchi!! 🫨

PENNY
I offered to make it for her instead so she wouldn't exert herself. 💪

PENNY
I've made a terrible mistake. 😵

PENNY
OMG, she's such a perfectionist. It's just f-ing kimchi! 😤 🤬

Goldie huffs in amusement. Even her friend's typically bubbly, easygoing nature is no match for her mother's sharp criticisms and exacting scrutiny. She texts back:

Thanks for everything, Pen! I owe you big time!

That just leaves one person for Goldie to talk to. It's a little early to go to the dealership and interrupt Tommy's work though. Maybe she can check a few emails while—

Suddenly, a rolled-up newspaper flies onto her desk and slides to a stop at her keyboard. The reporter jumps back and squeaks while looking to see where the projectile came from.

Amber's staring her down and pointing at the exit. "Get the fuck outta here, Goldie!!!"

Goldie grabs her purse and escapes out the door without looking back.

"YOU'VE CONVINCED ME, MAN. I'LL BUY THE CAR."

That was easier than Tommy expected. "Great, let me go—"

"*But*," the customer interrupts, "no offense, I have to at least try to make a deal. I'm not going to be paying sticker price like a sucker."

"Okay," Tommy says warily, "what price are you looking for?"

"This is the best I'm willing to do." He pauses and holds his hand out in a "wait for it" gesture. "No money down and no payments until 2035."

Tommy ponders possibly needing a hearing test and asks, "You mean the *year* 2035?"

The customer nods to confirm the stupid proposal.

The car salesman is rendered speechless for a full minute. By the time his tongue starts to work again, it's too late to explain basic market economics to the customer because someone screams for him from across the showroom.

"Tommy!"

He looks toward the entrance to see Goldie fast approaching, the clicks of her heels steadily getting louder.

"Oh shit," Tommy mutters.

The customer hears him. "You better run, dude. Your girl looks *pissed*."

Not for the first time, Tommy wishes he could legally and with good conscience use martial arts to break the noses of certain irritating customers. He shakes off the thought and grabs the closest coworker. "Hey, Reyes, do me a favor?"

"Uh, sure." Reyes gives a distressed look at the hand wrinkling his pressed dress shirt. "What's up?"

"I need you to inform this customer what the word *buy* means."

Tommy thrusts the poor guy at the awful customer and strides over to meet his friend. "Hey, Golds. What are you doing here?"

"You're taking an early lunch."

"Is everything okay? Is it your mother?"

"She's fine. She's busy bossing Penny around to make an impossibly perfect kimchi."

"Then what's going on?"

"Don't play dumb." Goldie gives Tommy a withering look. "You're going to explain why you sent Teo to the hospital to see me."

"Did it not go well?"

"It went fine. That's not the point. You plotted behind my back when I didn't want to see him yet."

"That's BS, and you know it." Tommy looks around the dealership and thinks better of saying anything more. "Look, let me tell the others I'm taking off for lunch early, and I'll meet you at Starbucks."

"Fine!" she shouts. The word echoes around the showroom, garnering more attention. Goldie does a quick turnaround on her heels and clicks right back out the door.

"You should have run like I told you!" the idiot customer heckles.

Tommy sighs and gets his keys.

When he arrives at Starbucks, Goldie's sitting outside at a table with an umbrella, sipping what Tommy suspects is her usual dirty chai latte. She motions to the chair next to her and a venti-sized cup on the table. "I already got your liquid heart attack."

Tommy snorts at the description of his usual order of a regular coffee with two shots of espresso and a shit-ton of Stevia. He sits and takes a few sips in the hopes it can offer the courage he'll need to get through this conversation.

"Why did you help him?" Goldie asks, picking their argument right back up.

"Why did you hide the truth?" he counters.

"You know why. You two barely got along, and I didn't need to worry about you fighting with him."

"I wouldn't have hurt him!"

"I'm not talking about you physically fighting him. I know you're better than that, but you would've tried to intimidate him."

"He lied to you!"

"And I'm a grown-ass woman, Tommy! I didn't want to worry about a confrontation between you two. I needed to deal with this on my own."

"Oh, you mean by not dealing with it at all? Because that's what you would have done. You would have shut me and the world out. Probably worked yourself to death too. I'm surprised you're not at the paper right now, even after what happened with your mom."

Goldie casts her eyes down. "My editor is forcing me to take vacation time."

The defeat in her tone reduces the heat of their exchange. Tommy blows out a breath and doesn't speak for a long time before admitting, "You're right. I would have pushed Teo around a bit if I hadn't met Eli and Jordan beforehand."

Goldie's mouth quirks at the mention of the duo. "They are way too adorable."

"I know, right!" Tommy exclaims. "It's some superpower they have."

"They could convince Republicans and Democrats to compromise."

"If they said aliens were real, the world would believe them."

They share a laugh, and Goldie's eyes twinkle with something wicked. "So, you and Eli, huh?"

Tommy groans. "Of course Teo told you."

"I was not prepared to hear that, especially with how much he looks like Teo."

"There are differences," he says, cheeks getting hot. "He's taller."

"That's the Nikes." Goldie chuckles. "How's it been going with you two?"

Tommy shrugs. "Not a whole lot to tell. We just met Saturday."

Goldie waits for him to admit more.

"And we spent most of Sunday together."

She waits again, this time impatiently winding her hand to reel more out of him.

"And we talked all last night." He rubs his tired eyes as evidence. "This past weekend has been exhausting."

"Worth it though?"

"Hell yes. He's so great, Goldie."

She gives a warm smile. "I'm really happy for you."

Tommy feels the sudden urge to reach out for her hand, but he fights it. Like he told Eli, it's something they don't do, a boundary they've never overstepped. Tommy wouldn't even be doing it for any reason other than friendly reassurance—especially now. "It's weird though."

"What is?"

"Me seeing your boyfriend's son."

Goldie's smile disappears.

Tommy matches her sudden frown. "How did it go at the hospital with Teo?"

"He said he wanted to check on me. He held me." She starts picking at the paper sleeve of her drink. "I'm sorry I got mad at you. You were right. I wanted to see him. I wanted to be comforted by him."

"Have you made any decisions?"

"No. I understand a lot more though. I get why Teo lied, but I'm still hurt. I feel ..." Goldie pauses and rips the sleeve off the cup. "I feel robbed."

"Of what?"

"The life I wanted with him."

Tommy, yet again, wishes he lacked a conscience so he could freely break noses. Teo is so lucky he has an attractive son. "I would be the last person to defend him or tell you how to deal with this situation—"

"You helped him find a way of seeing me without asking or informing me about it."

"Okay, I am not above making certain assumptions based on my history with you," Tommy admits. "Don't act like you haven't done the same."

"When?"

"When you didn't tell me the whole truth about Teo."

"You admitted I was right!"

"You were!" Tommy assures her. "And I'm right that you need to let go of this grudge sooner rather than later."

"What are you talking about?"

"You need to forgive him."

"What is with everyone pushing me to forgive him so soon? It hasn't even been ten days since Teo told me everything. I need more time."

"Don't you think we've wasted enough time though?"

"What do you mean?"

"Eli told me about the wreck that killed his mother," Tommy rasps. "God, Goldie, we can't keep holding on to how we think things *should* be. Life is too short."

He shoves his coffee aside and leans forward, wanting to get closer to his best friend while talking about something so emotional. Holding hands might have always been off the table, but proximity wasn't.

Goldie's jaw flexes in a concerning way, her molars probably on the brink of grinding to nothing. After a minute passes, her lips part just enough for words to trickle out. "Knowing he's a good guy who regrets his mistake isn't enough." She takes a breath, then adds too softly, "Not yet, at least."

Tommy can relate. He hasn't sorted out his opinions of Teo either. And now he's interested in the man's son? Yeah, the level of complicated could trigger migraines.

"Fair enough," he says. "Just don't shut me out again. Don't shut everyone out."

Goldie chugs the rest of her drink and suddenly finds the umbrella they're sitting under fascinating.

"What is it? What else haven't you told me?"

"Nothing! *You* know absolutely everything there is to know."

"Then why are you acting so shifty?"

"I, um, still haven't told my mom."

"Your mom doesn't know?! How could you not tell her?"

"She's been through a lot."

"What does she think is going on?"

"All she knows is that Teo didn't go to Europe and that I'm mad at him."

Tommy shakes his head.

"Oh, don't judge me! You try telling your mom that your boyfriend was hiding how much older he is and how he has a grown son and a granddaughter." Goldie folds her arms. "See how easy it is for you."

"Okay, yeah, your case is admittedly a bit extreme."

"Y'think?!"

"But you gotta tell her, Goldie! I know you hate confrontations with her, but she needs to know the truth."

"She'll say, 'I told you so,' and give me grief about how bad I am at judging people."

"She might surprise you."

Goldie responds with a glare.

"Fine, even if she does react like you think, so what? This is a huge dilemma you're facing. Don't leave the important people in your life out of it."

Goldie squints and tilts her head like she's scrutinizing him. "Not even three days since you met Eli, and love's already made you a sage."

"Quit labeling it love. We're just getting to know each other."

"And look where that got me and Teo."

Tommy rolls his eyes. "I still can't believe he's Eli's father. This is some *Twilight* shit."

"How is this like *Twilight*?"

"The beautiful, sad girl"—Tommy points to her (to which she rolls her eyes right back)—"falls for the stranger with a mysterious past who ends up secretly being ancient as dirt. Meanwhile, her *much hotter* best friend's feelings go unrequited, and he ends up bonding with their freaking kid."

Goldie's face goes slack. "My God, you're right."

Tommy throws up his hands. "We could have been married and divorced by now like normal people. But thanks to you, we're in a YA novel."

"Shut up!" She laughs and kicks him using the very pointy toe

of her black pump. "I can't unsee it!"

"I bet you even have a playlist of grandiose emo music."

Now Goldie seems totally offended. "My playlist is much more eclectic."

"*Of course* it is, you music snob," Tommy teases with a smile. Then his phone vibrates, and the smile grows to full wattage.

"Is it your Renesmee?" Goldie asks in a sickly sweet tone, then hums the chorus of (and Tommy has two younger sisters, so shut-the-fuck-up about him knowing this) "A Thousand Years" by Christina Perri from the last couple *Twilight* movies.

Tommy's face screws up in disgust.

"What? You're the one who compared Eli to the creepy vampire baby."

He groans and answers Goldie's mock question. "Yes, it's Eli. We're trying to make plans this week." He reads the message and hesitates before relaying it. "He says Jordan can't make it to Thursday's class."

"Why?"

"Teo's surgery."

Goldie pulls in her lips and stays quiet. With the sleeve gone, she starts tearing away at the empty paper cup.

"Are you going to be there?" Tommy asks when the silence stretches too long.

His friend closes her eyes, shutting him out the only way she can with them so close.

"Teo has Eli and Jordan with him," Goldie says, her voice noticeably rough. "He'll be fine without me."

———————

"Need more gochugaru," Goldie hears her mother say as she steps into the kitchen and takes in the scene on the floor.

Penny's eyes are burning with challenge. She looks ready to chuck the entire ten-pound bag of red chili powder in the garbage and abruptly declare the kimchi-making process complete.

"I put exactly the amount you told me to when I mixed the seasoning."

"No taste," Sun declares. "My kimchi always tasty. Should be so hot you spit fire." She tries to grab the bag to add more herself.

Penny pulls the bag away and practically hugs it. "Okay, I'll add some more," she says, and pours in an indiscriminate amount.

[pouring]

Holy cow, Ma still hasn't said stop.

[pouring]

Poor Penny. She looks seriously nervous.

[pouring]

Damn, Ma's stomach must be made of iron.

[pouring]

The freaking bag's more than half empty!

"Okay, stop!" her mother shouts.

"Oh thank God!" Penny slams the bag down on the floor and takes a breather to check on Tyler. Her youngest child is showing Lucky how to roll a treat ball to get the contents out. Serena and Corey are at summer day camps, so at least Penny hasn't had to keep tabs on her other children while committing Korean culinary crimes.

"Now, more salt," Sun commands.

"Absolutely not!" Penny shrieks, her cupid's bow lips forming a perfect circle of offense.

Goldie doesn't even need to taste the cabbage to know that Penny's right. "It doesn't need more salt, Ma."

Before her mother can come back with a jab about not knowing what the hell they're talking about because of their weak American tongues, Goldie checks on her condition. "How's your head?"

"How you think? Like someone hammer my skull."

Goldie winces sympathetically. Her mother waves it off.

"Why you home so early?"

The urge to pour more salt onto the cabbage to distract her mother is strong. Instead, Goldie succumbs to the talk that needs to happen and sits on the floor with the two women. "I'm on, uh, vacation."

Penny scowls. "You can't call taking a half day a vacation."

Goldie side-eyes her friend. "I was strongly encouraged by

my editor and very willingly agreed to take a month away from the office."

Jaws unhinge in close succession. You'd think a ship sank or a plane crashed or Bigfoot was spotted.

"You sure you not fired?" her mother asks.

Penny has the audacity to nod her mutual wonderment.

"I'm not fired, Ma! You got hurt, and you need to be watched. I can't ask Penny to stay with you the whole time."

"You really can't," Penny agrees. Sun's eyes narrow at her. "Uh, not that I don't enjoy seeing you, Imo."

"I'm fine! I take care myself."

Goldie full-on growls. "It's only been two days since your accident, and you're already trying to do physical work. Why do we need a two-year supply of kimchi all of a sudden?"

"I not die, so no excuse to be lazy."

"Jesus, Ma! It's not enough that you *didn't die*. You need to get healthy again, and I obviously can't trust you to do that alone right now."

Her mother stares her down for a solid minute. Typically, Goldie would shrink from her gaze, but she's very done with her mother's flippant attitude toward her health and stares back.

"Fine!" Sun surprisingly is the first to break eye contact. "You stay home and take care of me. You owe me anyway. Eighteen hour—"

"Of labor pain," Goldie finishes the statement. "Yes, I know."

"But why whole month? Really, I feel little better already. I not need that long."

Goldie remains silent and stares vacantly down at the deep crimson of the kimchi seasoning. Red happens to be her favorite color, representing love and passion to her. The all-consuming feeling she wanted with someone.

After everything that's happened, and despite the issues and doubts that linger, Goldie is certain of one thing—she found that feeling with Teo.

But maybe real love isn't meant to be that way.

"What else wrong?" her mother asks.

"I, um, need time to figure a lot out." Goldie takes a shaky breath and looks back up at her mother and Penny. She tries to school her face and catches herself sniffling and blinking away tears. "Teo and I are separated."

"Like, broken up?" Penny asks.

"For now."

"What he do?" Sun asks.

"This is going to sound unbelievable," Goldie starts, "but Teo's been lying about how old he really is. He's about to turn 62 and uses the Serum."

The astonished expressions return to the women's faces.

"He lied to you about that?" Penny squeak-asks. Goldie nods. "62? Really?" she asks, even squeakier. Goldie nods again.

"Wow, Serum do good work," her mother remarks.

"Seriously?!" Goldie barely holds herself back from screaming the word. "That's the first thing you have to say about it? Shouldn't you be full of outrage that he lied to your daughter?"

"Of course I'm mad. But I already know he lying about something. I'm surprised he lie about that. He have perfect baby face." Sun turns to Penny. "Can you tell?"

"No! I really thought he was in his 20s."

"Good to know I wasn't the only gullible one," Goldie bites out.

"How he pay for Serum?" her mother asks. "He just musician."

"He's been lying about that too. He's a retired investor."

"He rich?"

"He worked. He was successful," Goldie corrects, similar to how she was corrected by Teo, falling back on defending him despite her anger. "He also has a grown son and a granddaughter— and he lost a wife. He's lived a whole life that he hid from me."

"That why you mad?" her mother asks in her judging tone.

"Of course that's why! You don't think I should be mad?"

"That good reason, but I think you mad too 'cause he old."

Goldie wants to deny it at first without knowing why. She doesn't need to be ashamed that she's mad about that. "There's a lot that comes with being in your 60s. You know that, Ma. You take too many medications to count, and you're so fragile. You're lucky you didn't hurt yourself worse when you fell. And now I have to worry about Teo having surgery."

"Wait," Penny says, "you didn't say anything about that."

"It's why he had to confess about the Serum. He's getting surgery this week for cysts on his liver."

"Is he going to be okay?" Penny asks.

"The cysts aren't cancerous. He should be fine after getting them removed." Goldie second-guesses herself as soon as she finishes the sentence. She doesn't actually know the details. How long is he going to be in the hospital? Will recovery be tough? Could the cysts return?

"You go to hospital?" Sun asks.

"No. Teo's son and granddaughter are here in town to be with him for everything."

"You should go."

Goldie's eyebrows shoot up. "Why? He has his family. He doesn't need me."

Sun opens her mouth to say more but brings a hand to her head instead and winces in pain. She moans and takes a moment to regain control before addressing Goldie again.

"There two kind of hard heads. I have good kind; it save my life." She points at her head to get the meaning across, then turns her finger to Goldie. "You have bad kind. You most stubborn person I ever see."

"How am I being stubborn?"

"You love Teo?"

Hearing the words *love* and *Teo* in the same breath from her mother's mouth is jarring. "Um, yes," Goldie says around the lump that's formed in her throat.

"He love you?"

Goldie thinks back again to being held by him in the park outside the hospital. "Yes," she responds without a doubt.

"Then stop making stupid choice!"

"What stupid choice am I making?"

"Not go to hospital for him!" Her mother takes a few deep breaths, hopefully keeping the ache at bay. When she seems composed, she continues. "I say you stubborn 'cause you always do this. You hide in pain. I get you mad. You have good reason, but what more important is you still love him."

Goldie squeezes her eyes shut, her last defense when her mother wields her cutting words.

"If you not go, you regret it," Sun continues. "Don't worry about future. Be there now when you can—like you do for me."

Goldie hears rustling that forces her eyes back open. She catches Penny scooping some salt in her hand and spreading it over the cabbage. Her friend is teary and sniffling but tries to shrug off the emotions as she glances at Goldie's mother.

"That's all the extra salt you're getting."

CHAPTER 14

"HI, MAMI!"

Simone waves at Jordan on Eli's phone screen. "How are you two doing?"

"I'm having so much fun," Jordan says. "Tommy taught me how to punch a kidney."

"For fun?"

"For self-defense," Eli says. "Tommy's her martial arts teacher."

"And Daddy's new boyfriend."

Simone supernovas with glee. *"Boyfriend?!"*

Eli groans. "I can't call him my boyfriend. We're talking though."

"And kissing," Jordan adds. "They do a lot of kissing."

He pokes his daughter in the spot where her kidney should be. "You should focus less on the offensive part of Tommy's lessons and more on the defensive."

"I'm not supposed to protect my kidneys from my dad." She pouts and rubs the spot like it hurts.

"Ohhh," Simone crows. "Tell me about this Tommy."

Before Eli can open his mouth, Jordan starts gushing. "He's so awesome! He's a great martial artist. He can break big cement blocks with his elbows. And he's really funny too."

"He tells corny dad jokes," Eli says.

"They're funny!" Jordan insists. "Don't pretend you don't laugh."

Eli absolutely does not admit that he finds the endless stream of puns and wordplay at all endearing and part of the man's charm.

"I asked an I.T. person one time how to make a motherboard," Tommy *said after one of Eli's work calls.*

"What did they say to do?"

"He said, 'Tell her to watch paint dry.'"

Tommy easily ducked Eli's balled-up napkin. The quick bastard.

"What's he look like?" Simone asks. "I bet he's tall. Your daddy always goes for the tall ones."

Eli side-eyes the screen.

"I'll send you a photo," Jordan says, reaching for her phone to text her mother. She chooses one Eli took of Tommy and Jordan after class yesterday. She'd successfully split her first board, and she's proudly showing one piece while Tommy has the other.

The camera's off while Jordan's mother looks at the photo on her phone. "I knew it!" Simone shouts. "Tall!"

Eli rolls his eyes. "Yes, he's tall."

"And has the body of a *Greek god*," she says with an impressed whistle. Tommy's wearing a very tight white tank top in the photo, having discarded his uniform top since the class was over. "Honey, get over here! Check out Eli's hot new boyfriend."

There's some rustling, and then they hear her husband's voice. "Wow, good for you, Eli."

Eli groans for what feels like the hundredth time during this call. "Yeah, thanks."

"Hey, Jonathan!" Jordan calls out.

"Hey, baby! You having fun?"

"It's been great!"

The camera turns back on, and their faces—Simmy's lovely freckled nose and cheeks and Jonathan's unfortunate mustache—fill the screen. "That's good to hear," Jonathan says. "We miss you already."

"Miss you too. But it's just going to be a month. Abuelo needs us."

Their faces turn serious. "How is he?" Simone asks.

Eli shrugs. "He's doing his best to seem fine."

"He's worried about the surgery?" she asks. "Is it that serious?"

"He'll have to stay the night afterward. But I don't think it's just the surgery. It's everything with Goldie too. I haven't seen him this lost in a long time."

Simone frowns in thought before quirking her lips. "Don't worry too much, Eli. He'll get through this. There's one thing I know for sure about the Estradas. They get back on their feet better than ever."

Eli huffs at the vote of confidence. "Thanks, Simmy."

TEO METHODICALLY TURNS ON THE STAGE LIGHTS ONE BY ONE, leaving the rest of the bar dark. The space shrinks to this singular altar. A place to pray, to confess one's sins. To be absolved and redeemed.

He walks toward the lights as if being moved by an unseen hand and circles the modest stage a few times, tracing the circumference with the rhythm of his steps. When he comes to a stop, it's in front of the small plaque on the steps. The shiny bronze features a name with Greek origins that fittingly means light.

Helena was his guiding light in life.

"Oh, Montañita," Teo says, looking upward. "How're you doing in heaven?"

In his imagination, such a place can only exist in the clouds. It comforts him to think of Helena high above, watching over him, their son, and their granddaughter.

She's listening to him right now.

"I need to talk, Helena." Teo sits down on the steps next to the plaque, similar to how Goldie was sitting when he finally told her the whole truth. "You probably already know that I met someone. And, yes, I know it took me long enough. You can't give me grief about that. You *can* give me grief about how I completely screwed up the greatest love I've known since you."

Teo had told his son that it was pointless to regret the time that's gone by. Maybe he could have remarried sooner and lived out his days with someone, but it wouldn't have been with Goldie.

And he wants it to be with her.

Since he technically can't kick his own ass, Teo wishes there were rocks or something else to kick, some physical outlet for his frustration. "I just couldn't fathom the possibility of someone like her giving me a chance. Well, the real me." He groans before correcting himself with the word he actually means. "The *old* me."

He looks down at his smooth hands. "Fuck me, I can't believe I'm about to turn 62. When Jordan calls me abuelo, I just don't feel like it.

"I used to think of aging like it was a magical threshold that takes you from partying and living it up to making sure you get the senior citizen discount and always worrying about your prostate," he says, grimacing. "And you're supposed to be absolutely *fine* with it. The grays. The wrinkles and achy joints...

"But I was wrong. There's no one way of feeling and acting at this age." He thinks of Goldie's reaction to hearing he was almost 62. The ever-sensible journalist brought up some very good points about the realities of aging. "Or maybe I'm just fooling myself."

He runs his fingers over the etched letters on the plaque and smiles softly. "I wonder how you'd look now. I bet you would have held on to that sexy librarian style of yours. Pencil skirts and dress shirts with top buttons undone. Glasses and a glossy-straight bob. Would you have colored your hair or let it go gray? Maybe you would have colored it red like you always talked about doing."

He lets out a dreamy sigh, lost in the fantasy of a Helena who had gotten the chance to experience a body matured by time.

"I'm thinking of growing a beard. Give your brother a run for his money." Teo rubs over the stubble. "I wonder if Goldie would like it."

He leans forward and rests his elbows on his knees, again mimicking Goldie on the steps. "Fuck, the things I let her believe! I never thought I could do something like that. The last time I lied was on our first date when I said I knew how to ride a jet ski. Then I nearly *died*, and you dragged my ass out of the water only to insist I get back on the damn thing. 'You can't let one misstep stop you,' you said."

His laugh at the memory comes out hollow. "Does your advice work in this case? Should I try to get Goldie back after what I did?"

Teo gazes at the part of the bar where she sat the night they met.

He was entranced, feeling the thrill of mutual attraction again after a very long time. He couldn't risk losing it with the truth.

With a bone-deep sigh, Teo heaves up his young-old body to stand on the stage and looks out into the shadowed ring that surrounds him. He imagines the crowd enraptured by his performance, singing along and clapping to the beat

"When I'm up here, my age doesn't matter. How I look doesn't matter. I am the most"—he pauses to get the right emphasis—"*myself* up here." He looks at the microphone and stool that he's used for what must be hundreds of performances by now.

"In a way, I'm thankful for this surgery. It's made me face how I feel about myself. For the first time in a while, I'll see what the years have turned me into, and I'll have to decide if that's who I want to be."

Teo thinks he'll be comfortable with what he'll see in the mirror. The wild card is what Goldie will think.

"Goldie deserves a love she shouldn't have to compromise her true self for," he says before stepping off the stage and walking to the bar. He touches the space where his Golden Wonder stretched her hand out to him. "And so do I."

"What's taking so long?" Teo scratches under his papery dressing gown and checks the wall clock. "Do appointments mean nothing anymore?"

Eli arches an eyebrow. "You're in that big of a hurry to get cut open?"

"I'm in a hurry to get this over with. Stupid liver. It's been nothing but trouble for our family."

"Just be grateful it's not more serious like it was with Abuela," his son says.

"What if it had been more serious?" Teo wonders. "What if this were some sick twist of fate where I died, and you and Goldie ended up together after bonding over your mutual mourning of me?"

Jordan jerks her gaze up from the round of Candy Crush she's playing on her father's phone. "That's real messed up, Abuelo."

Eli full-body cringes. "Why would that happen?"

"You guys are closer in age. It would be ironic."

"But her having been with you makes Goldie the equivalent of a stepmother to me. Have you been watching telenovelas?"

"Korean dramas, actually. Thought they might help me connect with Goldie's mom."

"She didn't like you?"

"She didn't trust me." Teo looks away. "For good reason."

Eli gives his hand a squeeze. His phone then makes a non–Candy Crush noise.

"Papá, it's a text from Tommy." Jordan hands over the phone.

When Eli reads it, his eyes roll. "Tommy hopes the surgery goes well."

"And?" Teo prompts, knowing there's something smartass to follow.

"And that he bought a couple cases of Ensure so you can get the vital nutrients that old people need for a speedy recovery."

Despite his sullen mood, Teo snorts a laugh. "You got yourself a winner there, mijo."

The door opens with a couple of hospital staffers coming into the room.

"Mr. Estrada, are you ready?" one of them asks.

Teo looks at his son and granddaughter and engraves their faces onto his mind, heart, and soul—to fuel his fighting spirit.

He's being fucking melodramatic, of course. He'll be fine after this surgery. But the day will come—sooner than he'd like—when he won't be fine.

He'll be another tragedy for his family to overcome.

"Yeah, let's go," Teo mutters.

As he's swiftly prepared to transport to the operating room, Goldie, of all people, flies through the door.

"Thank God, I caught you!" she says, panting. "I would've been here sooner, but this flipping campus is always under construction, and I had to find a detour, which also means I'm basically parked in the next county, and then all the elevators were taking their sweet time, so I took the stairs." She pauses to catch her breath. "I am so glad I'm not wearing heels today."

Everyone in the room stares at her in silence until the meaning of her arrival fully sinks in, and Teo's face splits into a grin. "You came?"

Goldie's smile is less broad, but it's there. "Yeah, I came."

Teo seizes the opportunity to bask in her presence. The bright flush of her round cheeks—perfectly shaped for his hands to cup while angling their mouths in deep kisses. The wild lion's mane of her dark locks—long and silky and so very tuggable. The drops of sweat sliding down from her neck to her heaving chest, like how she gets while riding his—

Get a grip, you pervy old man.

It's just that he's *missed* her. In all the ways, Teo's missed her so much, and he hadn't realized how disappointed he was that Goldie wasn't here until he saw this unpolished, frazzled version of her standing in front of his gurney.

She's a vision—and he's so grateful to have her here.

"Thank you, Goldie."

She nods and pulls her gaze away from Teo to catch everyone gaping at her. "Oh, um, sorry."

Before Goldie can step aside of her own free will to clear the doorway, Jordan grabs her hand to pull her close. "Hi, Goldie!"

"Hi, sweetheart." Her use of the affectionate term for his granddaughter warms Teo to his core.

"Okay," the nurse says, wariness in her tone. "Are we really ready?"

Teo takes one last look at Goldie standing with his family. "Yes, ma'am. I think we definitely are."

THE WAIT WILL BE A FEW HOURS, SO ELI SUGGESTS A WALK OUTSIDE.

"I'm so happy to see you again!" Jordan gushes. "Does this mean you're getting back together with Abuelo?"

"Jordan," Eli says, "now's not the best time for that."

"But you being here is such a big deal, Goldie."

"Sorry, Jordan. I'm not here to get back together with your grandfather." Jordan's face falls, and Goldie's quick to add, "But I'm glad to see you again too."

Eli's daughter recovers quickly, holding Goldie's hand again to take advantage of having her new favorite person's attention.

"There's so much to tell you. I've been taking Tommy's taekwondo classes and can basically chop down trees with my fists now."

"She broke one board," Eli clarifies.

"I'm going to be a black belt by the time I leave here," Jordan proclaims, unfazed by the correction.

Goldie chuckles. "I don't doubt you're learning a lot from Tommy. He loves martial arts more than anything else in the world."

"He loves Daddy now."

"Ay, madre mía," Eli mutters miserably.

"Your grandfather told me," Goldie says with a smirk. "And Tommy might've said some things too."

"Did he say how much he loves Daddy? Because he totally does."

"Jordie, it hasn't even been a week since we met Tommy. You can't pressure these things."

"Why not?!" Jordan cries out. "You talk all the time and get along great. Just go ahead and admit you're falling in love. Goldie and Abuelo still love each other. Just choose to get back together already. Adults always make everything so complicated, I swear."

Eli glances at Goldie, who's not blinking, apparently stunned by his 11-year-old's blunt love advice.

"Um, well." Goldie seems to scramble for a response. "I still need to work out a lot of issues with your grandpa. But if it makes you feel better, I wish it could be so simple." She pauses for a moment, eyes going distant. "It *was* that simple," she says with a sigh, then leans close to Jordan's ear to speak low and conspiratorially. "And I think your dad and Tommy can be that simple too."

Jordan jumps up and down at the tantalizing possibility for gossip. "Ohhh, what do you know? Did Tommy say something?"

Eli tries to appear peeved by the shameless discussion of his love life but doesn't speak up to stop it. (Hey, he's curious too. Sue him.)

"Well, it's not so much what he said as what he didn't say. He wouldn't stop smiling when we talked about meeting you two. He was texting your dad and making plans with him, and Tommy's not a big planner. He doesn't like looking forward to anything. No expectation means no disappointment."

"That's no fun," Jordan says.

"He's protecting himself." Goldie winces, compounding Eli's

curiosity. "But thanks to you two," she continues, "he's excited again for what's to come."

The idea of being a definite part of Tommy's future should be scary to Eli. After all, they met less than a week ago. It's too much too soon. Instead, it seems … possible. And the more Eli considers it like a fact, something inevitable, possible is no longer a good-enough description.

It's just *right*.

Eli doesn't fight the dopey grin the thought inspires. "I'm glad you could be here today, Goldie."

Jordan's response is less reserved. "Forget only getting a black belt! When they get married, Tommy's going to make me a freaking *grandmaster*!"

TEO WAKES UP WITHOUT COMPLETELY OPENING HIS EYES, CAUTIOUS after his previous experience when a nurse cajoled him to full consciousness and didn't bat an eye as he puked from the nausea caused by the anesthesia.

This time, waking up thankfully involves less queasiness, but he still groans over the confused state of his body. When he feels that he can endure the eye-opening process, the first peek of light makes him groan again. *Fuck*, it feels like knives are stabbing his brain through his eyeballs.

"Abuelo, wake up already!"

The command does the trick to pry his eyelids apart. "Jesus, Jordan! You trying to give me a heart attack?"

"If you're going to have one, you might as well while you're in a hospital."

"That is so warped, Jordie," Eli says. "*Not* having one at all would still be better."

"I could have slapped him awake like they do in movies. Would that have been better?"

"You know it wouldn't!"

"Guys, guys," Teo interrupts, his voice croaky and sounding like he swallowed glass. "I'm just glad to be awake without having a heart attack or needing a slap in the face to make it happen."

"Sorry," Jordan says. "I was getting a little worried."

"It's okay, baby." Teo opens his hand for her to take. "I'm going to assume everything went well."

"Yes?" Eli hesitates, then admits, "Okay, there's good news and slightly less good news."

Teo pleads with his eyes for his son to tell him everything already.

"All right, less good news first. Your doctor had to be a little more aggressive than planned to get the cysts, so your recovery won't be quite as speedy as you were probably hoping. *But* the good news is that your liver is now spotless. Congratulations, Pops!"

The awkward attempt at enthusiasm makes Teo laugh, which triggers a hacking fit. When a straw in a much-needed cup of water is placed in his mouth, he drinks automatically. It's only when he's had his fill that he notices who provided the refreshment.

"Goldie?" His voice is clear as a bell now, the name a balm much like the water.

"Do you need more?"

"No, thank you." Teo takes note of her oversized black-and-white striped top and black jeans. Too casual for a weekday. "You took a day off?"

"Not exactly. I'm on vacation."

"You never take vacation."

Goldie's face twitches. "I was *voluntold* to take time off by my editor—and tangentially by Amber. Except for the Serum article, I'm off a month."

"That's awesome," Teo says. "You deserve it. What're you gonna do?"

"Just take care of my mom, mostly."

"You gotta do something fun too!" Jordan demands. "Can you come to Abuelo's birthday party?"

"Um ..." Goldie turns to Teo for some guidance, but instead of an out like she was probably hoping for, he mirrors his granddaughter's expectant, pleading doe eyes. With a sigh, she caves. "Of course I'll be there."

Teo smiles and offers her his free hand. To his relief, Goldie envelops it with both of hers.

Jordan starts squealing like a teakettle. "You two are sooo cute!"

"Okay, Jordie," Eli says, interrupting a follow-up squeal. "Since Abuelo's in good hands, why don't we fill that pit you call a stomach?" He angles her toward the door, not waiting for a response. "We'll be back, Pops."

Teo nods at his son and granddaughter but keeps his eyes on Goldie. When they're gone, he squeezes her hand. "Hey, thanks again for being here."

A corner of her mouth barely lifts in response.

"How's your mother?"

"She's better. Not a hundred percent, despite how she's acting. I've yelled at her way too many times to stop cleaning the house."

Teo chuckles. "Your mom's too used to working hard. Reminds me of someone else I know."

"That someone else probably hates how slowing down allows for too much time to think."

Teo frowns and wonders how much he should pry. He offers up some of his thoughts first. "I didn't think you'd come. You had every reason not to."

"I wasn't going to," Goldie admits. "You're not gonna believe this, but my mom convinced me."

That does surprise him. "Does she know the truth?"

"Uh, yeah?" she says, not looking at him.

"Really?"

"Okay, I didn't tell her everything until after her accident. But she knows now, and she's not happy with you. At. All."

Teo imagines Goldie's mother concocting creative forms of revenge involving an insane amount of plotting and deep criminal underworld connections.

He ignores the K-drama-fueled thoughts and addresses a serious concern. "Why'd she convince you to see me today, then?"

"She knew I'd regret not being here even after what you did."

Teo's left speechless by the familiar feeling of shame that lances him.

Goldie uses the quiet moment to study his face. The effects of the Serum shouldn't have worn off in any significant way yet. Teo must look like a wreck after the surgery, but he still looks impossibly young—like the person she fell for.

"I still love you," Goldie says in a whisper, somehow knowing where his mind meandered.

The words sound like a burden. Otherwise, Teo'd be elated to hear them. Still, he can't miss the chance to return the sentiment. "I love you too."

"You know, your granddaughter says that if we still love each other, we should just be together again."

"And what do you think?"

"I'm not ready to do that."

Even though Teo expected the answer, the weight of disappointment is heavy.

"But there is one thing I'm ready to do," Goldie says as she sits on the edge of the bed and holds his hand against her heart. "I forgive you, Teo."

"You do?" Teo feels a vulnerability that has nothing to do with his post-surgery state.

Goldie nods. "I've had to confront some brutal truths these last couple weeks. I understand myself better, that's for sure." Her lips quirk, the broadest smile she's managed since he woke up. "And I'm glad I get the chance to know you better too."

Teo's reminded of the time he was thrown off the jet ski during his date with Helena, because Goldie's words do what Helena had done—they save him from drowning. He feels like he can breathe again.

His lies severed the tether of their relationship, but now Goldie's throwing him one of the frayed ends. It's a lifeline to pull himself back up and forgive himself.

Teo takes it.

CHAPTER 15

THE SERUM INTERVIEWS NEED TO BE ORGANIZED INTO THEMATIC parts to roll out the week of the anniversary. Goldie figured out early on that there was no way all of them could be published in one edition, which was completely fine with Manning. After all, it's more content to hype.

The teasers have been running on the front page for weeks:

THE PRICE OF PERFECTION
Find out the real cost of the Crown Serum—
exclusively in the Daily Liberty Press.

FOREVER YOUNG—BUT STILL OLD
To some, the Crown Serum is a luxury. To others, a necessity.
Exclusive testimonials only in the Daily Liberty Press.

Manning also claims that having a weeklong series with user testimonials will build more excitement and drive up readership for the final part, the interview with Sarah Crown, which has been teased most of all:

THE HEAVY HEAD OF SARAH CROWN
THE DAILY LIBERTY PRESS *is the ONLY news outlet*
to have an EXCLUSIVE INTERVIEW with the maker
of the CROWN SERUM. SUBSCRIBE for the
SPECIAL SERUM ANNIVERSARY EDITION.

By the way, Goldie hasn't written that part yet.

Why did Sarah have to place such a decision in her hands? The Serum isn't her responsibility. She's barely making peace with what it's done to her life, and now she has to decide whether the world can handle a version that lasts forever. Goldie can't even judge what conditioner is right for her hair.

Besides the daunting task of writing that crucial last part, the user testimonials are causing her stress too. Throughout the editing process, the reporter has been getting introspective and emotional over some of the stories, especially Soledad Branigan's. Given recent events in Goldie's life, Soledad's interview reads very differently than the others. Her husband left her after she revealed all her scars. And here's Goldie contemplating whether she'll do the same with Teo.

The vibration of her phone pulls her attention away.

"Hey, Amber."

"How's vacation?"

"You mean mandatory freelancing?"

Amber scoffs. "Of course you've been working."

"I still have the Serum series to work on."

"I thought that was mostly done."

"Yes, *mostly,* which means there's still some left to do."

"You haven't done anything fun?"

"Between worrying about my mother's head and Teo's liver, there hasn't been much else I can do."

"I had a feeling that'd be the case, so you have two hours to get ready."

"What?" Goldie pulls the phone away like it had licked her. "What am I getting ready for?"

"We're going to a charity-auction-slash-dinner-slash-ball."

"Since when do we go to those?"

"The event's for the Environmental Vigilance Effort."

"EVE's a worthy cause, but I'm not paying the couple hundred bucks it probably costs for a plate of food I won't like."

"The Clean Clinic is a major sponsor. We're Connie's plus two."

"That's typically not the number of guests you get."

"Goldie, get glammed up. You're going." Amber hangs up.

The reporter gives the open documents on her laptop a final glance before shutting the lid and dashing to the bathroom to get ready.

After sliding into the one and only gown she owns for the few random times she reports on something big and fancy, Goldie goes to the living room to let her mother know that she's leaving.

Sun is watching an old *Unsolved Mysteries*–style TV show about airplane disasters that reenacts the circumstances of the crash and investigation. Even though they subscribe to every streaming service imaginable, her mother still ends up watching the most random stuff on YouTube.

"Ma, you gonna be all right tonight?"

"I'm not baby. I worry about you. You carry pepper spray?"

"I'm going to a fancy dinner at the country club, not for a run on the shady side of town."

Her mother's face says, "Don't play with me," without uttering the words.

Goldie pulls out her keys to show the small cannister attached. "I always bring my pepper spray."

Sun nods, satisfied, and holds out the puppy. "Tell Noona have fun finding new rich boyfriend."

Lucky does no such thing and instead moves his legs in a cute paddling motion, like he's swimming in air.

"That's not why I'm going! Geez, I've only been apart from Teo a few weeks."

"What you waiting for? You make it work or find new person. You 40. No more time to waste."

"What if I don't want anybody? What's so bad about being alone?"

"It not bad. I choose nobody after your daddy leave, and I can have anybody: rock star, pro wrestler, Orkin bug man." Sun holds up her fingers. "Even *three* soldier ask me marry them!"

"Why didn't you get remarried, then?"

"Because I like alone better. Why you think I move around world? I have too much family in Korea. Here, living hard, but I have room. I breathe."

"See? Why can't I do the same?"

Her mother looks at her with open pity. "It not what *you* want."

Goldie turns away and picks up her purse to shut down the

conversation. "Call me if you need me. Don't rearrange the furniture while I'm gone."

"Why? You think room look bad?" Sun asks, ignoring the passive-aggressive command for her to continue to take it easy.

Goldie slams the door behind her.

THE VENUE IS IN THE HEART OF GOLF COUNTRY, WHICH MEANS Goldie has to circumnavigate courses on one-way streets to get to the place.

Amber and Connie are at the main entrance waiting for her.

"Fashionably late?" Amber asks.

"It's your fault. You gave me two hours' notice," Goldie says as she checks out the couple. Amber is wearing an asymmetrical shimmery black dress, and her curls are barely held back at the sides by sparkly pins. Connie is wearing a royal-blue kimono-style dress with a plunging neckline. Her braids are piled high on her head to ensure no obstruction of the sexy view. Goldie compliments her co-worker's girlfriend first out of spite. "You look absolutely stunning, Connie."

"Thank you, dear." She smiles, opening her arms for a hug. "You look beautiful too. Black with gold-beaded flourishes. It suits you, Goldie."

"Thanks." Goldie's cheeks heat. "And thank you for letting me tag along. This looks like a great event."

"You don't have to front. I know Amber made you come."

"I could have said no."

"No, you couldn't have," Amber says. "I would have gone to your house and dragged you out."

"Quit playing," Connie chides her.

"She's not." Goldie side-eyes Amber. "She did exactly that one year when I decided to not go to the state journalism awards."

"You were journalist of the year!"

"It was a three-hour drive to the ceremony! They could have mailed me the dumb plaque!"

"All right, children," Connie says. "Do you two need a time out?"

Amber rolls her eyes at the patronizing comment.

Goldie takes the scolding seriously, however. "Sorry, Connie." She grabs her friend's arm in apology. "Thank you for inviting me, Amber. Care to escort me in?"

Amber squeezes Goldie's hand in silent return of the apology, then holds out her other arm for her girlfriend. "Let's go in already. We've got free plates of small-portioned, overdesigned food waiting."

As the trio walks through the propped-open double doors, Goldie's immediately swept away to another time. The building itself goes back more than two centuries and reeks of old Southern plantation money. The country club, however, has tried to rehabilitate its history by being the premier place for social justice organizations and for charitable events such as tonight's in honor of EVE. Adding to the throwback feel is the Regency-era aesthetic. It looks like someone on the party committee is a *Bridgerton* fan.

The tables reserved for Clean Clinic guests are already filled (Amber really should have given Goldie more of a heads-up). The women take the empty seats next to Amelia Gardner-St. Vincent and her family.

"Goldie!" Amelia greets her with a smile. "You came!"

Goldie's thrown by the Clean Clinic owner's enthusiasm. "Uh, hello, Amelia. It's nice to see you again."

"You too! Martin, honey, this is Goldie Hays, the reporter who's writing about the Serum."

Amelia's husband nods his very blond head in greeting. He's a Serum user like the rest of his family, but he doesn't lack evidence of his true age. His face has a fullness to it, reflecting the few extra pounds that he carries. His glasses are bifocals that sit on the bridge of his nose, and his posture is poor. He reminds Goldie of a young Ebenezer Scrooge.

"You remember my sons Monty and Mason?" Amelia asks.

The youngest Gardner-St. Vincent sons barely acknowledge her. Goldie thinks Monty at least grunts. Mason's watching something on his phone.

"Nice to see you two when you're not throwing up," Goldie says, not missing the opportunity to point out what dumbasses they are.

"And I don't think you got to meet my two oldest sons. This is

Martin Jr. and his wife, Claudia." The two exchange pleasantries. "And this is Marcus."

The man sitting next to Goldie extends his hand. "Ms. Hays, it's so nice to meet you."

"Nice to meet you too."

"I'm sorry I couldn't be there for your interview. My mother said you were trying to talk to us. Could I still add anything?"

"It's nice of you to offer, but I got a lot of insight from that day at your sister's birthday party. Besides, I'm currently organizing it all. The series comes out in a few weeks."

"I can't wait," Amelia says. "Did you talk to Sarah? She is so aloof. Barely responds to my texts."

"She's certainly busy," Goldie says, trying to be vague. "The interview was insightful, almost overwhelming."

"Ohhh, what did she say?"

"You'll have to wait for the article."

The staff begins to roll out the meals, saving Goldie from more questions. She sighs internally at the plate set in front of her: two thin strips of barely cooked beef drizzled with an unidentifiable sauce and garnished with some garlic.

Her disappointment must be written on her face because Marcus leans over. "Don't worry. That's only the first course."

"I totally knew that," Goldie lies.

He smiles with impossibly straight teeth that glow in the dim banquet room. "I'm sure you did."

Everyone digs in and finishes in less than five minutes, leaving plenty of time for chatter while waiting for the second course.

"Ms. Hays, can I ask a reporter a stupid question?"

"It's Goldie. Sure, shoot."

"Have you ever yelled, 'Stop the presses!'"

"Unfortunately, no."

"Ah." Marcus pouts.

"It turns out that people mostly get their major breaking news from their phones," she says, like this is uncommon knowledge. He plays along and mock gasps. "It just wouldn't be worth the hassle of stopping the press and redoing a page."

"How depressingly practical."

"That's newspapers these days."

Marcus's full lips tilt in a half frown, marring the perfect symmetry of his face. Along with being blond, he's also a Serum user like the rest of his family. Not a crease to be found on the 35-year-old living Ken doll.

"What do you do?" Goldie asks.

"I'm a Clean Clinic marketing specialist." He motions his head to the left. "Connie's my boss."

"And so's your mom," Goldie points out.

"Yes, obviously." He clears his throat. "I've always had an interest in journalism though. To write something with more depth than, 'Clean never gets old. Try our new pore scrub.'"

"Have you tried pursuing other kinds of writing?"

"No, I thought it'd be better to just join the family business. Not everyone can have such opportunities handed to them." Marcus looks at his younger brothers and rolls his eyes. "And certain siblings take their opportunities for granted."

Monty is talking very loudly on his phone, making it clear to everyone at the table that the person on the other end is his agent, and he's very pissed at him. Meanwhile, Mason is holding his phone out in front of him while speaking, which probably means he's livestreaming.

"I can see your point," Goldie concedes, "and I'm not the biggest fan of your brothers, but at least they're pursuing their interests. I complain all the time about my profession, but it's ultimately my passion. You sound like you're stuck with the opportunities, not gratefully embracing them."

Marcus blinks rapidly, considering her words. "This whole conversation took a very unflirtatious turn."

"What do you mean?" Goldie plays back their interaction. "Were you flirting with me?"

"Yeah, I opened with that silly question. Thought I could get some banter going, share a similar interest with you." He laughs with a shake of his head. "You're a very good reporter. You completely cut through to the deep stuff."

"Oh, um." She frowns. "Sorry?"

Marcus laughs again. "No, it's nothing to apologize for. It's refreshing."

"How so?"

"Look around. There are too many people here who look and act like me and my family. All wealthy Serum users pretending to change the world by stuffing our faces. All boring as hell."

"So, you thought you'd flirt with a commoner?"

"No, I thought I'd flirt with an attractive, interesting person."

Goldie stares blankly at him.

"And this whole conversation shows why I was not meant to work or interact outside this privileged bubble. I'm sorry if I offended you, Goldie."

The reporter immediately regrets her crappy, judgmental attitude. "No, I've got a lot of baggage right now."

The next course comes out at that moment. It's some kind of pasta dish with a striking imbalance of the noodle-to-sauce ratio.

"Let's make a deal," Goldie suggests.

Marcus quirks a blond eyebrow. "What kind of deal?"

"Don't let this experience with me keep you from expanding your horizons," she says, picking up her fork to point at her plate. "And I'll do the same with this ridiculous meal."

Her tablemate huffs a laugh. "Okay, deal."

They talk more throughout the other courses. Goldie tells him about her career, and she ends up quasi-interviewing him about the Serum when the topic comes back up. He has sentiments similar to his sister, Angel, both feeling ignorant and awkward around non-Serum users.

At the conclusion of the dinner, the event's organizers signal that the auction portion of the evening will begin shortly, and those who aren't interested can enjoy the bar and dance floor in the venue's east wing.

Since Goldie isn't going to spend money on whatever is up for bidding, she gets up and says her goodbyes to everyone at the table.

Marcus stands with her and holds out his hand to shake. "It was great meeting you, Goldie. I can't wait to read your article."

"It was great meeting you too. Take care, Marcus."

Amber and Connie get up from the table as well, and they move to the ballroom.

"You and Marcus seemed to get along," Connie says.

"Yeah, we had an interesting talk."

"It looked like a lot more than talking," Amber notes.

Goldie side-eyes her friend. "It really wasn't."

"If you say so," Amber placates her. "I was just checking that you were enjoying yourself."

Goldie's snarky response is overridden by La Bouche's "Be My Lover," triggering a piercing squeal from Amber. "This was the shit back in the day!"

She drags Connie and Goldie onto the dance floor to bounce and groove and act like fools for several songs straight. When the straps on Goldie's gladiator-style heels loosen, she signals to the women that she's going to the bar.

Once Goldie has successfully limped to the other room, she uses a stool to balance herself, undoing the shoe completely and slamming it on top of the bar.

"Whoa, that's an epic heel," the person behind the counter says as they pour a drink.

"Yeah, I like my shoes fashionable and borderline lethal," Goldie says as she plops down on the stool. "They're killing me."

Now that she's seated, Goldie checks out the bartender. They're wearing a black button-up, crimson vest, and black tie with subtle silver stripes. Their makeup is immaculate with eyeliner perfectly outlining dark, expressive orbs, and lips painted a shade of wine. Their short raven hair is swept back and styled high, adding an inch and a half to their height.

The bartender is gorgeous, and from their smirk, Goldie's attention hasn't gone unnoticed. "Can I get you something?"

"Uh, just a water. Thanks."

The bartender bends down and retrieves a bottle. "That's ten dollars."

"What?!" Goldie exclaims.

"It's for charity."

Goldie sighs and reaches through the slit of her dress to pull out a neatly folded twenty. "Give me two bottles, then."

Their mouth hangs open. "Where were you hiding that?"

"I've got a little pouch strapped to my thigh."

"Oh, wow." The bartender shakes their head while reaching down for another bottle. "You're the most interesting customer I've had all night."

Goldie snorts. "I think you mean weirdest."

"Totally." They smirk. "Hot and weird—a dangerous combo."

Goldie may have been naive when it came to Marcus's form of flirting, but even she's not so dense to the obvious come-on from the bartender.

"You wouldn't happen to secretly be a 62-year-old widower with a grown son and a precocious granddaughter?"

The bartender scowls. "Is that your way of asking if I take the Serum?"

"Sort of, yes."

"No, I'm a single, 26-year-old law student who never plans to have children, let alone grandchildren." They point to a name tag. "I'm Yasmeen, by the way."

"Goldie."

Yasmeen bats their long lashes and waits for more.

"Oh, um, I'm a 40-year-old reporter in a complicated thing with that secret 62-year-old."

Yasmeen leans against the bar. "Forget most interesting customer of the night. You're my most interesting customer *ever*."

Goldie rolls her eyes but can't help feeling a strange twinge of pride.

"So, they were taking the Serum behind your back?" Yasmeen asks.

Goldie nods.

"That's awful. You know there are legal recourses. I know some people who frequently handle that form of misrepresentation and fraud."

"That's not necessary." Goldie hates thinking of Teo like a criminal. She also hates that what happened to her has been happening to other people to the point that laws now exist to remedy the issue.

"Then how about revenge sex with a real 20-something?" Yasmeen suggests with a wink.

Goldie barks a surprised laugh. "I, uh, wow. Tempting." She gives them a meaningful once-over. Beautiful people in suit attire always make her weak in the knees. "*Very* tempting. But like I said, it's complicated."

"Would you like to talk about it? Bartenders are basically unlicensed therapists."

Goldie guesses it couldn't hurt to get an outsider's point of view. "He's really sorry about what he did, and I truly do forgive him. But now I have to figure out if I want to make it work with him, or if I'm afraid to let him go and be alone again."

"Would you be alone though?"

"What do you mean?"

"Did you miss how I propositioned you?"

"No, that came through loud and clear."

"So, if you decide to let him go and move on, you likely won't have a shortage of other options."

Goldie tilts her head in thought. "Okay, that's sort of true, but also not quite what I meant when I said I'd be alone again."

"What did you mean, then?"

"At dinner, there was this rich, handsome guy flirting with me, but I wasn't interested. You're stunning, and it pains me not to take you up on your offer, but I'm not looking for casual."

Yasmeen pouts playfully in response but otherwise doesn't interrupt.

"Even my best friend was in love with me, but I've never felt the same. There have always been people interested in me. I just never wanted them back. I've never felt a strong enough pull or profound enough connection. Not until Teo."

"And you don't think you could find that again with anyone else?"

"I had to wait until I was 40 to find it."

"That doesn't mean it's not possible again."

Goldie thinks of how Teo didn't find love after the loss of his wife until his 60s.

She doesn't want to be like him.

"And why bother betting on finding that kind of love again when you already have it?" Yasmeen asks. "It sounds like you have only one real option."

"Making it work with Teo."

Yasmeen nods. "If you love him this much, would it be so bad?"

Before Goldie can think too hard about the question, Amber and Connie approach the bar.

"Hey, there you are!" Amber cries out. "Why didn't you come back?" She notices Goldie's gladiator heel on the bar counter. "And why is your shoe up here?"

"My feet are done," she explains with a half truth.

Her friend seems to easily accept the excuse and homes in on the bottles next to the shoe. "Oh, good, water. I've been dying of thirst." Amber grabs both, handing one to Connie. "Here you go, baby."

Goldie looks forlornly as the ladies drink their fill. She turns to Yasmeen with an unspoken request for another bottle for herself. The bartender smirks and points down at her leg. Goldie groans and reaches back under her dress for another twenty.

BY THE TIME GOLDIE RETURNS HOME, HER MOTHER AND LUCKY ARE sound asleep. She uses the bathroom as quietly as she can, doing the bare minimum of wiping off her makeup and briskly passing the toothbrush over her teeth.

In her bedroom, she strips off the gown, leaving it on the floor, then pulls on her Wonder Woman sleep shirt and climbs into bed.

When she grabs her phone off the bedside table to plug into the charger, she notices a message:

JORDAN
hola goldie <3 i made this for the bday can't wait 2cu!!!

It's a picture of a birthday cake on fire. *¡FELIZ CUMPLE, ABUELO!* is written on top of the fire with party details appearing slightly too small at the bottom.

Goldie suspects Tommy had something to do with it.

She replies with a like for the image and "I'll be there! Can't wait!"

Goldie knows she should put her phone away and get to sleep. Instead, she looks through her gallery and taps open a video from a few months ago.

"I got a birthday request to begin the evening," Teo informs the crowd at Hank's. "Where's Tina Carter?"

Teo scans the room to find a woman waving her arms wildly and pointing at the woman next to her.

"There you are! Hey, happy birthday, Tina. And, Leslie, I see you now. You can cool it with the airport runway gestures," he says with a chuckle. "Tina, your wife came up to me before the show and requested the VIP birthday treatment for you."

A cry of "Oh God!" comes from the audience.

"That's right," Teo says. "Come on up here. Both of you."

Leslie pulls a very reluctant Tina onto the Helena stage. After climbing the few steps, Tina tries to keep her back to the crowd, but her wife forces her to turn around.

Goldie can see Teo mouth "Sorry" to Tina before speaking into the microphone again.

"All right, is everyone ready?"

The crowd whoops and begins singing "Happy Birthday" with Teo.

Leslie is the loudest and most enthusiastic, while Tina covers her face the entire time.

When the mercifully short song ends, Tina doesn't allow the shouts of "Happy birthday!" or the clapping to finish, grabbing Leslie's hand and immediately running back to their table.

"Leslie also asked that I sing a song that has special meaning for you two," Teo continues. "It's one that's got plenty of covers out there. Adele's is probably the most popular, but since she's busy being an international singing sensation, y'all are gonna have to settle for my version. I'll try to do it justice for this special occasion. Also, a shout-out to my girl"—Teo looks in Goldie's direction and winks—"who also loves this song."

Teo places a capo on his guitar's fretboard. Then, in a last-minute decision, tucks his pick in his pocket and hovers his curled fingers in front of the guitar. As if dancing, his fingertips cascade along each string, the gentle vibrations coalescing into "Make You Feel My Love."

Teo's voice isn't gravelly like Bob Dylan's, nor is it as wide-ranging as Adele's. Instead, it's a rumbling, rich tenor, an equivalent of honey for the ears, sweetening lyrics by turning them into honest, loving declarations.

During the performance, Goldie hadn't doubted that Teo would be willing to face any and all of the daunting tasks depicted in the song to express his love for her and that she would do the same for him.

But then the metaphorical storms came for them.

Now, all that can be done is to trust that Goldie and Teo can endure the bad weather on their own and eventually, hopefully, find their way back to the shelter of each other's heart.

CHAPTER 16

TOMMY IS NOT A BIG SHOPPER. SINCE HE MAINTAINS A STRICT DIET AT home, he gets the same bland food items every week at the grocery store, and the essentials are taken care of monthly at Walmart. Each trip is thirty minutes, tops.

As for his closet, he only needs dress shirts with his company's logo and khakis for weekdays. For nonworking hours, he has too many graphic tees to choose from, including one threadbare Superman shirt, one of Pink Floyd, two of AC/DC, three of NASA, various with skull themes, and one of Bruce Lee as a DJ that Tony Stark wore in one of the Marvel movies.

Tommy doesn't even feel the need to invest in items for his apartment. The exceptions include a king-size bed, a 4K television, and a curio crammed with his martial arts trophies.

All this is to say that Tommy avoids walking into stores if he can help it and would have bet his retirement savings on never seeing the inside of a Party City in his lifetime.

And yet here he is struggling with an armful of party decorations and dumb mylar balloons that whack him in the head every time he moves.

"We can get a cart," Eli suggests, his hands equally full.

"No!" Tommy says too quickly. "I mean, how much more could you possibly be getting? This is for an old man's birthday party."

Eli looks at him disapprovingly.

"Sorry, *your* old man's birthday party."

Eli sighs, apparently not satisfied by the correction, and turns to his daughter. "Jordan, what else do we need? The streamers, the banner, the balloons, the tablecloth—"

"Ooo, party hats!" A stack of paper cones is shoved into Eli's arms.

"You seriously want Abuelo to wear this?"

"No, I want *everyone* to wear them."

"Of course you do," Eli says with a shake of his head. "You know what? That's it. I'm cutting you off."

"But I still need to get socks with numbers on the bottom."

"Why?"

"So when Abuelo takes off his shoes and puts his feet up, they'll show 62."

"That is pretty sweet," Tommy admits.

"You two are so corny," Eli says, lips twitching with amusement. "But we still have to order the cake and get gifts."

Hearing that they have more things to do for her grandfather's birthday convinces Jordan to give up on her search for birthday socks, and they get in line to check out.

"Oh, I forgot to tell you," Tommy says to Eli. "I'm taking a couple days off and making a four-day weekend for myself."

"Yeah? How come?"

"It's been a pain working around my schedule to spend time with you two, so I thought I could take some extra days off here and there. I've got a lot of accrued vacation."

Eli smiles wide. "That's awesome."

Jordan does a little happy clap. "That means you can come to the party!"

Before Tommy can open his mouth to shoot down the idea, a bored-looking teenage employee beckons them to the checkout counter.

"So, where to next?" Tommy asks once everything's packed in his midsize SUV (affordable, sporty, phenomenal towing capacity).

Jordan points straight ahead. "The mall!"

Tommy can't help the pained noise he makes but hopes the sound of the V-8 engine he invested in adequately covers it up.

Luckily, they don't spend much more time in retail hell. The father and daughter duo already knew what they wanted to get the birthday boomer: a pair of aviator sunglasses from Jordan and a Guitar Center gift card from Eli. After a side trip to Foot Locker to check out the latest sneaker drops, they venture outside to the bakery for the cake order and grab a quick dinner.

By the time they get back to the Airbnb, all three need to decompress from the cacophony of humanity.

"You want to stay and watch a movie or something?" Eli asks.

Tommy typically ducks out on weeknights to get some sleep before the next workday, but tonight, that's not a problem. "Sure, sounds great."

"I'll go make popcorn!" Jordan dashes to the kitchen before her father can argue about eating yet again tonight.

As Eli opens his mouth to protest, he turns to Tommy, who's amused as hell and not hiding it. Jordan's father sighs, accepting the point loss on his parental scoreboard.

"I'm going to get changed," he tells Tommy.

Before Eli can turn completely around, Tommy grabs his hand and does a cartoony wag of his eyebrow, a silly seduction technique that, amazingly, works on Eli.

Their lips entwine with practiced ease. Sweet nibbles, light licks, smothered moans. This isn't the gentle press of mouths they shared when they first met. Eli and Tommy's kisses have evolved in intimacy—and hunger. A fact Tommy can't risk focusing on with the other man's daughter in the next room.

Before Tommy can pretend to be a semi-responsible adult and pull away, Eli surprises him with a playful shove to extricate himself. Tommy gasps mockingly, clutching his chest like he's truly wounded.

Eli gives him the laugh he's looking for. "Be right back. Make yourself comfortable."

When he disappears, Tommy lets go of a yawn he was somehow holding back during all the kissing. He slaps his face lightly before caving to the urge to flop down on the couch and shut his eyes.

A loud clanking forces his eyes to act like the spillways of a dam, letting in a flood of light.

Why is it so fucking bright? Tommy wonders inwardly while outwardly groaning like a dying man. *And why does my neck feel like someone tried to twist my head around but gave up halfway?*

"Oh, cool, you're awake," Jordan says from the edges of Tommy's bleary vision. "Daddy! Tommy's finally awake!"

Tommy winces at the unnecessarily loud relay of information. "I was asleep?"

"Yeah, you were like a corpse on the couch. Daddy and I had to sit on the armrests to watch the movie. Your abs made a great place for the popcorn bowl."

Tommy touches his stomach like he could possibly still feel evidence it was used as a table.

Eli comes into the living room then. "Sorry if I woke you. It's hard to make breakfast quietly."

Tommy notices how both Eli and Jordan are already cleaned up and dressed for the new day. "It's fine. It seems like I slept too long anyway. What time is it?"

"Almost eight," Eli answers.

"Oh my God! I slept for eleven hours?!"

"I told you, dude," Jordan says. "You were dead."

Tommy rubs his eyes and looks over at his shoes near the door. "I guess I should get back to my place and clean up."

"You don't have to," Eli says. "Use our bathroom. Shower if you need to."

It would be more trouble than it's worth to leave and come back, so Tommy agrees. He makes use of the bathroom offer for a quick break, then joins Eli and Jordan in the kitchen. His entrance is heralded by an embarrassing sound from his stomach thanks to the smell of bacon and eggs.

"That wasn't me this time," Jordan says to her father.

Tommy laughs. "No, that was me. I could eat a whole dozen eggs."

He bites back another laugh when Eli checks the carton to count how many eggs he has, as if Tommy had been serious. It's a mostly

full carton of eighteen, so even with the combined eating power of
Tommy and Jordan, they should have enough for this morning.

"I wasn't sure how you liked your eggs," Eli says. "I hope over
easy is good. I usually make them that way for an egg and avocado
sandwich."

"That sounds amazing," Tommy says. "Could you make me
that too?"

"Sure." Eli turns to Jordan. "Get more toast going."

"Right away, Chef!"

Tommy stays next to Eli to watch him move the perfectly oval,
golden-brown eggs to a plate and deftly crack three to fry. "You
like cooking?"

"I love it. I probably enjoy it more than eating."

"You're kidding?" Tommy gasps in honest surprise. "Jordan,
did you know your father thinks cooking is more fun than eating?"

"Weird, right? But it means I get so much good food when I'm
with him, so I just let him be weird."

"Smart," Tommy says with a chuckle, and leans down to kiss
Eli's temple. "I should have passed out on your couch sooner.
Looks like I've been missing out."

Eli glances at him in question and seems to catch Tommy's
real meaning. Their gazes stay locked for several rapid heartbeats
before Eli returns his attention to the eggs, cheeks puffing as he
blows out a breath, revealing how hot and bothered he is by the
moment. Like he's a pot on the stove that needed to let out steam.

Tommy clears his throat. "Can I help?"

"Just, uh, take a seat," Eli says, voice quavering. "My
apprentice and I will have your feast ready shortly."

"Excellent," Tommy says, sounding properly pompous to
lighten the atmosphere. "I am positively famished."

Everything is on the table in five minutes, and the trio
demolishes their first sandwiches in even less time.

"Since you're here already," Jordan says after a bite of her second
sandwich, "do you want to help set up everything for the party?"

Progress on Tommy's second sandwich halts as he holds it
midair while trying to think of an excuse not to go.

Eli notices the immense hesitation and comes to his rescue. "Hey, Jordie, why don't you and Tío Henry handle that? It'll give you a chance to spend time with Tía Riri too. We'll pick up the cake."

Jordan gives an okay and takes another huge bite.

Meanwhile, Tommy is still holding out the sandwich. He doesn't even react when an avocado slice plops to the plate. It's only when Eli points at the sandwich that Tommy starts to eat again. Unfortunately, it's with less of an appetite.

After breakfast, Tommy sheds his sleep-rumpled clothes and jumps into the shower. He uses the time alone to regroup from the off-kilter morning.

It's been a while since he's dated someone, and he guesses he's out of practice, except that implies he practiced to begin with. What makes Eli special is that Tommy doesn't feel like he needs practice with him. Everything is natural and carefree. The same goes for how Tommy is with Jordan.

Before meeting the pair, the idea of being a parent was laughable. After all, his paternal instincts are regularly satisfied by teaching a roomful of kids how to responsibly break boards with their bare hands.

There's also the matter of his father tainting the whole concept. Was the military to blame for sending him away often? Sure, but he was hardly home even when he didn't have deployments or duties. Ultimately, Dad didn't love Tommy and his sisters like he should have—like how Eli loves Jordan.

And Jordan doesn't only love her father right back. She is *devoted.* This girl adores movies and shows about superheroes, but in her eyes none of those caped and masked characters compare to her father.

Eli is Jordan's hero.

What's been a big hang-up for Tommy is how that same hero worship applies to her grandfather. He doesn't know how to avoid this birthday party without disappointing Eli's daughter.

"Oh, shit!" A rush of cold water rudely interrupts his speculative thoughts. "Fuck, how do I shut this off?!" His frantic attempts to push and pull all the knobs eventually stop the water. "Woooo!"

There's a knock on the door, followed by Eli's voice. "You okay? It sounded like Ric Flair somehow joined you in there."

"You know who Ric Flair is?" Tommy asks as he steps out of the stall.

"Of course I do!" His voice goes high with indignation. "I'm from Florida. Pro wrestling's a real sport down there."

Tommy wraps a large towel around his waist. "Did you ever go to any shows?"

"Yeah. Saw a couple matches with the Nature Boy himself."

"No way!" Tommy says as he swings open the door. "That's pretty cool."

Eli jumps back, his brown eyes growing big and his jaw going slack.

Tommy knits his brow. "You okay?"

"Oh, never better," Eli says, directing his answer to Tommy's bare chest.

Feeling helpful, Tommy places his hands on his hips to give the man an unobstructed view. "Sooo," he teases out, smirk evident in his tone, "I'm guessing you came here to bring me clothes." He nods toward the bundle clutched to Eli's chest.

"No, that'd be stupid," Eli says almost breathlessly, like all his energy was being diverted to the important task of gawking at Tommy's body. "I'm going to burn these and any other articles of clothing or fabric that could possibly be used to cover you up." His gaze travels downward. "That includes the towel on your waist."

"Is that so?" Tommy asks with a throaty chuckle. "Mind if I include your clothes in that fire?"

"Good idea." Eli drops the bundle and reaches for the hem of his shirt to pull off.

"Wait!" Tommy says, hushed. "Where's Jordan?"

"With Henry. I called him after breakfast to pick her up."

"Oh, good." Because Tommy could not live with scarring that girl for life (though knowing Jordan, she'd give an embarrassing thumbs-up of approval). "Then off shirt please now," he says in Neanderthal speak.

Eli obliges with a laugh, shucking his shirt to toss to the floor with the change of clothes. He reaches out again, but whatever expression Tommy's wearing stops him.

"What?" Eli asks.

Tommy gestures to Eli's chest.

He looks down. "Right, I forgot I didn't tell you where the tattoo is."

"You also didn't tell me which basketball player you had tattooed," Tommy says, shaking his head in disbelief. "I should have known."

The tattoo is line art of an open book. Above the left page, in script lettering that forms the shape of the page, is the name of his mother, Helena. On the right—Jordan.

"This does not count as a basketball player tattoo," Eli says.

"It does count, and I totally called it." Tommy wiggles his fingers to get the go-ahead nod from Eli to touch the ink.

The book is in the center of his chest with the pages swooping outward over the pectoral muscles. An anatomical heart is at the base, styled like a flower bud with leaves and petals etching its chambers, and in place of valves are vines emanating from it, sprawling and spiraling over the pages and behind the book.

On the left page, under "Helena," are lines written in Spanish:

El libro
de la vida
nunca se cierra

And on the right page, under "Jordan," are words in English:

In love,
our stories
live on

"Tell me about it," Tommy requests while tracing and retracing every line.

Eli seems too distracted to respond at first, eyelids fluttering with the attention. Tommy hears the whisper of a sigh before he finally speaks.

"Mamá had a massive collection of books. They were *everywhere*. And at first, after she died, Pops just left them wherever she last put them. The shelves were one thing; they were background noise. But there were Danielle Steel hardcovers on the kitchen table. Alice Walker and Jamaica Kincaid novels on her home office desk. A mess of classic lit on the living room coffee table.

"Eventually, being surrounded by her favorite things in the world got to be smothering. Most of the books were donated after a year, but Pops and I made sure to pick her absolute favorites to save. We've passed them on to Jordan, so she always has stories from her abuela to go along with the stories we tell about her."

Tommy glides a finger upward over Eli's sternum and the center of the book, traces along one of the protruding vines, and keeps going as if he were drawing it farther outward over his clavicle and around the base of his neck.

"It's a wonderful tribute, Eli. Thank you for letting me see it."

As he gets his fill of touching, Tommy thinks about how he never considered getting a tattoo before. But seeing this ink on this man?

Tommy desperately wants it on himself too.

He crushes their chests together and meets Eli's mouth once more. When their tongues come out to play, Eli moans and melds their bodies from head to toe. It's still not close enough for Tommy, but as he glides his hands down to grip Eli's ass, the other man tears his mouth away.

"Wh-huh?" Tommy whines, confused at the sudden ability to breathe.

"Sorry!" Eli exclaims. "But something's been bugging me, and I can't do this until we deal with it."

Tommy tries not to panic. "Um, sure." He lets go of Eli and steps back to give him space.

Eli takes a deep breath and cuts to the chase. "What's your deal with my dad?"

Oh. Shit.

"Uh, what do you mean?" Tommy plays dumb.

"I can tell you don't want to go to his birthday party."

"It just seems like more of a family thing. I don't want to be an intruder."

Eli places his hands on his hips. "He hurt your best friend. It's fair for you to hold some resentment."

"I don't! That's between him and Goldie."

Eli softens his stance and tone. "Look, I really like you, Tommy. More than I should after only knowing you for a few weeks."

"I really like you too." Tommy tries to reach for him again.

Eli gives a silent no with a shake of the head. "I need you to understand that my family is the most important thing in my life."

"Of course I understand. I adore Jordan."

"And I am so happy you do. Believe me, that has catapulted you above any other person I've ever been interested in. But you're forgetting about my father."

Tommy blinks, as if he really did just remember that Teo exists.

"I may not have his name tattooed on my chest, but I've told you all the things he's done for me. Don't doubt how much I love him."

The bile of shame roils Tommy's gut. He hates that he upset Eli with his issues with Teo. Determined to deal with it all, he bends over to pick up the clothes from the floor.

"Whoa, what are you doing?" Eli asks, sounding a little shrill.

"I'm going to get dressed."

"Why?"

"We're having a serious conversation instead of sex, so I don't need to be naked." Tommy thinks this is sound logic.

"But you should be."

"Wh-what? Why should I be naked for this?"

"Because I like the symbolism of it."

Tommy looks at Eli like he told him the Ford Pinto is making a comeback. "What symbolism?"

"Just like how the open book over my heart represents how I won't hide who I am or who I love or what I feel, you being naked means you're doing the same. You're baring your soul and have nothing else to hide." Eli folds his arms and holds his chin high.

Tommy squints, openly skeptical. "Okay, fine, but don't think for a second that I'm buying this symbolism thing."

He walks backward into the bathroom to give himself more space. He's an animated talker, especially on topics that he's passionate about or invested in.

This one's a doozy.

"I met Goldie more than ten years ago," Tommy starts, then pauses to reflect on the number and huffs a hollow chuckle. "Actually, probably more like twelve. Fuck, I can't believe I spent all that time in love with nothing to show for it."

Eli sucks in a breath but stays quiet.

"Don't get me wrong, I'm grateful to have her as a friend. It's just that we made so much sense as a couple. Can you see it?" Tommy asks, knowing it's weird to ask Eli to consider the man he's dating together with the woman his father was dating. (And, well, *shit*. Tommy might need to use the bathroom mirror as a dry-erase board to diagram all their relationship dynamics.)

Eli must need extra processing time too, because his brow cinches. "I have to admit," he says eventually, "yeah, I do."

"Everyone saw it. Even Goldie, I think. She always kept her distance though. She dug her very high heels into the ground and wouldn't budge us out of the friend zone. Eventually, I convinced myself that she didn't want anyone like that. It helped keep me from feeling like there was something wrong with me."

Eli opens his mouth, probably to object, but Tommy waves a hand to dismiss him.

"I was wrong on both counts, of course. There wasn't anything wrong with me, and I wasn't exactly *wrong* for her. I just wasn't *right* for her. I wasn't the big, sweeping, romantic love she wanted. She was willing to wait forever for that. Meanwhile, I was willing to do the same for her—wait forever. The big difference is that her waiting paid off." Tommy takes a breath to check on Eli. "Your dad never told you?"

"He knew?"

"Yeah, there was no hiding how jealous I was of Teo."

Eli shakes his head. "He's never said anything. Honestly, he only has good things to say about you. Albeit sarcastically sometimes."

Tommy rolls his eyes. "Of course he's being the bigger man in all this." *Not literally*, he adds petulantly to himself. Tommy's height advantage over Teo holds little solace, but he'll take whatever upper hand he can get, no matter how trivial. "When I first met your father, I hated him. He made Goldie so happy, and I wanted to axe kick him into the ground for it."

Eli's wince sends a twinge of guilt down Tommy's spine. He keeps talking honestly though. Unrequited feelings for a best friend are about the shittiest feelings a person can have, and Tommy can't hold back the hurt anymore.

"I felt so vindicated when Teo lied to her. A small part of me wanted to rub it in her face and be like, 'How does the disappointment feel?' But a bigger part hated seeing her so devastated. I'd do anything to take away the pain."

"Even encourage her to forgive my father," Eli points out.

"Yeah," Tommy mutters.

Eli studies his face before asking, "Are you still in love with Goldie?"

Tommy indulges in a final, wistful what-if where Goldie's concerned before focusing back on Eli. "I think I'll always be a little in love with her," he admits, then moves closer to the other man. "But I'm ready to find new love. Honestly, I probably already found it."

Eli's responding grin is gorgeously blinding and bashful. He tips his head down and darts his eyes away and back to Tommy. "Well, uh"—he clears his throat—"that's a relief, since I *definitely* already found it."

"Yeah?" Tommy steps even closer. "Are you serious?"

"We're headed there. I can feel it." Eli brings a hand up to Tommy's cheek. "Which is why you need to forgive my pops."

Tommy's broad smile vanishes. "Really?"

"Yes, Tommy, really. You still majorly resent him for his place in Goldie's life and what he did to her. You need to resolve it."

"But I said all that forgiveness stuff for Goldie's sake."

"So, do it for our sake too. Because I'm telling you right now—there is no me and Jordan without my father."

Tommy really wishes he had some clothes on right now, because Eli was right—being naked can be a way of baring one's soul. The rapid rise and fall of his chest, the hunch of his shoulders and neck, the tight coil of his muscles. They're all alarm bells from his psyche screaming that he realize something vital.

Tommy can't lose Eli and Jordan. The thought physically pains him.

"All right, I'll try," he says. "I need to."

Eli exhales a breath and barely gets a thank you out before they're kissing yet again, hands roaming far more than they had before. And although Tommy is very ready to get the sex ball rolling, he stops kissing as suddenly as they started, causing Eli to make the same whiny "Wh-huh?" sound Tommy had before.

"Sorry! I just want to check one last time that we're definitely having sex. I mean, we talked about a lot of heavy things. I won't be mad if you want me to get dressed and—"

"*I'll* be mad!" Eli shrieks. "Why do you keep bringing up clothes? I'm starting to think it's another issue we have to discuss."

Tommy scoffs. "You want to talk about that now too?"

"Hell no." Eli makes short work of stripping out of his jeans. "Now take off that towel already and show me what other skills you've got, *Master Rhodes*."

Tommy doesn't think twice after that. He practically carries Eli to the bedroom and takes seriously the other man's challenge to show him what other skills he's got (because martial arts makes a person *limber*).

Afterward, Tommy takes another shower but with Eli joining him this time. Then, to Eli's dismay, he puts on the change of clothes intended for him, and they leave for the party.

When they finally get to the bar, Jordan greets Tommy first. "I'm so glad you're here!"

Tommy worries the girl knew he planned to not come before. "Uh, yeah, of course I'm here. You knew your dad and I were coming with the cake."

"But now that you're here, you can help put up the 'HAPPY BIRTHDAY' banner. We need a tall person."

Ah, the great burden tall people bear—reaching shit.

"As you wish, my lady," Tommy responds gallantly, and goes over to help the daughter of the man he happily and wholeheartedly now calls his boyfriend.

TEO ARRIVES AT THE DARKENED ENTRANCE OF HANK'S BAR AT THE appointed time. He tries on his surprise face and embraces how ridiculous it is that Jordan's making everyone do this when it isn't a surprise party at all. He walks through the doors and turns on the lights.

"Surprise!!!"

"Oh. My. God!" Teo hams it up. "*Wuuut?!!!*"

Jordan sprints out of the crowd and slams into him. "Happy birthday, Abuelo!"

"Oof!" Teo folds over in pain. "My liver, baby," he wheezes out. "Ya gotta take it easy."

"Sorry! Are you okay?"

Teo's still groaning but manages to stand back up straight. "Uh, yeah, I think I'll live."

The guests gape with concern, allowing Teo to take in who came to celebrate his birthday.

There's Ruby with her husband, Spade, who plays drums for them when he can come out. It's only been a few weeks since Teo last performed, but seeing them makes him realize how much he misses it.

He sees Tommy, which is surprising, but Teo figures that he was forced to come by his son and granddaughter. There's Henry in his usual plaid, and Riri in one of his animal-print tops...

And there's Goldie. She's wearing a burgundy blouse and torn, faded blue jeans. Her hair is tied in a loose braid over a shoulder, and her face is cutely scrunched in concern.

Then he notices Goldie's mother sitting in a chair next to her. The expression on her face is distinctly not cute. In fact, she looks like she's trying to set Teo on fire with her mind.

"Jordie, I was wrong. Soy un muerto."

TEO MANAGES TO SURVIVE THROUGH LUNCH. HE SITS AT A GROUP OF tables with Eli, Jordan, Henry, and Riri, while Tommy joins Goldie and her mother in one of the booths. The distance is distracting, but Teo tries to maintain a positive attitude and simply appreciate that everyone came in the first place.

When it's time for cake, Rat Trapp plays the most intense rendition of "Happy Birthday" ever performed, and Henry makes Teo go on stage to blow out his candles.

He stares for a long time at the "6" and "2" flickering in front of him. He almost wants to rub his eyes to check if he's seeing things right. It's a lot more years than his parents or Helena got, and the thought overwhelms him.

Teo tears his gaze away and finds the lean figure of his son— his baby boy. The day of Eli's birth was filled with excitement and happiness and so much joy. The only dark cloud was not having his parents around and see them become grandparents.

But Teo has lived long enough to be not only a father but also a grandfather—Jordan's abuelo. The day she was born was just as joyous—and just as tinged in sadness. Like his mother, Helena had never lived to become an abuela.

With his mind heavy, Teo can't help but gaze over at Goldie. She wanted those kinds of days too, and she wanted them with him. He compromised all her desires.

Since he can't change the past, he makes an audacious wish now as he blows out the candles.

For all the joyous days ahead, Goldie.

"WHEN'RE YOU COMING BACK?" RUBY ASKS.

"I have about three weeks of recovery to go."

Ruby takes a cursory glance at Teo's midsection. "You don't have to move a lot to sing and play guitar. You're not Elvis. Shit, you're not even an Elvis impersonator."

Teo snorts. "Very true, Rhinestone. I'm not the King. I just need a break too. Work some things out."

"This have anything to do with Goldie? Because it has not gone unnoticed that you and her haven't interacted during this party."

Teo glances at Goldie and her mother talking to the lead singer of Clockwork Orangutan. Mrs. Hays's eyes don't blink as she gazes at Chester's facial piercings.

"I have a confession to make."

"About what?"

"Remember when we first met, and I told you right away that I use the Serum and was pushing 60."

"Yeah?"

"I didn't do that with Goldie."

Shock contorts his singing partner's face. Professionally arched eyebrows somehow climb almost to her hairline, and lips the shade of her name part wide to deliver a squeaked gasp that comes from the highest end of her vocal range. "You complete shithead! How could you fucking do that?"

"I was afraid she wouldn't want me if she knew my real age."

"But she still came to your party?" Ruby asks, puzzled. "Are you telling the whole truth? Did you really get surgery for some cysts, or did she stab you?"

Teo glares at her. "She's forgiven me, but there's still a lot to work through. I'm writing a song for her, and I need your advice on it."

"This better be the greatest song of the twenty-first century to get her back. I mean Taylor Swift levels of writing."

Teo frowns. "That's not the kind of advice I was looking for."

Ruby rolls her eyes. "Oh, stop looking like a kicked puppy. Of course I'll help."

Eli and Tommy approach. "Hey, Pops. Sorry to interrupt, but Tommy has something he needs to talk to you about."

Tommy looks terrified. "What, now?"

"Yes, now."

"Oh, is it more confessions?" Ruby asks. "Who else has been lying to their significant other about their age?" She looks at Tommy. "Is it you, hot stuff? Are you secretly an 80-year-old with amazing abs?"

"No, lying about their age is Teo's thing."

The comment earns Tommy an elbow in his "amazing abs" from Eli.

"Uh, sorry. Force of habit."

"In the meantime," Eli continues, "Jordan and I will go ahead and introduce ourselves to Goldie's mom and hopefully smooth things over for you some."

"Wow, mijo, that's, uh ..." The obvious word for what Eli is proposing would be *nice* or *generous*, but Teo looks again at Goldie's four-foot-eleven guard dog and answers honestly. "That's *brave* of you."

Eli shakes his head vigorously. "No, no, this is all Jordan. She's the brave one. There's no way in hell I'd be the first to approach the angry mother of a woman you wronged. I love you, Pops, but not that much."

Teo nods. "Good self-preservation instincts."

"You Estradas are something else," Ruby says with a laugh. "I guess I'll leave you boys to make your dramatic reckonings. Talk to you later, Teo."

"Later, Ruby."

Eli turns to Tommy and lays a swift kiss on his lips. "You can do this."

Tommy looks at Teo warily.

"And Pops?"

"Yes, light of my loins?"

Tommy full-body cringes, while Eli rolls his eyes and lets whatever he was going to say drop. Instead, he calls out to Jordan, who's hunched over the food table.

Her hand darts away from the cake. "Just one more piece!"

"Forget the cake!" Eli commands, and points in the direction of Goldie and her mom. "It's time!"

"Ohhh, okay!" She goes directly to Eli and takes her father's hand to lead away.

"¡Suerte!" Teo shouts after them, because they're going to need all the luck in the world.

When he looks back at Tommy, he notices the familiar shirt he's wearing. It's one of several brightly patterned button-ups that his son owns. But while Eli wears them with, well, more buttons done up, Tommy is letting the material hang wide open to frame his famously toned torso. The shape of his eight-pack is etched in the fabric of his too-tight tank top, which is riding up to expose a sliver of taut skin…

There's probably a special level of hell for ogling the boyfriend of his son/best friend and spurned love interest of his estranged girlfriend. (And forget telenovela or Korean drama; his life has officially become a V.C. Andrews book. Teo can imagine Helena glued to her cloud in heaven, absolutely riveted.)

Refocusing on what caught his gaze in the first place, Teo plucks the collar of the colorful shirt. "I'm guessing you and my son had a *very* good night. Because you might as well be wearing an 'I Heart Miami' T-shirt right now."

Tommy's face turns redder than Ruby's lipstick. After taking a deep breath, he side-eyes Teo. "Actually"—a corner of his mouth curves upward—"it was a very good *morning.*"

Teo's eyebrows lift in surprise.

Tommy shakes his head and huffs. "Being civil to each other is going to be impossible."

"No, it's not," Teo says. "We did it before for Goldie's sake, and we can do it again for my son's."

"That's not exactly the issue." Tommy cracks his neck and stretches his back, similar to what Teo suspects he'd do before a sparring match.

Oh, fuck. Am I about to get dropkicked in the teeth at my birthday party?

Teo takes a cautious step back before Tommy continues to speak.

"You called me out on my jealousy one time, which was fair, and I did better … I think. I was less of an asshole, wasn't I?"

"Yeah," Teo says. "Less looming. Only one or two smartass comments to my face."

Tommy looks pleased that his efforts had been noticed. "I thought that would be enough, but I didn't really address the feelings behind the jealousy, and everything that happened between you and Goldie made it worse. If I hadn't met Eli and Jordan at the same time, I would gladly never see your face again."

The open disdain stings and compounds the guilt and shame Teo's been wrestling with. Because despite the animosity the other man has shown him, Teo likes Tommy. He sees what Eli and

Goldie see in him—a hardworking, exuberant, upright person. To not even have Tommy's respect doesn't only bruise Teo's ego.

It breaks his heart.

"I don't hate you though," Tommy says, as if he can read Teo's mind. "I was even starting to like you. You're a hell of a musician; the way you support other musicians is awesome. And now that I know what you've been through, I can't say I would have handled things any better or worse in your shoes. You were wrong to lie to Goldie—but I get it. And if she can forgive you, then so can I."

With the air finally clear between them, Teo evaluates his relationship with the (yes, tall) man. Until recently, he had only seen Tommy as the third party, someone he was never directly connected to. He was his girlfriend's best friend. Now he's his son's boyfriend. The universe keeps tying them together through the people they love.

"Thank you, Tommy. I didn't know how much I needed to hear that until now."

Tommy considers him for a beat, then nods. "I didn't know how much I needed to say it either."

Teo takes another moment to absorb their exchange before extending a hand. "Let's start over. I'm Teo Estrada, a 62-year-old musician. I have a son who has a thing for gorgeous tall people and a granddaughter who can eat her weight in cake."

Tommy barks out a laugh and shakes the hand firmly. "Glad to meet you, Teo."

With that settled, Jordan's loud giggles and Eli's wild gestures grab their attention. Goldie's mother is bright-eyed and engrossed in whatever the duo is talking about. "And then the chickens chased Daddy into the house!"

"Ah, the chicken coop story," Tommy says. "That's a good one."

The returning dread of encountering Goldie's furious mom chokes any response from Teo.

"Hey, man," Tommy starts, probably noticing the terror in Teo's eyes. "I wish I could say that Mrs. Hays isn't as frightening as she seems, but you know better than most that she can make grown people cry."

"She's not that bad," Teo says unconvincingly. "Just a little critical."

"Goldie told me one time she reported a restaurant to county inspectors over some dust on a buffet table's sneeze guard."

"That's a bit harsh, sure."

"She worked at the restaurant and was close friends with the owner, who had to pay a 500-dollar fine."

"Damn." Teo winces. "Look, Tommy, I know our friendship is very new—like, thirty seconds new—but I'm gonna need some better effort from you. Any kind of encouragement or hope will do."

"Yeah, that's not the kind of friendship I see us building, lil' buddy." He slaps Teo on the back. "Expect to hear a lot more smartass old man jokes."

"Hmm," Teo intones, dread continuing to tie his tongue.

"But those two, on the other hand"—Tommy motions toward Eli and Jordan—"*they're* your hope."

Goldie's mom laughs loudly and claps when Teo's son and granddaughter finish the story. "Oh, that so funny! Now I want chickens." She looks at Goldie, who vehemently shakes her head no.

Teo's not going to come right out and say it because he's still a bit petty, but Tommy's right. Witnessing the most important people in Teo's life laughing and sharing a moment loosens the tight ball of anxiety lodged in his chest—and he dares to hope.

———

JORDAN HOLDS GOLDIE'S MOTHER'S HAND AS SHE LEADS THE WAY toward where Teo and Tommy are sitting. Eli and Goldie are close behind.

"Hi, Abuelo!"

"Uh, hi, baby." The chair scrapes loudly as Teo gets up.

"Halmoni wants to talk to you."

Teo and Tommy look at each other, confused by the unfamiliar word.

"It means grandmother. She said I can call her that. I know Korean now."

"One word," Eli clarifies.

"Nuh-uh. I also know kimchi and how to say, 'I'm hungry': Baegopa."

"Of course," Eli groans.

"Anyway," Jordan continues, "Halmoni and Abuelo need to talk. Tommy, can we get some food to take with us?"

"Heck yeah, we can." Tommy jumps up from his seat and holds it out for Mrs. Hays. He gives Teo a parting pat on the shoulder before taking Jordan and Eli's hands to escape.

Goldie looks at Teo and mouths "Sorry" before sitting next to her mother. Teo takes a deep breath before sitting down as well.

Mrs. Hays, surprisingly, isn't hitting him with her death glare right off the bat. It's a sober look, filled with disappointment and pity. "Happy birthday," she says.

Teo is unprepared for the sentiment even though it's the first thing everyone has uttered to him today. "Uh, thank you."

Goldie's mom shifts in her seat before continuing. "How you feel? Surgery okay?"

"It went well. I'm going to be sore for a couple weeks though. How are you?"

"My head fine. You my only headache now."

Teo winces at the barb.

"You know you do terrible thing to my daughter?"

Teo looks over to Goldie. "Yes."

"You do thing like that to her again?"

"Never," Teo vows.

Mrs. Hays nods. "You raise good son and granddaughter. You very lucky. Some people"—her eyes flick to her daughter—"not get so lucky."

Tommy had mentioned how Goldie's mother can make adults weep, and sure enough, that gut punch has Teo on the verge of tears.

Mrs. Hays doesn't notice, or if she does, she ignores it and looks off thoughtfully in the direction of Jordan, Eli, and Tommy. "But maybe they get lucky in different way."

Teo blinks rapidly, processing her words. Curious about Goldie's reaction, he turns to her but can't catch her gaze. Her eyes are locked on the trio her mother alluded to.

"I get more cake now," Mrs. Hays announces, signaling that she's done with the conversation. "You old and have bad liver. No need diabetes too."

And with that scorching takedown, she drops the metaphorical mic and leaves.

Teo blows out a breath he hadn't realized was trapped in his lungs. "Holy shit, Goldie, your mother could tell God how to get their act together."

Goldie nods. "She has a speech in that head of hers for when she passes. I just know it."

"I can believe that," Teo says, still reeling.

More used to her mother's ways, Goldie's quicker to recover and pulls out a card from her purse, handing it to Teo. "Happy birthday."

He smiles. "Thank you, honey."

Goldie looks away as he tears open the envelope. Teo knows she's shy about her writing despite being a professional.

The cover features a collage of music formats: records, 8-track tapes, cassettes, and CDs. On the inside is Goldie's semi-decent handwriting.

> *How old are you today?*
> *I'm going to take a guess and say you're*
> *in your mid-30s. After releasing a few of*
> *your original songs online, your mix of indie*
> *sensibilities and appreciation for folk music*
> *across nations will catch on, and you'll have*
> *a critically acclaimed, Grammy-nominated*
> *album out. You'll already have toured the US,*
> *Mexico, and Central America, with a few shows*
> *in Europe on the horizon ... for real, this time!*
>
> *As for us, our marriage is going strong. We*
> *finished renovating the fixer-upper we bought close*
> *to my mother so she wouldn't threaten to move in*
> *with us. It's nothing big, of course, but it's all ours.*
>
> *You still perform regularly at Hank's Bar,*
> *and we make those shows our date nights. You*
> *dedicate songs to me, we sing along with the*

other acts, and then we go back to our little
house to make music of a different kind.
        It's funny ... even though we have our own
house, I suppose music is our real home.

~~~

        I'm not sure how much of this fantasy can ever
become reality, but my gift to you should go far
in kick-starting your rise to respectable stardom.
The business card in the envelope is for Freddie's
Magic Studio. I'm paying for your studio time,
however long you need to make tracks you can
share with the world—and, more importantly,
for me to add to my numerous playlists.
        Happy 62nd birthday, Teo.

                                All my love,
                                Goldie

Teo turns the red envelope over and catches the little card. His chuckle at the studio's logo of a mustached microphone comes out gurgled and wet sounding. "This is perfect, Goldie. Thank you."

Goldie pulls a bunch of napkins out of the table's dispenser to hand to Teo, keeping a few to take care of her own tears. "Sorry it's not sex-all-day like we planned."

Teo almost falls off his chair from how hard he laughs.

CHAPTER 17

"In closing today," Pastor Paul says with a faint clearing of his throat, "I want to recite from Paul's letter to the Philippians, English Standard Version, Chapter 4, Verse 9: *What you have learned and received and heard and seen in me—practice these things, and the God of peace will be with you.*"

He looks up from his Bible. "It has been a privilege serving this church and ministering to you for the last year. Being back here has opened my eyes to my life's purpose. So, it is with a heavy heart that I'm announcing that I will be leaving this position."

Paul pauses to allow for the inevitable murmurs and gasps from everyone in the congregation. Goldie shares a surprised look with her mother.

"Now, this isn't my last day, but I wanted to share with you my decision as soon as I could. It was not an easy one to make, of course. However, the path that brought me here has also led me to a crossroads. But as Psalm 34:17 in the ESV says, *When the righteous cry for help, the Lord hears and delivers them out of all their troubles. The Lord is near to the brokenhearted and saves the crushed in spirit.*

"We are so lucky that God has our backs. That though we are vulnerable, He ensured our resiliency by giving us the heart—the body's greatest muscle. It not only keeps us alive but gets stronger all the time because it is constantly tested, and troubles of the heart are inevitable. No wonder it can hurt so much at times. But it's God's trusted instrument to deliver his love and guidance. And if you can only remember one piece of wisdom from me after these many, many Sundays, have it be this—always listen to your heart."

Goldie fights back a scoff. She's been trying to listen to that damn little drum in her chest, but it won't give her a clear answer. Should she take Teo back? She can admit that she still wants him after everything that's happened. She's just unsure if she wants everything that comes with him.

"As for my heart," Pastor Paul continues, "it says to join my family up north and find a parish there that is in need of my service. And to truly end today's sermon, one more bit from Philippians, Chapter 4:12–14, in which Paul thanks the people for the concern and care they've shown him: *I know how to be brought low, and I know how to abound. In any and every circumstance, I have learned the secret of facing plenty and hunger, abundance and need. I can do all things through him who strengthens me. Yet it was kind of you to share my trouble.*"

His lips curve upward with the last line. "Thank you, everyone, for your concern and care and kindness. Thank you for opening up your incredible hearts to me every Sunday."

———

"WHY YOU LEAVING?" GOLDIE'S MOTHER ASKS PAUL IN LIEU OF A greeting.

He looks at Goldie with an edge of panic before collecting himself. "It's good to see you at church again, Imo," he says, trying to ignore the loaded question. "How're you feeling?"

"Not dead yet," she says bitingly. "But God keep testing me. I grow up poor. I not have education. I live in boring part of America. I divorced. My daughter still not married. And when I think worst done, I hit head, daughter finally find man, but he *old* man, and now you leaving. Why you leave?" she asks again with no room for escape.

Paul's Adam's apple bobs with a hard swallow. "I want to be with Lily and the kids. Where they go, I should go too."

Sun's mouth twists into a sneer. "You love this church. You do good work here. Why you make sacrifice?"

"It's true that when I first took this path of service, I could only imagine ending up here. I tried to make that vision for myself and family work, but it didn't. I need to accept and adapt, and most of all, I need to cherish and hold on to what is most important to me—the love in my heart for God and my family."

Goldie thinks Paul's words have miraculously tempered her mother's bullish resolve. Her sneer turns into a petulant pout. "You better visit more," she commands with a wagging finger. "Not just Christmas."

"Yes, ma'am," Paul easily agrees.

"And you come to house for dinner before you move away."

"Um, sure, of course," he agrees less easily. "Do I have to do more laundry?" Paul had come by the house to check on Goldie's mother the first week after her accident and got roped into washing all the blankets and sheets. "Not that I mind helping you," he says without looking her in the eyes.

"Curtains need wash."

"Of course they do," he says, as if accepting his fate.

"Where's your mommy? I need yell at her for letting you go."

Goldie sees Paul hesitate to answer, but he raises a finger to unleash Goldie's mother on his own. "She's over there."

Sun turns in the direction he's pointing and starts walking away, yelling the Korean word for older sister. "Unni!" Paul's mother tries to move behind a pillar. "You can't hide! I already see you!"

Goldie shakes her head as she waits for her mother to get out of earshot before opening her mouth. "Sorry about that."

"I wish I could say I was prepared for the reactions I would get about leaving, but there is no preparing for your mother."

Goldie nods. "There really isn't."

"I am glad that she feels better. For her sake and yours, Goldie. I hate that you've been dealing with a broken heart on top of what happened to her." Goldie told Paul the truth about Teo when he came over to check on her mother.

"Things have mended some. I've gotten to know Teo's family too."

"That's great."

"Sure," she says distantly. "I still don't know what direction to take with him—if any."

"Did you listen to my sermon?"

"Yes, Pastor," Goldie says, teasing.

"So, let's cut to the chase. What's your heart saying about Teo?"

"I love him."

"There's your answer."

"It's really not."

"It really is," the pastor says. "You'll see what I mean. Just never lose sight of that love. The rest will fall into place."

———————

As CONTINUED PENANCE FOR HIS DECISION TO LEAVE, PAUL HAS TO sit with Goldie and her mother for lunch at the church and endure Sun's complaints about the food and the way the ajummas have been handling things without her.

As Goldie gazes around the room to detach herself from her mother's diatribe, she sees Penny rush toward the bathroom. She immediately goes to Jack, who was about to follow her. "Hey, I'll go check on her. You can stay and keep track of the kids."

"Thanks, Goldie. Just to warn you, she's probably throwing up. She hasn't been feeling great the last few days."

Goldie frowns and quickly makes her way to the bathroom. And, yeah, she definitely hears retching in one of the stalls. "Penny? Can I help? Should I hold your hair back like I did at your bachelorette party?"

She hears a gurgled laugh. Then the entrance to the bathroom opens, and Paul comes through.

"How dare you leave me alone with your mother?"

Goldie glares at her friend and motions to the closed stall.

Paul silently conveys that he's also here out of concern for their friend. "And are you all right, Pen?"

"Yup!" Her monosyllabic assurance is made echoey by the toilet bowl. "This is only the second time I've puked today. Yesterday, it was four before noon. Progress!"

"Why are you puking though?" Goldie asks. "If you don't feel good, you shouldn't be here."

Paul nods. "Yeah, I have it on good authority that God will

forgive you for missing church if you're sick. And besides, we can't risk spreading anything."

"I'm not contagious."

"How do you know?" Goldie asks.

"Pretty sure you can't catch pregnancy."

Goldie and Paul look at each other in astonishment.

"Really?!" Goldie exclaims.

Penny opens the stall door. "Yeah, I was like this with Serena. Not so much with the boys though. Wonder if that means anything," she ponders.

"That's, um ..." Paul hesitates. "Great? Congratulations?"

"Ugh," Penny groans. "What are we going to do with another kid? Jack does well, but he works enough hours as is. I'm going to have to up my Etsy game. I don't have enough hands to make more jewelry *and* feed four mouths!"

"You've done this three times already," Goldie says. "Sure, money will be a little tighter, but it's not like you're going to have to buy a lot of new stuff."

"Our crappy house only has four crappy bedrooms though."

"Have the boys bunk," Paul says. "Or maybe this is God's way of pushing you guys to find or build the home you've always wanted."

"Four kids though," Penny says with a far-off look. "I always wanted one. Jack and I were just going to have Serena, make sure she had everything she needed, and as soon as she grew up and went off to Harvard, we were going to retire early in the Caribbean."

"Trust me, Pen," Paul says, "you have a better chance of winning an entire Powerball jackpot than having every part of your future work out like you planned."

The friends stay quiet for a moment. Goldie wonders if they're all thinking the same thing, lost in the twists and turns their lives have taken recently.

"But you know what?" Paul continues, breaking the silence. "It sometimes works out better than you imagined. You've got three awesome kids. And now you're going to have another! A six-member household. No one will be the odd one out. There will always be even sides for game nights."

"Yes, that was always my biggest concern," Penny says with an eye roll.

"Paul's right." Goldie takes her friend's hand. "Having one kid probably would have been fine, but remember how lonely we were as kids? Yours are going to have bonds to support them for the rest of their lives."

"And at least you're not rich enough for a *Knives Out* situation," Paul mentions for some unfathomable reason. "You know, where they're all suspected killers who want your inheritance." He takes Penny's other hand and pats it. "Small blessings."

"Oh my God!" Goldie smacks Paul's arm. "You are the strangest pastor."

Penny has a good laugh. "Thanks for the support, you guys." She takes a few deep breaths. "Four still sounds like an awful lot. I'm probably going to be calling you for more babysitting favors, Golds."

Because she doesn't have any kids of her own to worry about goes unsaid. At least, it does in Goldie's mind.

"I'm always here for you, Penny. I've got no plans that would change that."

"Why so busy?" Goldie's mother complains while placing her blanket down onto the sand. They've been roaming around the beach for twenty minutes, looking for a spot that would satisfy her.

"It's summer, Ma." Goldie plops down the totes with supplies and food that fell on her to carry. "School's out."

Lucky stumbles around on the sand while the women set up the umbrellas for shade. The puppy is looking cuter than usual, dressed in a tiny striped tee and an even tinier bucket hat to help protect him from the sun. When things are situated to Sun's liking, she lies down with a satisfying thud, molding the blanket and sand underneath.

"Ah, sheewonhae," she says as the breeze from the water hits her.

Goldie pulls out a cold bottle of water and places it right next to her mother's head. "Drink some before you fall asleep. I don't want you to dehydrate. It'll aggravate your head."

"I not go sleep. Why come here and sleep?"

"So you can relax. It doesn't matter if you do it by sleeping. Enjoy the weather, the sound of the waves."

Her mother opens her mouth like she's going to argue but surprisingly drinks the water instead, dropping her head back down. "Okay, I take nap," Goldie hears eventually. "Watch your puppy brother."

Goldie does as she's told and watches Lucky have a great time digging a hole in the sand. With her two companions accounted for, the reporter pulls out her laptop to squeeze in more work on the Serum article.

After wrestling with Sarah Crown's interview, Goldie's now writing a commentary about the entire series—and she's struggling yet again. She needs to find the through line in the users' testimonials and with Sarah's part. Ultimately, what can be better understood about the Serum from these stories? Is there a bigger picture to be seen?

The answers start with her. Doing this story has undoubtedly affected her attitudes about the Serum and the people who take it. But what about her attitude toward herself? Goldie needs to look into a mirror and face what's looking back.

Since the ocean air doesn't seem to be clearing her mind like she had hoped, the reporter does some people watching. There's a toddler playing a few feet away at the line where wet and dry sand divide. Her dark limbs and navy-blue bathing suit are speckled with grains of sand, evidence of the hard work she's putting in, shoveling and wildly flinging mostly wet sand into an already full bucket. Looking torn, the girl pauses to study her work. Goldie thinks she was having fun shoveling, and now that she can't keep filling the bucket, she needs to make a decision.

Goldie wonders what her choices are. She could continue tossing sand on top of the bucket. She seemed to be having a lot of fun with that. Maybe the girl will dump the bucket of sand and start shoveling it back in. She probably liked filling the bucket as much as shoveling the sand, and without another bucket to fill, she would have to start again to be able to do both. Or maybe she'll abandon the whole operation. After all, a little girl has plenty of other options for a good time at the beach.

To Goldie's surprise, the girl does none of the above. She gets up while securely holding her shovel, dragging the bucket up the beach toward an area speckled with tiny mounds that Goldie hadn't noticed before. She sinks back to her knees and carefully tilts the bucket over without spilling too much, then she lifts it to reveal a sculpted mound of wet sand that joins several others. Goldie has no idea what the girl's making, but she claps excitedly.

Not too far from the little girl is an elderly couple walking hand-in-hand. Goldie can tell they're elderly because of their slow movements, hunched frames, and lack of muscle definition. She wouldn't have been able to know by their skin or hair color; both have smooth skin, no age spots, and plenty of non-graying hair. One wears an Aztec-patterned beach shawl and leans against the other, their head lolling on their companion's bare shoulder as they walk. Goldie can hear the more upright of the two talking about some "ghastly cottegecore ripoff," while the other seems happy to simply listen and be led at a glacial pace. The footsteps left in their wake are indistinguishable from one another.

As Goldie continues to scan the beach, her eyes latch onto a woman with hair color that matches the sand, sitting atop a large cushion, nursing her baby. Her piercing blue eyes watch two boys and a man toss a Frisbee. At once, the man lifts the smaller boy up over his shoulder and announces to the woman that they're going into the water. The other boy throws the Frisbee down next to the woman and runs to follow. The woman continues to nurse and watch.

Everywhere Goldie looks, there's another family, another couple, another person, another parent, another child, another body. Young, old, and in between. None more right looking than the other.

Goldie looks down at her hands, which have been hovering over her laptop the whole time. Right away, she notices the negatives: thick and prominent veins, unevenly trimmed nails. And she's always thought her knuckles were too big, ever since she was teased as a little girl for having "man hands."

After getting an inkling of the direction she wants to take for the commentary, Goldie puts her man hands to work. Only the groan of her mother waking stops the tapping of her fingertips.

"Wh-what time is it?" Sun asks. She swats her hands to her sides to reorient herself, accidentally hitting the snoozing puppy. "Oh, sorry, Lucky."

Lucky yips a few times before dropping his head into the dent he burrowed in the blanket and falling back asleep.

"It's lunchtime," Goldie answers, saving her document and shutting the laptop.

They brought a few sliced kimbab rolls—rice and strips of veggies, fish cake, and egg wrapped in dried seaweed—that her mother had made first thing in the morning.

As they devour the morsels, Goldie's mother casts her gaze at the water. "I spoiled when little girl. Your halmoni work at ocean, so I always see it."

"But she made you work too. That's not spoiled."

"I not appreciate when I have it. That is spoiled."

Goldie lets her mother's words linger while she looks at what remains of the kimbab. There are a few bright, neat pieces to choose from, along with the ends that are barely held together.

Sun's eyes remain on the waves. "I wanna see Korea ocean again," she says, rubbing the part of her head that hit the floor. "Before it too late."

After lunch, Goldie takes off the oversized linen shirt she was wearing for extra sun protection and stands up for the first time since they settled on their spot in the sand. "I'm going into the water," she informs her mother. "You going to be okay?"

Sun waves her off while looking at Lucky, who's trying to run and keeps face-planting in the sand.

Goldie walks a straight line toward the ocean. She focuses on the path as if it were the only way to reach the water. The sand she touches is meant for her feet only. The froth and foam are supposed to reach where she walks. The parts of the ocean that gradually envelope her can only mold to her body's shape, so when her feet leave the ground, she is not swimming. Instead, she chooses to be carried, letting the waves take her in whichever direction she's meant to go.

TEO RECEIVED A TEXT FROM GOLDIE ASKING IF SHE COULD COME over tonight with some dinner. He fired off a response as fast as his fingers could tap saying that would be great. She said she'd be over in an hour.

That was fifty minutes ago. He now has ten left to make his place look less like a hovel. Teo's been using his recovery as an excuse for not being as organized as usual, and Goldie hasn't been over in weeks—since he confessed everything to her at the bar.

Teo thinks he's been making slow-but-sure progress toward mending their relationship, and he'll be damned if his half-assed vacuuming is going to ruin it.

By the time he hears a knock, Teo has shoved whatever else that was out of place inside the utility closet. Attempting to look nonchalant, he places a hand against the wall and opens the door.

"Hey, Gold—" he starts before noticing that she has her hands very full. "Three pizzas?"

Goldie blinks quickly, like she's taking in the sight of Teo. He has a fresh haircut; his short curls, sprinkled with white wisps, are swept up and back. His beard is fully grown and neatly trimmed as of this morning. He's wearing a hunter-green Henley with the sleeves scrunched up to show his forearms and well-worn blue jeans that aren't skintight but still nicely outline his legs.

Teo fights the smirk tugging his lips, because Goldie's arms might be full of pizza, but her eyes? They're hungry for something else.

"Goldie? You okay? You want me to take those for you?"

Goldie shakes out of the sudden bout of wantonness. "Um, I'm fine. Can I come in?"

"Yeah, of course." Teo moves out of the way and motions for her to set the boxes down on the kitchen table. "Hey, so I'm glad you could come over, and I'm grateful for the food, but why three pizzas?"

"I thought Eli and Jordan would be here too."

"They'll be here later after Jordan's taekwondo class. And yeah, the girl could probably eat a whole pizza on her own, but that's still a lot."

"Pizza makes for good leftovers," she says with a shrug. "Plus, one of the boxes is specially made for you."

When Teo lifts the box top, a sweet smell fills his nostrils.

It's pineapple.

"Wow! Goldie, thank you."

Instead of saying "You're welcome," like he expects, Goldie stares at him with a meaningful expression.

"Why are you looking at me like that?"

She continues to stare, adding a head tilt.

Teo racks his brain for whatever she's trying to communicate so obscurely. Then he sucks in a breath. "Oh shit! Penny's pregnant?"

Goldie rolls her eyes and nods an affirmative.

"How is she?"

"She had a mini-freakout session with me and Paul. We talked it out with her though."

"So, not planned?"

"Definitely not. She and Jack are just programmed to procreate every three years for some reason."

"Well, tell them congratulations for me." He starts to move toward the cabinets for plates. "And thank you for my victory pizza, Golds."

"Sure, whatever," she says, sounding distracted.

Before Teo turns around, he catches Goldie's eyes traveling down his body. As he reaches upward, he flexes and clenches every muscle like the plates he's grabbing are discuses, and he's about to compete for Olympic Gold.

He doesn't bother fighting a smirk anymore as he turns back to catch Goldie darting her heated gaze away. "You ready to dig in?"

"Oh, um, sure," she says, still not looking at him. "Gimme a couple of veggie lovers."

"So you can pretend to eat healthy?"

"You have no right to criticize my choice in pizza," Goldie says as she takes her plate. "I'm not touching your gross pineapple."

"Fine." Teo shrugs and motions for them to go to the living room. "More sweet and savory goodness for me. It's like my birthday all over again."

"I'm going to be upset if you think a pineapple pizza is better than studio time. Because I have no problem asking for my money back."

"Don't you dare," Teo says as he takes note of Goldie's choice of the side chair instead of the center of the couch with him. "I'm already working on the instrument arrangements for a few of the songs. Got a new song I'm working on too."

"What's it about?"

Teo looks at her through his eyelashes. "You."

Goldie tries to seem aloof. "Same one you've been working on?"

"No, I scrapped that. It had a lot of allusions to our age difference. It was basically my way of confessing without really confessing."

She scoffs and shakes her head. "Oh, Teo."

"Pathetic, I know." He shakes his head too.

Goldie quirks her head but otherwise doesn't comment on his self-criticism. "Can I hear any of it?"

"You know you can't till it's finished."

"Play me something else, then," she says, voice low and vulnerable.

Teo gives their untouched pizzas a passing glance before placing his plate on the coffee table and getting up to grab his guitar. When he returns, Goldie's abandoned her pizza as well and lounges sideways on the chair with her legs and long skirt draped over one of the arms.

"Any requests?"

She catches the tip of her tongue between her teeth before answering with a huskiness not usually present in her voice. "Something sensual."

Teo's heartbeat picks up at the alluring request. "You got it."

He starts loosely strumming on the guitar, working out the right key, humming before committing to the style he wants. Goldie wanted sensual, so sensual is what she'll get.

"*Bésame*," he croons, "*bésame mucho ...*"

Goldie's eyes sparkle with recognition and what Teo hopes is pleasure. He's played this at the bar a couple times. It's a Spanish-language classic from the 1930s, written by a young woman who had never been kissed. The beginning of the song is a plea to kiss, a lot, as if it were the last time.

Teo imbues the lyrics and guitar strains with his longing for Goldie. The Spanish words might not be familiar to her, but his feelings are, and he hopes the song can wash away the pain and doubts that surround the two of them. Tonight, there is only the love and lust they feel for each other.

"Thank you," Goldie drawls when he finishes the song.

Teo nods to accept the thanks even though she can't see it. Her eyes closed at one point, and when the darkened irises finally show, Goldie sweeps her gaze over his face and down his body yet again.

"How old are you today?" she asks.

Teo has to swallow to keep the tremor of want out of his voice. "Early 40s," he says, then second-guesses himself. "Okay, *maybe* pushing 50."

"Middle age looks good on you."

Teo rubs his chin in response. "You like it? Graying beard and all?"

"I'm a little surprised by how much. I'm glad I get to see it."

A touch of guilt flares in Teo, but he doesn't waste time dwelling on it. This moment is a chance to further mend the rift he caused. "What's happening in our lives now?"

"Probably busy raising our kids."

Teo sucks in a breath. "Really?"

"That's how I saw things going for us." Goldie's eyes go distant for a moment. "Before everything."

Teo nods. "How many?"

"Just two. We're not Penny and Jack."

Teo snorts. "Two is plenty. Probably still don't get much time for ourselves."

"We try," she says with a hint of amusement. "We have them stay with their halmoni as much as possible. But you recently had to have surgery, so we can't even make do with some quickies."

"Oh no!" Teo gasps, playing along with the scenario. "I hope I'm doing okay."

"You look better than ever," Goldie says, searing him with her gaze.

It's a heated look as is, but Teo knows those beautiful brown eyes can burn even brighter. Hotter.

"You know, it's a shame we can't make love. Feeling your legs wrapped around me could heal me better than anything."

"These legs?" she asks playfully. Her long skirt inches upward to reveal bare limbs and a hint of her black panties. "I had no idea they held so much power."

"They absolutely do," Teo says, rough and throaty, not bothering to hide anymore how turned on he is. "I bet I miss those beautiful legs. How I would start from your feet and glide up to trace their shape with my hands. How I'd hook one over my shoulder and kiss the insides of your thighs. How I'd tease and torture you by worshipping them for too long. And then I'd gradually split them apart to nose around your mound while still holding your thighs on my shoulders—because it's not only my waist I love feeling you wrapped around."

Goldie grips the bunched material of her skirt with one hand while the other glides over one of her thighs. Teo hopes she's imagining it's his hand.

"I'd make sure I am completely in tune with your body when I finally placed my tongue on you. I'd spell out words of love and desire. Hell, I've written whole songs while I'm down there," he says with a breathy chuckle. "And the sounds that come from you— the sweet whines, bitten-off cries, and deep-throated moans—are the music I make."

Teo places the guitar next to the couch and leans forward. "I loved singing and playing for you tonight. I just hope I get a chance to hear the other kind of music I make when I'm with you."

Goldie's legs fall off the arm of the chair as she moves to stand, then collapse at the knees onto the cushion next to Teo, whose hands come up to her hips to steady her. He looks up into her beautiful face and licks his lips. A hungry gaze tracks the action while fingertips explore his facial hair.

"Does this new, older mouth kiss the same?" Goldie murmurs. The words inspire a groan from the very mouth that has her fascination. Her lips curve wickedly, and in a taunting lilt, she asks, "Does it *taste* the same?"

"Why don't you find out?" Teo rasps.

Goldie dips her head down.

Then the front door whips open.

"Abuelo, we're here!" Jordan's voice carries across the very short, barely out-of-sight distance to them.

"Oh shit!" Goldie freaks out and dives over the back of the couch.

"Goldie?" Teo watches as she disappears from his arms in a blink. He turns around to see her flat on the floor. "You okay?"

"Yes!" she hisses through gritted teeth.

Jordan comes into the living room followed by her father, who's carrying a gym bag. "Is Goldie here?" she asks. "We saw her car outside."

"And what's with all the pizza?" Eli asks.

Goldie pops up from behind the couch. "I brought them."

"Oh my God!" Both Eli and Jordan exclaim like a horror-film cliché. Eli even drops the gym bag and brings his hands up like he's about to full-blown scream.

"You *are* here!" Jordan jumps with excitement. "What are you doing behind the couch?"

"I was, uh." Goldie looks at Teo for an excuse. He shrugs helplessly. "I was looking for the remote! Thought it might have fallen back here. I had to check under the couch too, of course," she rambles. "Just saw a lot of dust bunnies. Teo, you really need to vacuum under there."

Teo groans. Of course, she was going to notice the one place he didn't vacuum.

Eli points toward the coffee table. "The remote's over there."

"Ohhh!" Goldie says, acting totally surprised and looking at Teo. "How did you not see it there the whole time?"

Teo feels completely out of his depth. "Well, I'm old. I probably need my eyes checked."

Goldie gives him a mean side-eye as she comes out from behind the couch and does a quick adjustment of her skirt. "It's good to see you guys. How was taekwondo?"

"Great!" Jordan says. "I made my first take-down. Soon, I'll be able to yeet even Tommy across a room."

Goldie chuckles. "That's awesome."

Eli clears his throat. "We weren't interrupting anything, were we? Because I was dropping off Jordan before meeting Tommy."

"No!" Goldie exclaims. "We were just about to eat pizza. That's all."

Teo wants to say that he was so close to eating something else, but he wouldn't dare say that out loud with his granddaughter there. Plus, Goldie would probably avoid him again for embarrassing her.

"Oh, good. I'm so hungry," Jordan unsurprisingly says. "Let me go change. We can watch the new Marvel show!"

When Jordan leaves the room, Eli tries to do some damage control. "I could take her with me if you two want to be alone."

Teo absolutely wants that, but he knows it's not up to him.

"That's okay," Goldie says to Eli while looking at Teo. She bites her bottom lip and gives his mouth one last heated look before tearing her gaze away. "Go out with Tommy. I'd love to hang out with Jordan again."

"Are you sure?" Eli tries one more time.

"Mijo, take advantage of this while you can." Teo loves having his granddaughter around, of course. But he was *so close* to being with Goldie that the disappointment is getting to him.

"Okay, but if you guys ever need me and Jordan to be scarce for *reasons*"—Eli air-quotes the word—"just give me a heads-up."

Goldie groans and covers her face.

Teo's more amused than embarrassed but takes pity on both Goldie and his son. "Sure, thanks. Now, go before I come up with a way to repeat what just happened but with you and Tommy instead."

The look of horror on his son's face is hilarious. "All right, I'm going!" He turns around, moving toward the door. "Bye, Jordie! I'll pick you up later!"

"Later, Papá!" she shouts as she comes back into the living room. "Have fun with Tommy!"

"*Oh, I will!*" Eli says over the shoulder, directing a glare at Teo.

When her father's gone, Jordan looks at the condition of the room. "You two haven't eaten your pizza?"

"We, uhhh," Teo drags out, "got distracted."

"I'll heat them up and get me some too." His granddaughter grabs the plates and heads to the kitchen.

Teo takes advantage of the little time they have alone. "You really okay with this, Golds?"

She sighs. "I'm a bit disappointed."

"Me too," he admits. "Next time?"

Goldie's lips form a thin line before she pops them open to speak. Whatever she was going to say gets interrupted though.

"Oh, yuck! Pineapple!"

Goldie takes the out and goes to the kitchen to help Jordan bring back the pizza. Throughout the rest of the evening, they binge the new Marvel show like Jordan wanted, but the real highlights include:

- Goldie and Jordan talking about which Marvel characters are in love. ("Peggy Carter is my girl," Goldie says, "but Steve should've been dancing with Bucky at the end of the last *Avengers* movie.")
- Jordan eating a whole slice of pineapple pizza. ("Tropical fruit just shouldn't be hot," she complains as she stubbornly takes yet another bite.)
- The positives and negatives of the *Star Wars* sequels. ("I didn't like Rey with Kylo Ren," Jordan says. "Me neither," Teo agrees. "But at least we got PoeFinn.")
- Teo showing Goldie braiding techniques on Jordan. ("How the hell did you do that fishtail?" Goldie gazes in wonder. "Do you have extra fingers I'm not aware of?")
- Advanced planning of Halloween costumes. ("Quit stealing my ideas, Abuelo! *I'm* going to be Spider-Gwen this year!")
- Teo teaching Jordan how to play poker. ("No se lo digas a tu papá.")

The laughter and spirited conversation is made all the sweeter with Goldie sitting closer to Teo than she has in weeks. Shoulders press against each other. Longing gazes exchange and linger. Hands trail across thighs on their way to reach for a drink. Goldie's lavender scent mingles with the air Teo breathes.

They're so close, in fact, that Teo imagines being able to hear Goldie's heartbeat. A beautiful thump, thump, thump that matches his, inspired by their proximity, the pull of attraction, the possibility of being in each other's arms again. The rhythm is loud and fast and strong, as sensual as his performance for her tonight. It can't be quieted or ignored.

But Goldie's the only one who can really hear that little organ within. Teo hopes she listens to it.

CHAPTER 18

"GOOD MORNING, ACTION NEWS NOW NATION. I'M MAX DORIAN, senior anchor and co-host of AN-NOW A.M. and AN-NOW MIDDAY.

"My apologies for interrupting the first of our ten weather segments for this hour, but I feel it is my duty to speak on the frankly exciting news to come out of the interview with the producer of the Crown Serum that was unfortunately not conducted by AN-NOW.

"Journalist and my close, personal friend Marigold Hays of the *Daily Liberty Press* had the privilege of interviewing Sarah Crown, the CEO and owner of Crown Cosmetics. She also had the privilege of interviewing me, which was the highlight of the series the newspaper published this week in celebration of the twentieth anniversary of the Crown Serum.

"While the interview with Ms. Crown contained incredible insight into the history and production of the Serum, readers like you and I were stunned by the revelation that a version of the Serum that lasts forever, brilliantly named the Forever Serum, has been immaculately conceived and will be available to the public.

"While no further details were unveiled, specifically the exact date of release and price, AN-NOW can speculate based on my intimate knowledge of Ms. Hays—*and* her work—that it will be sometime in the future. The cost, we can safely assume, will be the same as the current version of the Serum or more … or less. These are the facts.

"Now, you might be asking, 'Max, why are you giving this

news any of your precious air time? After reading your powerful and engaging interview, I thought you were skeptical of the need for the Serum and unfairly forced to take it after circumstances deemed it the only way to reach the lofty heights you so richly deserve.' And it is fair of you to call me out on all those nuanced points.

"I assure you all, I am not buying what Crown is selling … yet. The Forever Serum isn't on the market yet. What I am distilling from this latest innovation is a vision of the future. Gentlepersons, we are entering an age of agelessness. A brave new world free of the stigma that comes with looking older than 30. I was quoted, loosely, as rhetorically asking only what everyone thinks: 'Who wants to look old anyway?'

"It's a tough but fair question. Because, let's face it, Mother Nature cheated humanity. She gave us pathetically short lifespans, and we have to spend the majority of them weak and looking terrible. Why couldn't we live long, strong, majestic lives like giant tortoises? They look great at any age.

"We all want to believe that age ain't nothin' but a number because, until very recently, we had no choice but to accept the decay of our bodies.

"Not anymore. With the Crown Serum and the Forever Serum, we are tipping the scales. Neither product extends how long we live, but they can keep us looking like our best selves for however long we have left.

"Now, many of you might accuse me of being vain. You same people probably don't follow me on social media. If you did, which you can at the usernames and apps below, you'd know how super opposite I am of vain. Wanting to look fresh-faced and youthful and not bald for a lifetime isn't vanity. It's about *maximizing* quality of life.

"Twenty years ago, before the Serum existed, I was in my mid-30s and still looked great, even without the Serum. You don't see much drop-off in looks at that age, and besides, I'm a man, and men age more gracefully than women. We all know this.

"Anyway, I was the best reporter this station had. I was running out the door to a natural disaster one day, a city council scandal the next, and the opening of a new Super Target the next. Doing my best work and dating the hottest people around. I was living life to the *max*.

"Time took that away from me. I wasn't just losing my hair, I was slower. I'm never not tired. I need stupid reading glasses. I deal with back issues; hell, I'm in pain right now and take ibuprofen like it's candy. I was never able to return to that peak, even after taking the Serum. Don't get me wrong, I am at the pinnacle of my career and won't be removed no matter how badly certain Rachel Maddow wannabes try. But I miss that Max Dorian, and there's no getting him back.

"Or so I thought before this morning, when I read about the Forever Serum. Allow me to directly quote the *DLP* reporter—I like to call her Goldie—in her commentary: 'If you live on this planet, then you have been affected by the Serum—because it changed the world.'

"Today, the Forever Serum changed the world again. One dose, endless youth. If *that's* possible, then imagine what's next. The cures, the breakthroughs, the miracles. Not only a changed world—a better world.

"I hope we all live long enough to see it."

Max looks away from the camera and clears his throat. Goldie thinks the aside lasts longer than normal. He can be heard murmuring, "Yeah, give me a sec," probably in response to someone off camera. When he returns to the screen, he places a forearm on the desk and leans forward. His gritted smile shows both top and bottom teeth like a shark.

"When we come back, our first guest will be a baby otter named, strangely enough, Sealy."

Goldie pushes the remote's power button like she's jabbing someone's eye out.

Her mother squawks, "I wanna watch baby otter!"

Goldie gets up, handing her the remote.

"Why you mad? Max Dorian say your name on TV. He so handsome. Nice hair."

"He's using the Forever Serum as his 'The President's been shot' moment. He's, uh." She sputters to a stop, taking a moment to compose herself and consider why she's so mad at his statement. "I don't think he's being honest about his opinion on the Serum or the Forever Serum. If he really thinks it's all great, more power to him. But if he's just saying that to cater to what he thinks will be the side of society that will get him ratings and favors, then he's in no way the kind of serious journalist he idolizes."

"Hmph," her mother grunts, and narrows her gaze at Goldie before wagging the remote at her. "Why you really mad?"

Goldie flops back onto the couch and blows out a breath. "I'm afraid of people losing their minds over the Forever Serum. It's a permanent thing. It needs to be taken seriously."

"You think people not take it serious? That they gonna listen to Max Dorian and spend savings, and think, 'Oh nooo! I'm too young! I make big mistake!'"

Goldie frowns. "When you say it like that, it does sound a little stupid."

"'Cause it is stupid! You not give people credit."

"Oh, come on, Ma! People are going to misuse this stuff. It's happened with the Crown Serum. It happened to *me*."

"You still not over that?"

Goldie glares but admits, "I've mostly dealt with it. But what Teo did is still a good example of the messed-up things people can do with the Serum."

"What about stuff you write?" Her mother picks up the newspaper. "About how Serum not bad thing just because it take care of looks. You not mean that?"

"Of course I meant that. I also wanted people to make informed decisions and learn from the anecdotes." They're interrupted by Goldie's phone buzzing. She frowns at the name on the screen. "It's Sarah Crown."

Her mother grabs the phone to see for herself. "Why she call? You think she mad?"

Goldie shrugs and answers the phone. "Hello?"

"Oh, Pretty Reporter," Sarah says, "what have you done?"

Goldie scoffs. "I did my job."

Her mother whispers loud enough for Sarah to hear. "What she say? Put on speaker."

"Am I interrupting something?" Sarah asks.

"I'm with my mother."

"Let's do a video call! I want to meet her." Before Goldie knows it, her phone's screen is filled with Sarah Crown's porcelain face. "Hello, Mrs. Hays!"

"Oh no, don't look! I not even wash face yet," Sun says despite wrenching the phone from her daughter's hand to talk to the CEO. "I always buy your makeup and lotion. I loyal customer."

"Thank you."

"So, you can't sue my daughter. You owe me, and we not have money."

Sarah laughs. "You are everything I hoped for. Goldie did not exaggerate."

Sun looks at Goldie. "You tell Sarah Crown about me?"

"It was a long interview," Goldie says, trying to keep her explanation vaguely honest. "We talked about a lot of things."

Sarah saves her from saying anymore. "I'm not going to sue your daughter. I called to tell her I'm proud of her."

The mother and daughter stare dumbfounded at the phone.

"You proud of my daughter?"

"Hey!" Goldie squawks.

"Chill out," her mother says, showing off her surprisingly good grasp of idioms. "I mean people mostly cuss you out for news about them."

"Okay, yeah, that's true," Goldie concedes. "So, why are you proud of me, Sarah?"

"You made the choice I couldn't make."

Goldie's not so sure how she should feel about revealing the Forever Serum to the public, but proud doesn't seem to fit. "There was only ever one real choice to make," she says. "To offer others the choice. Besides, don't act like you weren't going to do the same thing eventually."

"Probably," Sarah admits, looking at something off screen. "I think I needed the added perspective. Just the right push."

It's impossible to tell what she's staring at, but the pause gives Goldie's mind a chance to wander back to her interview with the CEO in her homey office. She recalls the old ad on the wall of a butterfly emerging from its chrysalis. *A new beginning*.

Sarah looks back to the screen with a placid expression. "Thank you, Goldie," she says in an exhale. "Thank you for telling me your story."

To avoid the small crowd of people and cameras at the front and employee entrances of the newspaper, Goldie enters the building through the printing press. Manning warned her about them when he called at an ungodly hour in the morning to beg her to come back to the office to discuss the aftermath of the Forever Serum reveal and handle requests to talk to her.

The reporter does her best to stealthily circumnavigate the newsroom to get to her desk without fanfare. Her efforts prove to be futile the minute she passes Manning's window.

"Goldie, get the fuck in here!"

"Shit," she mutters, turning to cut through the desks for a direct path.

To her surprise, a few of her coworkers shout out, "Way to go, Goldie!" and other words of praise with a smattering of applause. She awkwardly waves at them as she hustles to Manning's office.

Amber rushes up to her side as she approaches the doorway and squeezes through with her. Before either Manning or Goldie can acknowledge her, she tears into the reporter. "How could you not tell me about the Forever Serum?! You interviewed Sarah Crown weeks ago!"

Goldie held on to her article until the last possible minute, only allowing Manning to edit it. Of course, he was ready to blast the news out on the internet immediately before she convinced him that waiting until the paper was delivered the next day would make the reveal all the more impressive.

"I couldn't tell anyone before the agreed-upon publication date. It was a condition of the interview."

"What the fuck!" Amber exclaims. "Did you see all those people out there?"

Goldie nods, looking at Manning. "What do they want from me?"

"They want the inside scoop on your inside scoop." The executive editor motions to his monitor and phone. "We're getting all kinds of requests to talk to you."

"But it's all in the newspaper!" Goldie argues.

"Since they couldn't be the ones to talk to Crown, they want the proxy, and they're gonna squeeze every last morsel out of our story." He picks up today's paper and waves it around like a flag. "You told the people why they should care about the Serum, and they fucking listened. This is huge for us."

"What do you mean?"

"You're doing these interviews."

"What?!" Goldie and Amber cry in unison.

"You'll have to do a few on Zoom, but we're sending you to New York to do the talk shows and news programs in person."

"You want me to go to *New York*?" Goldie asks, pronouncing the destination slowly like it's a foreign word. "This is ridiculous! I have nothing to do with the Forever Serum. That's what they really care about."

"You broke the story though," Amber says. "You're part of history."

In her commentary, Goldie touched on how the Serum affected her personally and how doing this story could change her professionally. She thought acknowledging the possibility would give her a head start on preparing for the change, but she seems to have forgotten another point she made.

Change often comes for us when we need it the most.

"Goldie," Manning says with unusual softness, "I know I can be a prick, but it's because I care about this paper and this industry. We need all the publicity and attention we can get, and you got it for us. This is your moment." He hands her the newspaper. "Make the most of it."

———————————

"SETTLE DOWN!" MANNING YELLS AT THE REPORTERS AND CAMERA operators after herding them into the newspaper's lobby.

"Lloyd, they better not break my displays!" Dottie warns from the reception desk. "Not one scratch against that glass. Y'all are gonna feel my boot against your backsides!"

"Thank you, Dottie! We got it!" Manning glares at the crowd and clears his throat. "All right, folks. Congratulations, your trespassing has paid off. You're going to be the first to talk to one of our finest, Marigold Hays, about her earth-shattering scoop on the Forever Serum and the intimate, sure-to-win-a-Pulitzer story on Sarah Crown that was found only in the *Daily Liberty Press*: 'Let Free Press Ring™.'"

Goldie can't help grimacing as Manning spouts the newspaper's slogan (even saying the "TM" for trademark out loud). She probably looks like a wounded animal in agony in front of all these people who want to speak to her. It is so weird being on the other end of an interview.

"We'll start with you, Candy," Manning says, taking on moderator duties.

Despite not being on camera, the TV reporter smooths her already perfect red hair and spreads her glossy lips into a fake-as-hell smile. "Hello, Candy Frost, WFNC Morning Matters."

"Yes, Candy," Manning says, "we know your ridiculous name."

Her glossy lips flash a sneer before settling into a more professional expression. "Ms. Hays, how did you of all people get this interview with Sarah Crown?"

Goldie plasters on her own fake smile. "Thank you for the snidely worded question. She contacted the paper and asked for me."

"Did the paper pay for the access?" Candy follows up.

"We did not. That goes against our policies."

"How could Sarah Crown know about your paper? It's not a national publication. No billionaire owns it. WFNC is a Fox affiliate, and my show is seen in more than a dozen markets."

"Luckily, Crown's headquarters falls within our coverage area." Goldie smirks. "And Ms. Crown is a fan of newspapers, especially the local kind. Besides, circulation and broadcast markets aren't the indicators of reach they once were. There's a little thing called the internet, Ms. Frost."

"But why *you*?" Candy asks.

"She wanted someone with a story to tell."

"What the hell does that mean?"

"All right, Candy." Manning holds up a hand like he's defending Goldie from paparazzi. "Let someone else ask a question. Tobey, you're next."

"Hey, Goldie, is it true that the Serum is for secretly injecting microchips into our bloodstreams to control our minds?"

Goldie squints in disbelief and turns to her executive editor. "My God, Lloyd, what have you gotten me into?"

AFTER THE IMPROMPTU NEWS CONFERENCE, MANNING AND GOLDIE work out a game plan for New York. Of course, Amber will be going as well to help chronicle the high-profile moment for the newspaper (and because Goldie threatened not to go without her).

The rest of the reporter's morning entails trying to manage her overstuffed email inbox. Her desk phone mercifully has been commandeered by Dottie and Manning, and she's blocked unknown numbers, which is why Goldie jumps out of her skin when her smartphone vibrates on her desk. Almost as surprising is the name that appears on screen—Terrance Bolan.

"Hello?"

"Uh, hi, um, Ms. Hays," the wellness guru and former Serum user greets stiltedly. "Sorry to bother you. I know you're probably very busy."

"It's no problem. What can I do for you?"

"Well, so, I read your interview with Sarah Crown today and how there's going to be a Forever Serum."

Goldie's stomach sinks. "Yes?"

"It didn't say when it would be released though."

"There's no date yet."

"Will it be soon though?"

"I don't know. Ms. Crown wasn't specific."

"You don't have any idea?"

"I'm sorry. I don't have any more information."

"Oh, okay," he says, almost too softly to hear. "I'm sorry to bother you again."

"It's no problem. Take care of yourself, Mr. Bolan."

There's a bitter huff before he responds. "Sure, thanks. Bye."

Goldie stares at the dark screen of her phone for a long time afterward. She eventually drops it into her purse and gets up. She needs to see how another former Serum user is handling the news.

THE PERSON AT THE FRONT DESK OF THE GARDEN'S WELCOME CENTER directs Goldie down a path underneath an array of arching tree limbs. At the end is a scattering of picnic tables with a familiar, fully covered figure working on a laptop.

"Hi, Soledad. Sorry if I'm interrupting."

The garden director looks up and blinks rapidly to adjust her eyes. "Goldie!" She gets up and hugs her warmly. "¡Hola, chica!"

Goldie laughs at the greeting.

"What are you doing here?"

"I wanted to check in on you."

"What? Why?"

Goldie second-guesses herself. "Did you read my article today?"

"Yes, of course. It's the only thing anyone's talking about. I had to get away to get any work done."

"Oh, I'm so sorry! I'll leave you alone."

"No, Goldie, stay. I'm just surprised you have time to come by. You're all over TV and social media right now."

"Yeah, I wasn't prepared for this level of attention."

"The Forever Serum is a big deal."

"What do you think about it?" Goldie asks.

"Is this another interview?"

"No, I'm genuinely concerned."

Soledad looks down at her covered hands and arms, then takes the mask off and touches the scarred side of her face. "Honestly," she says in a long exhale, "I don't like how people seem to treat wrinkles like they're scars."

Goldie nods. "That's fair."

"But reading those anecdotes showed me how intensely some people feel about their wrinkles. Like, honest disgust and shame. You said it yourself in the paper—billions feel that way. I can't say I have more of a right to my insecurities and pain about my appearance than they do. But now we're all going to have a permanent solution. This should be a great thing."

"You don't think it is?"

"We blame everything on the outside to avoid dealing with anything on the inside. The Forever Serum isn't going to heal my trauma. It's not going to fix my marriage. I let everything go slack while using the Crown Serum."

"You know better now," Goldie says.

"Yeah, but there are so many others who don't. They'll use the Forever Serum to smooth out their skin, then let their insides rot."

Goldie has to sit down after hearing such a bleak possibility. She pins it to her outsized mental board of worst-case scenarios involving the Forever Serum. She can't be responsible for the collapse of society. She can't even bear the guilt of occasionally going over the speed limit.

Soledad sits next to her, neither saying anything more for a while. Butterflies flit about the thick area of milkweed nearby, one flying fairly close to their table.

"Are you going to take it?" Goldie asks eventually.

"I think so. I just hope it's not going to cost me a fortune I don't have." Soledad turns her head to look directly at the reporter. "Are you disappointed in me?"

"What? No, of course not. I only want you to be happy with your choice."

"The choice I can live with," Soledad says, quoting Goldie's commentary with a deep, serious tone.

The reporter rolls her eyes. "Yes, exactly. So, you really read it all?"

"Of course, Ms. Hays. I read every word, including that bit about how you might consider taking the Serum for love. You have nothing to worry about with Teo. That boy of yours is gonna love you at this age and for all the years after no matter how you look."

Goldie stiffens. "He's, um, not quite as young as he looks."

"How old is he?"

"62."

Soledad jolts back. "Wow, I really couldn't tell."

"Yeah, neither could I."

"You didn't know?!"

"Nope."

"That son of a bitch."

Goldie snorts and laughs so hard that she starts gasping for air.

"What's so funny?"

After another painful snort, Goldie forces herself to calm down. "Sorry, it's just that it wasn't too long ago that Teo and I were here talking to you and calling your ex the same thing."

Soledad's mouth quirks at the reminder.

Goldie gazes wistfully at the garden. The gazebo they sat at for the interview peeks through the trees. "We were gonna get married here."

"Is it really over?"

"I wrote in my column about how great having a choice is, but I can't make myself decide one way or another about him. Which path of uncertainty do I take?"

"You're so full of it!" Soledad playfully slaps Goldie's thigh.

Goldie rubs the spot like it hurts. "Why do you say that?"

"You know what you're going to do. You wrote exactly what kind of choice people should be making."

"I meant with the Forever Serum!"

"It applies to this too," Soledad says. "Can you honestly see a future without Teo? Could you live with that choice?"

Living without Teo is a frightening thought. More than frightening, actually.

The possibility makes Goldie's heart *scream*. It beats fast and heavy, thumping hard enough to crack her sternum. Blood rushes in her ears; it's so loud.

She inhales deeply in a vain attempt to give the muscle more room, but it's been trapped for too long. Her heart's breaking free by any means. Or maybe just opening her up, chest splayed and gaping for the world to see.

No, not for the world. *For Teo.*

Soledad grabs her shoulders. "Are you okay?"

Goldie's mouth opens, but before words can be uttered, a relieved giggle escapes. "Well, damn," she says breathlessly. "I guess I do know what I'm going to do."

DISCOVERING THE FOUNTAIN OF YOUTH CHANGED US ALL

By Marigold Hays, Staff writer
The Daily Liberty Press

As I finish my work on this series, I feel a need to reflect on the entirety of this journey into the world of the Crown Serum.

This was not an assignment I took on lightly—or enthusiastically. Of the millions of journalists out there from the worlds of television, social media, blogs, websites, magazines, and my scrappy realm, newspapers, I was the recipient of the Golden Ticket.

The interview with Sarah Crown that you have just read could change my life professionally. I'll admit, it's already changed my life personally. More than two months ago, when my executive editor called me into his office and told me that I was going to do the interview of the century, I turned 40 and had almost 20 years of experience at the same newspaper. I wasn't looking to change anything.

That's not how life works though. We make plans, then plans fail. The most mundane expectations often never come to fruition. Storms real or metaphorical come and go.

And change occurs. It not only occurs, it *comes* for you, and a lot of the time it's when you need it to happen.

In the beginning, I didn't want this assignment. Now, after all the interviews and hours of research and writing and debate, I know that I needed it.

Asking why

Going into any story, a journalist must address the five W's: Who, What, When, Where and Why. The Why is probably the trickiest. Strictly speaking, Why should apply to the subject of the story. On another level, Why applies to the reader.

Why should you care?

Addressing this Why for the 20th anniversary of the Crown Serum meant talking to users and nonusers alike and learning about their experiences with a product that has been marketed and hailed as a miracle.

Now, there's no doubt it does exactly what it is supposed to—eliminate wrinkles and other signs of aging. This series was never going to be some grand exposé on the product's lack of effectiveness or previously unknown side effects or evil schemes by the big, bad corporation.

There are no villains in this story.

The bigger picture I wanted to address as part of the fundamental Why question was whether aging, something we all endure, required any miracle at all.

A changed world

While I did my best to get diverse voices, the majority of Serum users are wealthy and affluent, and my pool of anecdotes reflects that. Often, the lack of availability to lower-income people is a focus of Serum debates. The concern is valid. Most can't afford the Serum, so why should you care if you're never going to be able to take it?

Let's take into account how monumental the Serum is. No wrinkles, no white hair and no hair loss. These achievements were unimaginable 20 years ago. Sure, other products have tried. All the creams, lotions, oils, wands, scrapers, acids, light therapies, surgeries, microneedles, charcoal, rose quartz—none of it was enough. But the Crown Serum worked for everyone without fail.

You may have never taken the Serum, but up to 20 percent of people have. Laws have been made to adapt to circumstances related to it. Workplace human resources have made adjustments because coworker dynamics have changed. Because of the Serum, relationships and families have been made and unmade.

Again, why should you care if you're never going to be able to take it? Well, if you live on this planet, then you have been affected by the Serum—because it changed the world.

Fair criticism?

It's wrong to make a blanket statement on the ethics of using the Serum. There are no absolutes in the world. Look at birth control pills, which are known to have a variety of uses. The pill can regulate or eliminate periods, address hormonal issues, and even clear up skin. It's no more ethical to use birth control pills for any of those reasons than for their primary purpose—to not get pregnant.

The same can be said for taking the Serum. Soledad Branigan used it to eliminate the physical scars she received from a fire. We understand this choice. We would not shame her for it or insist she learn to live with the scars.

People who use the Serum purely for ridding themselves of wrinkles face a different kind of scrutiny. They are accused of vanity or selfishness. I know because I was one of the people throwing such accusations.

The cost of the treatment is a factor. There are so many worthy causes that could use the money that goes to the Serum. They also could use the money that goes to the sports car you dreamed about and worked hard to save for. They could use the money that goes to the engagement ring for the love of your life. They could use the money that goes to all the streaming services you pay for because you need the escape from your stressful job. They could use the money that goes to the makeup you use to make you feel a little bit better about yourself.

Matilda Crown, the founder of Crown Cosmetics, didn't like how she looked as she advanced in age. It's a feeling shared by billions, and she found a solution, yet I and countless others criticized how she used her own money because we weren't one of those billions who felt a need for the Serum.

It's funny how we can criticize them and not see the same need to criticize ourselves for our own "vain" uses of money.

Looking in the mirror

How old are you today? It's a question I've been asking a lot lately. Aging used to not be a choice. I was never truly aware of this fact until I turned 40.

Being a woman means living with an expiration date. So much

of our bodies is tied up in our ability to reproduce, and as our ability to have children declines, there's an implication that our physical attractiveness declines as well. The value placed on our looks in connection with our ages is astounding and unfair.

I've always seen issues with my face and body. There is extra weight, dark circles, gaping pores and oily skin. As I get older, I see every new wrinkle and every new white hair. I track whether the skin under my chin is getting loose. I even need to convince myself that I'm not seeing cellulite on my legs, only marks from sitting down funny. It's been an awakening of sorts, understanding how I see myself. I was never a fan of looking at myself in the mirror, but now, as I get older, I absolutely dread it.

But what's so scary about looking old? For me, it was about love. I had found it while looking the way I did. If I changed, wouldn't he stop loving me? I started to see how we can often tie our appearances with what's going on around us. We don't so much like how young we look. We like what happened or what we attained while looking that way.

We too often leave the fun, exciting, wild stuff in our youth. We should be living our best lives for *all* our lives. Then maybe we can look at ourselves in the mirror at any age and say, "I look great today. Same as yesterday."

Choices

But maybe you can't wait for attitudes to catch up. You know that you'll be a happier person if you never see your wrinkles again. Then you have the choice to take the Serum.

Maybe you're like Amelia Gardner-St. Vincent, who is happy with her successful company and beautiful family but likes looking young too. Then you have the choice to take the Serum.

Maybe you're like Thandie Fox and want to play the roles the Serum-using actors don't want. Then you have the choice not to take the Serum.

Because that's ultimately what the Serum is all about—choice.

However, we must weigh this choice carefully. As the anecdotes from the series have shown, choosing to use or not use the Serum comes with fallout. While eliminating wrinkles and scars, physical attributes we see as issues, we might let internal issues go completely unaddressed. Our desire to look a certain way also can blind us to how we affect those closest to us. And then there's the danger of believing that your choice is the right choice for everyone.

That's a lot to think about when deciding whether to take the Crown Serum or the Forever Serum. Make the choice you can live with—and one you won't regret.

CHAPTER 19

"HEY, BABE?" TOMMY CALLS OUT AS HE COMES INTO THE KITCHEN. "You almost done? I think Jordan's about to eat her foot."

Eli holds up a spatula in a silencing gesture and motions to the phone to his ear. "Sir, why do you think there's a poltergeist in your computer?"

Tommy snorts at his boyfriend's latest work call.

"Uh-huh," Eli responds. "I agree, it's always good to ask whether there's been a murder on the property when looking for a new home, but I don't think you have a poltergeist. It sounds like your browser has a text-to-speech program operating. Just go into the settings to turn it off. Thank you for calling Tiger Computer Repair. Don't forget to take our survey."

Eli taps his phone screen to end the call but doesn't pocket the device like Tommy expects.

"What are you looking at?"

"Just another headline about the Forever Serum." Eli hands Tommy the phone while turning back to the burgers on the stove.

Tommy's not sure which headline caught Eli's attention, because the news app has plenty of clickbait to choose from:

- *"Lots of meditation and sweet massage chairs": Crown interviewer tells all about secret lab*
- *A childless, middle-aged spinster: Everything you need to know about journalist who talked to Crown*
- *After cracking youth code, could Crown give us shapeshifting next? "That'd be cool, but no," says DLP reporter*

"Sorry about the work call," Eli says, interrupting Tommy's doomscrolling.

"It's no big deal. I overheard you give detailed instructions on how to cleanly wipe and reset a computer while shooting a perfect eighteen in mini golf. Your ability to multitask is phenomenal."

Tommy had been annoyed about losing, but Jordan was so jealous, and Eli had been cocky as hell. Seriously, he acted like the special-edition red golf ball he won was the same as the US Open trophy.

Even now, there's a smirk on his boyfriend's face after mentioning his victory. It's only the barest of curved lips though.

"Hey, what's up?" Tommy asks.

"Just annoyed. The calls remind me that we've gotta get back to Miami soon."

Tommy's chest feels too tight all of a sudden.

"Jordan's mom and stepdad have plans for the rest of her summer vacation, and I have to go into the office at least once a month."

The duo's departure hadn't seriously crossed Tommy's mind until now. What is he going to do? The mundane paperwork and rude customers became more bearable because he had Eli and Jordan to cheer him up. He wants to be the one to award Jordan a yellow belt too—and every belt after. He especially wants to wake up with Eli every morning, whispering how much he loves him in his ear.

When Eli finishes plating the burgers and looks up, he seems to notice Tommy's heavy breathing. "Are you okay?"

A loud, groaned-out declaration of "Daddy, I'm dyyying" interrupts a response.

Eli keeps his attention on Tommy. "What's wrong?" he whispers.

What must be the dopiest grin spreads across Tommy's face as he makes the best and easiest decision of his life. Leaning down to swiftly kiss Eli's pouty, perplexed lips, he whispers back, "We have a lot to talk about."

TEO HASN'T TAKEN A BITE OF HIS BURGER SINCE SITTING DOWN, TOO busy scrolling and tapping on his phone.

"Pops, you're gonna drive yourself crazy."

"I can't believe these idiots. Listen to this: *Hays's woke agenda obscures the real issues with the Crown Serum and Forever Serum—an impossible standard of innovation. How are other companies expected to compete? Sure, they could fairly compensate their employees, foster supportive work environments, and prioritize creative freedom over mass production, but they're wisely spending their money and resources on safer bets such as political influence and meme coins.*"

"It's pretty awful," Tommy says. "I shut off my phone after I saw a viral post accusing Goldie of making up the Forever Serum to get attention because she wasn't hot enough to be a TV reporter."

"But she's been all over TV too," Jordan says around a mouthful. "I think she looked super hot."

Eli shakes his head. "Everyone's just picking on Goldie so they have something extra to say about the Forever Serum."

"Abuelo, are you going to use it when you're all better?"

Teo pulls his eyes from his phone. "I haven't thought about it." He's totally lying, of course, but he doesn't want to burden his granddaughter with the debate raging in his head.

"I don't think I'd take it if I was old," Jordan says. "Being young kind of sucks."

Teo huffs. "What makes you say that?"

"I can't go anywhere by myself. I can't buy whatever I want. And school is boring ... except for science."

"Trust me, Jordan," Tommy says. "Being a young adult is very different."

"Would you take the Forever Serum?"

Tommy takes his time chewing and swallowing before responding. "I think Goldie was right about how we link our looks with what's going on with us. I don't think I really care about looking 20-something again. I was stereotypically young and dumb back then."

"What'd you do?" Jordan asks, ever nosey. Teo's son also looks very interested.

Tommy hesitates again, his mouth hanging open before shaking his head and answering. "Senior year in college, a bunch of dudebros and I got our hands on a dirt bike, got drunk, and messed around on an abandoned racetrack. Someone was bound to get hurt."

"And that someone was you," Eli assumes.

Tommy nods but can't seem to look directly at Eli to answer. "I lost traction and ended up sliding with the bike on its side. Luckily, I wasn't a complete dumbass and had a helmet on, but I fractured my right calf bone. I couldn't compete in the taekwondo championships that year. I was a real mess. I'll gladly keep that version of me in the past."

"Ah." Eli pouts. "So there's no hope of riding on the back of a motorcycle and holding you tight as we ride into the sunset?"

Tommy jumps at the idea. "I can arrange that! I know a few guys at the Harley-Davidson dealership across the street at work."

Eli subtly nods before digging into his burger.

"Daddy, you're the only one who hasn't said if you'd take the Forever Serum."

"I, um ..." Eli borrows Tommy's delaying tactic of slowly chewing and swallowing. "I don't think I could take it even if I wanted it."

"Why?" Jordan asks.

"Since it gets rid of all scars, it would heal my tattoo."

Tommy looks at Eli's chest, although it's covered. "What would happen if you took the regular Crown Serum and then stopped?"

"The faint scarring from the needle would come back, but there'd be no color since the ink would have been purged from the skin."

"That'd be so weird," Jordan says, nose scrunched. "But what if you didn't have the tattoo? Would you take the Forever Serum?"

Eli rubs his chin, taking a few beats before answering. "You know, most of my 20s were a blur. I was just looking to stay numb. Still, I don't want a chance to do it all over again. My life's only gotten better as I've gotten older. I get to see my daughter grow up. I still have my pops looking out for me. Now I have a gorgeous goofball for a boyfriend." Tommy snorts at the jab. "I welcome aging and everything that comes with it."

Teo thinks about his own reasons for taking the Serum. The fresh start excuse he told Goldie was true. Looking young motivated him to live out his dream of making music, and it gave him confidence to stand in front of a crowd night after night. Using the Serum also helped him find new love, despite how badly he messed up.

Now that he looks more like his actual age, he surprisingly finds that his confidence and drive haven't disappeared, which causes Teo to wonder if the Serum obscured what was always there in him. Has he always had the capability to build a music career? Maybe he could have won over Goldie despite the wrinkles (or maybe even because of them).

His life over the past five years has been great and fulfilling. But maybe he gives the Serum a little too much credit and should start giving himself more.

Teo shelves the thought for later and picks up the ketchup bottle to drench his burger. Before one drop can escape, his phone vibrates. He checks the screen and drops the bottle on the table.

"Geez, Pops, what's up?"

"It's Goldie."

"Oh, answer it! Answer it!" Jordan demands.

Teo sits up straighter for some reason and clears his throat. "Hey, Goldie!" *Nope, too chipper. Dial it back some.* "So, um, what's up?"

"Hey, Teo. Uh, hi."

Teo waits for more to be said but only hears some unidentifiable background noise. "Goldie, you still there?"

"Yeah," she says, barely above a whisper.

"Are you okay?"

"What's wrong?" Jordan asks.

"Am I interrupting anything?" Goldie asks.

"I'm with Eli, Tommy, and Jordan. We were having dinner."

"Hi, Goldie!" Jordan leans over to get closer to the phone. "You should come over too. Daddy can make you a burger."

"I wish I could, sweetheart."

"She says she wishes she could," Teo relays.

"Put her on speaker," Jordan says.

Teo sighs. "Goldie, are you okay with being on speaker?"

"I guess. Sure."

Teo hates that she doesn't sound happy about it but goes ahead and taps the speaker button. "Okay, everyone can hear you now."

Jordan is the first to take advantage of the impromptu conference call. "Why can't you come over?"

"I'm on my way to the airport."

Tommy's jaw drops. "You're actually going somewhere that requires air travel?"

"Yes, Tommy." Teo can practically hear the eye roll in her voice. "I'm going to New York City for a week. It's really last minute."

"Why New York?" Tommy asks.

"I'm going to be on a few talk shows and news programs."

"That's so cool!" Jordan exclaims. "You're a star! Are you in a limo now? Is a private jet taking you there?"

"No, I'm in an Uber and got stuck with a middle seat in the bowels of economy class."

"Is your mom going to be okay?" Tommy asks.

"Yeah, she's pretty much a hundred percent, and Penny and Paul are planning to visit. Paul's going to love the yardwork my mother has planned for him."

"Can we visit?" Jordan asks.

An "Oh" escapes Goldie, then a few beats of silence that make Teo nervous. Before he can give her an out, she answers. "Sure, sweetheart. My mom would love to see you again."

"Abuelo, let's go tomorrow."

"Baby, I'm not sure—"

"Ma would love to see you too, Teo," Goldie says surprisingly.

Teo bets she'd love to see him—see him fall into a fiery pit, that is.

He imagines a hole in their backyard that Goldie's mom dug

herself. She would hand-chop the wood for kindling too. And instead of matches, she would dramatically toss down a Zippo to light him up in the most badass way possible. (Along with Korean dramas, Teo also watched way too many Korean gangster movies.)

Teo huffs at his ridiculousness. For Goldie, he'll face the flames. "Okay, sure then. We'll go."

Silence lingers before Goldie says anything else. "I guess I'll go. I'm almost at the drop-off."

"Have fun, Goldie!" Jordan says. "Byeee!"

Tommy and Eli say their goodbyes as well.

Teo is a hair slower with his. "Talk to you later?" Instead of the usual sendoff, he leaves it as a question. A request.

He thinks he hears a slight chuckle before she responds. "Yeah, definitely. Bye, Teo."

"Bye, Golds."

Teo looks at the dark screen for a wistful second before setting it on the table and picking the ketchup bottle back up.

"You know what this means?!" Jordan cries, startling Teo and almost making him drop the bottle again.

For everyone's safety and benefit, he forgets the ketchup and sets it in the table's center. "What does what mean?"

"You have to go after her."

"Why would I do that? She's coming back in a week."

"That could be too late!"

"Too late for what?"

"To tell her how you feel and that you want her back!"

"She doesn't need that kind of pressure. She's got enough to deal with right now."

"Abuelo, she could have just texted to tell you she was leaving, but she *called* you. She wanted to talk to you before she left."

"And whose fault is it that I never got to hear why she called, huh?" Teo points an accusing finger right at Jordan.

"Okay, yeah, my bad. You know I get super excited about you and Goldie."

"That's an understatement," Eli mutters.

"But you don't have to hear it on the phone now," Jordan

continues. "Or wait for her to come back. This is your big 'get the girl' moment from every rom-com movie ever. You can't miss it."

Jordan's right. Goldie reached out to Teo. She wanted to tell him something. Teo can't be sure of what, but it couldn't have been for him to permanently get lost. She wouldn't have welcomed the chance to talk to him again later—right?

In an instant, Teo's shaky outlook on his relationship with Goldie completely changes. He needs to get to the airport or he'll regret it.

Teo gives his granddaughter a loud, smacking kiss on her head as he gets up. "I am so lucky to be your abuelo."

"Yeah, you are," Jordan agrees, not missing a beat.

"Okay, I'm going. Save my burger."

"No way, old man." Tommy goes ahead and takes Teo's plate. "It's forfeit. Jordan and I are splitting this."

"Fine, whatever," Teo says while grabbing his keys and wallet. "I gotta go channel Hugh Grant and magically drive across town in record time without getting pulled over."

"You can do it!" Jordan yells as Teo blindly waves behind him before shutting the door.

ELI NUDGES HIS BOYFRIEND UNDER THE TABLE WITH A FOOT TO GET HIM to join in on serving judgy glares at his daughter.

Before Jordan can return to her burger, she notices the attention. "What?"

Eli scoffs. "You're pushing them back together before we go to Miami. You're cheating on the bet."

"I'm just being a supportive nietecita."

Tommy places Pops's burger onto his plate. "I'm not sharing this with you anymore. It's my consolation prize."

"Hey! You still have a chance to win!"

"I'm obviously not going to now. 'Go get your girl, Abuelo!'" Tommy mimics. "I should've known better than to bet against you. Goldie used to be so reliably hard-headed. She would have brooded for a year before. Now there's clearly no stopping this romantic trope train."

"WE SHOULD TRY OUT THIS BAR TONIGHT." AMBER SHOWS GOLDIE photos of the place on her phone.

"We're supposed to land at 10:30 tonight, and I have to be at the first morning show by 6:30."

"And the problem is?"

"Lack of sleep?"

"Pfft," Amber sputters dismissively. "You don't go to New York to sleep. There's literally a motto about it."

"I'm not going there to party either."

"Oh, but you will," Amber promises, looking back at her phone. "I am putting this place on the to-go list."

Goldie groans but doesn't argue anymore. She shifts her butt in the unforgiving plastic seat and returns to blankly staring at the travelers as they come and go. In the distance from the direction of security, Goldie thinks she sees a familiar figure running and zigzagging around people. "Hey, Amber?"

"What?" she asks, still looking at her phone.

"I think I see Teo."

That gets the photographer's attention. She swivels her head, her curls flying out and thwacking Goldie's face like car wash brushes. To make her stop, Goldie points where her eyes were tracking Teo's fast approach.

They get up when he almost completely runs past their gate. "Teo!" the women shout.

He slides to a stop and hunches over to catch his breath.

"Thank God you saw me! This place is a damn maze." He pats around his heaving torso. "Okay, I think the liver's mostly fine."

Goldie's at a loss for words and can only gawk. In the meantime, Amber starts asking the important questions. "You grew a beard?"

Teo stands upright and touches his face self-consciously. "Uh, yeah."

"It's just that I haven't seen you in weeks." Amber's gaze furtively takes in Teo's appearance. His hair and beard are mostly white, and deep lines etch his forehead and around his eyes. "You changed."

Teo shrugs and looks at Goldie, probably to see how she's handling his sudden appearance (in every sense of the word).

"I should let you two talk," Amber says, taking the handle of her carry-on. "I'll be at the Cinnabon."

Teo and Goldie don't give her passing glances as she walks between them. They're locked into place, staring at one another. It's a duel of sorts, where both parties have reached their breaking points, and it's now or never for a resolution. Hopefully, this duel will end in a *Hamilton*-esque musical number and not so much with death and tragedy.

"How did you get through security?" Goldie asks.

"One of the TSA workers is a regular at Hank's. I had to promise to perform 'Your Body Is a Wonderland' for his boyfriend the next time they're at the bar."

Goldie cringes. "You didn't have to do that and come all this way. I was going to call again later."

"This is all Jordan's fault."

"Oh, really? Did your 11-year-old granddaughter drive the car here too?"

"She would have jumped at the chance. Car keys aren't allowed unattended in her presence." Amused, Goldie chuckles, while Teo's laugh is more nervous. "Okay, maybe I didn't need much convincing to come see you one more time before you fly off to New York City."

"You're acting like I'm going away forever. It's just a week."

"I also thought that maybe you needed to say something important to me. You haven't called me much lately."

"That's true," Goldie says. "I wanted to ask what you thought of it all. The article, the Forever Serum."

"You want to know if I'm going to take it?"

Goldie nods.

"Do *you* want me to take it?"

"Teo, I don't want you to take it for me. I was mad enough you felt you had to hide taking the Crown Serum from me. I want you to do what's right for you."

"And what if you don't like what I decide?"

"That doesn't matter."

"Yes, it does!" Teo looks around to see how many eyes he attracted from raising his voice but doesn't seem truly concerned and shifts his gaze back to Goldie. "What you think matters to me because I love you. Whether I look young or old while loving you"—his big brown eyes bore into her—"*that's* what doesn't matter."

Goldie swallows hard and looks down. "Did you read my commentary?"

"Of course I did."

"Including the part where I said looking older was scary because I thought you might stop loving me because of it?"

"Goldie, I fell in love with you as you are now: a 40-year-old workaholic journalist, music snob, and superhero fanatic with permanent worry lines on your forehead and bags under your eyes. And I would have fallen in love with you even if you were a 40-year-old Serum user without a line or shadow on your face.

"I will love you at 50, whether you start dyeing your hair because you don't like going gray or decide to just leave it be. I will love you at 50 even if you don't ever have to worry about your hair color changing and only have to worry about how frizzy it gets.

"I will love you at 60 when you complain about frown lines, and I will make you laugh all the time so you complain about those kinds of lines instead. I will love you at 60 even if you still look 25, and I will still try to make some laugh lines last.

"God willing, I will be able to love you at 70, whether you look convincingly young or obviously old. Goldie, I will love you for as long as I live—no matter how you choose to look."

Goldie takes a deep, steadying breath, controlling the swell of fear and hope. "You deserve someone who can love you that way too."

The new-old crease between Teo's eyebrows deepens with worry. "Can't you?"

The boarding call for the flight is, of course, announced then. Teo's eyes flick over to the opening that leads to the plane, but Goldie's are locked on him as she feels a familiar stirring in her chest.

On the first night they met, Goldie's heart had made a permanent impression of Teo with his wild, dark curls, strong jawline, and brow that only wrinkled for ironic effect. She compares it to what she sees in front of her now. The white hairs and wrinkles. The looser skin around his jaw and neck. The prominent veins and unique creases of his hands.

Goldie feels her heart trace every line, wrinkle, and crease, carefully carving out a space for this version of Teo too.

"How old are you today?" Goldie asks out of nowhere.

Teo purses his lips, looking disappointed that he's apparently not going to get an answer to his question. "I turned 62 recently."

"Really? Wow, you don't look it."

A bark of laughter cracks the sullen expression. "Thanks, I make sure to use lots of sunscreen."

Goldie thinks her smile should be bright enough for him to really need the stuff.

Teo notices the look, his eyes alight with curiosity. "We're getting kind of old now, aren't we?" he muses.

"Yeah, we are," she answers without hesitation. Goldie keeps smiling, honestly unbothered by the thought.

"What's happening with us now?"

Goldie gazes off into the distance and says with a note of awe, "I have absolutely no idea." Her smile turns into a sly smirk before looking back. "But I can't wait to find out."

Teo sucks in a sharp breath.

Goldie begins walking backward toward the gate doors. "See you in a week, Teo."

A bubble of laughter escapes as a grin stretches Teo's gray-bearded, wrinkled cheeks. "I'll be waiting, Golden Wonder."

CHAPTER 20

GOLDIE WIPES THE FOG FROM HER BATHROOM MIRROR. TYPICALLY, she leaves it to disappear on its own and puts off looking in a mirror until the last minute, but she's in a hurry.

She takes the towel off her head and riffles through the hair on top, noting a couple of white strands that are clearly visible. After combing, she lets her hair air dry a bit before using the blow-dryer.

Her face is wonderfully clean and oil free, and she takes a moment to appreciate the nakedness before tackling her skincare routine, starting with the eyes. The stuff she dabs on has algae to help with the dark circles. She then places gel eye masks on top and imagines it all actually working.

Her acne hasn't been too bad lately, but she still makes sure to swipe on some medicated toner before picking up the new Crown Retinol Topical Serum that her mother bought (clearly labeled so as not to be confused with the Crown Serum, which requires a scary needle). She traces over every forehead line and the crescents of her cheeks. Then she dabs all around for good measure.

She ditches the eye masks early so she can smooth on the moisturizer that apparently "plumps" the skin to further lessen the appearance of lines. She makes sure to use it on her neck too.

After all that is done, Goldie inspects the progress and sighs. "Still 40," she murmurs.

The last step is the powder foundation ... which she immediately drops because her mother pounds on the door.

"What take so long?! I already dress and ready. You slowest person ever. You try and win world record? Ppalli nawa! Hurry up!"

The grumbling continues as her mother retreats from the door.

The powder is a goopy mess in the wet sink. Goldie flicks off the light and leaves the bathroom without bothering to clean up or give her reflection a final glance.

The stuff probably wouldn't have made much of a difference anyway.

———————

ALTHOUGH IT'S EARLY EVENING, THE PARKING LOT OF HANK'S BAR IS pretty packed. Goldie ends up weaving between rows a few times before finding a decent spot.

"This not happen if you not so slow." Her mother scoops Lucky out of his carrier and gets out of the car. "We gonna be late."

"We are very much not late. The music won't start until eight." Goldie looks up at the marquee and smiles at the name spelled out in big, black letters against the field of white. "Besides, he wouldn't start without me."

Her mother stands beside her and looks up too. "You sure about this?" she asks.

"No," Goldie admits, and keeps staring at the name. "But I can live with that."

As they step through the doors, Goldie catalogs the familiar faces and features of the place. Henry is easy to spot, effortlessly handling drink orders behind the earthy red-brown wood of the bar. Her eyes move on to the wall of signed headshots and album covers that showcases the talent the place has fostered. She looks above at the crisscrossing beams that remind her of weaving, like the bar is a giant basket containing the precious odds and ends of the city's music scene.

When the stage lights are on, the beams disappear, and the expanse turns into the night sky. The spotlights become the stars shining down on the little mountain of a stage at the center.

"There you are!" Amber is the first to find them. "What took you so long? Connie had to stop me from calling the cops."

"I told you," Sun says, smug.

Goldie ignores her mother. "You were that worried?" She folds her arms. "I'm not even late!"

"No, I wanted you arrested for being criminally antisocial. You gotta mingle!"

"I did enough of that in New York."

"You had a great time. Don't even front."

"I got called a fascist shrew who hates America and then also somehow got called a self-hating sellout in the pocket of big corporations."

"I'm talking about when you weren't on camera. I still can't believe you got into that DJ booth and had them mash up ABBA with Dua Lipa."

"They fit together so well!"

"Girl, I was exhausted!" Amber looks at Goldie's mom. "Your daughter was a machine out there. She faced down pompous A-holes during the day, then went to every museum, tourist trap, and hot nightclub in Manhattan."

Sun gives her daughter a profound look. "I very proud of you."

Goldie glances at Amber to confirm that she heard right. "Uh, really?"

"Yes," she says, nodding, "because you not boring now."

Goldie hangs her head and groans. She should have seen that coming.

"Look." Her mother points to a corner. "Penny and Jack here with babies. We go say hi."

"Sure," Goldie agrees, but takes a moment to give Amber a hug before following. "I'm so glad you're here. Thanks for coming."

"Are you kidding me? I wouldn't miss this night for the world." Amber lets go and gives her shoulder a final squeeze. "I always got you."

Goldie goes to join her mom with the Song brood, who are occupied with the puppy.

"Ah," Serena pouts, "we should have brought Rex too."

"He doesn't do well in strange places," her father says, and looks thoughtfully at the furry bundle in his daughter's hand. "And he probably would confuse Lucky with a toy."

"Hey, Penny," Goldie says to grab her friend's attention.

"Oh, hey!" Penny gives her a quick hug before pulling away and appraising her.

"What are you looking for?"

"Just checking for anything missing. No injuries, right? Still got all your teeth?"

"What? I'm fine! Why were you so worried?"

"You were in New York City, Goldie! There are, like, fifty crime shows and podcasts that use it as a setting. I was watching every show you were on just to make sure you were still alive."

"And apparently watching and listening to every one of those crime shows and podcasts too." Goldie shakes her head. "You're almost as bad as Ma. She tried to put a tracker for lost luggage on me."

"What you mean 'try'?" Goldie's mother asks.

Goldie pats her body like she could still have it on her. "Where did you put it? How?"

Sun shrugs and turns back to the children, pulling out a treat bag from her purse. "You kids wanna see Lucky do trick?"

Serena and Corey shout, "Yeah!" Meanwhile, Tyler is already busy on the floor, rolling a ball to the puppy and squealing when Lucky jumps and attacks it.

With a low growl, Goldie lets the topic drop into the dark inner void for things she has every right to be mad about but aren't worth the extra grief from her mother.

Goldie addresses Penny again. "How're you feeling? Still got morning sickness?"

"The last few days have been better. Also, panicking over you helped distract me from panicking over having another baby. Jack and I looked at some properties the other day."

"That's great, Pen." Goldie smiles and hugs her one more time.

"Hey, Goldie!"

She turns toward who's calling and sees that it's Paul with, surprisingly, his whole family. "Lily! You're here!"

The pastor's wife waves. "Yeah, we came for Paul's last sermon."

Goldie manages to maintain a neutral expression despite how sad she is about her friend's imminent departure. She got a lot of practice using the look during the media tour.

Her mother, however, is not so well trained. Her face is burning mad. Goldie's tempted to check for the nearest fire extinguisher.

While all the kids are busy greeting each other, Goldie tries to get Paul's attention to address her mother's current state. They've known each other long enough that he picks up on what she's communicating.

"Uh, Imo, it's good to see you well and enjoying yourself."

Her mother doesn't respond, which might be a good thing. Flames would undoubtedly shoot out if she opened her mouth.

After the embarrassing failure of his opening tactic of showing pastoral concern, he tries a more secular approach involving incentives. "Lily and I would love to bring you lunch tomorrow and help wash the curtains you mentioned."

His wife glares at him. "What?"

Goldie's mother remains quiet for a full minute to ironically instill the fear of God in the pastor.

Paul acts as Lily's human shield and moves in front of her.

When Sun finally speaks, it's a commandment, not a suggestion. "You come at 11."

"Yes!" Paul instantly agrees. "Whenever you want."

The promise seems to slake her anger, and she returns to ignoring everyone but the children and puppy.

"So, Goldie," Lily begins, "Paul says I'm going to witness the voice of an angel tonight."

"Tell her the rest," Paul insists.

Lily rolls her eyes. "And hear songs so profound that they should be etched in stone for future generations to discover—or at least made available on SoundCloud."

Goldie snorts a laugh. "You're in luck, Paul. Teo has plans to record some stuff."

"Oh yeah? That's so awesome." Paul's gaze turns in the direction of the back room. "Look, it's him! You think I could get his autograph? Like, even on a napkin would be great."

Goldie turns to see for herself. Teo's talking with Eli and Jordan.

When she doesn't respond to his request, Paul taps her shoulder. "You doing okay, Golds?"

She checks herself and smiles with genuine warmth. "Don't worry, Pastor. It's going to be a good night."

Goldie turns back in time to see Jordan noticing her.

"Goldiiiie!" she shrieks, waving her hand wildly. She drags her father in Goldie's direction, and before she can register what's happening, the 11-year-old is wrapped around her. "I'm so happy you're here!"

"I think you've made that obvious," Eli says in amusement. "Give Goldie room to breathe. It's good to see you, by the way."

Goldie flashes him a smile.

"It's our last night here, and I haven't seen her for a whole week!" Jordan hugs tighter. "I'm going to miss you so much!"

Goldie suddenly does have trouble breathing but not from the hugging. She swallows hard. "I'm going to miss you too, sweetheart."

Luckily, the puppy's sudden yipping offers a distraction from all the emotions.

"Lucky's here too!"

"And my mom."

"Halmoni!"

Her mother makes an "oof" sound after the girl wraps her in an embrace. "Jordie, hi," she says with a laugh. After letting the girl get her fill of hugging, she pulls away to bend over. "I have gift for you."

"What? No way!"

Sun hands over a tote with Tupperware. "It Korean rice cake. You take home."

Jordan immediately tears open the container top and takes a piece.

"Or eat now," Goldie's mother says, eyes wide.

"It's soooo good!"

Sun smiles and makes a pleased sound.

"What's the Korean word for it?"

"Tteok."

"Daddy, you gotta try this tteok," Jordan says before shoving a whole piece in his mouth.

Eli takes a while to give feedback. "It's really chewy," he explains, still chewing.

Goldie's mother is on high alert for any criticism, which doesn't go unnoticed by Eli. "It's great," he assures her, mouth *still* full. "Can you teach me how to make it?"

Sun lights up ... well, like the *sun*. "You cook?"

"Yes, ma'am. I love to cook all kinds of things."

Goldie sighs at the inevitable.

"Thank you, God!" Sun exclaims, looking up to the ceiling. "You finally give me child who cook and not explode kitchen!"

Eli looks at Goldie with alarm. "You exploded a kitchen?!"

"No! I just burned ramen one time."

"Same thing!" her mother accuses. "I throw out good pot because of you. House smell like smoke for month."

"Okay, um." Eli stifles a laugh and takes out his phone. "I promise to write down everything you say to do so I don't explode my kitchen. I just need a favor from Goldie first."

"Yeah?"

"Do you mind sitting with Tommy?"

"Where is he? I was wondering about him."

"He's guarding our table near the stage. He, uh ..." Eli gives her a sheepish smile. "He needs to talk to you."

The reporter fights her natural urge to ask for more clarity and quickly goes to find her friend.

It's hard to miss Tommy most of the time with the height he likes to brag about and the toned body he likes to flaunt with tight tees. He especially stands out tonight in an open button-up colorfully covered in palm tree leaves and his legs and arms spread out as wide as possible.

"Excuse me, can I have this seat?" Goldie asks, pitching her voice high.

"Sorry, I'm saving them," Tommy says without looking up from his phone.

"Is your lap taken too?"

"What?!" Tommy's head shoots up.

Goldie laughs a little too hard at his scandalized expression.

"What the hell, Goldie? That was"—he starts laughing too—"not bad. Okay, you got me. Gold star for the Golden Girl. Welcome back, by the way."

"Thanks." She smirks, taking the seat next to him.

"Maybe I should start calling you Wonder Woman instead. I loved how you took down that pig on *The Early Hour*. 'Women who actually want to keep their wrinkles have no self-respect,'" Tommy mimics the anchor's now infamous quote.

"It wasn't the cleverest comeback. I just called him a pretentious moron."

"And reminded him that his network's president is a woman who doesn't use the Serum. The look on his face! I'm so proud of you, Goldie."

"Um, thanks." Her cheeks heat. "Was that what you wanted to talk to me about? Eli was adorably shy about it."

Tommy is the one who blushes this time. "I, uh, have some big news."

Goldie holds her breath.

"I'm moving to Miami to be with Eli and Jordan."

"Like, tomorrow?!" She tries and fails not to sound panicked.

"No! Not that soon."

"Oh." Goldie finally exhales.

"I have to take care of a lot of things here first. Make sure my mom has everything she needs. She travels half the year anyway, so she can just plan an adventure in Florida if she wants to see me. Take her alligator wrestling or something."

Goldie cringes. "Pretty sure there are other things to do in Florida."

"Yeah, I should probably ask Eli for suggestions." Tommy's brow cinches. "I have to talk to my dad too. Try to salvage some of that relationship."

Goldie's head nods, although she can hardly feel the movement. Her body, mind, and heart all start to feel numb to defend against the dread pervading her.

"I'll try to go to Florida for a visit sometime soon, and Eli and Jordan will be back up here during fall break. By then, I think I'll be ready to move."

Goldie swallows the lump in her throat. "It sounds like a good plan. I'm happy for you."

Tommy frowns. "You don't sound happy."

"I said I was happy *for you*. For me, I feel like I lost a limb."

"You know I wouldn't consider leaving you if I didn't think you were going to be okay here."

"How I'm doing shouldn't play any part in this."

"I love you, Goldie," he says with no room for awkwardness or attempts to play it off as a joke. "You will always be a major part of my life."

Goldie blinks back tears. "I love you too."

"Am I right though?"

"About what?"

"Are you gonna be okay?"

Henry comes out from the bar to the stage at that moment, while Eli and Jordan, pulling Goldie's mother, approach their table.

Goldie grabs Tommy's hand, startling him, but she smiles through his reaction. He smiles back and gives her hand a solid squeeze before everyone settles into their seats.

"Ahem." Henry clears his throat to get the audience's attention. "Thank you all for coming to Hank's Bar for this special family night. I hope you're enjoying the Coke products and sparkling water."

A few people holler and clap. A child makes an especially high-pitched whine.

"I'm not much of a talker, so I'll let our headliner explain what's so special about tonight. After several long weeks away from the Helena stage, give a warm welcome back to Teo Estrada!"

Teo comes out from the back room with the other musicians to loud cheers and applause. He's wearing a plain white tee layered under an unbuttoned short-sleeve beige shirt. Combined with his mostly white hair and beard, under the stage lights, he almost glows.

"Thank you, guys! Thank you!" Teo shouts. "Thank you all for coming out tonight. I've missed you."

More whoops and even one "Missed ya too, baby!" can be heard.

"First off, let me introduce the band for tonight. You all know my partner in crime, the crowning rhinestone of this classy establishment and vocalist extraordinaire, Ruby Florence. On drums is her hubby and heavy hitter, Spade Taylor. And for extra rhythmic backup, we have Byron Lafayette on bass."

The musicians do short intros with their instruments to greet the crowd.

"So," Teo continues, "you regulars have probably noticed I look a little different since the last time you saw me. Well, I got a haircut, grew a beard," he says, rubbing his chin, "aged more than thirty years in over a month."

There's a smattering of chuckles from the audience.

"I had minor surgery recently and had to stop using the Serum. Nothing too serious, but my son and granddaughter came up here from Miami to be with me during recovery. There they are in the front," he says, pointing. "Everyone, say hi to Eli and Jordan."

Members of the crowd applaud and laugh at Jordan, who bounces up to wave. Meanwhile, Eli's rooted in his chair and barely raises his hand.

"Oh, come on, mijo," Teo says into the microphone. "Properly greet everybody. Do you wanna come up onstage?"

"Not a chance, old man!"

Teo snickers. "Tommy's such a bad influence on you."

"*I* wanna go onstage!" Jordan shouts.

"Later, cielo." He winks. "I promise."

With her wish granted, Jordan sits back down and cedes the spotlight back to her grandfather.

"They've been here for several eventful weeks," Teo continues, "and have to get back home tomorrow. This night is partly in honor of them. I'm gonna miss you guys so much."

"¡Te quiero, Abuelo!"

Teo blows a kiss to Jordan, then turns to Goldie. "There's another special guest here tonight." He takes a long breath. "This first song is dedicated to her, but before we get to the music, I'd like to share a little background. This stage that I'm standing on is named after my late wife, Helena, who was also Henry's sister. Helena died way too soon, more than twenty years ago, before her 37th birthday."

He pauses to let the audience absorb the tragedy before continuing. "She and I met way back when at the University of Miami. I was two years ahead, so when she was finishing up her bachelor's, I was doing grunt work at my first company. One seemingly ordinary day,

Helena calls me at work. She says, 'Henry's in town.' I innocently go, 'That's great. I can't wait to see him again.' She comes back with 'You wanna get married?'"

The crowd laughs.

Teo smiles at the memory. "You gotta understand: Helena was unflinching and uncompromising. She never did anything in halves, and when her mind was made up, there was no stopping her. This meant that even though she was technically asking, the only choice was to say yes. Plus, you know, I loved her and planned to ask her after she graduated. Silly me, I should've known she'd beat me to it." He rolls his eyes and looks upward, like he's trying to ensure that she sees him doing it from heaven.

"Her proposal might have lacked romance, but she made up for it with the wedding. We got married on the beach at sunset with her family there. And when the vows came, I sputtered out something forgettable, but hers were unmatched."

Teo's face goes slack and soft. Goldie knows he's back on that beach in front of Helena, repeating her words to the audience as she speaks them to him.

"It's impossible to encompass how much I love you in the few simple words within these vows. There isn't a book big enough to contain all the words I would need. Not ten books, nor a hundred. A whole library wouldn't have enough. No language is expansive enough, and even if such a perfect language existed, time would literally run out and the world would end before I could say all the words I would need to say.

"So, since it is an undeniable fact that I will never be able to say how much I love you, I've decided to marry you and simply show you every day for as long as I live."

Teo blinks out of his reverie, tears unabated, and looks back at Goldie. "There aren't enough words in this song to encompass how much I love you, Goldie—but it's a start. Today and every day after, I will show you how much I love you for as long as I live."

He turns to cue the band. Spade counts them down with his drumsticks, and in an instant, a blast of sound explodes from the speakers. It's a rousing, heavy start that Goldie can feel in every part of her body, then the music drops as quickly as it started.

Again, Teo looks directly at her:

In the golden wonder
I haven't the heart, haven't the mind
To deserve such a goddess
So skilled and divine
A thousand good deeds would be of no use
My worth's in your touch
I submit to you

The instruments come back in force for the chorus:

Your soul's in the lyrics
Your heartbeat's the drum

Spade beats a steady rhythm, mimicking a heartbeat.

I've sung every word
But you ARE THIS SONG!

Teo and Ruby shout more than sing the last three words of the chorus, each of the words further punctuated by Ruby, who strikes the tambourine at the same moment her husband hits the drums.

The instruments don't drop off again like they did when Teo first started singing. Instead, they enhance his ardent vocals.

In the golden wonder
I haven't the strength, haven't the will
To deny such pleasures
I'll drink to my fill
My sins and my wrongs, paid for in the end
You deserved so much better
My lover, my friend

Teo barely lets the lyrics breathe before singing the chorus again. There's a subtle yet noticeable increase in intensity throughout it, and a beat or two added to the end before he starts the next verse.

In the golden wonder
I haven't the life, haven't the time
To waste on my pain
The shame of my crime
Having loved and lost isn't better at all

In the cruelest of lessons
True love suffers the fall

Again, they perform the chorus, and again, the intensity increases. Goldie is getting exhausted just listening to them, but Teo and the band do not let up, even for the quieter verses.

In the golden wonder
I haven't the right, haven't the voice
Two flames burn apart
You're left with a choice
United, we're brighter, warm and aglow
But together's not forever
And my fuel's run low

The lyrics are starting to get to Goldie, and she finds herself imagining the beat of the song influencing the incredible beat of her heart.

In the golden wonder
I haven't the pride, haven't the edge
To demand your forgiveness
But here I will pledge
I'm the man you had known, you loved no lie
Our love is the truth
Please don't say goodbye

The chorus kicks in—three times in a row this time, each refrain louder than the last—until everything just stops.

Only Teo's heavy breathing in the microphone can be heard. He looks back down at Goldie with pleading, wide eyes.

This song has no end
Words are yet to be sung
So, tell me, O' writer
What do we become?

When faced with a decision, Goldie typically hesitates. She'd go over the facts and figures. Put everything in a neat list. She'd weigh and reweigh every bullet point before making the safest choice, which more often than not meant making no choice at all. But that's her reliably hard head talking. It's had more than enough to say on the matter of her relationship with Teo.

With fully formed wings, Goldie flies onto the stage—and listens to her heart.

(And as she kisses Teo, amid the whoops and cheers and whistles, Jordan can be heard shouting joyfully … that she totally won the bet.)

The End

SPECIAL EPILOGUE

TOMMY STARES INTO THE CAVERN OF HIS BEDROOM. A VERITABLE abyss, if you will.

Strike that. He has no idea where his brain pulled those words from or if he used them correctly.

His bedroom's fucking empty is what Tommy's getting at.

Three-and-a-half months have passed since deciding to move to Miami to be with Eli and Jordan. Tomorrow, he'll be leaving this apartment, his place for as long as he's been able to pay his own bills, and he's feeling nostalgic—and remorseful, surprisingly.

Not about leaving the apartment, which is arguably pretty shitty and small. (Good luck to the place's next residents.)

No, if he's being honest, Tommy's remorseful for the many years of his adulthood spent here living in limbo. ...

WANT MORE?

Get the entire special epilogue at **Gloria-Holt.com**.

ABOUT THE AUTHOR

GLORIA HOLT IS A FORMER JOURNALIST TRYING OUT THIS AUTHOR THING.

While *Youth* isn't a memoir, it has elements of her life: a love of superhero cinema, a Korean mother and her Chihuahua named Lucky, and a snobbish admiration for music.

She holds a master's degree in English, which she is finally getting use of. *Youth* is her first novel, but another is on the way. This journey has just begun.

To learn more or keep up with her projects, visit **Gloria-Holt.com** or find her **@AuthorGloriaHolt** on Instagram.

www.ingramcontent.com/pod-product-compliance
Lightning Source LLC
Chambersburg PA
CBHW050012120726
47903CB00006B/1734